continued . . .

"Near perfect."   —*Midwest Book Review*

"A stellar read . . . the kind of book that will make one sigh with satisfaction, and make for enjoyable rereading over the years . . . Superb."   —*Romance Reading*

"Hysterical to read. Gracie's humor is as engaging as ever."   —*All About Romance*

"With wit and tenderness . . . Gracie entertains and satisfies her fans."   —*Romantic Times*

Praise for the other novels of Anne Gracie

An Honorable Thief

"She's turned out another wonderful story!"
   —*All About Romance*

"A true find and definitely a keeper."   —*Romance Reviews*

"A thoroughly marvelous heroine."   —*The Best Reviews*

"Dazzling characterizations . . . provocative, tantalizing, and wonderfully witty romantic fiction . . . Unexpected plot twists, tongue-in-cheek humor, and a sensually fraught battle of wits between hero and heroine . . . embraces the romance genre's truest heart."   —*Heartstrings*

How the Sheriff Was Won

"Anne Gracie provide[s] pleasant diversions."
   —*Midwest Book Review*

"An excellent story with an engaging plot and well-rounded characters."   —*Romantic Times*

THE
Perfect
Stranger

Anne Gracie

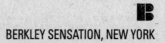

BERKLEY SENSATION, NEW YORK

THE BERKLEY PUBLISHING GROUP
Published by the Penguin Group
Penguin Group (USA) Inc.
375 Hudson Street, New York, New York 10014, USA
Penguin Group (Canada), 90 Eglinton Avenue East, Suite 700, Toronto, Ontario M4P 2Y3, Canada
(a division of Pearson Penguin Canada Inc.)
Penguin Books Ltd., 80 Strand, London WC2R 0RL, England
Penguin Books Ireland, 25 St. Stephen's Green, Dublin 2, Ireland (a division of Penguin Books Ltd.)
Penguin Group (Australia), 250 Camberwell Road, Camberwell, Victoria 3124, Australia
(a division of Pearson Australia Group Pty. Ltd.)
Penguin Books India Pvt. Ltd., 11 Community Centre, Panchsheel Park, New Delhi—110 017, India
Penguin Group (NZ), Cnr. Airborne and Rosedale Roads, Albany, Auckland 1310, New Zealand
(a division of Pearson New Zealand Ltd.)
Penguin Books (South Africa) (Pty.) Ltd., 24 Sturdee Avenue, Rosebank, Johannesburg 2196,
South Africa

Penguin Books Ltd., Registered Offices: 80 Strand, London WC2R 0RL, England

This is a work of fiction. Names, characters, places, and incidents either are the product of the author's imagination or are used fictitiously, and any resemblance to actual persons, living or dead, business establishments, events, or locales is entirely coincidental. The publisher does not have any control over and does not assume any responsibility for author or third-party websites or their content.

THE PERFECT STRANGER

A Berkley Sensation Book / published by arrangement with the author

PRINTING HISTORY
Berkley Sensation edition / June 2006

Copyright © 2006 by Anne Gracie.
Cover art by Voth-Barrall Design.
Interior text design by Kristin del Rosario.

ISBN: 0-425-21052-9

BERKLEY SENSATION®
Berkley Sensation Books are published by The Berkley Publishing Group,
a division of Penguin Group (USA) Inc.,
375 Hudson Street, New York, New York 10014.
BERKLEY SENSATION is a registered trademark of Penguin Group (USA) Inc.
The "B" design is a trademark belonging to Penguin Group (USA) Inc.

PRINTED IN THE UNITED STATES OF AMERICA

10 9 8 7 6 5 4 3 2 1

For my sisters, Jan Westerveld and Jill Graham.
And for all my "sisters of the road"—you know who you are.
With love and thanks.

Chapter One

∞

Long is the way and hard, that out of hell leads up to light.
JOHN MILTON

VOICES. THERE WERE VOICES IN THE DARK, IN THE SAND HILLS. Men's voices.

Faith Merridew sat up. A light bobbed in the sand hills above her. It was moving slowly, unevenly toward her hiding place.

"Où es-tu, ma jolie poulet?" (Where are you, my pretty hen?) The man sounded drunk, whoever he was.

She heard another man stumble in the dark, crashing into one of the low bushes that dotted the sand hills. He cursed. "Are you sure she's here?" he asked in rough French.

"Oui. I watched her go in and not come out. She's waiting, snug in her little nest for us." The speaker laughed coarsely. Two others laughed with him. Three men, maybe more.

Faith didn't wait to be sure. She snatched up her homespun woolen cloak and her reticule and, keeping low, began to creep away as fast as she could.

Behind her lay the town; before her, who knew? But

she had no intention of heading back to town. Not at night. The town would offer her no sanctuary. She'd discovered that the hard way. The town was full of men like these. Men who'd driven her to hide in the sand hills in the first place.

There was no alternative. She made toward the beach.

"Là-bas!" (Over there!) They spotted her and gave chase.

It was too late to worry about noise. She ran as fast as she could, weaving through scrubby bushes and low grasses. Her skirt caught on twigs and spiny thorns. She snatched it up in desperate fists and ran on. Sticks and thorns slashed at her legs, but she was oblivious. Behind her, men crashed through the undergrowth. They were gaining on her.

Thump! Faith tripped over a root and crashed into the ground. Pain exploded in her face. She lay on the sandy ground, winded, her empty lungs gasping frantically for breath that would not come. Finally air gushed back into her, and she could breathe.

She scrambled to her feet and listened for her pursuers. And that's when she heard it. Music. Soft, but not far away.

Where there was music there were people. People who might help her. Or not. They might be like the men in the town, like the ones who were chasing after her.

No choice. She could not let herself be run down like a hare by hounds. She had to risk it. She would run, run to the music, and pray for safety.

Music had once been her refuge. And lately her downfall.

Risking everything for the sake of speed, she plunged onto the open beach, down to the very water's edge where the sand was firmest. Shafts of pain jabbed her ankle with every step. She heard shouts as her pursuers spotted her. Faith ran, ran for her life, ran toward the music.

Her heavy boots slowed her down. They'd protected her feet in the rough scrub—her own slippers would never have stood that punishment—but now the soft sand sucked at them. No time to stop and take them off. Her breath came in great gasps. Pain bit sharply into her side. She ignored it and fled on.

She rounded a small headland. Fire glowed in the base of the sand hills. Lungs heaving, she ran toward it. A campfire. A cooking pot hung above it. Fishermen?

A solitary shadowed figure sat beside the fire, playing music softly; Spanish-sounding music that rippled out into the night like water, or wine. A man. A gypsy? A huge dog rose out of the shadows. Faith froze. She'd had dogs set on her twice in the last week. This one was of a size to rip out her throat in one bite.

"Là-bas!" Her pursuers came crashing across the headland. Nothing, not even a hound from hell, could be worse than what these men planned. Terror drove her forward.

"Aidez-moi!" she gasped raggedly as she stumbled toward him. *"Aidez-moi . . . je vous implore!"* (Help me, I beg of you!)

The music stopped. The dog's low growls blossomed into a frenzy of rage.

"Silence, Wulf!" The deep barking stopped instantly, though the dog kept growling.

"Aidez-moi!" she gasped, her breath sobbing from exhausted lungs. The words came out as a whisper.

Somehow, he heard her. He held out his hand toward her, a dark lifeline etched in flame. *"À moi, petite,"* was all he said. (To me, little one.)

His voice was deep and calm and sure, and it seemed to speak to something deep inside her. And so, despite the fact that she could not see his face, despite the huge snarling beast at his side, Faith gathered the last of her strength and stumbled toward him. He was so tall and solid, and that voice, she imagined, held strength and reassurance. He could be no worse than those behind her, she thought, and besides, she had reached the end of her tether.

The toe of her boot caught again in the undergrowth. Her bad ankle buckled, and she pitched forward and crashed into the man. He caught her hard against his chest, but the impact knocked him backward and brought him down, flat on his back.

She lay for a moment on top of him, exhausted, gasping for breath on his big, hard body. Beneath her, the man lay still, as if his breath, too, had been knocked from him. His arms had closed around her. Hard, strong muscles. He smelled clean, of salt and woodsmoke and soap.

The dog barked again, but now its menace was directed into the darkness. Her pursuers must be almost here.

As she scrambled off him, Faith tried to think of the words in French to explain, to beg for help. Not a single word or phrase came to her frightened brain. She knelt beside him in the sand, struggling to pull her wits together.

His features were in shadow, silhouetted against the fire. "Mademoiselle?" His voice was harsh, deep.

Her mouth opened and closed helplessly. "I'm sorry, I'm sorry," she whispered in English. "I can't think of the words. Oh God!" She could not see his face. Her own was lit by his fire.

His voice sharpened. "You're English!" He stood abruptly. He seemed immensely tall.

Faith nodded. "Yes. Yes, I am. And you—" His words pierced the fog in her brain. He was English, too.

"Thank God, thank God," she whispered. Though

why she should feel safer with him just because he was English as well as clean was a mystery. But somehow, she did.

The dog suddenly broke into a renewed frenzy of barking, and she pulled herself together. "Those men, they'll be here any minute—"

He did not so much as glance away. He bent down and held out his hands to her. "Can you stand?" Distantly she realized he spoke with no hint of an accent. Spoke, in fact, with the tones of a gentleman.

She nodded, though her legs were shaking. He helped her to her feet with strong, gentle hands. She stared fearfully into the darkness. The dog snarled and growled, clearly sensing her pursuers, though they'd gone very quiet. "Enough, Wulf!" The dog stopped, and silence fell.

Three silhouettes were dimly visible against the glimmer of the sea and sky.

"They're after me."

"So I presumed. But why are they chasing you? Did you steal—"

"No!" she said indignantly. "They want—they think—they think I am—"

His gaze ran over her, coldly assessing. "I understand," he said in a clipped voice.

He did, too, she could tell from his tone. She hung her head, too mortified to speak.

"Sit down over there, near the fire," he ordered. "I'll deal with them."

"But there are three men! Maybe more."

His teeth glinted in a savage smile. "Good."

Good? Faith stared at the shadowed face, wishing she could see him properly. What could he possibly mean by *good*?

A voice from the darkness shouted roughly in French, "Hey, you there! That woman is ours."

"*Oui*, give her back, and there will be no trouble," another added.

The tall man answered in French. "The woman is mine." The dog snarled, as if to reinforce his words.

"*The woman is mine.*" An implacable statement of fact. Faith shivered. Did she now have four men to flee instead of three? She glanced up at him, a tall, featureless silhouette. A spurt of anger shot through her. She was no man's woman. Since she'd walked out on Felix all sorts of men thought she was theirs for the taking. Was it only ten days ago? It seemed like an endless nightmare, getting worse each time.

The first man swore. "The whore is ours. We found her first." He spat. "You can have her when we've finished with her."

They were planning to *share* her? Oh God! Faith began to shake again. She looked around her for a weapon, a knife, or even a heavy stick, but she could see no sign of anything useful. The biggest pieces of wood had been thrown on the fire. She would have to run. Again. The stitch in her side had eased, and her breathing had returned to normal—almost. Her face ached and her ankle throbbed, but she was in a better state to keep running than ten minutes before. Surreptitiously she bent and began to unlace her heavy boots. She would be faster on the sand barefoot.

The tall man bent sideways and took her wrist with a firm grip. "Stop that," he ordered softly, drawing her upright again. "You won't need to run. You have my word you will be safe."

He raised his voice and announced with quiet menace, "The girl is mine, and I don't share. She stays with me." He said to Faith in an undertone, "See those saddlebags over there on the blanket beside the guitar? There's a pair of pistols in them. Fetch them for me, there's a good girl. I can't take my eyes off these swine."

"There's a good girl?" That didn't sound like a potential rapist talking.

"We found her first," a man yelled furiously.

"You want her? Then come and take her. But you'll have to kill me first." And to Faith's amazement, he smiled again. There was nothing gentle or humorous in it. It was purely ferocious; a savage baring of teeth in anticipation of a fight.

A scornful laugh came out of the darkness. "Bah, Englishman, we are three to your one. We will feed you to the fish!"

Faith's Englishman smiled that terrible smile and shrugged, as if to say, *We'll see.*

Faith found the pistols and hurried back and thrust them into his hands. The men in the shadows muttered, speaking in indistinct voices. As if they were arguing. Or planning.

He checked the pistols unhurriedly. Faith stared at him, marveling at his calm. One man against three. He was tall and broad-shouldered, but not as heavyset as the three. They were probably the sort of ruffians who positively bristled with knives, too. And though he had his pistols, they would only account for two, at best.

He seemed perfectly unworried by the atrocious odds.

Suddenly a wave of self-disgust washed over her. This man, a stranger whose name she didn't even know, was risking his life for her. She shouldn't cower behind him, letting him and his dog defend her from attack. She'd made some resolutions during the last week about learning to take care of herself, about not depending on others—not for anything! Now was the time to put her resolutions to the test.

She hurried to the fire, selected a thick, long branch, and pulled it, still burning, from the fire. Stiffening her shaking limbs, Faith stepped up to stand beside her unknown champion.

"I'll fight you, too!" she shouted and shook her blazing brand fiercely at the shadowy Frenchmen. Sparks flew everywhere.

Her protector gave a bark of laughter, with real humor this time. "Good for you!" He raised his voice, "A man, a girl, and a dog! Three against three! So come on, swine, let's see what you're made of!"

Faith waved her stick in what she hoped was a threatening gesture. Light from her blazing brand danced over his features, and for the first time she glimpsed his face. She had an impression of strength. A bold nose. Dark hair, thick and tousled, in need of a cut. High cheekbones. A firm, unshaven chin, dark with rough bristles. His eyes glinted, reflecting the flame. It was almost as if he relished the prospect of a fight. Which was, of course, ridiculous.

He raised first one pistol, then another. Twin silver barrels gleamed as they caught the firelight. He brandished them with a casual expertise that even Faith could appreciate. There was a sudden hush from the three men in the dark.

"Not so brave now, my buckos?" His face hardened. "Then take yourselves back to whatever gutter you slithered from, or taste a little English metal."

Faith waited, hardly breathing. It was a bluff, of course. He couldn't possibly see to shoot them from such a distance and in the dark. If anyone was an open target, he was, silhouetted against the fire.

The silence from the darkness lengthened. "Very well, monsieur, you win," one called. Heavy footsteps crunched through the undergrowth, moving away. Faith heaved a sigh of relief.

"Don't move." The tall man beside her whispered. He stood braced, tense, like his dog, his head craned forward, his expression intent.

Faith froze.

"Toss that thing away and crouch down for a moment," he ordered her softly. "I need you out of the firing line."

She flung the half-burned branch into the sand and crouched motionless, straining her eyes to see. The dog's ears twitched. Faith watched as her Englishman closed his eyes and cocked his head, as if listening. She could hear nothing.

She jumped almost out of her skin when he suddenly shot over her head into the dark. There was scream of pain followed by a flurry of cursing.

"Lucky shot, but can you fight on three sides, Englishman?" came a taunt from the opposite side.

"With pleasure," he answered and shot in the direction of the voice. There was another burst of swearing.

"The devil, Englishman, how can you shoot like that? It's pitch-black."

"I have the devil's own luck, and I can see in the dark," he said calmly. He tossed the second pistol onto a blanket and said to Faith, "Fetch me another burning brand."

She hurried to obey, and as she passed it to him, the firelight glittered on a wicked-looking blade. The fishermen were not the only ones with knives. He lifted the brand and twirled it easily around his head like a baton. Sparks flew everywhere, but he took no notice. "Come on, you cowards, let's have a look at you!" He strode forward. Faith grabbed her stick and made to follow. "Stay back," he commanded. "You'll just be in my way."

He strode forward, twirling the brand as he moved, faster and faster in a barbarous display. His ferocity and control were mesmerizing: a mythical warrior, bathed in fire and a hound from hell baying at his side.

He looked utterly terrifying. And utterly magnificent.

Suddenly he hurled the brand at a shadowed figure,

even as the other two leaped on him. He warded off one of them with a kick. His fist smashed into the other. Faith could barely see what was happening; it was all shadows and horrible sounds—the sounds of fists smashing into flesh, of bones crunching, and the guttural gasps and groans of men fighting.

Incredibly, her Englishman seemed to be winning. He landed two frightful blows on the biggest man, then picked him up bodily and hurled him into some bushes. The man screamed again as he landed in a prickle bush.

As her champion wrestled with another man, the third man limped up from behind. A knife glittered. Faith screamed a warning, and the Englishman swung around and shoved his assailant at the attacker. There was another scream and further cursing.

And then suddenly there was silence. "Keep her then, English," one of the men wheezed. "I hope she gives you the pox!" The three attackers stumbled off into the darkness.

Man, woman, and dog waited until no further sounds of retreat could be heard. The dog's growls died away. His hackles dropped, and soon there was only the sound of the fire crackling and the distant splash of waves.

"They've gone," the tall man said curtly.

"A-are you sure?"

"Yes. Beowulf wouldn't relax if they were anywhere in the vicinity, would you, Wulf?" The dog looked up as he addressed him. He glanced at Faith, and a low growl emitted from behind those appalling teeth. Faith shuddered. The terrifying creature was huge and woolly and the size of a small horse. Beowulf? He looked more like one of the legendary monsters the hero of that name had fought.

"Don't worry. He doesn't like women, but he won't· hurt you. Now, are you all right?"

"Yes, thank you. But what about you? Are you hurt?"

"Me? Of course not." He said it as if the idea was ridiculous.

At the realization that she was safe, Faith's legs— her whole body—started shaking. "Th-thank you for r-rescuing me." It was totally inadequate for what he had done.

"Nicholas Blacklock at your service." He put out his hand, and she placed hers in his. It was trembling like a leaf. Her whole body was. She tried to control it.

He frowned, noticing, and his hand tightened over hers. "You're safe now." He said it as if it was an order.

"Yes." She bit her lip to stop it trembling. "I know."

He examined her face and scowled, a black, intimidating look. "Come over to the fire, and we'll see to that." He grimaced at her. "Can you walk?"

"Yes, of course." She started toward the fire, but for some reason her legs didn't seem to work properly. A horridly pathetic sound escaped her as she stumbled and nearly fell.

He made some exclamation under his breath, and before Faith knew what was happening, he'd scooped her up in his arms and was striding toward the fire.

Nick caught a flash of something—fear? surprise?— in her eyes. She stiffened in his arms, as if bracing herself to escape. He tightened his hold and growled, "Little fool! Why not tell me you were hurt? I can see your face is, but I didn't know about your feet!"

She gave him an uncertain look, but her body relaxed slightly. Her arms wavered, as if she didn't know what to do with them, and then she hooked one arm gingerly around his neck, watching his face with a wary expression. When he made no objection, she tightened her hold and clutched at his shirtfront with the other, afraid he would drop her. She wasn't used to being carried in a man's arms, he thought.

That surprised him. Her green dress was low-cut

enough to show slight but very feminine curves, and it was torn at the neck to reveal even more. It was silk or some fine fabric, though stained and ragged in places. Her cloak, on the other hand, was thick, coarse, and heavy; hand-woven wool, he guessed. An incongruous combination.

Tucked up close against his chest, he couldn't help but inhale the scent of her. His body reacted the same as the first time, when she'd knocked him flat to the ground. Arousal. Intense and immediate. His nostrils flared, taking in the scent of her like an animal.

Thank the Lord it was dark. His body was rampant. He forced his mind to concentrate on the mystery. She smelled fresh. Female. Not a trace of perfume, just that tangy female scent that sent him hard and aching. She looked like a ragged streetwalker, her clothes were grubby and torn, and yet she herself smelled fresher than a number of ladies he could name. Too many people he knew doused their bodies with perfume rather than bathe. Yet in the unlikeliest situation, this waif had somehow kept herself clean.

Fool woman! What the devil was she doing in French sand hills anyway? An assignation goné wrong? He doubted it. Despite her bizarre clothing she didn't seem the assignation type. Then what was she up to?

She sounded gently born. Her accent was pure, untainted by any regional burr, even when she was shaking with fear. In Nick's experience, affectations disappeared when people were in terror for their lives. So the aristocratic accent was natural to her.

But gently bred English girls did not venture anywhere unaccompanied, let alone into French sand hills after dark.

He set her down on the blanket near the fire, pushing aside the guitar he'd dropped when he first heard her cry for help.

He watched for a moment while, with shaking hands, she tried to straighten her clothes, smooth back her hair, assume some semblance of poise. She was thin and on the scruffy side. Her nose was peeling, her skin was blotchy and scratched, and her face was lopsided. Swollen, he thought, looking closer. Her hair was scraped back in a tight knot. Loose strands straggled untidily from it.

She didn't weigh much. She wasn't much to look at either, he thought, wondering again at the state of his body. Her only claim to beauty were those big, wide eyes fringed with dark lashes. Clear as water and showing every passing thought. Eyes a man could drown in—if he had a mind to. Nick had no mind to drown in any woman's eyes.

And then there was her mouth. He could barely look at her mouth. Soft, lush, and vulnerable, it was simply the most kissable mouth he'd ever seen. Not that he was planning to kiss it, either.

"Th-thank you. I'm sorry; I did not mean to—" Her voice wavered and broke, and Nick braced himself for female hysterics.

She surprised him by taking a deep breath and mastering herself. In a shaking voice she managed to say, "I'm very sorry for involving you in my troubles, but I didn't know what else to do. I'm so grateful you helped. You were so brave, taking such a frightful risk for—"

"Nonsense!" he interrupted brusquely. "I am—was a soldier. I don't mind a fight, and those three were hardly a serious threat."

Her lower lip trembled. She bit it. Nick reached into his coat pocket and drew out a flask. "Have a drink. It will help settle your nerves."

"Oh but I—"

"Even hardened soldiers can get the shakes after a battle." He thrust the small silver flask into her hand. "Don't argue. Drink."

She gave him a suspicious look. He rolled his eyes and said impatiently, "I'm not planning to get you drunk, girl. Just do as you're told and swallow a mouthful or two. It'll do you good. Settle the nerves and keep out the cold."

"I'm not cold," she said, but she took the flask anyway.

He squatted down in front of her and reached for her skirts.

"Stop that! What are you doing?" she squeaked and tried to bat his hands away.

He caught her flailing hands in his and gave her a hard look. "Don't be stupid! How the devil can I look at your ankle if I don't lift your skirt?"

She glared back at him. "Wh-why do you want to look at my ankle?"

"Because it's injured of course!"

She glanced doubtfully at her ankle. "Actually, it does hurt, rather a lot," she admitted, sounding almost surprised.

She'd probably been too frightened to register pain, he decided as he released her hands. It happened that way sometimes. People carried on with injuries, unaware, until the fighting was over. He picked up the flask she'd dropped. "I told you to drink! It will help the pain."

The flask was silver, scratched and dented with hard use and warm from being carried on his body. She unscrewed the stopper and raised the flask to her lips. Fiery liquid burned its way down her throat, and she choked and coughed, shuddering as it hit her empty stomach.

"Wha-what was that?" she gasped once she had recovered her breath. "I did not expect—"

"Brandy. Not precisely a lady's drink, but you need it after the shock you sustained."

She wiped her streaming eyes. "You mean you replace one sort of shock with another." Her voice was hoarse from coughing, but Nick recognized a brave attempt at humor when he saw one.

"You'll do," he said softly.

The quietly spoken words of approval stiffened Faith's spine. There was something about the way he spoke—somehow compelling. He'd said he was a soldier. An officer, she decided. He had that sort of effect, an unconscious habit of command.

Now that the first burn of the brandy had passed, a warm glow was building inside her. She could feel its effect smoothing out her jangled nerves, warming her blood.

"Thank you." As she handed the flask back she saw that his knuckles were scarred, the skin raw from the recent fight. "Your poor hands—" she began.

He shrugged. "It's nothing." He put the flask to his lips—the place where her own lips had been a second before—and took a mouthful, not choking in the least.

"What is your name?"

Faith hesitated.

"I gave you my name before—Nicholas Blacklock," he reminded her.

"Faith Merrid—M-Merrit," she amended. It would not do to reveal her real name. It was bad enough that she had disgraced herself, but she wouldn't taint her sisters' reputation.

"How do you do, Miss . . . Merrit." The deliberate pause told her he'd noticed her amendment. But he made no other comment.

"Now, let me check on that ankle."

Faith jumped when his big hands slipped under her skirt and touched the tender skin at the back of her knees. "What—?"

"I was trying to undo your garters, get your stocking

off." His voice was so noncommittal she knew at once he'd felt she wore no stockings.

Faith hung her head. No respectable woman would be without stockings. "My stockings were a mass of holes. I used them to pad the boots."

"I see." He lifted her skirts and folded them back over her knees. Feeling shamefully exposed, she tried to tug them down, but he stopped her with a look. How did he do that?

The light from the fire fell on her legs, and his mouth tightened as he unlaced her boots. She knew at once what he must be thinking. No lady would wear such rough footwear.

"My own slippers were too flimsy. I traded them for the boots," she mumbled. He didn't respond.

Cupping her calf in one hand, he gently drew her boots off one by one. She heard his breath hiss in. He carefully untangled the stockings she'd wound around her feet but stopped when she winced.

He sat back on his heels and glared at her. "How the *hell* did you get into this state?" He spoke quietly, but she shivered at the anger she heard banked down inside him.

She looked away. "Bad judgment."

"Who is looking after you?"

"I am."

He muttered something under his breath and pulled off his own boots, then shrugged out of his coat. Just as she was wondering nervously what he would remove next, he bent forward and scooped her up against his chest again.

"What—?" She clutched at him.

"I'm taking you down to the sea." He sounded furious. "The salt water will hurt like blazes, but it will clean your feet and legs like nothing else."

"I know they're dirty, but there's no need to be so cross. I didn't ask you to take my shoes off."

"Dirty! Soaking your feet in water is the only way to get these damned rags off you. They're stuck to your feet with your own blood!"

"Oh."

"And your legs are a mass of scratches and cuts."

"I pulled up my skirts when I was running. The fabric kept catching on thorns. I suppose that's how it happened."

"Oh, yes!" His voice was almost savage. "God forbid a tatty old skirt gets caught on a few thorns! Far more sensible to get your skin torn to pieces."

"It wasn't that," she explained with dignity. "My skirts kept getting caught on bushes, slowing me down."

He grunted. "And what about the boots? Your feet are a mass of blisters!"

"I had a long way to walk," she began and then stopped. It was none of his business. He had no reason to be cross. They were her feet, her legs, and her boots. If he didn't like the state of them, he could ignore them. She didn't have to explain herself to anyone. Anyone except her family.

He stalked the rest of the way to the water in silence. When they came to the water's edge he didn't stop. He waded in until the water was up to his knees.

"Brace yourself. This will hurt like the devil." His voice was both furious and gentle as he said it.

Faith gasped as the cold salt water bit savagely into a hundred scratches, cuts, and blisters. It was all she could do not to scream. She gritted her teeth and forced herself to endure it.

All the Merridew girls could take pain without crying. A legacy of Grandpapa's upbringing.

He stood there in the water beside her, not saying a thing. It was some time before she realized he was holding her upright. And that she was clutching onto him in a death grip. The worst of the pain was receding by that time.

She opened her eyes and saw him staring down at her, his face a grim mask. "Better?"

She still couldn't speak. She nodded.

"Good girl. I'm going to carry you to that rock over there, see if I can get that mess of rags off your feet." He carried her to a flat rock and seated her gently on it. "Keep that ankle in the water. I know it's cold, but it will help reduce the swelling."

He lifted one of her feet from the water, and with amazing sensitivity for hands so big, he peeled the rags from around her feet. She watched. Her feet really were a mess—raw and bleeding in places. No wonder the salt had stung. She hadn't realized how badly blistered they were. She supposed the worst damage had been done in that panic-stricken flight from her attackers.

He cleared the last of the rags off her feet and straightened up. "Keep your feet in the water as much as you can. You can warm up at the fire later on. I know it hurts, but salt water heals." He gave her a long look. "I'll be back in a few moments. Stay there." He waded back up to the beach, leaving Faith perched on her rock like a bedraggled mermaid.

Chapter Two
∞

And with him fled the shades of Night.
JOHN MILTON

"BETTER?" NICHOLAS BLACKLOCK WADED OUT TO FAITH'S ROCK.

"Yes, thank you. You were right. The seawater does help."

"I expect you're cold by now. I've built up the fire." He scooped her into his arms and waded ashore. Faith clung to him, not knowing what to say. Until tonight, she'd never been carried by a man. It was very . . . nice.

As they drew close to the fire, Faith became aware of a glorious smell. Stew. As her nose caught the scent, her empty stomach rumbled loudly. She gave an embarrassed glance at Mr. Blacklock.

"My friends will return shortly."

"Your friends?"

"No one to worry about," he said, reading her face. "Only Stevens and Mac, my groom and my old sergeant." He set her gently on the blanket, which he'd shaken out and neatly respread. "You'll dine with us, of course."

"Oh, but—"

He gave her that look. "You will dine with us," he repeated as if daring her to argue.

Faith was so hungry she had no spirit even to demur politely. "Thank you. I'd be delighted."

"Good. Now, let's see to that ankle." Without ceremony he flipped back her skirt and took her injured ankle in his hands. Faith felt less embarrassed this time at the exposure of her calves and ankles, but it was still an odd sensation to have her feet and limbs bare, his dark, tousled head bent over, so close to her body, just inches from her breasts.

"Good. That cold seawater has done the trick. The swelling has gone down quite a bit. Now, a little bit of liniment—" He glanced up with a dry expression. "Horse liniment, but just as good for humans." He dipped his fingers into a pot of salve standing nearby and very gently spread it on her ankle. The salve was cold, with a pungent odor that made Faith's eyes water, but as he lightly massaged it into her ankle it seemed to heat up. Faith watched his hands, mesmerized.

They were big and calloused and should have been clumsy, but not the tenderest of her sisters could have handled Faith's feet more gently. She looked at the scarred knuckles and recalled the brutal sounds they'd made smashing into the fishermen. Felix's hands were long and elegant but also strong and calloused from playing violin but they'd never handled Faith with such delicate care. She pushed the thought from her mind . . .

It did no good to repine over the past. She had only herself to blame. Such a terrible mistake she'd made. And all because of the dream. The dream . . . it tasted bitter in her mouth even now.

Years before, when Faith and her sisters had been miserable under Grandpapa's terrible guardianship, she and her twin had a powerful, simultaneous dream. They'd woken together and shared their dreams—the same, yet different—and they knew their dead mother had sent them as a reminder that all would be well. Mama's dying promise had been that all her girls would find love—love and laughter and sunshine and happiness.

Hope's dream had been of a man who danced—waltzed his way into her heart. Faith had dreamed of a man who made music.

And then they'd escaped Grandpapa and come to London. And Hope had found her dream man, her darling Sebastian, and had married him not three months ago. And in the same week Faith had heard Felix play and had known—believed—from the first glorious chord that he was her dream man. But the dream had become a nightmare . . .

Her stomach rumbled again, jerking her into the present. He had to have heard it that time. His head was only inches from her belly. He made no sign.

She sniffed at the aroma coming from the pot. "Um, I think that stew might be about to burn. Shouldn't you check it?"

He finished bandaging her ankle and looked at his liniment-covered hands. "How about you check it, and I'll wash this stuff from my hands? Try out your ankle now, see how the bandage works."

She stood and found it was much better. While he strode down to the sea to wash liniment from his hands, she checked the pot. Hot, fragrant steam enveloped her, and she almost fainted from the mouthwatering smell. How long had it been since she'd eaten a proper meal? Days, she thought. A small piece of dry bread and cheese last night. She stirred the luscious mix with a wooden spoon, inhaling the scent rapturously. It was almost as good as eating. Almost.

He came back, wiping his hands on his thighs. "Is it burned?"

"No, but it was about to catch. It's very thick. Is there any liquid I can add?"

"Use the wine in that bottle."

Faith splashed in a generous quantity of red wine and stirred. Fragrant winey steam gushed up, and she almost swooned from the glorious fumes. As she replaced the lid, her stomach growled again, protesting.

"We shall talk after dinner."

Faith swallowed. "Talk?"

"Yes, about how you got into this mess and how best to restore you to your loved ones."

"Restore you to your loved ones." Faith felt her face and her knees crumpling. She hid her face from him as she sat with a thump on the blanket.

There was a small silence, then he said quietly, "Have another mouthful," and held the flask out. She said nothing—was unable to—and did not take it, so after a minute he replaced the flask in his pocket.

He picked up his guitar and started to pluck soft notes. His hands moved surely over the instrument. He played without looking, simply staring into the fire.

Faith stiffened, then forced herself to relax. Music had no power over her now. It was no longer the voice of love. It was just music. A pretty sound, like the rhythm of the lapping waves or the wind soughing through the long grass.

She let the music, the hush of the waves, and the rustle of the breeze wash over her, balm to her ragged spirit.

"If that stew is burnt a'cos of your bletherin' on to that female, Stevens . . ."

Faith jerked upright as two men stepped into the light of the fire. One was small and wizened and nearing fifty, the other young, she thought—under his concealing red beard—not yet thirty. And huge. She blinked. She'd thought Mr. Blacklock was tall.

The small man gave Faith a curious glance and a quick, "Evenin' miss," but it was clear where his priorities lay. He whipped the lid of the pot off, peered in, gave it a quick stir, and looked up, grinning. His face was badly scarred, and his grin twisted it in a peculiar way, but his eyes twinkled, and Faith warmed to him instantly.

"Thank you, miss, for the saving of me stew."

Faith was surprised. "How do you know I did anything?"

He snorted. "Mr. Nicholas? Remember to stir the stew?"

"I told her to add the extra wine," Mr. Blacklock said with mild indignation. "Miss Merrit, let me introduce you. The culinary doubting Thomas is Wilfred Stevens, and the bearded giant is Mr. Dougal McTavish, otherwise known as Mac."

Faith greeted the two men. Mr. Stevens gave her a warm smile as he shook her hand, but Mr. McTavish stood like a stump on the edge of the firelight, ignoring the hand she held out to him. He looked her up and down from under bushy red brows, and Faith shriveled a little inside at his expression.

She knew what he was thinking. His opinion of her was no better than that of the men who'd pursued her in the dark. Only *he* wouldn't touch her with a ten-foot barge pole. She raised her chin and gave him back stare for stare.

"Mac? This is Miss Merrit." Mr. Blacklock repeated. There was that tone again.

The big fellow growled a reluctant, "How d'ye do," before peering narrowly at Nicholas Blacklock. "Ye have the look o' a man who's been in a fight, Cap'n."

Nicholas Blacklock explained about the three attackers, only he called them unwelcome guests and said nothing at all about his heroism, only that Faith had taken up a burning branch to the villains, and they'd run off. The big man wasn't fooled, though, and gave Faith another hard look. "Aye, well, bad meat will always attract vermin!"

"That's enough!" snapped Mr. Blacklock.

"Aye, well, I'll go an' check that the 'unwelcome guests' are gone, for certain.' He stomped back into the darkness.

Faith blinked at the big man's hostility.

"Ignore him, miss," Stevens said, as he fussed over the pot. "These days Mac doesn't have much time for ladies—for females of any sort. He suffered a disappointment a few years back and has been like a bear with a sore head ever since. But his bark is worse than his bite."

"He'd better not bark or bite again within my hearing," Nicholas Blacklock said with soft menace as the big man returned from checking the brush.

Mac gave him a shocked look and hurriedly sat down. "Can I pass ye some wine, miss?" His voice was grudging but polite.

How did Mr. Blacklock do it? she wondered as she accepted the mug of wine. He never raised his voice, spoke quite mildly and softly, and yet she—and now apparently this giant—found themselves obeying without thought. *Drink this. Stir that. Sit on this rock. Stay for dinner. Be nice to this woman.* Was it that very deep voice he had? There was something mesmerizing about a deep, masculine voice.

Stevens handed her a bowl of stew and a chunk of bread. "Here y'are, miss, eat it while it's nice an' hot."

"Thank you, Mr. Stevens." She waited for the others to be served. Fragrant steam rose from the bowl. She longed to just dive in.

As soon as everyone had been served, she closed her eyes to say grace. The noise of vigorous slurping interrupted her.

"Miss Merrit, will you say grace, please?" said the man at her side.

There was a sudden suspension of chewing sounds. Stevens froze, his spoon halfway to his mouth. "Sorry, miss," he mumbled, his mouth still full. He put down his bowl and waited.

Faith, her cheeks aflame, quickly recited grace, then devoted her attention to the stew. It was the best meal she'd ever eaten. The meat was tender and tasty, studded with chunks of potatoes and flavored with wine and herbs.

"It's wonderful, Mr. Stevens," she said. "I don't know when I've eaten a tastier stew."

Stevens's battered face crinkled with bashful pleasure. "Have some more, miss. There's plenty."

"Perhaps Miss Merrit would like a cup of tea, Stevens," suggested Mr. Blacklock at the end of the meal.

Tea! Faith did not know how long it was since she'd had a proper cup of tea. The French made it differently, and Felix detested tea. He only drank wine or coffee.

"Would you, miss?" asked Stevens.

"It would be lovely, th-thank you." Her voice broke as emotions suddenly came welling up from nowhere. Faith bit her quivering lip and blinked furiously to keep back the tears. She had been through so much already without crying one drop; it was ridiculous to be brought undone by something as simple and homelike as the offer of a cup of tea. Especially now, when she'd just had a delicious meal and was warm and safe for the first time in weeks.

It would be utterly missish to give in to tears now! And she would *not* be missish! She pulled out her handkerchief and blew into it fiercely.

Nicholas Blacklock watched, frowning. She was like no female he'd ever met. Young, gently born and delicately built, she'd escaped gang rape by a hairsbreadth and afterward had fought to control her emotions. She'd endured the pain of salt water on a hundred cuts and scratches and not made a single complaint. She'd borne his ministrations on her twisted ankle without a sound, and yet now, at the simple offer of tea, she was fighting off tears.

She was quality through and through.

In the last few years he hadn't come much in contact with young ladies of quality—his mother's recent efforts notwithstanding—but he'd known such ladies on the peninsular, during the war. Even by their gallant standards, Miss Faith Merrit seemed extraordinary.

Something or someone had brought her to unforgivably desperate straits. And it wasn't just three drunken fishermen.

Nicholas Blacklock was determined to find out what had happened to her. And fix it before he moved on.

He waited until she'd finished her cup of tea and then gave a silent gesture to his men that he wished to be alone with her.

"Now, Miss Merrit, I think it's time we talked."

It was as if he'd stung her. "Sorry, it is late and past time I took my leave." She scrambled to her feet as she spoke, stumbling in her haste. "I can never thank you enough for rescuing me from those men. And could you please convey my thanks to Mr. Stevens for that delicious dinner?"

"I shall escort you." Nick rose.

There was a short silence, then she stammered hastily. "No, no, thank you very much. My—er—my l-lodgings are but a step from here, and I feel quite safe now. Those men are long gone; I feel sure of it."

"You are too full of pride for your own good, I think," he said softly.

There was a long silence, then she whispered, "You know, don't you?"

He didn't answer. There was no need.

"Are you also without funds? Is that why you are forced to sleep on the beach, too?"

He closed his eyes briefly. Dear Lord, she was sleeping on the beach! He shook his head. "No, that was my choice. I have felt rather . . . hemmed in lately, and since the weather was so fine, I wanted to sleep under the stars." His mouth twitched wryly. "My men are less than impressed with my choice, I might add."

"Oh. So you are not obliged to."

He grimaced. "In a way I am. Put it down to having a surfeit of civilization recently. When I was in the army, sleeping under the stars was a matter of daily routine. I suppose I wanted to . . ." His voice tailed off.

What was he trying to recapture? His youth? By most accounts he *was* young. Or was it a way of avoiding the implacable future? Pretending a freedom he knew he didn't have. All he knew was that he had to do it. To stay in England, watching his mother's dreams die again, would kill him.

A snort of bitter laughter escaped him. *Kill him.* What a joke!

"So you will not leave me to my threadbare pride and my sand hills?" she asked softly.

He shook his head. "No, although your pride is in no way threadbare, Miss Merrit." He added in what he hoped was a lighter voice, "But if we are discussing sand hills, mine are, I believe, safer and more comfortable."

She still hesitated. He wished he could read her expression, but he couldn't. He added matter-of-factly, "I have no intention of letting you leave unprotected, so you may as well give in graciously." A spasm crossed his face.

She frowned. "What is it?"

"Nothing. Just a headache." His brow was suddenly

deeply furrowed, and he spoke as if he had to force each word.

"You are ill," she insisted.

He began to shake his head but froze in midmovement. "I get . . . headaches. Forgive my rudeness, but—" He staggered to where a roll of blankets lay near the fire. He kicked it, and it unrolled into a bed. "Make sure . . . you stay here. My men . . . take care of you." He carefully lay down on the bedroll and closed his eyes. He looked dreadful.

Faith looked around wildly and called for help.

McTavish appeared.

"What is the matter with him, Mr. McTavish?"

McTavish ignored her. He pulled a blanket over Mr. Blacklock, as gently as if he were a child. Stevens arrived, took one look at his master, and began to build up the fire.

Mr. Blacklock opened his eyes, gripped the big Scotsman's wrist, grated, "The girl . . . stays with us," and closed his eyes again.

"Dinna fash yersel' lad. I'll see to it." McTavish turned to Faith. "You stay here. I'll fetch ye a blanket tae sleep in." He gave Faith a hard look, as if daring her to take one step away from his custody.

Not that she had any intention of leaving now. He looked really ill. His face was dead white, even in the firelight, and his forehead was deeply furrowed with pain. She knelt down beside him. Had his head been injured in the fight? Was it her fault he lay here like this?

His thick, dark hair was tumbled in all directions. She smoothed it back. His skin was clammy. She took out her handkerchief, still damp with seawater, and wiped his face gently. With those penetrating, watchful eyes closed, he seemed younger than she'd thought at first. Not yet thirty, she thought.

Had the furrowed brow eased a little? She could not

tell if it was wishful thinking or not. She straightened to find McTavish eyeing her, his bushy brows knotted in grim suspicion. He dumped a bundle of gray blankets on the ground, like tossing down a gauntlet.

"I hope ye don't mind sleeping under the stars, on the sand and all, miss," said Stevens, laying driftwood on the fire in a complicated pattern.

Faith gave him a rueful smile, but she couldn't bring herself to explain the depths to which she'd fallen. "What is wrong with Mr. Blacklock?"

Stevens opened his mouth to speak but was interrupted by McTavish. "Hush up, ye bletherer! If he wants her to know he can tell her himself in the morning!"

"He will be recovered by morning then?"

The big Scotsman gave her a surly look. "He will, aye!"

"The headaches pass. You can sleep here, miss," Stevens picked up the bundle McTavish had dumped and shook it out.

Faith hesitated. It was rather close to Mr. Blacklock, even if he was currently insensible.

Stevens continued, "It's best you stay near the fire. I can see you've been troubled by midges. The smoke will keep them away."

Faith put her hand to her face, which was covered in midge bites from the previous night.

"Mac will sleep over there." He pointed to where McTavish was rolling himself in a blanket, far from the fire.

"Midges don't bother him. And besides, he snores somethin' shockin'. I'll be over here, on the other side o' the fire."

"What about Mr. Blacklock? Shouldn't someone watch over him?"

"No. Wulf will watch over us all; he'll rouse us all at

the first sign of any trouble—from Mr. Nicholas or from anyone else."

Faith recalled the way the big dog had growled and barked earlier and felt better.

"Now you get yourself some sleep, miss. You look as if you could do with it. Mr. Nicholas will sleep soon enough. He usually does once the headache passes."

"Thank you, Mr. Stevens."

He hesitated. "Just Stevens, if you don't mind, miss. I'm Mr. Nicholas's groom, y'see. Watched him grow up."

Faith nodded. "Very well, if you'd prefer it."

"I would. Well, if you've got everything you need, I'll be off, then. Good night miss."

Faith bade both men good night and sat down. She brushed the sand from her damp feet and from between her toes, then wrapped herself in her blanket and settled down for the night. She took one last look at Nicholas Blacklock.

He was breathing more regularly now, so perhaps the headache was passing, as Stevens had said it would. His strong profile was limned by the bright gleam of the fire. He looked gentler in sleep, not so grim and somber.

Beowulf gave a longing look toward his bearded master, turned three times in a circle, and dropped down on the sand beside Mr. Blacklock and closed his eyes with a big, doggy sigh.

"Good dog," Faith told him.

The dog opened one baleful eye, looked at her, and bared his yellow fangs in a low growl, warning her to keep her distance.

"Like master like dog," she told him in a whisper, feeling better for the defiance.

She wriggled a bit to make the sand conform to her shape, then lay in the dark, watching the flames throw dancing shadows, and thought of her sisters.

Where were they now, and what they were doing? Probably worrying, she thought ruefully. They would have received her letter saying she was leaving Felix. They'd have expected her home days ago.

She closed her eyes and tried to send good thoughts to her twin. They could sometimes do that; feel each other's emotion. Faith concentrated, not knowing if it would work but helpless to do anything else.

That had been the worst of these last weeks, the feeling of helplessness. She'd had no idea what to do. All her life she'd let others to look after her: older sisters, her much bolder twin, her great-uncle, and finally, Felix.

Felix. What a naive, trustful fool she'd been!

She lay in her borrowed blanket, staring up into the velvet dark sky. One star seemed a little brighter than the others, standing alone, yet bright and sparkling. She would be like that star, she decided. She would learn— somehow—to take care of herself. She would never be so wholly dependent on anyone again.

The fire crackled gently, the dancing flames making a bright glow against the night sky. Beyond the fire, the waves hissed and shushed, hissed and shushed in a soothing rhythm, and soon Faith, too, was asleep.

She was woken in the middle of the night by a sound; she did not know what. Cautiously she raised her head and looked around. She could see nothing. Beowulf was sitting up, though, watching Mr. Blacklock with ears pricked and a worried expression. The big creature whined softly and pawed at the man's body.

Faith moved closer to see what the matter was. The dog growled low in its throat, but she ignored it. Mr. Blacklock's head turned restlessly back and forth as if he was trapped. His expression was far from peaceful, but it wasn't a rictus of pain as it had been earlier. A bad dream, perhaps, rather than pain. Faith was well acquainted with the effects of nightmares. Her twin had them often. Faith, too.

She felt his forehead. It was no longer clammy. She stroked it softly, smoothing it under her fingers. "There, there, all is well," she whispered. His eyes opened wide and stared at her, unseeing.

"Hush now," she repeated softly. " 'Tis just a dream. There is nothing to worry about."

He looked blindly around him as if searching.

"Hush. Everyone is safe and well. There is nothing to worry about. Go back to sleep."

His hand came up and grabbed her hand, imprisoning it fast in his big fist. He stared fixedly at her a moment, then his eyes closed again. His grip on her tightened, and he gave a big sigh and relaxed with her hand clamped against his chest.

Faith made several attempts to tug her hand free of the warm, hard grip but could not move her hand. His heart beat under her fingers, steady, a little fast. As soon as he slept again, his fingers would loosen their hold on her, she thought.

She lay down beside him, her hand imprisoned by his, and waited for him to fall asleep again.

It was very soothing feeling his chest rise and fall with his breathing. Like the waves of the sea, going in . . . and out . . .

Nick awoke to the first rays of sun on his skin, a rare feeling of contentment and a sour taste in his mouth. He was hard, aroused, rampantly so; a state he had not woken in for some time. His mouth curved. It must have been some dream. He wished he could recall it.

He stretched and was immediately aware of a small, feminine hand tucked against his chest. The reason for his arousal became clear. No dream, but a soft female body that lay pressed against the length of him, curled against his side, warm and trusting. Intimate.

Who the devil was it? He had no recollection of taking a woman to bed. The only woman he recalled—and then the events of the previous evening came flooding back. He remembered the girl fleeing those swine, and the fight—God, but he'd enjoyed that!—and he recalled eating dinner beside the fire and the girl's prideful pretense of having somewhere to stay . . .

The rest was a blank. The reason for the unpleasant taste in his mouth suddenly became clear. He'd had another one. Already. Damn!

His contented feelings dissolved, though the state of his body remained unchanged. He sat up cautiously. His movement disturbed her, and she cuddled closer, mumbling something in her sleep.

Why had she reached out to him in the night? He was still in breeches and shirt, so nothing had passed between them. She was cold, perhaps? Or frightened. Needing a feeling of protection. Probably.

Beside him the thump, thump, thump of a tail told him Beowulf was awake and raring for exercise. Nick stretched again. He needed to clear his head. He glanced down at his body, which had not abated in the least. A swim would take care of both problems.

"Fetch Mac," he whispered. The dog bounded off, tail swaying joyfully. Taking care not to disturb the sleeping girl, Nick rose and looked down at her. She lay bundled in her blanket, sound asleep. All that was visible was a small, pink, peeling nose and a tangle of fair curls. No doubt she was exhausted after her trials the night before.

The morning was still chilly, despite the sun. She'd miss his warmth. Nick picked up his coat and spread it over her. She'd sleep for hours yet, plenty of time for him to decide what was to be done with her. One thing was clear; she couldn't go on as she was.

A splutter of Scottish curses came from the far side of the camp. Nick grinned. Wulf invariably woke Mac by licking his nose.

Faith awoke to the smell of man in her nostrils. Man and coffee. Could there be any more heavenly scent in the world? She inhaled deeply, luxuriously, and sat up, discovering as she did that she was wrapped in a man's greatcoat. Mr. Blacklock's? He was gone from his bed, she saw immediately. There was no sign of him or the dog. He must have recovered from his bout of . . . whatever it was.

"Sleep well, miss?" Stevens was bent over the fire.

Faith stood a little stiffly and stretched. For such an unconventional bed she had slept remarkably well. She shook out the greatcoat and blanket and laid them over a bush to air.

"There's hot water in that pot, miss. If you want to wash and so on before breakfast, you can go up in there, behind those bushes. No one shall disturb you. Mr. Nicholas and Mac are down at the beach. Mr. Nicholas wanted a swim. They should be back by the time you've finished."

"A swim? Really?" Too cold for swimming, she would have thought. She took the hot water and made her way deeper into the sand hills where she made her ablutions. It was heavenly to have hot water to wash in.

She brushed down her clothes as best she could, wishing they were clean and fresh. She felt suddenly nostalgic for a petticoat freshly pressed and smelling of starch and soap and the iron. She tidied her hair. Something at least had come of those years of growing up in Grandpapa's house, where no looking glasses were permitted. She could do her hair without one.

She touched her cheek gingerly. The swelling seemed better, but it was still sore. She was probably sporting a huge, unsightly bruise. She felt her skin and grimaced. A looking glass was the last thing she needed just now, with her nose sunburned and peeling and the midge bites. And freckles, too, probably. Aunt Gussie would have a fit.

Faith hadn't thought of freckles when she'd sold her bonnet. Only of the money it would bring. And the food she could buy with it.

Still, freckles beat starvation any day. And speaking of starvation . . . that bacon smelled heavenly. Despite her sore ankle and her blisters, there was a definite spring in her step as she returned to the campsite.

"Coffee, miss? If you don't mind waiting, I'll cook your breakfast along with Mr. Nicholas's and Mac's. They shouldn't be long." Stevens glanced impatiently down at the beach as he handed her a steaming mug. "I was sure they'd be out before now."

Faith sat by the fire, sipping the hot, black brew. It was amazing what company, a full stomach, a good sleep, and a cup of hot, strong coffee did for one's spirits, she reflected. She was just as destitute as yesterday, just as thoroughly ruined. It was true what people said; morning did bring the dawning of hope.

If Mr. Blacklock was indeed a gentleman of means, he might lend her the fare to England. England. She so longed to go home, home to where she was loved and she belonged, home to her sisters and to Great Uncle Oswald and Aunt Gussie. She missed her family so much, she ached.

But would home ever be the refuge it had once been? When she returned she'd be a social outcast, a ruined woman. She'd have to face the full weight of her foolish recklessness.

Faith drank her coffee and pondered her situation. She could not return to her former life. She would be forever coming into contact with people who *knew*, and she didn't think she could bear that. It had been hard enough when she was one of the Virtue Twins and people stared so. Now it would be much worse; in addition to being a twin, she would be that curiosity and source of malevolent gossip: a fallen woman.

The thought of having to face, over and over, the look on people's faces when they *knew*. The look that called her whore. It flayed her, every time. She wanted to explain that she'd been tricked, that she thought she'd married for *love*.

Her precious, romantic dream sounded like a cheap excuse now.

With foreigners, strangers, it was bad enough, but at home, with people she knew, people who'd been friends . . .

She couldn't face them, couldn't face their pity or scorn or worse, the smug glee that one of the beautiful Virtue Twins had fallen. There would be such play made with that name now. People would forget it had come about because the twins—all the Merridew girls— were named after virtues. Now the name would be an ironic statement, an added twist of the knife.

She took a final sip of the strong, bitter brew and tipped out the coffee grounds. The spent grounds stained the clean, white sand. She scooped up a handful of sand and drizzled it over them until the stain was buried.

A pity her errors could not be as easily dealt with. She would never be able to slip back into her old life. She would have to make a new one. But as what?

Charity and Edward could take her in, find something for her to do in their remote corner of Scotland, where the gossip might not follow her. Faith could help with her little niece, baby Aurora. She would like that. And Prudence, too, was expecting a baby soon. Faith could help her, too. She loved babies, had dreamed of having her own little ones one day . . .

She bit her lip. Another dream in the dirt. No decent man would want her for the mother of his children now.

She heard Stevens swearing softly under his breath. She glanced at him in surprise. He stared down at the beach, and his brow darkened. "Damn! They must think you're still asleep," he muttered. She turned to see what had so annoyed him.

"No, miss! Don't look!"

Faith stared at him in surprise.

Stevens hastened to apologize. "Sorry, I didn't mean to shout." He moderated his tone. "Ah, please don't look at the beach, miss." He grimaced, looking horribly embarrassed. "It's no fit sight for a lady."

He speared a thick slice of bread onto a wire toasting fork and handed it to Faith. "Make some toast, please, miss. I'll just nip down and tell those two you're awake! And don't turn your head, miss. Trust me!" He hurried down the beach.

Bemused, Faith took the toasting fork and held the bread over the glowing coals. But she was so very intrigued, she had to look—just one little peek—and so she turned, craning her neck to see what had so upset Stevens down on the beach.

The toasting fork drooped in her suddenly slackened grasp.

Nicholas Blacklock and his big Scottish friend had just emerged from their swim and were walking back up the beach toward a pile of clothing. Water streamed from their bodies. Faith swallowed.

The toast turned a perfect golden brown. Faith didn't notice. She was too dazzled by the gleam of morning sunshine on wet male bodies.

Wet, *naked* male bodies. Nicholas Blacklock and McTavish were totally naked. They strolled up the beach, talking and laughing, naked, unashamed, proudly masculine. Magnificent.

The toast blackened, then started to smoke. Faith didn't move.

Not that she had eyes for the brawny, bearded Scotsman. It was Mr. Blacklock who drew her eyes irresistibly. Faith's mouth dried as she watched.

Mr. Blacklock was a Greek statue come to life under her gaze; all hard, masculine elegance and lean, whipcord power. His dark hair was wet, slicked carelessly back from his face, sleek against his head, gleaming in the morning sun.

His legs were long and powerful, his chest broad and deep. She'd touched that chest. She swallowed at the thought. She watched the bunch and flow of muscles as he moved, lithe and full of the joy of life. His skin glowed. Sheer, naked, masculine beauty, strolling unconcerned up the beach toward her.

The toast burst into flames.

Chapter Three

∞

Luck affects everything. Let your hook always be cast; in the
stream where you least expect it there will be a fish.

OVID

"THE TOAST, MISS!"

Faith jumped. "Oh, heavens!" She hastily knocked the burning toast into the fire. "Sorry." Her cheeks must be flaming, too, she was certain. Had he noticed where she'd been looking?

"Never mind. 'Tis no worse than if Mac had done it—he's useless, the big gawk!" Stevens broke off and glanced at Faith. "I'm sorry, miss, I didn't mean—"

"It's all right," Faith said ruefully. "I deserved it. Will you trust me with another slice?"

He shrugged his agreement. "If you like. We can scrape any black bits off. It'll all get eaten, black or not."

Faith, on her mettle now, silently vowed there would not be a speck of black on any future toast. If she hadn't been so distracted . . . Thank goodness the fire would account for any extra redness in her cheeks. Whatever would they think of her if they knew how she'd stared? Stared at naked men. A true lady would have turned away, as Stevens had suggested. She concentrated on the toast.

It took great concentration, too, with the image of a naked Nicholas Blacklock still firmly fixed in her mind.

Stevens placed a dozen thick, streaky rashers of bacon into a pan, then thrust it into the coals. Soon they were sizzling, and the smell was heavenly.

Faith tried to concentrate on the toast but could not prevent an occasional quick glance at the two men coming up the beach, now dressed. Even clothed, he still looked magnificent.

Even clothed. How depraved had she become! She dropped a perfectly toasted slice on a tin plate, buttered it, and skewered another on the toasting fork.

Last night she'd seen him in firelight, a man of shadows, hard and strong and fierce. A fearsome warrior, yet she recalled the way he'd tended her hurts, with repressed anger and gentle hands.

This morning, his face and body gleaming and wet in the morning sun, he did not seem the same man. The man of the night seemed all dark and brooding mystery. Now he looked like a sea god risen out of the waves, powerful, exhilarated, full of life.

Clad only in buff breeches and a white linen shirt, he looked the essence of strength, of masculinity. His shirt clung to his body. His skin was still damp. His chest was broad and powerful, his legs taking long strides in the sand.

A whiff of smoke caught her attention, and she hastily turned the toast. Slightly scorched did not count.

"Breakfast's almost ready," said Stevens as the men arrived at the campsite. "Bacon's cooked, miss is making the toast, and I'm just doing the eggs now." As he spoke he broke eggs into the sizzling pan.

"Good morning, Miss Merrit." Nicholas Blacklock bowed gracefully.

For a moment, Faith did not recognize the name she'd hastily claimed. "Good morning, Mr. Blacklock, Mr. McTavish." McTavish made some sort of noise, which Faith decided was a Scottish greeting. She stared up at Nicholas Blacklock. His eyes were gray, darker gray than the dawn sky, lighter than the gray and glassy sea behind. His skin was lightly tanned. Tanned evenly all over, she recalled. He must swim naked often. Their eyes met, and she blushed and looked away, as if he could read her thoughts.

He squatted down beside her, took her chin between finger and thumb, turned her face to the sun, and examined it intently. Faith squirmed. "I know; I look a sight."

He said seriously, "No, the scratches are healing, the swelling has gone down a bit, and the bruises are a good color."

"A good color?" She was inclined to be indignant.

"Yes, they'll fade soon. You're obviously a fast healer." He released her chin and reached for the hem of her skirt. Faith, her hands encumbered with the toasting fork, managed to swing her knees away. "My feet are perfectly recovered, I thank you," she said in a firm voice that told him she had no intention of baring her limbs to him again.

His lips quirked, and he sat down beside her in an easy movement. "I trust you slept well."

She checked the toast. "Yes, thank you. Amazingly well—better than I had expected. And you—have you quite recovered from your indisposition?"

"I have." His tone made it clear the subject was off-limits.

"Did you enjoy your swim?" She flushed as she recalled the sight he'd made emerging from the waves and added hastily, "Um, Stevens told me you went for a swim. Not that I saw you swimming, you underst—" She broke off, flustered, when he gave her a piercing look. What did it mean? Did he know she'd peeked? She hurried on, "It's a beautiful morning. Was the water cold?" Oh heavens, what had made her ask that? She'd *seen* it was cold! Her whole face flamed.

"Och, give it here!" Mac grabbed the toasting fork. The toast was smoking gently.

"Oh dear, I'm sorry! I was not looking!"

"Aye, I noticed," he grunted. "I'll have tae scrape this lot wi' a knife!" He pulled a knife from his boot and with a long-suffering expression started to scrape toast.

It was only one piece and not that badly burned and Faith was inclined to tell him so, but Stevens interrupted. "Don't worry, miss. Mac is a rare talent at scraping toast. As he said, he's our usual toast maker." Stevens winked at Faith, and she felt better.

"Now, here's yer breakfast. Eat it while it's hot." It was a feast; golden scrambled eggs, thick slices of bacon, and toast, carefully scraped and lavishly spread with the rich local butter.

"Now, Miss Merrit, I think it's time you told me your story," Nick said when they'd finished breakfast.

"My story?" she said, with a not-very-convincing air of innocent surprise.

"You know very well what I mean," he growled. "The story of how a gently bred young English lady comes to be alone, hungry, and sleeping among French sand hills. At the mercy of any passing villain." His bluntness was deliberate. This was no time for false pride. She could not be allowed to continue like this. The consequences of last night—had he not been there to prevent them—were unthinkable.

"None of us will repeat a word of what passes here. You have my word."

She looked down and mumbled a thank-you. "I suppose the story will be all over London in a few weeks anyway . . ." She hugged her knees and wiggled her bare toes, stretching them toward the fire. The slender, dainty feet were a mess of blisters. Healing blisters, Nick saw, but still! He made a resolution to do something about those big ugly boots at the first opportunity.

When it seemed she wasn't going to say any more, he said, "Come on—spit it out! What the devil are you doing in this mess?"

She raised her head and gave him a cool look. He attempted to moderate his tone, make it sound less like a prisoner interrogation. "I mean, who is responsible for your current predicament?"

She shrugged. "I have no one but myself to blame."

Nick's brows knotted. It was his experience that most people's problems were invariably someone else's fault. "How so?"

She hesitated, then said, "I fell in love." She broke off, and for a moment it seemed as though she would leave it there. Nick opened his mouth to prompt her further, but she said, "I fell in love in England, but he was—well, I *thought* he was a Hungarian violinist. He asked me to marry him, to elope with him! And . . . and so . . . I did."

"I see." *Damned fool romantic notions!*

Stevens swore under his breath. "You didn't even think about the disgrace, miss?"

She gave him a rueful look. "It never even occurred to me, Stevens."

"Why ever not, miss? Surely you knew what people would say!"

"No," she said simply. "The thing is, eloping is something of a tradition in my family. My mother and father ran away to Italy to get married." She hugged her knees, and her voice grew wistful. "I grew up hearing about it. They were completely and wonderfully in love until they day they died . . ."

The fire sputtered, and far away, seagulls fought over some morsel of food.

"You said you thought he was a Hungarian violinist," Nick prompted. "Wasn't he?"

"No! Well, yes—he is most definitely a violinist and an extremely talented one, but he wasn't Hungarian at all! He was *Bulgarian*."

Nick frowned. "And it mattered—his being Bulgarian?"

"No, of course not. What mattered was that he has *five children*! Five!"

"Five children?" he nodded. "Rather a quiverful, I agree. I gather you're not fond of children."

"Of course I'm fond of children. I love children! It wasn't the children!"

"Then what?" He was puzzled.

"He was *married*. His wife and children are living back in Bulgaria. He *lied* to me."

"So when he refused to marry you—"

"Oh, he married me. I would never have lived with him without being married. I am not so lost to propriety as—"

Nick leaned forward. "But you just said—"

"The thing is, I *thought* we got married." Her voice was a mixture of desolation and anger. "He faked the wedding."

"How the devil did the bast—" Nick bit off the word and tried again. "Er, how does one fake a wedding?"

"He bribed a priest for the use of the church, and he got a friend of his to dress up as a minister and perform the ceremony."

Nick carefully unclenched his fists. He wanted to throttle the bastard. "How did you discover the cheat?"

She sighed. "It was our one month anniversary, and I wanted to do something to celebrate. Felix was busy, so I decided I'd go to the church and take some flowers there. I took a bottle of wine for the minister, too. But when I asked for him . . . I found the real priest and . . . well, it all came out. He said he hadn't realized what Felix wanted the church for . . ." She shook her head.

Nick flexed his fists. Two people to throttle; a Bulgarian fiddler and a crooked priest. "What did you do then?"

"I went home and confronted Felix about it. I . . . I thought it would all turn out to be a misunderstanding, but . . . he didn't deny a thing." She bent over so he couldn't see her face. Trailing sand through her fingers, she said in a low voice, "I discovered he'd never loved me, had never really cared about me at all."

Nick said nothing, just waited for her to explain.

"I was a bet, you see."

"A *bet*?" His body was like a coiled spring.

"Yes. He bet one of his friends he could elope with me." She added in a tight voice, "Actually, any well-born English girl would have done. But I was the stupidest girl in London that season. I thought I'd found my true love, just like Mama."

There was a long, awkward silence. If he ever met him, the violinist was a dead man! To ruin a sweet young girl *for a bet*!

Nick could imagine it. A shy, sheltered, naive little creature, raised on stupid romantic fairy tales. She'd be no match for a slick Continental flatterer. She ought to have been protected from such a villain. "Did your parents not see what was in the wind, try to stop you?"

"My parents died when I was seven."

Nick dismissed them with a curt mumble of sympathy, but he was not to be distracted. "Did no one try to stop this impostor from targeting you?"

She shook her head. "The thing is, Felix had assumed the name of a real Hungarian family. The Rimavska fam-

ily is well-known, very rich and aristocratic, so he was
accounted a good match. Great Unc—"

She bit off the sentence unfinished, but Nick could
put two and two together. The lax guardian was her
great-uncle. It made sense. Only a very sheltered girl, a
girl brought up by an elderly man, would have been so
easily deceived.

And it would account for why the guardian was
willing to turn a blind eye. Anything for a chance of a
fortune, he thought savagely.

She continued, "He wasn't Felix Vladimir Rimavska
at all. His real name was Yuri Popov."

"I'd bloody well pop him off!" muttered Stevens
angrily.

Mac noisily shoved some wood onto the fire. It
blazed, creating a gush of smoke, before the wood
caught.

Nicholas, coughing, gave Mac an irritated look but
turned back to the girl sitting hunched and desolate next
to him. "That still does not explain why you are apparently destitute and abandoned, unprotected. Do you tell
me this"—he carefully unclenched his fists again—
"this *violinist* threw you out with not a penny to your
name?"

"Oh no." Her voice was dull. "He wanted me to remain as his mistress."

Nick swore.

"Feli—" She caught herself up. "*Yuri* did not see
why his wife and children should be any sort of an im-
pediment to his pleasure. After all, they were in Bulgaria."

"Did the fellow have no shame at all?" exclaimed
Stevens.

"No. He was not the slightest bit put out by my dis-
covery of his lies. He knew I was ruined, that I could
never return to my former life. He thought I had no

choice but to stay with him until he tired of me. So many people knew we had run away to get married, you see." She added in a brittle voice. "I cannot believe the extent of my folly now, but when we eloped, I wrote to everyone to tell them. I thought it was the most romantic experience of my life." She gave a dry laugh. "I even thought Mama and Papa would approve if they knew."

Mac crashed around, rattling dishes noisily. "For God's sake, Mac, will you stop your dammed noise!" Nick said irritably.

"The dishes need tae be cleaned."

"Then take them down to the beach and wash them there!"

"Aye, I will that!" There was another lot of rattling and clashing of tin implements, and then he heard Mac stomping away, his displeasure evident. Nick ignored him. He wanted the whole story.

"So what did you do?"

"I could not stay there another minute. As soon as he left for his concert—he really is extremely talented, you know—I packed a few things and fled. I did not take the diligence—it was booked out and—"

"Do you mean to say you left Paris at night, to travel back to England on your own and in the power of complete strangers?"

She gave him a narrow look. "I had no choice."

"Didn't you have a maid?"

"No."

"What? But—"

"Look!" she flared. "I was upset, and I wanted to leave Paris as soon as I could. I didn't think it through, and I haven't had much experience of planning journeys. I did the best I could at the time, and yes, I know it was a stupid and dangerous thing to do. Does that make you happy?" She glared at him.

"Not a bit." Nick glared back at her. Why the devil

should she imagine he'd be happy that she'd put herself in danger? He thought he'd made it quite clear that he didn't approve of her being in danger.

"So what happened, miss?" Stevens asked in a soothing tone.

"I found—well, someone in the boardinghouse arranged it for me—a private carriage taking passengers. It was very old and rather dirty, but I did not care." She paused for a moment, then added in a defensive voice, "Yes, I know! I should have cared. I will in future!"

"Why? What happened?" Stevens prompted.

"After they'd dropped the last of the other passengers off, I heard them talking—they did not realize I understood French. They—they planned to rob me— and worse. I managed to escape them but had to leave my baggage behind. Which is how you find me now," she said with an air of having finished her tale.

Nick disagreed. She hadn't left Paris in those disgusting big boots. She hadn't left Paris half-starved. She'd left out several significant details. But he hadn't been a wartime serving officer for nothing. Skilled questioning could elicit unexpected details.

"How did you escape?" Blunt questions could also do the job.

"I jumped out of it."

"Out of a moving carriage?" Nick caught himself up and followed the explosion with a mild. "And don't tell me—it was dark, too, correct?"

"The moon was bright, though luckily it went behind the clouds for all the time I was hiding in the vineyards. And as soon as they stopped searching for me and went away, it came back out, and I could see to walk."

Nick closed his eyes. Dear God, she'd jumped from a moving carriage in unknown territory in the dark. He heard himself say, "You little fool! You could have been seriously injured!"

She retorted with an edge in her voice, "I might have been hurt, but I wasn't. If I'd stayed, however, I would definitely have been hurt, for I would have fought them."

He had an instant image of the way she'd stood beside him last night, waving that burning stick, attempting to look fierce. He sank his head in his hands and groaned.

Faith didn't notice. She shivered as she recalled that terrifying time after she'd jumped from the moving carriage, crouching between rows of vines in the dark, praying for the moon to stay behind the clouds. It was hours before the driver and guard gave up. And then she was alone in the dark, somewhere in northern France, with no money, dressed only in a thin silk gown, a Kashmir shawl, dainty kid slippers, and a tiny, elegant bonnet. She shivered. It wasn't until they'd left that she started to feel the cold.

"Whereabouts was that, miss?" Stevens interrupted her thoughts.

"Somewhere past Montreuil."

"Montreuil!" Mr. Blacklock's head snapped up. "How the devil did you get from Montreuil to here?"

She gritted her teeth. She was not some—some skivvy to be snapped at. She answered pleasantly, a counterpoint to his rudeness. "I walked."

Stevens whistled, impressed.

Mr. Blacklock muttered savagely, "Hence the atrocious state of your feet!"

Embarrassed, Faith tucked the atrocious feet under her skirts so he wouldn't have to be offended by them any further. How on earth had she imagined him as kind? He was rude and bossy, and she just itched to get up and walk away. But after all he'd done, she did feel she owed him an explanation—even if he spoke to her as if she were a criminal in the dock.

She said with dignity, "I traded my kid slippers and

my Kashmir shawl to a farmer's wife for these boots and the cloak." And some soup and bread and cheese, but she wasn't going to tell him that. He'd probably snap her nose off again for the crime of needing to eat.

"It was a good trade. My slippers would never have lasted the distance; I could feel every stone through their thin soles. She offered me her sabots—wooden clogs—but I could never have walked in them, so I held out for her son's Sunday boots. And my Kashmir shawl was very fine, but not warm enough for the nights."

"Did no one offer you shelter? Assistance?" Mr. Blacklock said.

"No." She hung her head. "People . . . when they see a young woman on foot in a dirty silk dress and peasant boots . . . they . . . misunderstand. They took me for . . . for—"

"We know what they took you for."

She felt her face reddening. "Yes, so I learned not to ask. But I did ask some English ladies in Calais—I mean, I was speaking *English*—but they, too, seemed to think . . ." She swallowed and looked down at her boots. She would have to—somehow—accustom herself to being despised by respectable ladies.

"Forget the stiff-rumped English ladies." Nicholas Blacklock sounded almost bored. "The solution to your difficulties is clear."

"Oh, is it?" Faith was nettled by his calm announcement. Her future seemed clear to her, too, only she didn't feel half as sanguine about it. "What is so clear? Would you care to share this solution?"

"It's obvious. You will marry me."

"*Marry you?*" Faith choked. She jumped to her feet. "Marry *you*?" With great dignity, she stalked off.

The trouble with stalking off, Faith reflected some time later, was that while it was very satisfying in some respects, it would have been a lot more effective if she'd had somewhere impressive to stalk to. A castle, or a tower: a place from where she could sit and glare loftily down at him.

Sitting on a rock, even quite a big, impressive sort of rock, did not have the desirable remoteness. Nor that feeling of solid impregnability combined with superiority that a tower in a castle could bestow on her. A rock on the next beach was not the sort of place from which you could extract a groveling apology.

She hovered between fury and tears.

"You will marry me" indeed! Did he think she was a complete fool? Totally gullible and naive? That she would fall—again!—for such an obvious ploy!

She thought of the way he'd tended her injured feet last night—with gentle hands and a savage diatribe about her foolishness—and wanted to weep. With anger, of course. She would not give him the satisfaction of tears. Arrogant brute. And quite impossible, of course.

Because even if he was sleeping under the stars, he was obviously not a poor man. His clothes and boots were of the best quality, and he traveled with a servant. He was educated and well-spoken and he had that air of command—not to mention arrogance!—that informed her he was a gentleman born.

And what gentleman born would offer to marry a destitute woman of unknown background who, by her own confession, was a fallen woman? It was inconceivable, impossible. Ridiculous. And Faith would not stay to be mocked.

Because even though she knew he hadn't meant it, it hurt. And why on earth the careless words of a stranger she'd known for less than a day should be allowed to hurt her was something she didn't care to think about.

A tear rolled down her cheek. She dashed it angrily

away. Stupid man! He probably thought it was a joke! She never wanted to speak to him again!

The trouble was, her boots and her cloak were back at his campsite. She had no choice but to return. She set her jaw and marched around the small headland, determined to collect her belongings and leave in dignified silence.

The campsite was deserted, though everything remained in place. The fire was still burning; in fact, something smoked dreadfully, and the stench was horrible. Faith peered through the smoke and gave a gasp of indignation.

"My boots!" She stared in stupefaction. Her boots—or rather, what remained of them—were sitting in the middle of the fire, a blackened mass of misshapen, smoldering leather.

She looked around for someone to blame, but the camp was still deserted. How dare he burn her boots! Now she was trapped here, for she'd already tried walking in bare feet, and once she stepped off the sand onto stony paths or prickly vegetation, it was impossible. Besides, she'd look even more of a beggar if she were barefoot. When she got her hands on Nicholas Blacklock she would—she would—! She clenched her fists angrily. She would *force* him to buy her a new pair of boots!

She spotted Stevens fishing near the headland. She stormed down the beach toward him.

"He's gone into town with Mac, miss," Stevens said the moment she came within earshot. "On business."

"He burned my boots!" she exclaimed indignantly.

Stevens nodded. "Yes, miss, I saw him."

"But they were perfectly good boots!"

"Yes, miss, that's what I said, too."

"He had no right to burn them. They were my boots!"

"Yes, miss. I think that's why he burned them."

Faith clenched her fists. There was nothing worse than being angry and needing to yell at someone, and the only person available was not only innocent of any crime, but kept agreeing with you in the most infuriatingly placid way.

"Do you know how to fish, miss?"

"No, I don't—" began Faith in frustration.

"Here y'are then. It's easy." He shoved a fishing line into her hand. Faith was about to explain in no uncertain terms that she had no desire whatsoever to learn to fish, when he added, "Now that we've got an extra mouth to feed . . ."

She shut the extra mouth and fished. After a few minutes, she became aware that Stevens was observing her from the corner of his eye. "Yes?" It came out rather snappily.

He shrugged. "Oh, nothing, miss. I was about to observe what a very soothing activity fishing was . . ." He darted her a wry glance. "Only mebbe I've changed my mind."

She had to laugh then. "I'm sorry. I did not mean to be rude, only I did so want to speak to Mr. Blacklock. I am furious with him, but I didn't mean to take my frustration out on you, Stevens."

"S'all right, miss. You didn't say nothing to upset me."

They fished then for a while in silence. Faith glanced across at him. He really did seem to find fishing soothing. It was quite pleasant sitting here on a rock and looking out to sea, but it was also just a little bit . . . boring. Especially when she needed to throttle someone.

After a while, Stevens said, "Don't you mind Mr. Nick's high-handedness, miss. He always has done what he thinks is right, no matter what anyone else says. Always, ever since he was a boy."

Faith sniffed and fished. High-handedness indeed! He could be high-handed with his own possessions.

"I've known him all his life, see."

Faith waited for him to say more, but he seemed intent on his fishing. Curiosity got the better of her. "You've known Mr. Blacklock all his life?"

"Ever since he was able to escape his nanny and head for the stables. Loved horses, he did, right from when he was a little lad. All animals, really, even the wild creatures—especially the wild creatures." Stevens frowned over his cane and wound the line in. "Cunning beggars! They've nibbled me bait off again." He pulled something out of a pail that sat beside him in the sand and threaded it on his hook. Faith averted her eyes, trying not to notice that whatever it was wriggled. When he'd tossed the line back in, he continued, "Master Nicholas was the same age as my boy, Algy."

"You have a son?"

"Had. He got killed in the war." He tugged at the line. "When Mr. Nicholas got sent off to war, my boy followed him. Ran off without so much as a by-your-leave and joined up wi' Master Nick." He shook his head in wry reminiscence, "He couldn't let Mr. Nicholas go off by hisself, you see. The pair of 'em was inseparable—bin getting up to mischief together since they was old enough to run. Mr. Nicholas, he got Algy into his own regiment. Old Sir Henry had bought him a commission, you see."

"I'm sorry you lost your son, Stevens. I suppose they thought the army would be a big adventure—boys often do, I believe."

"Nope." Stevens gave her a look. "Master Nicholas, he was sent, miss. Didn't want to go. Didn't have no choice about it. Old Sir Henry was furious with him— he'd got up to mischief again, y'see. Old man reckoned the army would learn him a lesson."

"What sort of mischief?"

He shook his head. "Harmless stuff, boys' stuff, but it drove the old man wild with rage. Wanted Mr. Nicholas to be more like his brother—in other words, more like Sir Henry."

Faith would have liked to ask about the brother, but Stevens was deep in reminiscences, and she didn't like to interrupt.

"Mr. Nicholas was desperate angry about bein' forced to be a soldier. Never hurt a fly, he wouldn't. Not then, at any rate. So young he was—and Algy, too. Just boys." He shook his head. "They'd have both been killed in their first battle if it hadn't been for Mac."

"Mac?"

He cast her a look. "Don't let Mac's bitterness blind you. He's a good man, missie. Ruined he was, by a heartless Spanish light-skirt." He shook his head again. "That big Scottish lummox has a heart of marshmallow."

"Mac?" She couldn't believe it.

Stevens grinned. "Hard to believe, I know, but he risked his life, diving into the river—he couldn't swim in those days—to rescue a misbegotten mongrel pup that had been tied to a brick and slung in. Mac fished it out and nearly drowned himself. He would have if Mr. Nick hadn't dived in when he saw Mac was in trouble. Tch! And all over a dog!" He jerked his head back toward the camp. "That Beowulf. Mr. Nicholas, Mac, and Algy palled up a'cos of that ugly pup, and the three lads became mates, even though Mr. Nick was an officer and the other two naught but common soldiers. Best thing that happened to Mr. Nick and my Algy, Mac was. See, they were the same age, only Mac had started soldiering at twelve."

"Twelve!" Faith was shocked.

"Yes, as a drummer boy." Stevens shrugged. "There's

lots of Scots lads in the army—it's that or starvation in the Highlands. So by the time my two green lads arrived on the peninsular, Mac was a seasoned soldier. He showed them both the ropes, taught 'em enough soldiering tricks to stay alive by the time they faced their first battle. Three lads, and all just sixteen."

He was silent for a long while, thinking of his son, Faith thought, then he added bitterly. "Old Sir Henry Blacklock was right. Army did learn Mr. Nick different. Changed him. Killed something inside him. Killed every one of his blessed friends, too, didn't it? Includin' my Algy. That's when I went over to Spain to join Master Nick." He snorted with self-mockery. "Thought I'd look after him, but got this instead." He rubbed the scar on his face as if it itched. "And it was Master Nick and Mac what looked after me." Then his tone changed. "Now, d'you see how your cane is bent over and you can feel something tugging—"

"Oh! You mean I have a fish! Help! What do I do?" All other thoughts flew from Faith's head as she struggled to land the wildly fighting fish. Stevens waded into the water, brandishing a small net, and Faith found herself following until she was knee-deep in the sea. Laughing, shrieking, and hanging on to the line like grim death, she attempted to follow Stevens's instructions, and by the time the fish was safely landed, both she and Stevens were extremely wet—and had become fast friends. She looked at her fish with satisfaction. It flipped in its bucket, big, fat, and furious.

"It's a beauty, isn't it, Stevens?"

"It surely is, miss. Now, here you are." He handed her a knife.

"Don't we cook it first?"

Stevens laughed. "Yes, but first you've got to kill it. And then to gut it and scale it."

"Me?" Faith squeaked in horror.

"Yes, miss, you. You caught it, you kill it."

"But I've never killed a thing in my life! Not even a spider. And I wouldn't know where to begin."

To her dismay, Stevens didn't budge from his position. He was a groom, not a gentleman. He didn't think a lady should be sheltered from the realities of life. Especially not one who was sleeping in sand hills, his look seemed to say. "Never know when you might need to fish for your supper again, miss. Best to know the whole process."

Faith was thoroughly appalled by the idea, but it was barely a day since she'd resolved not to rely on others so much, to be more independent, to have control of her life. She stared at the fish, madly flipping in the pail. This was her first chance to prove she could do for herself.

She watched him as he took a dead fish from the pail and showed her how to hold it. Gingerly she picked up her fish as he instructed, slipping her fingers into its gills and gripping hard. It wriggled and flipped and felt cold and slimy and completely disgusting.

"Good girl," he said.

Faith's resolve firmed.

"Now hold the fish down here, on the sand, and slip the point of the knife in here, nice and gentle." He demonstrated on his fish. "It won't feel a thing, miss. It's all any of us can ask, a quick and painless death."

She wrinkled her nose and nodded, unconvinced. It seemed a perfectly disgusting thing to do, but she was determined to leave helpless Faith in the past. Independent Faith could do anything.

"V-very well." Faith took the knife and braced herself. She raised her hand, screwed up her face, and brought the knife down.

"No!" Stevens grabbed her hand.

She stared at him in surprise. "What?"

He gave her an incredulous look. Slowly his face dissolved into a mass of crinkles. And then he started to laugh.

"What is it? What did I do wrong?"

Still chuckling, he removed the knife from her grasp, and killed the fish in one quick movement.

Faith watched with a mixture of revulsion and relief. "I thought I was supposed to—"

He interrupted her gently. "Yes, miss, but the thing is, it's not a good idea to stab the fish—stab anything, really—with your eyes closed."

She gave him a sheepish look. "I couldn't bear to watch."

He laughed again. "Come along then. I'll gut and clean it for you. But watch how I do it so you know how, if you ever need to, all right?"

She thanked him humbly and received her lesson in gutting and scaling with a minimum of squirming. "And if you need any sewing or darning done, Stevens, I'll do it for you in exchange."

He cocked his head and considered. "Depends, miss. Do you sew with your eyes closed, too?"

She said primly, "I'll have you know, sir, I am accounted a very neat hand with a needle.

He laughed. "You'll do, miss, you'll do. Now, you keep a'fishing and I'll kill 'em and clean anything you catch. You'll probably never need to do it yourself anyway, now you're marrying Mr. Nicholas, but—"

"Marrying Mr. Nicholas? I'm not. I'm sure he didn't mean it. He couldn't."

"Never says nothing he don't mean, Mr. Nicholas."

"Well, I'm not marrying him! The very idea is ludicrous."

He stopped scraping at fish scales and gave her a long, skeptical look from under his beetling brows. "You don't look daft to me, miss. Why wouldn't you wed him? He's the finest man I've ever known—and I've known 'im all his life."

"Perhaps, but *I've* only known him a few hours."

He gave her another look and sniffed. "Mighty picky, aren't you? For a lone female what's been sleeping rough in a foreign country."

Faith flushed. "Just because I—I am in temporary difficulties, doesn't mean I should be rushed into marriage with a stranger."

He sniffed again and resumed scaling the fish. He looked offended, so she said, "Look, I've already made a dreadful mess of things with my inability to judge a man. I don't mean to insult your master, but I don't wish to jump from the frying pan into the fire." She recalled a grievance. "Even if that's where he put my boots!"

"Lor', miss! Mr. Nicholas isn't no fire! He's a good man—one o' the best! If I was you, I'd be jumping with both feet and hanging on tight to him!" He swished the cleaned fish in the sea, tossed it into the bucket, sat back on his heels, and stared at her. "I don't understand your hesitation, so help me, I don't! He's offered you a free ticket. You don't have to do nothing—he'd be the one what's giving you everything!"

Faith bit her lip. "That's the problem," she admitted. "Even if he meant it—which I cannot believe—I couldn't accept such an unfair bargain. There'd be nothing in it for him that I can see—nothing!" She waited for him to contradict her, to offer her a fresh insight into Mr. Blacklock's extraordinary offer, but Stevens just cast a new line and thrust the fishing rod into her hand again.

"Don't fret on it, miss. Just keep on fishing. Good opportunity for thinking things out, fishing—as well as fillin' the pot."

Faith fished. And thought. And fished some more. Stevens was right. It was a good way to think. But sometimes thinking did no good. No good at all. Her thoughts veered all over the place.

Their business in town concluded, Nick and Mac walked back to the campsite. Mac adjusted the bulging string bags he was carrying and said for the fourth time. "I canna believe ye mean tae do this, Cap'n! It's pure folly!"

"I don't think so," Nick said.

Mac made a scornful sound. "She'll be after your money! I've seen her kind before! Takin' advantage of your better nature wi' that pathetic tale—and that blasted female catch in her voice! Guaranteed to tweak at a man's heartstrings! And you let her tweak awa' on ye, like a great gormless harp!"

The harp strode on, unmoved. "She's a lady, Mac, fallen on hard times."

"Pah! A lady? I doubt it!" He snorted. "In that tatty silk dress cut down to indecency. You're no well enough acquainted wi' the wiles o' women, that's your problem!"

"Indeed?" Nick was unmoved. Mac's opinion was reliable about most things, but not about women. Not since a certain señorita from Talavera had taken him for everything he had. Until then, the big Scot had been the biggest soft touch, rescuing widows, orphans, and strays of all sorts—witness Beowulf. But Pepita— damn her larcenous little soul—had trampled on the big man's pride and broken his heart into the bargain. Mac had been sour on women ever since.

"Aye, well, a plain wee thing like her needs wiles, I'll admit, wi' that lopsided purple face o' hers and that terrible case o' spots."

"The swelling will go down, and the bruise will fade. And they're not spots, they're scratches and midge bites and will disappear. Once she's restored to England she will be quite pretty. In any case, you'll not have to look at her long. I'm sending her to my mother."

Mac said with dark foreboding, "And how will your mam cope when yonder lass brings shame and disgrace to your name?"

"How will she do that, pray?"

"Dalliance—and worse! Wi' other men!"

Pepita had done just that with Mac, so Nick kept his tone mild. "She won't shame me with other men. And after a while it won't matter anyway."

There was a short silence.

"She's already run off wi' one man—and who's to say whether he was the first or not? Mebbe that's what had happened last night wi' those chaps on the beach— only she wasn't prepared to go through wi' it at the last minute! Females are contrary. Ye know that."

"Some females," admitted Nicholas. "But not Miss Merrit. I think she's exactly as she represents—apart from the false name—"

"Ye see!"

"Now, Mac, you've said your piece and cleared your conscience, and I'll hear no more disparagement of her. The lady is to be my wife."

"Och, but Capt'n, she's a—"

"I said, enough!"

After that, Mac said not another word on the subject, but his silence was like himself: large, Scottish, and disapproving.

Chapter Four

∞

*It is always incomprehensible to a man that a woman
should ever refuse an offer of marriage.*

JANE AUSTEN

FAITH HAD CAUGHT SEVERAL FISH AND DONE A GREAT DEAL OF thinking by the time the men returned from the town. She felt a distinct lurch in her stomach as Nicholas Blacklock's tall figure strode around the cape. His gleaming black boots ate up the distance between them. He looked relaxed, unworried, totally in command.

Yes, she could easily imagine him as an officer. He had an air about him, a faint unconscious arrogance, a natural authority. He was used to dominating other men. Deciding what was best for others. Burning their boots.

If she chose to let him, Nicholas Blacklock would dominate Faith, too. *If* she chose to let him.

"You burned my boots!" She accused him the moment he was close enough.

"They needed burning." There was not a trace of contrition in his voice or demeanor.

Her anger sparked back into life. "They were *my* boots!"

He glanced at her feet. "They gave you blisters. How are they, by the way?"

She hid her feet under her skirt. "None of your business. You had no right to burn my boots."

"I know. It was an impulse that I couldn't resist."

She blinked at his calm admission. "Well, what am I going to do without boots? I can hardly walk into town in my bare feet!"

"No, I know." He turned to his friend. "Mac?"

Mac dumped several bulging string bags on the ground beside Faith, pulled two breadsticks free, and stomped off toward the fire without a word.

Nicholas Blacklock squatted down, pulled out a brown paper parcel, and handed it to Faith. "Here."

Disconcerted, she accepted it. It was oddly shaped, both squashy and hard. What on earth could it be? And what was he up to?

"Well, go on, open it."

She pulled off the paper and looked at what he'd bought her, what the horrid, arrogant, boot-burning, bossy pants had bought her. She felt her eyes fill with tears. She blinked them furiously away.

"I hope they fit. I had to guess at the size."

They would fit, she knew. If she didn't know better, she'd think they'd been made for her.

"Don't you like them?"

She managed to whisper, "Yes. Thank you. They're lovely." And they were. Her new boots. Her beautiful, new, soft, blue kidskin boots.

"Well, try them on."

"I—I'll wait until I wash my feet. I don't want to ruin them." She was reluctant to put them on. They were so beautiful, and her feet were so ugly. And she was still angry with him in a strange sort of way.

He shrugged and turned to Stevens, who had been observing with a fatherly told-you-so beam. "How was the fishing?" He turned back to Faith and added in an afterthought. "It will be tomorrow morning, by the way."

"What will?"

"The wedding. It's all settled and arranged for to-morrow morning."

Faith's jaw dropped. "But we haven't even discussed it!"

He raised his black brows at her. "What is there to discuss?"

She gave him a fulminating look. He glanced at Stevens, then held out his hand. "Come, let us walk along the beach then, and discuss whatever it is you wish to discuss. Stevens can pack up here."

His hand closed, big and warm and strong around hers. She felt both trapped and—annoyingly—soothed.

She pulled her hand free. "I didn't believe you meant it!"

"I always mean what I say."

"But why would you wish to marry me?"

He arched a sardonic eyebrow. "I don't *wish* to marry you. I don't *wish* to marry anyone. It will be a ceremony, that is all. A mere form. You must admit, your current situation is impossible."

Faith didn't have to admit anything of the sort. Nothing was impossible. She just hadn't yet worked out what to do. "But to marry a perfect stranger? It's ridiculous!"

"It's unusual, but it's the perfect solution." He was completely calm. It was very annoying!

"Solution for whom? What do you get out of it?"

Nicholas Blacklock frowned, then said stiffly, "It would be a white marriage, naturally." He meant it would not be consummated.

"Would it?"

"Yes, of course. After the wedding, I will send you back to England where you will be safe and protected. We would go our separate ways."

For some reason she found this even more annoying. "Oh, would we?"

He frowned. "Are you angry with me?"

She shrugged. She was, but anger was only one of

the emotions that roiled around inside her at the moment, and she hadn't a hope of sorting them out while he stood there like a—a masculine sphinx! "I don't know what I feel."

Marry this man, this stranger who she'd known for less than a day? Who was he, truly, this Nicholas Blacklock? She knew nothing about him except that he rescued fallen women without a thought, then proposed marriage to them in a manner so disinterested as to be extremely irritating.

"It will be a ceremony, that is all. A mere form."

She shook her head. "I . . . I'm sorry. I cannot think what to do."

"What is there to think about?"

Her jaw dropped. "What is there to think about? Only everything! I've almost destroyed my life by trusting one man—and I thought I knew him"

"I am a man of my word and was an officer in Wellington's army. You may trust me. By all means take some time to think. A moment's reflection will convince you."

"Oh, will it?" His calm masculine assumption of rightness exacerbated her already tense nerves. "Then I'd better go off and reflect, hadn't I?" Faith lifted her skirts and marched into the water, enjoying the cool water against her skin, knowing he could not follow because of his boots.

He waited on the shore, picking up stones and skimming them across the glassy surface of the sea, as if he hadn't a care in the world.

"You may trust me."

Trust me? The last man who'd said that had also been trying to coax her into marriage. Not that Nicholas Blacklock was exactly coaxing. The way he'd put it was more like an order. But whether a blunt, unemotional order or a wildly romantic proposal, the effect was the same; she must trust herself and her future to a man.

Never again, she'd sworn. Never again put herself in the power of a man. She'd escaped Grandpapa's harsh rule, only to hurl herself into Felix's web of lies and humiliation. Both of them had left her scarred. She would be mad to trust herself to another man, particularly one she didn't know.

A small voice reminded her that she hadn't done too well with men she'd known. What was the difference in trusting a stranger?

She couldn't afford to put her fate in a man's hands. Any man's. And especially this—this stranger!

But could she afford not to? She'd made such a mess of her life. Could he truly make it worse?

Yes. He could. There were worse things than those she'd experienced. Those men last night, for instance.

"It would be a white marriage, naturally." If he truly meant it, a white marriage with his name as a gift, what would he get out of it? He had to get something. No man would offer what he offered without some reward.

She turned back to him. "You know nothing about me. I could be a . . . a criminal, for all you know."

He snorted. "Nonsense!"

She splashed back toward him. "I might be! You cannot tell I am not!"

"Believe me, I can tell." Nick kept his expression bland. She sounded almost put out at his refusal to consider her a criminal. "As for myself and what I get out of marrying you, well, for one thing, it will please my mother."

"Your mother?" She sounded just as put out by that.

"Yes. For the last few months she has flung eligible young ladies at my head in the hope that one of them might interest me."

"Why didn't they?"

Why didn't they? He thought of the young ladies his

mother had brought home for him. He couldn't imagine
any of them looking such a gift horse so suspiciously in
the mouth. They'd have jumped at his offer, no matter
what. It was only he who knew the gift horse was no gift
at all.

"That bad, was it?" Her soft voice interrupted his
thoughts.

He grimaced. "The process was unfortunate. And so
my mother did not get the daughter-in-law she wanted
so badly."

"Did she have a particular girl in mind?"

"No, anyone would do—as long as I was married."
He picked up a handful of sand and trailed it though his
fist onto his boots, listening to the soft hiss it made. "I
should add that since my older brother Henry died of a
fever three years ago, I am the last of my line. It is not
so much a bride my mother wants—it is a grandchild.
A grandson."

"Oh!"

He realized at once what she was thinking. "It was
not, however, an heir for Blacklock Manor that I was
thinking of when I proposed to you. I care nothing for
that. That was my brother Henry's job, and if he did not
secure the succession before he died . . ." He shrugged.
"I simply thought that since you were in need of a husband and my mother was desperate for me to wed, I
could kill two birds with one stone. I should add, I have
been something of a disappointment to her all my life.
You could live safely and securely at Blacklock Manor,
and you would be company for her."

"But what would she think of having a daughter-in-
law foisted on her who was not really your, um—"

"She need not know that there was no marriage bed.
My cousin will inherit the estate when I die, but my
mother is amply provided for. As will you be."

"I could not take your charity—"

He snorted, "It is not charity. You would be doing me—it would be a mutual favor." He shifted his position on the sand and crossed his legs restlessly. His mother would have a fit! The heir to Blacklock and a waif of the sand hills! Nicholas imagined the letter he could write:

Dear Mother,

I have found the new mistress of Blacklock. I found her hiding in some French sand hills, courtesy of a bogus Hungarian swine called Yuri Popov. She is a dear little soul, and I think she will make a very nice daughter-in-law. I hope this compensates for my running away.

Your loving though disobedient son,

Nicholas.

"Is your mother an invalid? Lonely? Is that what you want—someone to take care of her?"

"Lord, no, she's as fit as a flea! Nor is she lonely; she has dozens of friends. I am not after a nurse or companion for her."

"Then I don't understand! I would have my reputation saved and a home—in exchange for what? It seems a very unequal proposition." Her voice softened, "Forgive me if I seem rude or ungrateful, but my recent experiences have taught me not to trust people's words so simply.

He shook his head. "No, you are right to question me. For a start, it is no great thing I offer. I am no great catch, if that's what you are thinking. You would simply get my name, a place to live, and a comfortable allowance. And I would get . . ." He frowned, wondering how best to convince her.

Convince her? Nicholas caught himself up on the thought. Why would he want to convince her? She was nothing to him. At least she ought to be. And yet . . . he did want her to marry him. It was the only way he could think of to protect her from her folly. He could not continue his journey knowing he'd done nothing to ease her lot. It would rest his mind considerably to know she was safe and well provided for at Blacklock.

"Almost all my mother has talked about for the last few months is my wedding. Instead, I left England, unmarried. And I left in a hurry."

"I see."

"No, you don't. It is a bigger oversight than you realize. I am only now realizing how much my actions will have upset my mother. If I can send her my bride . . ." He shrugged. "I don't know—I suppose it would be a form of apology for the abrupt way I left."

There was a short silence. Her voice trembled as she said, "You don't think a bunch of flowers and a nice little note might be easier?"

It took him a few seconds to realize. "Are you laughing at me?" he asked suspiciously.

"I am sorry," she said eventually, her voice still shaking. "It is just that I have never thought of myself as a living apology before. It takes a little getting used to. Tell me, would I expect to be wrapped up? And would you wish to pin a note to my skirt, or would I be required to repeat your apology, parrot style. I must warn you, I never was very good at recitation."

The chit *was* laughing at him! He didn't know how long it had been since someone had actually had the temerity to laugh at him.

"You, miss, are a baggage!" he said severely.

"Yes, sir," she said in a docile manner that fooled him not at all.

"I simply wish to please my mother, to show her that her attempts to urge me into marriage had not been in

vain and that I am not completely the ungrateful, undutiful son she no doubt thinks me."

Her voice sobered. "But you would still be undutiful,
for if we made a . . . a paper marriage, it would be a de-
ception. You said she wanted grandchildren."

Nick made a dismissive gesture but said nothing. Her
logic was impeccable, dammit!

She pondered his silence for a few moments and then
said, "So if we were to marry, I would go to England
and be foisted on your mother. What would you be
doing in the meantime?"

"Me?" He shrugged again. "I will continue my journey, of course."

"I see. To Paris?"

"No. We shall make our way down the coast to Spain
and then travel inland."

"Oh?"

He hesitated. It would do no harm to explain his
route. "In Spain and . . . and beyond, I will be visiting
some sites of the late war, places I fought in . . . battlefields where some of my friends died."

"You must miss your friends very much."

He shrugged. He did miss them. More than he could
explain, even to this soft-eyed girl.

"And when your journey is completed, shall you return to Blacklock Manor then? To your mother and—if
I married you—to me?"

He picked up another stone and threw it far out to
sea. "I doubt I shall return to Blacklock. My journey
will go on. You will be free to do as you wish."

"I don't understand," she said after a moment. "Do
you mean we would get an annul—?"

"Those are my terms. Now choose," he said in a hard
voice.

Faith's thoughts were in turmoil. She sat in the sand
and thought and thought. It seemed all wrong. It was not

how two people should marry—without love, without knowing each other, for the sake of appearances. But she'd married for love once and ruined her life by it.

"I know it's not ideal, but I must press you for an answer today. It is just that I don't have much time."

"There is no need to delay your journey because of me," she said, knowing she sounded snippy and ungrateful. But really, would he leave her no choice, no say in her own wedding? Did he think she had no pride left at all? "Besides, you haven't even asked me!" She sighed. "I know it is irrational, that I have no choice, but—"

"You *always* have a choice!" He bent and picked up another stone. "Forgive me. I am anxious to get on my way, and I was so certain of the rightness of this, that I did not consider your feelings."

"Oh, but I—"

"No!" He skipped the stone along the surface of the water, and they both watched as it skipped four times before sinking. "There is *always* a choice. Always!"

She was surprised by his vehemence. "I know, but not for me." He opened his mouth to argue, and she stopped him with a finger on his lips. "No, don't. I—I suppose I'm just being missish and contrary." His lips were cool and firm, and his breath was warm against her fingers. An odd tingle ran through them. She dropped her hand hurriedly. It was just—

"It is a habit of mine, to see a problem and solve it."

She winced.

"Oh Lord, I didn't mean you were a problem, I meant—oh hell. Let me tell you what I've arranged, and you can tell me whether it is acceptable to you or not." His voice was rueful as he added, "I might be an insensitive clod, but keep in mind that I would be honored to marry you."

Faith felt tears prickle at his words. Honored, to

marry a scruffy, homeless, fallen woman. He was such a gentleman.

He continued in a brisker voice, "It will—if you agree—be a civil ceremony. In France these days one is married by a town official—the mayor. There is normally a three-week wait—the banns, you know—but," he rubbed his thumb and fingers together in the age-old symbol of bribery, "I was able to convince the mayor that the marriage of two foreigners could be expedited with greater haste, and it will be done tomorrow. Do you mind a civil wedding?"

"No." She quashed the pangs she felt. As a little girl, she'd always dreamed of a church wedding, with flowers and lace and everything. As she'd had with Felix. Ironic that her dream wedding had been the false one and that her real wedding would take place in an office.

He grinned. "Our interpreter was very glum—he is an elderly priest, you know, who is appalled by this notion of civil weddings—it is against God, you understand. But since we are Protestants, we must register in the town. So, Miss Merrit, what is it to be? Will you marry me tomorrow morning or not?"

The moment of truth had arrived. Faith stared at him a long moment. He was looking straight at her, his eyes gray and unemotional. She scanned his face, searching for an answer. It was severe and unsmiling, but it was a good face, she thought. Strong. His lips were firm and fine-chiseled, his nose long and aquiline, his chin square and somehow dependable looking.

Oh, what did she know about men? One couldn't tell by looks. Grandpapa had been just such a big, strong-looking specimen. And Felix was positively beautiful! Looks meant nothing. Her mind was in turmoil.

"Miss Merrit?" His hand reached out and touched hers. "I give you my word, no harm will come to you from this marriage." His voice was deep and sincere.

She kept her eyes closed and grasped his hand. It was a strong hand, warm, a little battered. She felt safe holding it. A small thing, but it was enough. It would have to be.

Eyes still shut tight, Faith made her leap. "Mr. Blacklock, if you are certain it is what you want, I would be very honored to marry you tomorrow morning. And I thank you for it, from the bottom of my heart. I am well aware that I don't des—"

"Hush!" He lifted her hand to his lips and kissed it. "Thank you."

A tremor passed through her. He kissed her hand as if she'd done him the most tremendous favor. As if she were redeeming him, instead of the other way around.

There was a lump in her throat. She swallowed. He would not regret his chivalrous deed; she would make sure of that. She gripped his hand and made a silent vow.

"Well done, miss!" Stevens said when they returned to the camp and announced Faith's decision. "It's the right thing to do. You'll not regret it, I know. You can put the past behind you now."

Faith smiled at him tremulously. Yes, it was the right thing to do. The moment she'd held his hand and agreed to marry him, she'd known it. It was as if a load had been lifted from her shoulders. And Stevens was right; she could put the past behind her. She had a new future now, one worth fighting for.

Nick watched the small exchange. So Stevens approved, too. He was surprised by the intense feeling of satisfaction he himself felt, now that she'd agreed to marry him. "We shall be married in the morning at nine o'clock. I hope that isn't too early for you, but the mayor—"

"It isn't too early."

"Good. You will sleep the night at an inn in the town.

I have arranged it all. Stevens will accompany you for
protec—"

"Oh, but I am quite happy to stay here."

Nick recalled the way he'd woken that morning, the
feeling of her soft curves cuddled up to him. His body
leaped at the memory. He'd promised her a chaste marriage. He'd sleep better if she was locked well away
from him, out of temptation's way.

"Nonsense! Stevens will be very glad to have a bed,
for he is getting on in years and dislikes sleeping on the
ground. And would you not prefer a bed and a bath and
a civilized meal at a table?"

"A bath! Oh, what I would give for a lovely hot
bath . . ." She sighed, and he had a sudden vision of her in
a bath, naked, pink, and glowing. He clamped down on it.

She continued, "That and a warm, dry bed with real
sheets would be most welcome, I admit, but I would
like to dine here, with you—if you don't mind. I have
never before eaten fish that I have also caught."

"You were fishing, too? I thought you were just
keeping Stevens company."

She laughed at his surprise. "Stevens taught me. I
must say I thought it was rather a dull occupation until
I caught my first one! After that it was very exciting. I
caught seven fish, you know." He caught a tiny crow of
pride in her voice.

"Seven? Excellent. In that case, of course, you must
dine here in rustic style. I well remember my own first
fish. It was small and rather bony, and we cooked it over
an open fire—or should I say we burned it—but you
know, I never tasted a better fish. "

"I am looking forward to my first fish, too—only not
burned, I hope. Or bony. I'm not fond of fish bones."
There was a small pause, then she said, "You said 'we.'
Who was your companion in this great historical
event?"

The moment of gentle reminiscence vanished with a rush. It all came crowding back on him. He dropped her hand, vaguely surprised that he'd held it all that time, and turned away. "I . . . I must speak to Stevens about the arrangements."

"Oh, but—"

He walked away toward the smell of the fire.

She called after him, "But what about these bags? Shall I put them somewhere for you?"

"The contents are yours," he said brusquely. "You deal with them."

Faith watched him leave, dismayed. What had she said? One minute he was almost smiling at her tales of fishing. The grim lines about his mouth and eyes had softened, and his whole face had lightened. And then she'd asked about his fishing companion, and it was as if he'd slammed a door in her face.

She recalled what Stevens had told her, and abruptly she knew. His youthful companion was Algy, Stevens's dead son.

She turned to the string bags. They were stuffed with brown paper parcels. For her, he'd said. He was such an odd man—arrogant, abrupt, kind. He'd roused her to such anger when he'd burned her boots and then brought her almost to tears with their unexpectedly beautiful replacement. She sat in the sand and began to open the parcels.

The first parcel was small and squashy; it contained stockings, fine silk ones, like the ones she'd ruined. The next contained underclothing: chemises, pantaloons, and a petticoat in soft cotton, all prettily trimmed with eyelet lace. She blushed to think of Mr. Blacklock and Mr. McTavish choosing such intimate items for her. But she was enormously grateful. Tonight she'd have a proper bath and be able to put on these pretty, clean new things. She hadn't realized how difficult it was to keep clean. Washing in seawater might be good for scratches, but it left an uncomfortable film of salt behind.

She opened the next parcel. Soap! She smelled it rapturously. It was plain and unscented, but she didn't care, she'd be clean! There was a brush and comb and several handkerchiefs.

He'd bought her another pair of shoes: dainty kid slippers in a pale fawn color. And two dresses, one periwinkle blue and the other a deep carnation pink, both loosely and plainly cut. Made of soft cotton, they buttoned high to the neck and down to the wrists. She shook the dresses out and held them against her. They looked a bit large. She could take them in if she could get hold of a needle and thread. Grandpapa had made all the Merridew girls sew all their garments, and Faith was a competent needlewoman. She'd done most of the sewing for herself and her twin. Poor darling Hope loathed sewing.

Faith sighed. She couldn't wait to see her sister again.

She searched through the parcels and found a needle and thread and a packet of pins. They'd thought of everything! Perhaps they hoped she'd do some mending for them. She would do it, too, happily.

She smoothed the crisp fabric of her new dresses. There couldn't have been a greater contrast to the clothes that Felix had bought for her. Felix had insisted all her dresses were silk or some other glamorous fabric, and he favored her in low-cut necklines and close-fitting, revealing gowns. She'd never felt comfortable in them.

These were probably all they could buy in a hurry, she decided. She didn't mind at all. She liked pretty dresses, but just now she'd feel happier wearing these plainly cut, high-buttoned dresses than any of Felix's glamorous choices. They positively shrieked respectability, and Faith had been so short of that in recent days that she was grateful to have them. People were judged by their clothing. In any case, she might be able to find some pretty buttons or ribbon perhaps to brighten them up.

These plain dresses might even, in an odd way, help her to discover her new self, the one she was determined to become.

Faith had never given a thought to the way she'd looked until she and her sisters had come to London. They'd grown up in a house where vanity was not simply a sin, it was a punishable crime! There were no looking glasses at the Court, the grim old house in Norfolk where she'd spent most of her youth. It had been a shock to come to London to find that she and her sisters—except for Prudence—were regarded as beauties.

Her twin sister, Hope, quite enjoyed the attention it brought them and cared not a snap of her fingers for people's expectations. Even the shyest of her sisters, gentle Charity, hadn't minded men flocking around her, as long as her Edward was one of them, but Faith had always felt a little uncomfortable at the way people stared. She would tell herself that half the interest was because she and Hope were mirror images of each other, and that golden hair and blue eyes were all the rage in the ton at the moment, but still, it was most unsettling. Being the cynosure of all eyes did not come at all naturally to a girl whose childhood sense of safety had come from striving to be invisible.

Felix had enjoyed the attention her looks received and after their elopement had dressed her in clothes that drew attention to her even more. She'd forced herself to wear them for him, because she loved him . . . thought she loved him.

No, her looks had brought her only trouble, and not just from Felix. The English ladies she'd approached at

Calais Port had taken one look at her bright gold hair and oddly assorted clothing and decided she was a tart, ignoring what she told them and that her English was spoken with their own cultivated accent. The men in the town had noted her bright looks and the low-cut, ragged emerald silk dress and drawn the same conclusion.

But in these plain, respectable dresses, nobody could imagine she was out to entrance them. She wouldn't be on show anymore. She could go back to being invisible again if she wanted. She thought about it a moment. No, she didn't want to pretend to be invisible again. She didn't want to pretend to be anything.

Two years ago, she'd escaped the yoke of Grandpapa's fearsome rule. Now she could escape the pressure of being one of the Merridew beauties, pretending to a sophistication she'd never had. And best of all, she would be safely married, so she could never again be swept away by mad, blind, love. It was such a relief.

In these clothes, away from all she had known before, and married to a man who wanted nothing from her, Faith could simply be herself—whoever that might be.

"Was that not the inn I am to sleep in?" Faith glanced back, puzzled, as Stevens, carrying her belongings, peeled off to the left. Mr. Blacklock escorted her past the inn without pausing. Mac and his dog were back in camp clearing up after their delicious dinner of crispy, golden fish.

"Yes, it is the one." Mr. Blacklock did not so much as break stride. He had her arm clamped in his. Faith had to skip to keep up. She was wearing her new fawn kid slippers.

"Then where are we going?"

"Monsieur le Curé asked to meet you this evening."

Faith stopped dead. "The priest wants to meet me? Why? You said the mayor was going to marry us."

"Yes, but Monsieur le Curé assisted me in expediting the matter. And he insists on meeting the bride tonight. I could hardly refuse."

"But I'm not dressed to visit a priest!" Faith's hands crept to her bosom, still partly exposed by her low, ripped neckline. She hadn't wanted to wear any of her new clothes until she'd bathed. She'd had to wear her new slippers, but her feet and legs were bare under her dress.

"He won't care. I told him a little about your situation."

"You told him about me?" Faith pulled the edges of the cloak together. "He will imagine the worst."

"Probably, which is why I offered to bring you to meet him. It will set his mind at rest."

"You offered to bring me to meet him? For heaven's sake, why? And why did you not warn me?" Faith turned and headed determinedly back toward the inn.

He took two steps and grabbed her around the waist. "Where are you going?"

"To the inn."

"You don't have time to bathe and change and be back in time. Besides, he won't care what you look like. He's a priest."

She glared at him over her shoulder. "I wasn't planning to be back in time. I'm not going to meet him at all. I refuse to have some—some priest condemn me! I've had quite enough of that over the past few days! Oh, will you let me go?" She struggled angrily against the iron band that imprisoned her.

"He's expecting us. He promised us tea."

"I don't care! I'm not going!"

Nicholas Blacklock turned her in his arms, still keeping a firm grip on her. "Stop making a fuss! You are coming with me, and that's final." Before she had time to argue any further, he said, "If he is the slightest bit rude to you, I will have you out of there in a jiffy. He won't be. He is a gentle, kindly old man, and I promised him I would bring you. Now come on!" He headed toward the church, propelling her ruthlessly on.

Faith dragged her heels rebelliously, but he simply hitched her off the ground and kept walking.

It was a small stone house next to a large bluestone church. Faith felt trapped, anxious, and furious with the big blockhead beside her. As Nicholas knocked on the door, Faith felt her fury drain away. Dread took its place.

A thin, elderly woman dressed in severe dusty black opened the door. The priest's housekeeper, smelling of lavender with a hint of camphor, nodded briefly to Mr. Blacklock.

She looked Faith up and down with a sour expression on her face. Obviously, she knew their story, too. Her long-nosed stare took in Faith's bright gold hair, the bruised cheek, the tattered emerald silk dress with the low neckline. She sniffed. It was as good as a slap in the face.

Faith swallowed and stiffened her backbone. She knew exactly what the woman was thinking, what the priest would think, too. Faith was a harlot, escaping from the wages of sin by deceiving a poor fool. It was a look she would have to get used to.

Sticks and stones will break my bones, but names will never hurt me, she repeated over and over in her mind. Grandpapa had used his stick. She'd survived him by hiding from his anger. She was not going to be a coward anymore. She would not hide. She would not let anyone make her ashamed of something she could not help. She could survive any amount of scorn and contempt.

She hoped.

She squared her shoulders and stepped into the priest's house.

Chapter Five

∞

Teach me to feel another's woe,
To hide the fault I see,
That mercy I to others show,
That mercy show to me.

ALEXANDER POPE

THE WOMAN INTRODUCED HERSELF AS MARTHE AND USHERED them into the parlor. Monsieur le Curé jumped out of his chair to greet them. He was spare and elderly, with a bald pate and shrewd brown eyes.

When they were all seated, he regarded Faith with a solemn expression. She braced herself. *Sticks and stones.*

"*Eh bien*, mademoiselle, you are to marry this fine fellow in the morning, yes?"

"Yes, monsieur."

"He has told me a little of your story. A lucky coincidence that you met, no?"

"Very lucky, monsieur." She had no intention of justifying herself.

Marthe arrived with a pot of tea and a plate of small cats' tongues biscuits. "Ah, *bon*," said Monsieur le Curé as she set down the tray. "*Le thé*. The English are fond of *le thé*, are you not? Mademoiselle, would you care to pour, please?"

Faith obediently poured and handed cups and biscuits around, aware of the critical gaze of both Marthe and Monsieur le Curé. She did her best to ignore them. The sooner the tea was drunk, the sooner she could escape to the anonymity of the inn. She stirred two lumps of sugar into Mr. Blacklock's tea—she'd seen on the beach he had a sweet tooth—and handed it to him.

When she sat down again there was a slight frown on the priest's face. She drank her tea.

"So, mademoiselle, you are from England, yes? And Monsieur Blacklock tells me you will return there after this marriage? To stay with your *belle-mère*, yes?"

"My mother, yes, that's correct," agreed Nicholas.

Faith glanced briefly at him but didn't comment.

The priest steepled his fingers and tapped them thoughtfully against his chin. He regarded Faith with an unwavering stare, meant, she decided, to disconcert her.

She put up her chin, refusing to be disconcerted.

"So, mademoiselle, you told Monsieur Blacklock here you were married before in a sham wedding."

Faith did not like his tone. "That's because I *was* married before in a sham wedding." Mr. Blacklock placed his hand over hers. She wasn't sure whether he meant it as reassurance or as a silent signal to keep calm. She shook it off crossly. He'd got her into this.

"Where did this wedding take place?"

"In Paris. At Saint Marie-Madeleine's church."

"Ah, the church of Ste. Marie-Madeleine. And who is the priest there, if you please?"

She answered with composure, "Which priest do you mean? The false one who married me—he called himself Father Jean—or the real one who was bribed to allow it to happen? He called himself *Père* Germaine." She gave him a look that said she had no opinion of French priests, real or false.

The priest nodded affably. "Ah, *oui*, *Père* Germaine

of the church of Ste. Marie-Madeleine, I know him. A short, fat, jolly fellow with white hair, *non?*"

"*Non.*" Faith said bluntly. "The *Père* Germaine I met was tall, thin, stooped, and with a large red nose. He was completely bald."

Monsieur le Curé frowned. "And this *Père* Germaine, he did not perform the ceremony?"

"No, the false one did."

"And were the banns called beforehand?"

Faith shook her head. "I don't know. The first time I visited Ste. Marie-Madeleine's was on my wedding day. My false wedding day."

He pursed his lips. "And that day you did not sign *Père* Germaine's register? A big black book, about so big?" He gestured with his hands.

Faith shook her head. "No, I signed nothing."

The elderly priest nodded thoughtfully. "Then, mademoiselle, I think perhaps you are indeed free to marry Mr. Blacklock. You have described the real *Père* Germaine exactly. Veritably, his nose is of a profound redness; he drinks, that one. Always he has. A bad business, a very bad business. I shall report it to the bishop."

He gave her a straight look. "And now, you wed this man willingly?" He gestured to Nicholas Blacklock.

"Yes."

"He has not coerced you in any way?"

Faith shook her head. "No."

The priest leaned forward and took her chin in gentle fingers, tipping her bruised cheek to the light. "He is not responsible for this, I hope?" His honest old eyes bored into hers, and she knew he was offering refuge if she wanted it.

"No, Father, he is not responsible for it," she said softly. "He saved me from men who would have hurt me much worse than this."

"*Eh bien*, it is good." The elderly priest sat back.

Faith looked at him uncertainly. The priest began to discuss tomorrow's arrangements with Mr. Blacklock. Faith found her body shaking with relief. She was not to be reviled as a whore after all. She'd been braced for a moral harangue, but he just wanted to be certain she was not committing bigamy. And was choosing freely, uncoerced.

She drained her cup and stood on legs that felt a bit wobbly. "Monsieur, I am feeling a little hot from the fire. I shall step outside for some fresh air, if I may."

Monsieur le Curé frowned, glanced at Nicholas Blacklock, and when he said nothing, replied, "As you wish, mademoiselle. Marthe will show you the way."

"Thank you, but I can find it myself," said Faith hurriedly. She had no wish to have Marthe's prying and disapproving eyes on her. She needed a little peace, and she knew just where to find it.

She slipped out of the house and entered the church from the side, through a heavy, dark, oaken door. It was cool inside, and dark, with two large candles burning by the altar. The familiar scent of incense, brass polish, and beeswax washed over her, and she was taken back in time to when she was a little girl, and Mama and Papa and sometimes Concetta, their nurse, took her inside the village church in Italy. Mama used to go in there to pray, though she was not a Catholic. God was everywhere, Mama said, but she felt closer to Him in a church.

By the door stood the votive candle stand, the spent ones and stubs; dribbles of wax in the sand, mute testimony to hopes and prayers and memories. Sleek fresh candles lay in a box on the side, ranging from the slenderest wisp of a taper to thick columns of wax, waiting to be chosen and lit with a prayer.

When Faith was a little girl in Italy, Concetta had explained the candles to the Merridew girls. She lit them regularly for the soul of her dead husband. The children knew the ritual well.

Faith had not been inside a Catholic church since she was seven. Grandpapa said Papists were devils. Years later and all grown up now, Faith understood the comfort the candles could bring. She suddenly had an overwhelming desire to light a candle for her mother and father. She looked at them longingly. But she had no money.

She slipped into a pew on the side, knelt, and prayed. Mama and Papa had been dead for so long—more than twelve years—and yet tonight she missed them so very much. She remembered the way Mama used to hold her, all soft and pretty and smelling wonderful. And Papa so strong and big and smelling of cigars. And when she rode on his shoulders, she was safe from everything and on top of the world.

"I've made a terrible mess of things, Mama," she whispered. "I thought I was doing what you and Papa did, thought I'd found a love like yours. But I was wrong, so terribly wrong." Mama would forgive her, she knew, but she would be very disappointed. She'd promised all her girls love and laughter and sunshine and happiness. Faith had let her down badly.

"I'm going to be married tomorrow, Papa. He's a good man, I know. He's doing it for me, to help me, even though he knows nothing about me. I don't know if it's the right thing to do or not . . ." She felt her face crumple. Hot tears spilled down her cheeks.

She didn't know how long she knelt there in the dark, but finally, feeling a little more peaceful, she rose to leave. She hesitated again at the tray of votive candles, picked up a candle, and sent a small, silent message to Mama. She kissed the candle and gently replaced it in the box, unlit. The next person who lit a candle would send Mama's message to her.

A shadow moved in the darkness. Faith jumped. "Wh-who's there?"

The shadow moved into the light. It was Marthe. "I thought you were an *Anglaise*?" she said in French. "I didn't know there were members of the True Faith in England."

"There are some," Faith responded in the same language, "but I am English, and not Catholic."

"You know our ways, though." Marthe jerked her chin toward the votive candles. "You wanted to light a candle."

Emotion filled her throat so that Faith could not speak. She nodded.

"I did not think the English Protestants lit candles."

Faith shrugged. "I was born in Italy. Our nurse lit candles in church. She showed us what to do. It seemed to bring her comfort."

"*Oui*, it does," Marthe said after a minute. "So . . . you need comfort, do you?"

Faith bit her lip.

"Why did you not burn a candle then?"

"I had no money."

"But you thought you were alone. Nobody would have seen you, nobody would have known."

Faith just looked at her.

Marthe nodded slowly. "So . . . who did you want the candle for?"

Faith hesitated. She didn't want this sour, critical old woman to know any part of her story, but the silence built, and eventually she muttered, "My mother and father."

"They are dead? Both of them?"

Faith nodded, battling with tears again. She would look a fool if she said they'd died when she was seven. How could a grown woman of nineteen possibly miss her parents when she only had a few scattered memories of them in the first place? But right now she did miss them, terribly.

Marthe said nothing more, just came forward, dropped some coins in the box, selected two thick candles, and shoved them brusquely into Faith's hands. "Light them, then. I will await you outside."

When Faith returned to the priest's house, Monsieur le Curé regarded her with a severe expression. "Marthe told me you went into the church and prayed," he said in French. It sounded like an accusation.

Faith nodded.

"She said you wanted to light some candles, but you didn't because you had no money."

Again, Faith nodded.

He addressed her in Italian. "She said you are knowledgeable about our Church. And that you were born in Italy, and I see you understand me, so it must be true that you lived there for some time. So explain to me, if you please, where were you baptized?"

She shrugged and answered in Italian, "In the local church. There was no other alternative."

"The local Catholic church in Italy?"

At her nod, he jumped up, suddenly wreathed in grins. "Aha! Did I not say it, Marthe?" He switched to English and addressed Nicholas Blacklock, who had been trying to follow the conversation with little success.

"Monsieur, I can marry you and your young lady after all. You must let the mayor do his civic duty, but afterward come to me, and I will marry you in God's eyes. Your bride was baptized in The True Church; I can marry you!"

Mr. Blacklock's eyebrow rose. "Is this what you want, Miss Merrit?"

Faith looked around, as if an answer would come to

her. If it came right down to it, she'd prefer not to get married at all—not an obligatory marriage of convenience to a man she hardly knew—but since she had no real choice . . .

She'd felt peace in the church. She'd lit candles for Mama and Papa. She'd wanted them with her; perhaps this was the closest she could come to it. "I would prefer to be wed in a church. But it is your decision, too. Do you have any objection?"

He shrugged. "Makes no difference to me." He turned to the priest. "Will ten o'clock suit you? The civic ceremony is at nine."

As the elderly priest bowed in assent, the knocker was heard. As Marthe went to answer it, Nicholas stood. "That will be Stevens. Come along, Miss Merrit, we shall escort you to the inn."

"The inn?" Monsieur le Curé looked affronted. "She cannot stay at the inn. It is not fitting. She shall stay here. Marthe will chaperone her," he added with dignity.

"Oh, but—" began Faith. She had no desire to spend the night under Marthe's gimlet eye. The woman may have been momentarily kind about the candles, but she still seemed cold and disapproving of Faith.

"The matter is settled," said the old man firmly.

"Very well. I admit, it is preferable to the inn. My man Stevens would have stayed with her, but she will be safer here. And a woman needs the company of another woman on the eve of her wedding."

Perhaps, but not the company of an old woman who still disapproved of her, thought Faith, but she did not argue. The thought of staying at a public inn was a little frightening, given her experiences of the last week or so. No one would bother her here.

Mr. Blacklock took her hand and bowed over it, planting a light kiss on her fingers. "We will come at half past eight to collect you, Miss Merrit." He held her hand a long moment and added softly, "Sleep well, my dear."

His kindness and gallantry brought tears to her eyes. She just nodded.

"Never fear, monsieur, we shall take good care of her for you."

Nick plunged naked into the sea. The cold brine scoured him; it was freezing, bracing. He swam away from the shore, breasting each wave, swimming out as far as he could. He always did this, swimming blindly out to sea, without thought, without care. There were times the thought crossed his mind that he should just keep going, keep swimming until he was too exhausted to swim back, let the sea take him.

But it was not in him to give up. A wave broke over his head, and he shook his head like a dog, laughing, exhilarated. He loved swimming; sometimes imagined he was part seal, like the Scottish legends of selkies. In the water he was free. He could do anything, go anywhere, be anyone.

When he was a young soldier and facing death every day, he and his friends would sometimes talk about what they wished to do before they died. They were often silly things, dreams of greatness, Matt wanted to bed a hundred beautiful women before he died. George wanted to taste every wine in France. Albert to read all the works of Shakespeare.

Nicholas never could decide. Yes, it would be fun to bed a lot of women, but really, a hundred was too many. After the first dozen, surely it would stop being special. And he didn't want to taste all the wines in France— just the best ones. He'd seen a couple of Shakespeare's plays, but he'd enjoyed the comedies before them more. In their group he was the only one without a burning ambition to achieve before he died. The only burning ambition he had was one he was too ashamed to admit to them: he wanted to live. He didn't want to die.

He'd worried that it made him a coward. Surely a soldier shouldn't mind about dying. Nicholas threw himself into battle to hide his cowardice from the others. Always at the front, always in the thick of the battle. Fighting not for king and country, but for his life.

He'd gotten his wish. His friends had died around him, died like flies, cut down in their youth and their prime, their ambitions unfulfilled. Only Nicholas lived.

He swam until his arms ached and his eyes stung with the salt. He floated there for a while, letting the waves wash over him, drifting aimlessly, a piece of human flotsam. He thought of that other piece of flotsam, Miss Faith Merrit. She would no doubt be in that bath now, warm and flushed, all curves and soft, clean skin . . .

His bride to be. But not to be his wife.

He turned and swam wearily back to shore. He waded out of the water, shivering as the cold night air bit into his warm, wet flesh. He whistled for Wulf, and he bounded up and butted his rough, damp head against him.

"You'll catch your death one of these days, sir," grumbled Stevens.

"No such luck, I'm afraid."

The words hung in the air for a moment. Stevens thrust a towel into Nicholas's hands. "Go up to the fire anyway. You don't want to take a chill."

Her bridal morning dawned fine and clear. Faith rose, washed swiftly, and dressed in her new clothes from the skin out. The evening before, to her surprise, Marthe had provided her with a small hip bath, several large cans of hot water, a small cake of fine, rose-scented soap, and a healing lotion to rub into her skin. Now, as she dressed, she relished the feeling of fresh new clothes on her clean body. The act was symbolic, she thought. She was beginning a new life. She would take only what she wanted of the old life.

She bundled up her old clothes and wrapped them in the ruined green silk dress. She would give them to Marthe to burn or to be used as rags.

Marthe knocked on the bedchamber door. "Are you awake, mademoiselle?"

Faith opened it. "Yes. Good morning, Marthe."

Marthe's beady black eyes ran over Faith critically. She sniffed. "That dress! You do not look like a bride."

Faith shrugged. She didn't feel like a bride either.

"Just because it is a hurried wedding does not mean you should not dress to be pretty for him," said Marthe severely. "Did you use the soap I gave you?" She leaned forward and sniffed. "You did. Good." She bustled into the room. Faith saw her eye the bundle of emerald silk, but she said nothing.

"You should be grateful to have such a man willing to marry you!"

"I am."

"Then show your gratitude! It is your duty to make him happy, to please him in every way a woman can!"

Faith felt herself blushing. She didn't know where to look. Was Marthe referring to what Faith thought she was? Marthe had to be well past sixty at least. She had the appearance of a dried-up, sour old woman. She was housekeeper to a celibate old priest, for heaven's sake!

"A bride should be beautiful on her wedding day. You are well enough in yourself, but that dress!" She snorted. "The color is pretty enough, but the cut! It is an abomination!"

"I only had that thing left," Faith gestured toward the green silk bundle. "All my baggage was stolen. Mr.

Blacklock bought me this dress and another, in pink."
She smoothed the blue cotton dress. "I don't mind it
being plain."

Marthe sniffed again. Without a word she stalked out
of the room. Faith tidied her hair and gathered her few
possessions together, but before she could leave,
Marthe was back, bearing a small pot, a jar, a hare's
foot, a bunch of tiny pink roses fresh from the garden,
and a white satin ribbon.

She caught Faith's look and muttered, "Don't look
like that! 'Tis nothing. Just a few bits and pieces, flowers from the garden and an old piece of ribbon."

She began with the pot, smoothing a cream over
Faith's bruised cheek, covering the purple and yellow
marks. She dabbed some on the last of the midge bites,
then dusted the whole of Faith's complexion lightly
with the hare's foot dipped in some powder. When she
showed her the looking glass, Faith gasped. It was a
miracle. Her usual face looked back, her skin apparently
clear and unmarked. So this was what it was like to be
a painted hussy. Not at all the hideous thing she'd been
led to believe. She grinned at Marthe's reflection.

Marthe sniffed and, pushing Faith down on the bed,
threaded the ribbon through Faith's curls then tucked
dozens of tiny roses into her hair. She frowned critically
at her handiwork and nodded. "That's better. You look
more like a bride, now. Your *maman* would have wished
it so."

Faith could not speak. She put her arms around
Marthe's gaunt waist and hugged her. The woman stood
stiff for a moment, then softened. She patted Faith on
the shoulder and said gruffly, "Go downstairs now,
mademoiselle, for your breakfast, and then it is off for
your heathen ceremony. I shall see you again when you
come to the church for your true marriage."

• • •

At half past eight, Nicholas Blacklock arrived at Monsieur le Curé's. "Ah, monsieur," Father Anselm said, "Your bride is waiting. See, here she comes."

His men fell silent. Nick felt like someone had punched him in the stomach. She was beautiful. He stood stock-still, staring at her until Stevens nudged him. Nick stepped forward and raised her hand to kiss it.

Her skin was soft, and she tasted of roses. "You ta— smell of roses," he blurted.

"Yes. I am wearing real roses in my hair," she explained in a shy voice. "Marthe picked them from the garden and wove them into my hair." She smoothed the fabric of her dress. "And I'm wearing blue, because my mama was married in blue."

She'd dressed up for their wedding. Roses in her hair. And she was so damn beautiful his voice didn't work. Her hair was gold, spun, shining pure gold, tumbling in artless curls around her face.

"You will have a lifetime to stare at each other, *mes enfants*," the elderly priest broke into his thoughts. "The time it marches on, and the mayor will demand more money if you are late. I will see you back here when you are finished."

Father Anselm refused to let them enter the church together. "Ma'm'selle"—despite their legal marriage, he insisted on calling Faith mademoiselle until she was married properly, in church—"Ma'm'selle will be escorted down the aisle by one of these two fine gentlemens . . ." He looked expectantly at Mac, who looked away.

"I'll do it." Stevens stepped forward.

"*Bon!* Now you two gentlemens . . ." The elderly priest led Nick and Mac around the side door and into the church.

Mac practically frog-marched Nick around the back

of the church, growling in his ear, "I pray ye'll no live tae regret this, Cap'n! There's still time tae change yer mind, sir. We can just keep walking."

"And abandon my wife at the church door?"

Mac snorted. "She's no' yer wife—not yet!"

"The mayor seemed to think it legal."

Mac's snort dismissed the seedy little mayor. "That mumbled bit o' official lingo didna fool me, sir. I canna believe it was a wedding at all."

"I can."

Mac marched another six paces, then burst out, "Och, Cap'n, ye canna mean tae trust yon stray lass wi' yer name and worldly goods, sir. Ye know nothing about her! Nothing!"

"My worldly goods are in England, Mac. I don't need them."

There was a short silence, broken only by the sound of their boots on the flagstones. "What about yer Mam?"

"My mother is well provided for. Miss Merridew—I *knew* the name she gave us first was a false one—Miss Merridew—no, she's Mrs. Blacklock now, isn't she? At any rate, she already has my name and is welcome to my worldly goods. As for my mother, I have no doubt she'll be delighted to have a daughter-in-law at last!"

"'Twas an heir she wanted, no' just a daughter-in-law."

"One needs one before one can have the other. And half a loaf is better than no loaf at all."

"But—"

"Enough!" Nicholas's voice was sharp. "The deed is done. There will be no more discussion, Mac. And my wife will be treated with respect!"

It was an order, and Mac grunted in reluctant assent. But as he pulled open the side door of the church, he added in an undertone, "I still reckon ye're crazed, Cap'n!"

Faith paused at the doorway of the old stone church. Logically she knew she was already married, but this— this felt like the real thing. Her hands were shaking. She laid one on Stevens's proffered arm and gripped the folds of her skirts with the other.

"One moment, *ma petite*." Marthe stepped forward and waved Stevens aside. "You will wear this, perhaps? If it pleases you, that is." She gruffly offered Faith a small parcel folded in aged tissue. Faith opened it carefully. Faded rose petals floated to the ground as she unwrapped it. She bent to collect them, but Marthe stopped her with a hand.

"No, it is fitting. She gave it to me wrapped in tissue, the same as now, with dried rose petals from her garden in between. She grew beautiful roses, my *maman*. But these petals are from my own garden. One must change them every year, you know."

Faith pulled back the last layer of tissue. In it lay a folded square of lace. She opened it out with trembling hands. The lace was creamy with age, yet still perfect and so delicate it resembled cobwebs as it spilled across Faith's hands. The region was known for its fine lace-work, Faith recalled, but this was the finest she'd ever seen.

"It is old, but . . ." the old woman trailed off.

"It's beautiful," Faith whispered. "I've never seen such a beautiful piece of lace. Never." She examined it reverently. "I wonder who made it? It's very old. I doubt you could get such fine lace today."

"*Ma mère*, she made it. She was the finest lacemaker in the district," Marthe explained with pride. "People used to come all the way from Paris for her lace. Great ladies in the old days." She fingered the exquisite piece of lace tenderly. "This piece she made for my wedding, nearly fifty years ago." She contemplated it for a long moment, then she shrugged. "But *le bon Dieu* never blessed me with daughters. It is time *Maman*'s lace was brought out again for a new young bride. You will wear it, yes? For the sake of my mother and yours, who are both dead, but who loved their daughters very much."

Faith could say not a word. She nodded and stood, unbearably moved, as Marthe took the lace from her nervous hands and draped it carefully over her hair.

The soft, lacy folds caressed Faith's skin. The veil smelled faintly of roses, not the fresh scent of the new-cut tiny roses that remained in her hair, but an older, more enduring fragrance. The scent of roses. And of love. She felt her eyes fill.

"Enough of that! No tears, please!" The old woman said, frowning severely. Faith did her best to blink the tears away. Marthe made the final adjustments to the veil. "*Enfin!* Now you look like a bride should look. Your man, he will thank the *bon Dieu* for his luck."

Faith had her doubts about that but said nothing. "I wish Mama—and my sisters—could have seen me, too."

"Pah! What nonsense is this?" said Marthe briskly. "Your sisters I know nothing about, but your *maman*, she is here now, assuredly—and your papa, too. Did you not light the candles for them last night? Then of course they are here! Now, go, and do not keep your man waiting any longer. A little waiting, that is good, but men are impatient creatures. So go!" The old woman gave her a small push.

Faith took two steps and turned back and embraced Marthe. "Thank you, dearest Marthe," she whispered brokenly. "I will never forget your kindness this day."

Marthe made a dismissive sound, but she returned the embrace strongly, and when she stepped back, her eyes were wet. "Go now, *petite*," she said gruffly. "Your man awaits."

Her man.

Faith took a deep breath, took Stevens's arm, and set out down the aisle. The journey seemed to take forever. The church smelled of incense and beeswax and roses. Only a few days ago she'd had nothing. She'd been robbed of everything, even her faith in the basic goodness of people.

Now suddenly she was showered with gifts from all directions, and her newfound cynicism was floundering. Who would have expected the sour, suspicious old woman she'd met last night to be such a comfort, so sensitive to Faith's fears and anxieties?

The scent of roses beguiled her. If she closed her eyes, she could almost imagine she was in the small church of St. Giles, where her twin, Hope, had married Sebastian two months before, surrounded by family and friends and roses.

Twice now Faith had been married without a member of her family present, without her sisters, without her beloved twin, without even a friend. Now Marthe had stepped in with her words of comfort and her mother's exquisite veil, and Stevens's arm was warm and sure under her hand, and suddenly Faith felt as if this time, she was not alone.

She opened her eyes. Not at all alone. The biggest gift of all—Nicholas Blacklock—stood waiting, tall, dark and somber.

Nicholas Blacklock, who married an unknown girl to save her reputation. Nicholas Blacklock, securing Faith a future out of gallantry. How could she ever repay such a gift?

She wasn't sure, but she was determined to try.

Chapter Six

*Human nature is so well disposed towards those who are in
interesting situations, that a young person, who either marries
or dies, is sure of being kindly spoken of.*

JANE AUSTEN

"I NOW PRONOUNCE YOU MAN AND WIFE. YOU MAY KISS THE
bride."

Faith turned to face Nicholas. She knew what to expect; she'd already been kissed in the mayor's office. A
brief, hard kiss. A mere pressure of firm, cool lips on hers.

Even so, it had been memorable. It had tingled, that
almost impersonal kiss, sending a slight frisson through
her that started in the tender skin of her lips and left her
tingling with awareness of him. Her husband. The faint
taste of him had remained, the scent and texture of his
skin, the look in his eyes as he'd kissed her.

He reached for the veil and lifted the delicate folds
carefully back over her hair, taking care the lace did not
catch in the roses or fall to the floor. While his attention
was on the arrangement of the veil, Faith examined his
face. He was sending her back to England tomorrow.
She wanted to memorize every detail.

His dark brows puckered with concentration, his
mouth firm and serious, his lips cleanly chiseled. He

was freshly shaven, his skin lightly tanned and fine-grained. His dark whiskers showed barely a hint of shadow just now. By the morning they'd be rough and sandpapery. She'd felt them that first evening, when he'd looked like an unshaven pirate, dangerous yet exciting. There was a tiny silvery scar across his chin. She'd probably never find out what caused it.

He reached around her to adjust the veil, and she inhaled the scent of him, her husband for a day. His smell was already familiar to her, familiar and somehow right—no doubt because she'd woken that first morning wrapped in his coat. Now he also smelled of some tangy fragrance, shaving soap or cologne water.

Nicholas Blacklock, her husband—it did not feel real. She had known him two days, and yet in some ways it was as if it had been forever.

He took her by the waist, holding her firmly, possessively. He drew her close against his body for the bridal kiss, close so they were standing thigh to thigh, breast to chest. She could feel the warmth of his body even through her sensible blue dress. Feeling suddenly breathless, Faith raised her face to receive his kiss.

His hard, gray eyes bored into hers, and he bent and gave her a kiss that was brief and hard and possessive. It zinged through her, and dazed, she clutched his shoulders. She swallowed, staring up at him, and licked her lips, shivering as she tasted him on her tongue.

His eyes suddenly blazed with intensity. He slid one arm around the small of her back and with the other cupped the nape of her neck, sliding his fingers up into the curls of her hair. Slowly, so slowly, he bent and captured her mouth again, first a warm claiming, then a deep, thorough possession of her mouth, until she was breathless and dizzy, tingling all over and clutching him tighter than she'd ever clutched anyone. The church shimmered around her.

"Congratulations, *mes enfants*!" The voice seemed to come from a long way away. The priest. Monsieur le Curé.

It was the signal for everyone to come forward and congratulate them, Marthe, and Stevens. Mac hung back, his face more fit for a funeral than a wedding.

Faith, blushing furiously, battled for composure. She did her best to respond coherently to their felicitations, hoping that Nicholas would keep his arm exactly where it was, firmly around her waist, otherwise she wasn't sure if she could stand, let alone walk back down the aisle and out into the autumn sunshine.

She darted a sideways look up at him. He looked as calm and severe as ever. She wanted to thump him. How could he kiss her—in church!—in a way that sucked all the strength right out of her knees and made her toes curl right up inside her new blue kidskin boots, and yet remain unmoved himself? The man was inhuman.

After the wedding, they retreated to Monsieur le Curé's front parlor. Marthe had prepared a light repast.

"Let us toast the newlyweds." Father Anselm opened a bottle of wine and poured, while Marthe passed glasses around. The wine was ruby-colored and rich with sunshine.

They all drank the toast, and then Marthe disappeared, presumably to tend to the kitchen. However, a few minutes later she appeared with a parcel and handed it to Faith.

"What is this?" Faith asked, puzzled. She made to unwrap the parcel, but the old woman stopped her.

"No. Open it tonight, when you are alone," she said gruffly.

"But, Marthe," she began. "You have already given me so—"

Marthe waved away her protest. "Pah! This is not some precious thing, like the veil of my *maman*. It is just an old item, no use to me any longer." She gave a very French shrug. "Perhaps you may find a use for it."

Father Anselm stepped forward. "I, too, have a small gift for you, my child." Beaming, he presented Faith with a small, dark red leather-bound book.

"Poetry!" she exclaimed as she opened the book. She scanned the contents excitedly. "In English! Oh . . . It contains some of my very favorite poems! Oh, thank you, Father, I will treasure it always. Please, would you inscribe it for me?"

He took the book back and, smiling, wrote on the flyleaf in a crabbed hand. He handed it back with a smile and said, "When one is in a foreign land, one of the small pleasures one misses most is the pleasure of reading in one's own language."

Faith hugged it to her bosom. "You are so right. I have missed reading very much since leaving . . . home."

"Now, now, miss, you're not allowed to cry on a happy day like this," declared Stevens, stepping forward. "I have a small gift, too, miss—that is to say, Mrs. Blacklock." Stevens corrected himself with self-conscious humor and handed her a small cylindrical parcel.

"But why is everyone giving—?"

"A weddin' present, o'course, miss—I mean missus."

"A wedding present." Touched and a little embarrassed, Faith accepted it. She'd already been given so much, and it wasn't as if she were a proper bride. She was being sent home in the morning.

She glanced at Nicholas Blacklock and was startled to find him frowning blackly. Obviously he did not think she should be getting presents, either. She hesitated. "Should I not—?" she began.

"Just open it!" he snapped.

She blinked at his bad humor. Obviously he was embarrassed, too, that the others were treating this as a real marriage. Best get it over quickly. She unwrapped the parcel. It was a small wooden, handmade flute. Her eyes flooded.

"I know it's not much, miss, but you told me you liked—"

"Stevens, it's beautiful. I had one like this when I was a young girl, and I loved it more than anything. My grandfather smashed it. He—he did not like me to play music."

There was a small silence. "Play it now then, miss."

And Faith played. It was the first time in months she'd played any music. Felix hadn't liked it when she played music. Her role was to listen and admire his genius, and Faith did admire it. It was only now, as the notes flew from the little flute that she realized how much she'd missed making her own music.

When she finished there was a short silence, then her new husband said, "You're good. You're very, very good." The others joined in, but Faith didn't really hear, she was storing up that small piece of praise like a squirrel storing nuts for the winter.

He took her by the arm and said, "Let us go outside. I have something to say to you in private."

Nick led her into the priest's small, walled garden. Here, in this sheltered spot, autumn was not so far advanced. The garden was ferociously neat, with straight rows of well-tied-up vegetables and precise squares of herbs. The only discordant note in this sea of neatness lay in the center, a four-sided arch formed by a luscious tangle of late roses; the only visible outlet for Father Anselm's romantic soul. A stone bench had been placed directly beneath the point where the four arches met.

"I see this is where you got your wedding roses."

Nick gestured to the small pink roses in her hair, now sadly wilting.

"Yes." She sat down on the bench, eyes downcast, and folded her hands neatly. She looked like a schoolgirl awaiting punishment. A very beautiful schoolgirl, he thought. How had he not seen how truly beautiful she was? He'd hardly looked past her hurts, the cuts and bruises and blisters and the sadness in her eyes.

Nick stood in front of her, hands clasped behind his back. He felt very uncomfortable. He took his fence in a rush. "I didn't get you a present."

She looked up, frowning.

"I'm sorry. I should have."

She jumped up and clutched his arm. "I thought you were cross with me. I thought you thought I shouldn't be getting any presents, since it's not a proper wedding."

"It *is* a proper wedding!"

She waved an impatient hand. "You know what I mean, I'm not a proper bride and you're—"

"You're a very beautiful bride."

She stopped and stared up at him. And then she smiled, a glorious, dazzling smile that dried Nick's throat.

"Thank you," she whispered tremulously. "I felt beautiful, too, with Marthe's exquisite lace veil."

It wasn't the veil that made her beautiful. She wasn't wearing it now, and she seemed to glow from within. With an effort Nick managed to clear his throat of whatever was obstructing it and say what he'd come here to say.

"I didn't think of getting you a wedding gift, but I'll get one for you this afternoon. What do you want?"

Her smile vanished.

"I don't want anything. You've already given me so much."

"Nonsense!"

"But you have. You gave me every single item of

clothing I am wearing today, including these lovely boots." She lifted her hem to show him the boots. "They fit perfectly, by the way—"

He cut her off with a curt gesture. "Necessities don't count, and besides, I am your husband now; it is my duty to provide you with whatever it is you need. However, I intend to buy you a proper wedding gift—something you don't need, but that you would like to have. What would you like?" *Pearls*, he thought. *Or maybe a sapphire necklace to match her eyes.*

"But I don't want any—" He gave her a hard look, and she subsided. "Oh very well, but I cannot think what to suggest. I have everything I can think of."

He gave her an incredulous look. Her possessions, she was wearing half of them, would barely fill a string bag, and she thought she had enough?

She thought for a minute. "What about some writing paper and a pen and ink?" She broke off at the look he gave her and said defensively. "I need to write some letters."

"I'll buy you a ream of bloody writing paper but *not* as a wedding present!"

"There is no call to swear at me!"

"I apologize," he said, not sounding the least bit penitent. Writing paper indeed! "Now think of a proper present."

She gave him a look from under her lashes. "Some people think a person should think up their own presents. Some people think the value in a present is the thought behind it."

"Those people have never been given hideous items they never wanted!" he retorted.

She giggled. "You're right. Oh very well. There is something I'd very much like, but it will be quite expensive, and you might not want to buy it for me."

"Hang the expense!" Nick heard the words come out

of his mouth with a faint sense of disbelief. Mac could be right. He had gone crazy, telling a woman he barely knew that expense didn't matter. "What is it?"

She hesitated, twirling a vine around her finger. "You might not like it."

Exasperated and cross with himself for being so remiss as to forget to buy his bride a present, especially when everyone else except Mac had given her one, Nick snapped, "I promise you, Mrs. Blacklock, whatever it is, I will like it! Now tell me what you want and, if possible, I shall buy it this afternoon."

She looked at him with wide blue eyes, then took a deep breath and said in a rush, "Very well, and I want you to remember that you promised! I want a pistol."

Faith heard his sharp intake of breath and hurried on, wanting to get her explanation in before he could refuse. "My mother always carried a small pistol in her reticule. She traveled a great deal in Italy, and having her own weapon meant she could protect herself, and us, if she needed to."

She tried to read his expression. It had returned to grim and wooden-faced. He was probably shocked. No doubt he was like most other gentlemen of her acquaintance who thought that proper ladies did not carry weapons. They found the notion offensive, as if the lady in question did not trust her masculine protectors.

But the women in her family did carry weapons! Her mother had. Her oldest sister, Prudence, did. Aunt Gussie did. And Faith would, too!

She folded her ams and set her jaw pugnaciously. Her safety was more important than his masculine pride. "You carry pistols and who knows what else. Mr. McTavish and Stevens positively bristle with knives and other weapons—in fact, for all I know, McTavish carries a knife in that horrid big beard of his! I want to be able to protect myself, so I need a gun of my own."

He was silent for a long moment. Faith was about to unleash another barrage of arguments when he said, "You will be perfectly safe on the Dover packet, and a private coach will take you to Blacklock Manor, but after your experiences on the journey from Paris, I can see why you might be nervous. A small pistol is an excellent suggestion—though *not* as a wedding gift. I will see to it this aftern—"

He didn't finish. She jumped up and, flinging her arms around his neck, kissed him exuberantly. "Oh thank you, Nichol—I mean Mr. Blacklock. You won't be sorry, and I promise I'll be very careful, but oh! You don't know how this makes me feel."

Nick knew exactly how she felt. Soft, warm, and female. His bride. His arms tightened around her.

His bride in name only. He forced himself to put her gently aside.

True to his word, Nick purchased a pistol for his bride that day, and after lunch he took her a short way from the camp to teach her to use it. An offshore breeze had sprung up, which was a pleasant change from the still air of the past few days.

"Oh what a beautiful little pistol!" Faith exclaimed when she saw it. "Look at this engraving—and the inlay work on the handle is exquisite. I assumed it would be a plain weapon, not something so pretty."

"It's a weapon, and its value is in its effectiveness, not its decoration," Nick said in a dampening tone. Truth to tell, he was embarrassed to have selected such a pretty little pistol. He was a soldier, not a dandy. "This was the smallest, most accurate, and easy-to-use weapon available. The fact that it is pretty is neither here nor there."

She gave him a mischievous look from under her lashes. "Don't you like pretty things?"

The minx was teasing him. Nick did his best to ignore it, though the way those soft lips pouted was enough to drive a man wild. He forced his mind back to the matter at hand: giving a lesson in handling a weapon. "It's designed to be carried in a reticule or a fur muff. Now, let me show you how to use it."

"Oh, but I—"

"It's not difficult."

"No, I didn't think it would be but—"

"Just listen and watch. Questions later. First the powder . . . just this much . . ." He demonstrated as he spoke. She watched obediently. "Then the ball along with the paper wadding. Now, you will need a ramrod, and in this model it is here, specially concealed."

"Oh how ingenious!"

"And now it is loaded. Now to learn to prime, cock, aim, and fire it." He handed it to her, saying in a reassuring tone. "It is perfectly safe at the moment."

She gave him a wide-eyed look and took it from him with extreme care.

"Prick the touchhole—that bit there—to make certain it is clear. Place a few grains of priming powder into the pan—not more than a third full, a little less is best."

Frowning with concentration, she did what he told her. "Now, close the frizzen."

"The what?"

"This bit here. That's right. Now, carefully, cock the hammer. Pull it all the way back—don't be frightened—yes, that's it."

"And now I'm ready to fire?" She gave him a big smile and aimed at a nearby rock, squinting down the barrel.

"Not like that!" He came around behind her, placed one hand on her waist and the other on her shoulder and positioned her so she was facing the rock directly. "It's all very well for duelists and soldiers to stand side-on—

that's to make themselves a smaller target. Your situation is different. Your advantage will be surprise and accuracy. Now, brace both feet apart and hold the gun with both hands if possible."

"But it's so light I'm sure I could—"

"Yes," he said patiently. "But for now, you need to learn to shoot straight. Both hands make for a steadier aim. Besides, there will be a slight recoil." The pistol threw a little to the left, but he doubted it would make any difference to her.

He brought his arms around and guided her hands to the correct position. The brisk breeze stirred her freshly washed golden curls so that they tickled his jaw and chin. It was most distracting. He'd instructed many a young soldier in how to fire a pistol, but none of them had golden curls that smelled of roses.

"Oh, yes, I see." She leaned back against him a little.

Nick stiffened. "Now, brace yourself for the recoil, and squeeze the trigger. It will make a very loud noise, so try not to be alarmed."

There was a report and a puff of fumes. The recoil was slight, but she fell back hard against him, gasping. "Oh, that was a very loud bang, wasn't it? But utterly thrilling! How soon can we do it again?" She turned in the circle of his arm, her eyes lit with excitement, the pistol in one hand, the other clutching his arm. There was a small smudge of gunpowder residue on her cheek, and without thinking, he brushed it off. She smiled into his eyes, and suddenly Nick realized she was close, too close. Her mouth was just inches from his. She licked her lips.

He stepped back, trying to picture her as a sixteen-year-old newly commissioned lieutenant, and said firmly, "Before you load it again, you must brush the pan free of all residue from the last shot, using this pan brush. I will show you how to clean it properly when we have finished, but for the moment, this will do."

She gave him a brisk, mischievous salute. "Yessir!"

Nick scowled as she wielded the little brush obediently—almost too obediently. He explained, "You must keep your pistol clean at all times—otherwise you will get what's known as a flash in the pan—the initial flash and then nothing!"

When the pan was clean, he said, "Now, show me how you load it."

She loaded it exactly as he had shown her before, perfectly and without the slightest hesitation. Then she looked at him with wide eyes. "Was that correct?"

He nodded. "Very good. Now, see if you can hit that rock."

She turned and aimed, but the gun wavered in a most unsoldierly fashion. Nick endured as much as he could and then stepped forward and put his arms around her again, to show her how to aim properly. This time she leaned back comfortably against his chest, her head tucked under his jaw.

"Will it make the same big loud bang?" she breathed and rubbed her cheek against him.

A sudden suspicion crossed Nick's mind. He dropped her hand, stepped back, and regarded her through narrowed eyes. She turned with a look of innocent inquiry. Too innocent for words.

"You've shot a pistol before, haven't you, minx?"

She laughed. "Why yes, quite often, sir. I told you—my mother had one that my sister uses now. Prudence taught each of us how to use it—and to clean it thoroughly, too."

"Why didn't you tell me?"

She gave him a reproachful look. "I tried—twice!—but you wouldn't listen. And then you were so enjoying giving me instruction, I didn't like to interrupt. I must say, you make a lovely officer."

Nick folded his arms and gave her a severe look.

She'd led him merrily down the garden path, and he had no one to blame but himself. "Dare I suppose you can hit that big rock without too much trouble?"

She nodded. "Too easy. See that small piece of wood sticking up out of the sand?" She raised the pistol, squinting against the wind, which was becoming quite gusty, and shot. It bit into the sand just left of the piece of wood. She frowned.

"I forgot to warn you," Nick said, quashing an ignoble feeling of smugness. "It throws slightly to the left. That is enough practice for today. I think a storm is brewing."

She glanced up at the gathering clouds. "I hope you are wrong."

Nick had bespoken two bedchambers for several nights at the inn, the same inn where his horses had been stabled since they'd arrived. Only one of the rooms had been used the previous night; Stevens had slept at the inn while Faith's room remained empty. Nick hadn't been able to tear himself away from sleeping under the stars.

But for his wedding night Nick planned to use Stevens's room and send Stevens back to camp. He had no intention of sharing a bed with his bride; he would not have that on his conscience, and he'd given his word.

By the time he and Faith returned to the camp, the wind had picked up, and black storm clouds began to build, and they were greeted with the news that Stevens and Mac had decided to pack up the camp and remove to the inn as well. Nick had no objection.

However, when they reached the inn, they found it was crowded. The storm had come after several days of windless weather, and ships had been stranded in port for days. As a result many of the inns in town were full. As some ships raced into port ahead of the storm, the Dover packet, which had set out earlier, turned back, and now every inn in the town was filled with stranded passengers clamoring for a bed.

As Faith and Nicholas entered, the innkeeper came hurrying up. "*Bonjour, monsieur.* As you can see, we have a problem. I was wondering, would your good lady perhaps care to share her bedchamber with these two English ladies? Very genteel they are, monsieur, of a respectability unquestioned—the finest quality leather *bagages*, a majordomo who will share the attic room with my son, and a superior maid who will sleep with my daughter. But these two grand ladies, they have no place to stay, and all my other *chambres*, they are filled to bursting point. All that remains are the two rooms you have paid for, and since you did not use both last night, I thought, perhaps . . ." He spread his hands in an eloquent gallic shrug.

Nick had no objection. He would share the other room with Stevens and Mac. He turned to Faith. "Whatever you decide, my dear." As he spoke, a clap of thunder shook the building, and the heavens opened. Wind and rain buffeted the inn furiously. Windows and doors rattled. Faith shivered and clutched his arm convulsively.

"Madame?" the innkeeper prompted.

She gave a shiver and straightened. "Of course I don't mind shar—" she began, turning to smile in welcome at the two fashionably dressed ladies the innkeeper had pointed out. Her smile froze, and she tightened her grip on his arm.

"What is it?" Nicholas asked in a quiet voice.

Deliberately she loosened her fingers and said in as relaxed a tone as she could manage, "It's nothing. Yes, innkeeper, I don't mind—"

A cool, upper-class English voice cut across her. "Look, Mama, isn't that the beggar gel we saw in town the other day—the one who speaks English?"

The older lady turned and swept Faith with a disdainful look. "You mean the strumpet who had the temerity to accost us? I see she has found . . . protectors. Unfortunately, my dear Lettice, men, even so-called gentlemen, have lower standards than we!"

She turned to the innkeeper and said in a carrying voice, "Innkeeper, I trust that *creature* will not be staying here. I thought this was a *respectable* inn."

Faith's earlier happiness shriveled, but Nicholas's grip on her tightened. He said coldly, "I will need both rooms, innkeeper. My *wife* stayed last night in the care of Marthe Dubois, in the home of Monsieur le Curé, but she is well again now. Thus I will need both rooms, one for my wife and myself, the other for my men."

"But monsieur—"

Nicholas arched an eyebrow and said in a voice of faint hauteur that carried just as well as the English lady's, "My good man, I really can't ask my wife to give up her privacy and comfort for the sake of a couple of stray females of dubious background."

"Well really!" The older lady drew herself up. "I'll have you know that—"

"Madam, I do not believe we have been introduced, so kindly refrain from badgering me or my wife," Nicholas said in an icy voice that carried all the sting of a whiplash. "I was addressing the innkeeper."

Faith blinked. She knew he'd been a soldier; she'd seen the fighter in action on the beach two nights ago. She thought she'd met the officer, but now she knew she hadn't. Not fully.

The lady flushed and set her teeth. The daughter's jaw dropped to see her mother so casually and effectively silenced.

Ignoring them, Nicholas took Faith's hand in a firm grip. "Come, my dear, let us retire to our bedchamber and compose ourselves before dinner."

The English lady recovered her poise and pounced on

the hapless innkeeper, "This is an outrage! How *dare* you prefer that little slut and that man before us! I will have you know that I am Lady Brinckat of Brinckat Hall in Cheshire, and I *demand* you provide us with a bed."

Nicholas ignored her and walked steadily up the stairs, Faith on his arm. Just before the turn, Nicholas paused and said casually, "Oh, innkeeper."

The man hurried to the foot of the stairs, his face hopefully upturned. *"Oui, monsieur?"*

In a cold, slow drawl, Nicholas said, "Those English women can sleep in my second bedchamber if they wish."

"You will turn your men out for the English miladies after all? *Oh, merci, monsieur,*" the innkeeper began joyfully.

Nicholas's brows rose in faint incredulity. "Turn my men out? For a pair of unknown females? I should think not." He added silkily, "The women can bunk in with them. My men won't mind sharing."

"I had no idea you had such a wicked sense of humor!" Faith exclaimed as they entered the small, well-scrubbed chamber. A crooked, whitewashed ceiling sloped unevenly to meet a casement window set into the wall. The shutters rattled in the storm.

He arched an eyebrow sardonically. "What makes you think I was joking?"

"Oh, you could not possibly have meant such a dreadfully improper thing!" she declared blithely. She crossed the room to check that the windows and shutters were firmly fastened. "When you said that about your men not minding sharing, I thought Lady Brinckat would explode!"

"That would account for the rumblings I heard as we mounted the stairs." Nicholas began to open a bottle of wine that had been placed, along with glasses and an opener, on a side table. "Would you care for a glass of wine?"

"She was positively gobbling with fury, the horrid old trout! No, thank you, I don't much care for wine." Faith laughed again and bounced onto the high bed. It was very high and wonderfully soft, with a deep, thick eiderdown quilt in pink. And then she froze.

The bed. One bed.

She looked around to see whether there was perhaps a truckle bed, or a pallet on which she could sleep. The room was minimally furnished. A chair, a small table, a cupboard, a bed. A lantern burned on a plain oak bedside table. She opened the cupboard, hoping a pallet might be stowed there. No pallet. She pretended to fiddle with her shoes and glanced under the bed, hoping to find a truckle bed.

No truckle bed. No pallet. Only one bed.

Faith glanced at Nicholas. Her husband. He drank his wine, unaware of her concern.

"To future victory over all such harridans, Mrs. Blacklock." He raised his glass and waited. "Nothing at all to drink?"

"No, I'll have a cup of tea later. Thank you for standing up to Lady Brinckat and her daughter for me," she said shyly. "I—I seem to be not very good at st-standing up to that sort of thing. I'm very grateful for your support." And she was. More than she could say.

He gave her an intense look and said quietly. "No thanks needed. You're my wife, Faith. I'll support you against all comers in all situations."

Faith's eyes prickled with emotion, but before tears could spill down and embarrass her, he added, "Besides, it was a pleasure. I can't stand puffed-up, bossy old bats like that. And the daughter was just as bad. You'd run into them before, I gather."

"Yes, the other day, in town. I could see they were

English ladies, so I asked them to help me." She felt the humiliation rising again and fought it back down. "But they thought I was a—a—"

He made a scornful sound. "I can imagine. Add stupidity to their list of crimes. And you were still ready to share a room with them?"

"Oh, well, that was before they were so horrid to me. I thought perhaps I could explain—I can understand how they misunderst—" She broke off at his sardonic look and added lamely, "They had nowhere to sleep, and the storm was so awful . . . I know what it is to have no place to stay."

"You are very forgiving, Mrs. Blacklock. Be warned: I am not!" He drained the glass.

Mrs. Blacklock. Again. As if she were in truth his wife. He'd assured her it would be *un mariage blanc.* But legally they were married, and husbands had rights. And there was only one bed. She swallowed.

Outside the storm raged. There was a small enameled stove and in it kindling was set, ready to light. Faith found the tinderbox and lit it, glad to have a reason to keep busy.

She would try not to think about the bed until it was time to sleep. It was cowardly, she knew, to put it off, but at the moment things were pleasant and easy between them, and she wanted to savor it while it lasted.

They sat for a moment in silence, listening to the storm. "Would you like to play chess?" he asked.

She grimaced, remembering the agony of childhood lessons where Grandpapa, confined to a sickbed, had forced them all to learn, in order to entertain himself. Only they were all too frightened of his temper to be able to concentrate. "I know the moves, but I'm not very good at it. But if you would like . . ."

"No, don't worry." He rose and paced around the room.

He filled the small room with his presence. It was terribly distracting, the storm howling outside and the silent pacing within. In an effort to break the growing tension, she blurted out the first thing that came to mind. "Stevens told me your father forced you into the army."

He went still, then shrugged. "I was young. My father understood me better than I did myself. The army suited my nature more than I understood at the time."

His words, for all their apparent acceptance, were said with bitterness and a thread of self-disgust. She recalled Stevens's words about how the army—or was it war?—had affected him. *"Changed him. Killed something inside him."*

"In what way did it suit you?" she prompted gently.

He turned abruptly and went to the door. "If you don't mind, I'd better check on Wulf and the horses. That dog of Mac's goes crazy in thundery weather, and Mac doesn't take nearly the care that he should. He will not believe that his blasted dog gets frightened. He said he would shut him in an empty stall, but if he hasn't, the blasted dog will frighten the horses to bits."

"I don't mind," she lied. Oh, she didn't mind him checking on the dog; that was perfectly understandable. It was the feeling of having a door slammed in her face she minded.

"I'll be back at seven to take you down to dinner."

It was foolish to mind, she told herself as he left. Married or not, they were still relative strangers. It was none of her business what he'd thought about his father sending him into the army. He was entitled to his privacy.

She'd kept secrets back from him, after all.

She shivered as the wind and rain buffeted the building. Adding coal to the fire, she fetched her writing materials and sat down at the small table to write to her family. Her twin, Hope, first, then Prudence, then Great Uncle Oswald and Aunt Gussie.

Plenty of dogs panicked at the sound of thunder, but not Beowulf. He didn't mind thunder or guns. Checking on the dog was an excuse. He had to get out of that small room with its big, high bed: the storm beating outside and the soft-voiced, soft-skinned girl inside.

Damn those English harpies. He could have throttled them both, and not only for the way they'd treated Faith. If it hadn't been for them, he wouldn't have committed himself to sharing a bedchamber with his bride. Now, if he chose to share a chamber with his men, it would reflect badly on her.

He'd promised her a *mariage blanc* and was honor bound not to touch her. Even though her soft, gentle voice opened up chasms of need in him he'd thought were gone forever.

And the scent of her drove him wild.

The sooner this blasted storm was over and he could send her on her way to England, while he headed south to Spain, the happier he'd be.

He and Mac headed for the stables. Stevens had earlier braved the kitchen in order to meet the innkeeper's widowed sister, a cook of some reputation. Having breached that lady's defenses by begging to know the source of the glorious aromas coming from the kitchen, he was then questioned by Madame herself, exhaustively. His answers, even for an Englishman, were not totally despised, and thus he was graciously allowed to assist Madame herself, performing menial tasks as he learned her particular way of preparing *moules à la crème*.

Nicholas returned to the small bedchamber some time later and knocked on the door. "Dinner will be served in fifteen minutes. Do you want me to have a tray sent up, or would you prefer to come down?"

She opened the door. "I'll come down."

With all the extra, stranded guests, the inn's resources were stretched to the limit. The dining room was crowded, but the innkeeper had broken it into two areas, one for the upper class and one for the common folk—never mind the effects of republicanism. The common folk served themselves; the others were served and paid extra for the privilege. As Nick and his bride threaded their way to their table in the superior dining area, they saw that Stevens had been pressed into service. He bustled past carrying a huge tray of dishes and threw Faith a wink. He looked hot but happy.

Nicholas shook his head philosophically as he seated Faith. "He's hopeless. Never could stand to be idle. Loves to be needed, Stevens."

Faith smiled. Everybody loved to be needed, she thought.

Lady Brinckat and her daughter were already seated. The landlord whispered that someone else had been willing to give up their room.

As Stevens passed the two ladies, Faith heard the girl say, "Oh, Mama. Look at his face! How beastly ugly!"

The girl was talking about Stevens, Faith realized, horrified. Referring cruelly to his war injuries.

The mother said in a loud, spiteful voice, "Avert your eyes, my dear. A fellow like that has no business in a dining room. If his master had any delicacy of mind, he would keep a grossly deformed servant like that out of sight, so that ladies with true sensibilities would not be offended."

She was using Stevens to get back at Nicholas, Faith realized, and suddenly her temper flared. She flung back her chair and marched over to the women's table.

"How *dare* you!" she raged. "How *dare* you refer to a man injured fighting for king and country—*and your-selves*—in such a callous, unfeeling way! Call yourselves *ladies*? You should be ashamed of your lack of sensibility! You should *honor* a man like Stevens—yes, servant or not! You should honor *every* man who has risked his life for your comfort and defense!"

The two women stared at her, stunned, as if a mouse had turned on them.

Faith glared at them, her chest heaving with emotion and her eyes prickling with angry tears. "And if you ever—*ever!*—make a nasty remark about Stevens's face within my hearing again, I'll—I'll *slap* you both, *very* hard!" She wished she could think of a worse threat, but she was so upset, she could hardly think straight.

To think that anyone could use dear, kind, Stevens's scars as a way to get back at Nicholas and her for refusing to share a bedchamber—it made her blood boil.

There was a fraught silence. Faith braced herself for further nastiness from Lady Brinckat and her daughter, but they seemed to be so shocked at her unladylike outburst that they said nothing. Lady Brinckat's face was white, her daughter was flushed.

The sound of clapping came from the corner table. Everyone stared. Nicholas Blacklock stood, applauding. Faith stared at him, shocked.

The door to the kitchen burst open, and a large woman dressed in a white apron and mobcap stood in the doorway. Madame, the cook. Arms akimbo, she demanded in French, "What happened?" Her brother, the innkeeper, hastily translated what the English ladies had said about Stevens.

Madame swelled to even greater proportions and, enraged, began to march purposefully toward Lady Brinckat's table. Just as she reached it, her brother finished translating Faith's words, and she stopped in midstride. She made him repeat what Faith had said, and when he had repeated it to her satisfaction, she embraced Faith, kissing her heartily on each cheek. Suddenly everyone in the dining room started to applaud. Faith was flushed with embarrassment but could not escape.

Finally Madame finished embracing Faith. She turned on the English ladies and glared. "You!—old bitch and young one!—out!" She jerked a thumb. "I do not feed swine such as you in my dining room! Get out before I kick you out!"

Shocked by such blunt vulgarity, not to mention the implicit threat of violence from a large, sweaty, irate Frenchwoman, Lady Brinckat and her daughter hurriedly rose and scuttled from the room.

"And good riddance!" the cook declared. "Now, *ma petite tigresse*, my brother will give you some champagne." She glanced at Nicholas, still standing, a look of amusement on his face. "The friends of Stevens are most welcome here."

Stevens said something in her ear, and she started and then beamed with all her chins. "It is a *bridal*? Why did you not say?" She turned and announced it to the room in French. "*Ma belle tigresse* and this handsome man were married only this morning by Father Anselm. *Eh bien*, a wedding, my friends! We must celebrate!"

And so the party began. An absolute feast poured from the kitchen, dish after dish of wonderful food, the best morsels coming first always to the blushing bride and groom, washed down with bottle after bottle of champagne. And once the food had been eaten, a fiddle, an accordion, and a flute were produced by patrons, and there was music and singing. Enthusiastic hands removed tables and chairs, then dragged Faith and Nicholas out to the center of the floor, and the dancing began. The celebrations drowned out the sound of the storm that raged outside.

Finally Faith decided it was time for her to go up to bed. She whispered to Nicholas that she was tired and wanted to retire. Her voice trembled a little when she told him. He knew why she was nervous.

"Go now," he said. "And lock your door. I will share a room with Stevens and Mac. Don't worry."

She gave him a look of relief and slipped quietly away.

But when Nick, an hour or so later, attempted a discreet exit, he was caught, amid much raucous and bawdy laughter. It seemed half the room had seen Faith's exit. There was no possibility, no question of Nick being allowed the same. It was a *bridal*!

Fifty-seven happy, drunken people escorted the groom up to his nuptial chamber. Dozens of well-wishers carried him up the stairs, shouting gleeful and explicit French advice. Nick devoutly hoped his bride could not hear it.

Dozens of exuberant fists pounded noisily on Faith's door, calling to the bride to come out and behold her master. And when she finally opened the door and peered nervously out, dressed in a long white lacy nightgown and wrapped in an eiderdown, Nick was thrust in the door with happy congratulatory cries and further, very French suggestions. He shoved the door closed on the happy throng behind him and bolted it, panting slightly.

Chapter Seven

∞

If one scheme of happiness fails, human nature turns to another;
if the first calculation is wrong, we make a second better:
we find comfort somewhere . . .

JANE AUSTEN

THE ROOM LOOKED DESERTED, THE ONLY SIGN OF OCCUPATION
the rippling bed-curtains, testament to a nervous bride's
hasty retreat.

"Sorry about that," Nick said. He had to raise his
voice to be heard over the storm and the noisy celebrations continuing outside his door. He parted the bed-
curtains, and in the soft light of the turned-down lantern
he saw her, huddled to her ears in the eiderdown.

"Don't worry," he assured her. "I'll just wait here
until they go away. As soon as the noise dies down, I'll
slip out and go to the other bedchamber."

But the noise continued. A group of men had decided
to continue their celebrations on the stairs outside the
bedchamber, and the sounds of drinking and talking and
laughing continued.

Nicholas stuck his head around the door. "Do you
mind leaving?" he attempted in his imperfect French.
"My bride cannot sleep."

This was greeted by a roar of laughter and many

lewd congratulations. He tried again, but everything he said seemed to amuse them heartily. Nick, nettled, withdrew. He could get men to do almost anything, but not in another language and not when they were drunk. He could throw them bodily down the stairs, he supposed, but it seemed ungrateful to commit violence on men for overenthusiastic celebration of his good fortune and future happiness. He decided to wait them out.

An hour passed. Nick was getting chilly. He wished he'd built up the fire, but it was out now. He peered behind the bed-curtains.

"Are you awake?" he asked the mound in the bed.

There was no answer.

Nick pulled off his boots, shrugged off his jacket, took one of the extra eiderdowns, and sat on the bed, his legs stretched out. He could at least be warm and comfortable while he outwaited the merrymakers.

Another hour passed with no abatement of the noise on the stairs or the storm outside. He'd have to stay the night. He removed his breeches and shirt and slipped into bed, taking care not to touch her. He'd promised a *mariage blanc* and, even if it killed him, he would deliver it, for this night at least. And tomorrow, they would be on their separate ways.

He could smell the elusive fragrance of roses that seemed always to hover around her. He felt anything but chaste.

She lay there, unnaturally still. Her breathing seemed to have stopped. She was awake. Had she been awake all this time?

The sheets were cold and thin. The coverings were heavy. There was no pillow, not even one of the long thin tubes the French used as a pillow. He was sure he'd seen one on the bed earlier. Long and round, like a bolster. He felt around in the bed. And then he found it, the long French pillow. Not placed across the top of the bed for two heads to sleep on. Placed down the center of the bed, to separate two bodies.

She went even stiller than before, if that were possible. She knew what he'd found. She was no doubt braced for his reaction. Did she expect him to explode with rage? Rip the bolster off and seize his husbandly rights? Probably. She didn't know him very well.

"Go to sleep, Mrs. Blacklock," he said softly. "I may be trapped here by our well-wishers outside, but I am a man of my word. Your virtue is safe."

She lay as quiet as a mouse, but somehow, he felt her slowly relax. Nicholas laid his head back down and closed his eyes. Sleeping with no pillow would be no hardship.

Sleeping next to a silken-skinned girl who smelled of woman and roses was quite another thing.

They lay in bed, side by side, separated by the bolster, listening to the storm and the rise and fall of voices on the stairs, punctuated by bursts of occasional laughter. Most men got little sleep on their wedding night, Nicholas reflected ironically, only not quite for the same reason . . .

He finally got to sleep, but was awoken before dawn by the feel of a soft, feminine body burrowing against him.

"Changed your mind, have you?" he murmured, and turned over to take her in his arms. As he did, a flash of lightning illuminated her face, and he froze. She was still asleep. Her face was crumpled with some emotion, the flash was too quick for him to read it, but her eyes were tight shut.

"Faith?" he asked softly.

Thunder followed the lightning, crashing down so close around them that the building shook. She gave a start and burrowed hard against him like a small animal seeking safety, or warmth, or comfort.

Nicholas gritted his teeth even as he drew her into his arms. His new bride was no coy seductress. She was scared of the thunder. Sound asleep and scared of the thunder. His promise to her still held, dammit. Even though his body was afire to take her.

Her cheek was silken soft against him, and he could feel her breath through the fabric of his shirt. Her hair smelled of roses. Her night rail had ridden up, and her lower limbs twined around one of his legs. Her feet were cold, and he felt them slowly warm from the contact with his skin. Her scent surrounded him. He was hard with wanting, and his reckless promise of chastity racked him.

But a promise was a promise. Just one night to get through. Less than a night, and she'd be gone from this place, gone from him. He'd return to living with men and dogs, creatures who troubled his sleep not at all.

She snuggled against him, and her breathing evened and relaxed. Her head was pillowed on his chest, tucked under his chin. Where was the damned bolster now? he wondered.

Faith woke to a wonderful feeling of warmth and safety. She lay for a moment, savoring it. The world seemed peaceful and quiet, and it took her a moment to realize that the storm must be over. There was no sound of wind or thunder or pelting rain. She was wonderfully warm and comfortable, and she had no desire to move, but then it all came flooding back to her. She'd married a man called Nicholas Blacklock yesterday. And today she was going back to England, to her sisters and Great Uncle Oswald. She had better get up and get ready. Ready to go home and face the consequences of her actions. Still with her eyes closed, she stretched.

And froze as she encountered a big, warm, masculine body, lying practically beneath her.

She hadn't only married a man called Nicholas Blacklock yesterday, she'd shared a bed with him last night. And she distinctly remembered putting a bolster between them in the bed.

The heavy weight of his arm curved around her back, keeping her pressed against the full length of his body. She could feel something pressing into her thigh, and it certainly wasn't a bolster.

"What do you think you are doing?"

He groaned and stirred beneath her. Faith hurriedly shifted position.

"Stop that at once! You promised!"

He stretched and opened his eyes. "Looks like I got some sleep, after all," he murmured.

His skin was rough with stubble, his hair was rumpled, and his skin a bit crinkly with sleep, but his eyes were as gray as a misty morning. Windows to the sky, though never a sunny sky.

She belatedly realized he was watching her with an intense gaze. Her heart started thudding. She felt herself flushing, and the look sharpened. There was a gleam in his eye she didn't trust, and she suddenly recalled exactly what was pressing most insistently against her thighs.

She tried to scramble off him, but his arm tightened around her.

"What are you doing?" her voice squeaked.

"Good morning, Mrs. Blacklock."

"Good morning," she babbled and tried to move off him again.

His arm didn't budge.

"I trust you slept well." His voice was deep and a little raspy. Not unlike his raspy, dark chin.

"Yes, thank you," she said politely, willing him to let her go. "I would like to—" She pushed against him with her hand on his chest. He seemed unaware of it.

"Storm didn't bother you?"

She shook her head stiffly, feeling uncomfortably aware of the intimacy of their relative positions. "No. Not at all." As she shook her head, the tips of her hair brushed against his skin. She strained her head back away from him. But his arm didn't budge, and the action arched her body, pressing her lower half more closely against him. She immediately stopped pushing.

"Not afraid of storms, are you?"

"N-no. Not since I was a little girl," she said firmly. It wasn't quite true; they still made her nervous. But she had managed to conquer her childish terror of them.

"Thunder doesn't bother you at all then?"

"I am no longer a child, to be frightened of such things." He was wearing a shirt, but the front had come unbuttoned and fell open to the waist. It was very hard not to be distracted by the muscular planes that rose and fell under her hand. And not to notice that the center of his broad, firm chest was covered by dark hair that looked appealingly soft. She forced her fingers to remain still.

"No, you are no longer a child. You're a married woman."

Faith swallowed. "Yes. And now I would like to get up, please."

"Not yet. There's a small matter of your wifely duty."

"W-wifely duty?" Faith squeaked. "But you promised—"

"Every wife has a morning duty to her husband. I'm sure you know what it is."

Faith had a very good idea of what it was. Something to do with the part of him pressing so insistently against her thigh. His arm remained locked around her waist, loose, yet immovable.

"Surely you don't mean . . ." She licked her lips anxiously. She barely knew him.

"Surely I do." The gleam in his eyes intensified. She

pushed against his chest, but his other hand came up and gently, implacably brought her head down. His lips came up to meet hers.

His lips were cool and firm, and the taste of him was hot and dark and spicy. The taste of him spiraled through her in a heated shiver, shuddering through her bones in a dizzying wave and curling her toes up tight. She opened her eyes, and the room dipped and wavered around her, exactly as it had in the church, and she quickly closed them again. She heard a soft chuckle, then he kissed her again, quickly.

And suddenly Faith found herself freed. She blinked, still a little dazed.

"Good morning, Mrs. Blacklock," he said softly and surged out from under her. He swung his legs over the side of the bed and reached for his boots.

A kiss. That's what he meant by her wifely duty. Just a kiss. She felt shaky laughter well up in her. She was relieved. Of course she was. He hadn't meant her to . . . break his promise. Yet, even as relief swamped her, she had an odd feeling of . . . disappointment. Of being let down. It baffled her.

His back to her, he pulled on his boots and his jacket but left his shirt hanging loose. "I'll get myself shaved and presentable and have some hot water sent up to you. Would you like your breakfast brought up—Stevens can fetch it—or would you prefer to come down?"

The cool, businesslike tone, as if they hadn't just shared a stunningly intimate kiss, and more—it felt as if she could still feel the imprint of his . . . his *desire* against her thigh—threw her quite off balance. For after she had said quite calmly that she would come down for breakfast, something caused her to sit up and blurt, "What—why did you remove the bolster?" And to her mortification, it sounded like an accusation. As if she were offended. Or disappointed. Or something.

He paused. "You burrowed under the bolster to get to me in the night."

Her mouth fell open. "*I* burrowed—?" she began indignantly.

His mouth quirked. "You haven't conquered your childhood fear of thunder as well as you like to think you have. Last night you came to me in your sleep, and lay shivering up against me with every clap of thunder. I held you to comfort you; that is all."

She glanced at the rumpled bedclothes, and there was the bolster, behind her, half hanging out of her side of the bed.

He took a couple of steps toward the door, then stopped, turned, and came back. He stared down at her a moment, frowning, and said abruptly, "Do not read anything into what just happened. Nor what happened last night or this morning. I know women are apt to spin fantasies out of moonbeams, but this marriage is a wholly pragmatic arrangement, intended for the eyes of the world and nothing else. There are no—no *feelings* involved here."

His voice hardened. "You are not an innocent, so I will not beat about the bush. The state in which I awoke this morning is a normal one for any healthy man, particularly a man who has been celibate for some time. Don't imagine I have any tender feelings for you. I don't. And don't imagine you have any for me, because you can't. We part after breakfast. Do you understand me?"

Faith swallowed and nodded. The transformation of the man was astonishing. From teasing husband to stern and distant martinet, warning her off.

"I'll see you at breakfast, Mrs. Blacklock. And then I'll escort you to the docks. I have obtained a passage for you to England." He closed the door quietly behind him as he left.

Mortified, Faith pulled the bedclothes over her head. She might never come out again.

He'd made it very clear their marriage meant nothing to him. She knew it, but to hear him say the words out loud . . . it was a shock.

In a few days she'd be in England, explaining to her family that she hadn't in fact married Felix. That was bad enough. But how could she explain that she'd married a stranger she'd met on the beach, married him to save her reputation, and then left him? She couldn't even explain it to herself.

And then there was his mother.

How could he expect her to go back to England and take up a life of comfort at his expense? Faith shivered at the thought.

Comfort? Cold comfort, with no man or child to love or care for. For though he'd hinted she would be free to, she would never betray him.

She lay there, in her chaste marriage bed, thinking.

The first time she'd repeated the marriage vows, she'd spoken them from the heart. Yet that marriage had been a lie and a sham, and the love she thought she felt for Felix had evaporated like a puddle in the sun.

Could she bear another sham marriage?

Yesterday she'd married Nicholas Blacklock in a beautiful little stone church, before God and—according to Marthe—in the presence of her mother and father. And she'd worn Marthe's exquisite handmade lace in the place of the daughter Marthe never had.

Whichever way Faith looked at it, those vows were holy.

There were hidden depths in her new husband that unnerved her. The way his eyes could turn from warmth to cold implacability in a flicker. And the feral light of battle that lit them when he fought was such that . . . She shivered. His ancestors were probably Vikings.

Yet despite his avowal that he had no feelings for her, he'd protected her, not just from her three brutal attackers but from the public scorn of people like Lady Brinckat. He'd tended her hurts with a gentleness that brought a lump to her throat. He made beautiful music with those hands, too. And he'd held her close in the night because she was frightened. And though his body strained, hard and wanting, against her, he hadn't taken her, because he'd given his word.

He'd ordered her not to feel anything for him. How could she possibly obey?

She'd vowed to love, honor, and obey. Did he expect her to keep only one of those vows?

What was he planning to do in Spain? It sounded serious—and very gloomy if it involved revisiting the places where hundreds of men he'd known had died. He was very unforthcoming, almost secretive about his intentions. He'd been a soldier. Perhaps he was one still, traveling with his sergeant and another soldier. He might be on some sort of mission.

Faith huddled down in the bedclothes, smelling the faint scent of his body on the sheets. For years she had been like the child in the story, pressing her cold nose against the glass; only she gazed hungrily not at food, but at the glowing private worlds of lovers. Words that echoed with hidden intimate meanings, glances that caressed and made private promises. She had been waiting years for her turn to love and be loved.

She had a choice to make, here and now: live in the ruins of her past or make a new future. Yearn pointlessly for what could not be or try to build something practical and real.

She hadn't married a dream; she'd married Nicholas Blacklock, a stern, hard, honorable man. And if he had depths that alarmed her, other aspects of him touched her.

Nicholas Blacklock might have no feelings for her,

but he desired her. And though it embarrassed her to admit it, his desire was not unwelcome. She swallowed. She would never forget the feeling of waking up pressed to his big, hard, aroused body. And the blaze of desire that had lit his eyes, before he sternly banked it down.

Desire. Many marriages started with less.

"Women are apt to spin fantasies out of moonbeams."

Was she spinning another fantasy? It was her weakness, she knew. She'd spun them all her life. Yet, without fantasy, without hope that things could get better, life would be just a matter of grim endurance.

The more Faith thought about it, the more Faith believed that if they tried—really tried—she and Nicholas Blacklock could make a life together; not a foolish golden fantasy, but something solid and workable. Something real.

And perhaps . . . She closed her eyes and, hugging her knees, sent up a silent prayer for a child. She longed for a child. She needed so desperately to love.

They reached the wharf before Faith plucked enough courage to tell him. "I'm not going back to England."

He came to a sudden halt. "Nonsense!"

"I'm coming with you."

He looked taken aback. "You can't come with me. Now get on that ship at once."

Faith said nervously, "If it's money you're worried about, I—I come into some money on marriage. I will send a copy of our marriage lines to England and my, um, trustee will send some money to wherever I am. So you see, it will not cost you very much extra."

He said stiffly, "Money is not the issue!"

"Then what is?"

He gave her a look of frustration, then glanced at the people crowding onto the wharf. "Madam, I will not stand here and bandy words with you. Remember what I said to you this morning about the purpose of our arrangement. You can't come, and that's that."

"I will not be returned to England like an unwanted piece of baggage."

"It's what we agreed! You are to make your home with my mother."

"You agreed. I didn't." She laid an arm on his sleeve and said earnestly, "I can't take everything from you and give back nothing."

He said in his deadly quiet, officer whiplash voice, "You will board that vessel now, Mrs. Blacklock!"

Faith lifted her chin, screwed her courage to the sticking point, and said, "I refuse to go." She braced herself. For such a piece of impertinence, Grandpapa would have knocked her flat.

Nicholas Blacklock gave her one look and picked her up. Ignoring her struggles, he marched up the gangway and onto the deck. "Blacklock. Private cabin," he snapped to a seaman watching goggle-eyed. He followed the man to a cabin, apparently oblivious of Faith's fists pounding his back and her toes kicking at him.

He dumped her unceremoniously onto a narrow bunk and said, "Your fare is paid. Your baggage will follow." Before she could get her breath back he tossed a leather pouch onto the bunk beside her and said, "There should be enough money here to hire a private coach to take you to Blacklock, for any accommodation you may require on the way, and for any other needs you may have. Here also is a letter that contains a draft on my bank for whatever you may need. I have left all the necessary letters of introduction with the captain. I have also made arrangements for him to assist you in Dover with the hiring of a coach, a chaperone, and outriders."

"But I don't want to go to England. I want to stay with you. Oh why can't—"

"You are spinning nonsensical fantasies, madam."

"I'm not!" Faith declared passionately. "I want to build a future with you. I'm sure we can if we tr—"

"We have *no future*, madam!" His voice was hard, cold, and implacable, his eyes bleak and empty. "Get that through your head; *you and I have no future*. It is quite impossible!"

"How do you know if you don't try?"

"I know." He shoved his hands in his pockets and stared at her, his gray eyes boring into her, silently bending her to his will. He moderated his tone. "Now, let us not make this a parting of hard words and futile argument."

"But—" Faith tossed her head, frustrated.

"You know what we agreed, madam. Let us kiss and part with dignity and goodwill. You will regret it if you don't."

She eyed him thoughtfully. He was absolutely right. She would regret it. "Very well," she said at last. "Kiss me then."

He kissed her, hard and briefly, as if it meant nothing to him. But it shivered through her as it had each time, and she couldn't help but weep.

It was better this way, Nick told himself for the twentieth time, trying to banish from his memory the picture of a pair of big blue eyes awash with tears and a mouth soft and trembling with emotion. When he'd finished kissing her, he'd used his handkerchief to dry her cheeks, knowing he was prolonging the moment.

Her tears had dried easily, he reminded himself. He would soon be nothing but a memory to her, a chance-met stranger who'd helped her and sent her home to safety. She could build her future without him.

"Do you want to make camp tonight, Cap'n, or will ye stay in an inn?"

Mac had cheered right up once they'd left Calais. Nick hadn't waited to watch Faith sailing away. He'd marched down the gangway without a backward look, fetched the men and horses from the inn, paid his shot to the landlord and, ignoring the questions about the whereabouts of his bride, had ridden out of town. His journey had finally begun.

"Camp, I think," Nick responded. "It looks as if it's going to be a fine and mild night." They'd passed through Boulogne, and the glitter of the sea was visible between the curves of the horizon. Tomorrow they'd turn inland and head south, toward Spain. It was longer this way, but Nick had a fondness for the sea. It was so fresh and clean, and in some mysterious way he felt it renewed his spirit.

Mac threw him a glance. "Ye did the right thing, Cap'n, freein' yeself o' that wee entanglement. Women tie a man in knots. It's best to be shed o' them."

Nick didn't respond.

"I don't know; I miss her," chimed in Stevens. "She had some mighty sweet and pretty ways about her, Miss Faith did."

"Aye, all women have sweet ways, and it's best for a mon tae stay clear o' the whole pack o' them," Mac said sourly.

"Miss Faith was one of the good ones," Stevens insisted. "Mr. Nick couldn't have picked himself a better girl, not out of the whole of London, I reckon."

Mac made a rude sound.

"Precious few young ladies would've faced up to that old griffin lady, let alone to defend someone like me the way Miss Faith did." Stevens's voice sounded a bit thick. He was touched.

As well he might, thought Nick. She'd been more willing to defend Stevens than she was to defend herself. As if she thought Stevens didn't deserve the treatment Lady Brinckat had dealt him, but she somehow did. Nick's fists tightened around the reins. That Bulgarian bastard had a great deal to account for.

"Aye, it was good she stood up for ye, and I honor her for it," Mac said in a begrudging voice. "But that doesn't mean the Cap'n had to marry—"

"Enough, both of you!" Nick snapped. "My marriage is behind me now, and that's where it will remain. The subject is closed, for now and the future."

The men rode on in silence, but after about five minutes Stevens, his voice rich with amusement, said, "Mr. Nick, your marriage may be behind you, and your bride is, too—only not quite as far as you thought. Look."

"What?" Nick slewed around in his saddle, following the direction of Stevens's pointing finger. To his stupefaction, he saw his bride of a day, not more than a few hundred yards away, mounted on a bay horse and wearing a slate-gray riding habit. She was cantering toward them.

He swore. "Stay here," he ordered his men. "I will deal with this." He galloped to meet her.

"Where the devil do you think you're going?" he roared the moment he'd reached her. And regretted it instantly.

His shout, combined with the way he'd thundered down to meet them, frightened her horse. It reared and plunged in alarm. Nick reached out to try to grab its rein and control it, but it danced out of reach. It reared again. His heart was in his mouth. Good God, he might have killed her. He watched helplessly.

He was furious, Faith saw as she fought to control her mount. With himself now, as well as her. She hadn't expected any different. Her heart was pounding, and it wasn't because of her horse. Men did not take well to outright defiance.

By the time she'd brought her horse under control, they'd both calmed. The moment her horse stood trembling, all four feet on the ground, Nicholas dismounted and pulled her from the saddle. In silence he tied the reins of both horses to a bush, then stalked over to Faith and grabbed her by the upper arms.

He repeated his question, only this time in a lower voice. He sounded shaken but still furious. "What the devil do you think you're doing here? I left you on that blasted ship! You should be nearly in England by now!"

"Yes, but I didn't want to go. I told you."

He swore and gave her a small shake. "For God's sake why not?"

Faith chose her words deliberately. She'd rehearsed them all the way. "I married you yesterday. I am your wife, and 'whither thou goest, I will go; and where thou—'"

He cut her off angrily. "Don't spout that nonsense at me—"

"It is not nonsense! You are my husband and—"

"Only on paper."

She shook off his hand and declared passionately, "Not only. I experienced a false marriage once, and I don't intend to live a second one. Yesterday in that beautiful little church I made my vows before God and our friends. And I intend to honor them."

"We are traveling overland on a rough journey, woman!"

She nodded. "I know. You plan to travel through Spain and Portugal, sleeping on beaches and in stables. And I will travel with you." Her voice softened, "'Whither thou goest, I will go; and where thou—'"

"Will you stop quoting that at me, damn-dash it all!" Nicholas clenched his fists in frustration. The catch in her voice was most unsettling. That, and the incipient sheen of tears in those big blue eyes as she stood there, shaking like a little leaf, defying him with biblical quotes. Damn, damn, damn! He'd never been any good with women. Men and animals, that's what he understood.

"It will be a very hard life. You have no conception of how hard."

"I am tougher than I look," she said, and he recalled that she had walked all the way from Montreuil to Calais. He also recalled the state of her delicate little feet at the end of that journey, and he hardened his heart.

"We will travel long hours on horseback, without the comfort of a carriage."

She gestured to her horse. "As you see, I can ride. I will do my best not to slow you down."

He ground his teeth. He knew she could ride—damn well as it happened. But it wasn't about slowing people down, it was about her having to endure discomfort and hardship. When she did not need to. "We will travel in all weathers, sun and rain, and there may even be snow in the mountains. We'll be living as soldiers do: sleeping out of doors, in all sorts of weather."

She nodded. "I understand. I can be a soldier's wife."

"It will be dangerous. Risky. Perilous."

"Yes, I realize that."

Nick shook his head. The stubborn little wretch. She'd barely survived one appallingly dangerous journey. And he didn't want her to risk herself again, dammit!

"What you experienced was *nothing* compared to what awaits us on this journey! If you have any sort of a brain you'll take yourself back to safety! I'll send Stevens to escort you."

"No, thank you." She said it as if he'd offered her a piece of cake.

Nick threw up his hands in disgust. "Dammit, Faith, you'd have a very much safer, more pleasant time of it if you went to my mother." And he would be a lot happier. Well, if not happier, less—less *bothered.*

She shook her head. "I didn't marry your mother. I married you." She took his hand in both of hers and squeezed it. "Please let me come with you."

Nick stared at her, frustrated. Now she'd got the bit of a blasted biblical heroine between her teeth, there was going to be no stopping her, he saw. Blasted women and their blasted fantasies, spun out of the veriest blasted nothing. He should never have kissed her!

"Let me try, at least. If I cannot keep up, then you can send me away." She hesitated, then added, "You spoke before about regrets; if I went home now, I would always regret it."

"Why? There is no point in you coming. We have no future together, you and I."

She said nothing, but he could see she didn't believe him.

"I feel nothing for you!" he insisted.

"I wouldn't want you to feel obliged to feel anything," she responded. "I'm not asking you to love me. I'm telling you I'm coming with you."

Nicholas rolled his eyes at her stubbornness, noting the change from asking to telling. Defeat stared him in the face. Why would any woman willingly take a long, uncomfortable, dangerous journey, sleeping on the ground and facing all sorts of perils when she could live in comfort—luxury!—with his mother?

He recalled the bolster in the bed last night and the way she'd trembled in his arms. In desperation he played his final trump card. "If you insist on traveling with me, my promise of a *mariage blanc* will be null and void. I would fully expect you to share my bed, madam. As a true wife does."

She gave him a wide-eyed look and swallowed. He

felt the taste of victory in his mouth. Tasting somewhat of ashes, but victory nonetheless.

"Very well. A true marriage all the way. Like Ruth in the Bible." She held out her hand to shake on the bargain.

Nicholas's whole body clenched in shock. Or something. She wasn't supposed to agree. He had an instant vision of the sight she'd made waking up in bed, all beautiful and rumpled and warm in his arms.

He rallied and said in a brusque tone, "I have one final condition. You are *not* to get attached to me. If you cling or in any way begin to fool yourself into thinking that what we have between us is love, then you must leave. If I notice it happening, I will ask you to leave, and I want your solemn promise that you will go— without argument." He cast a glance at her horse and added, "Or trickery."

She looked stunned. "Why would you want to refuse love? I've told you I don't expect you to love me, and I'm not promising to love you, but if it happened, why would you reject it?"

"That, madam, is my business. This marriage is nothing but a convenient arrangement, and there will be no talk of l—attachment between us. Such a thing is impossible. If you cannot agree to my terms, then you must leave now."

She looked unhappy, her smooth brow furrowed, and for a moment Nick thought he had her beaten. He added, "And I want no talk of the future."

"No talk of the future." She thought about it for a moment, and gradually her face cleared. She said slowly, "My twin sister, Hope, has a philosophy she lives by, which is to seize every moment of joy that comes her way, to live in the moment and wring every morsel of pleasure from it."

She regarded him gravely, "You don't want to think

about the future, and I don't want to dwell on the past. Are you saying you want us to adopt my sister's policy and live only in the present, taking what life brings us and enjoying it if we can?"

Nick thought about it. Live for the moment. He could do that. He nodded gruffly, and she held out her hand in a determined way. "Very well then, I agree to your terms."

He did not take her hand but said in a severe tone, "I make no concession to female weaknesses, mind. You may travel with us as far as the port of Bilbao, and if you cannot keep up, or if you find the discomforts too much, you will depart on the first boat for England without further argument. Is that agreed, Mrs. Blacklock?"

"It is indeed, Mr. Blacklock." And to Nick's amazement, she didn't just shake his hand, she stood on tiptoe, put her hands on his shoulders, and kissed him. On the mouth. It was barely a kiss, just the faintest brush of her lips against his and a whisper of warm breath. He was disconcerted to feel the soft imprint of it clear through to his toes.

He stared down at her. "No."

Her brow wrinkled. "What do you mean, 'no'?"

He said slowly, "If you're going to stay with me, that's not the way we're going to do that anymore. You need to understand that any kisses between us will not be soft and sweet baby pecks." He wrapped his arms around her and lowered his mouth to hers.

He'd intended it to be a sort of threat, a way of frightening her off with his horrid masculine appetites, but the moment his lips found hers, he forgot. She tasted sweet, meltingly sweet and hot, just as he'd remembered. He'd hungered for one more taste of her, but now she offered him a feast.

Her mouth trembled open under his, and he plunged

in boldly, hungrily. She met his passion with a shy generosity that stunned him, as if she welcomed the masculine invasion. She clutched him hard, pressing her supple body against him, stroking his face with soft fingers and returning kiss for kiss until he was hard and wanting and utterly disconcerted.

He released her and stood back. She looked dazed and slightly mussed, and as he watched, she gathered her composure together shakily. She was breathing heavily, as was he.

She blinked at him, then smiled. "I think that will be quite satisfactory, Mr. Blacklock." Then she smiled with a mischievous light in her eyes that made him want to snatch her back and kiss her again. But they were on an open road, and besides, his men were watching.

His kiss was supposed to make her cut and run; he'd deliberately made it as carnal and demanding as he could, given their lack of privacy, and now here she was—dammit!—smiling at him, an open invitation to do it again. And the worst thing was he couldn't help himself. He kissed her again, hard—just to show her who was in charge here—and stepped back.

In as curt a voice as he could manage, he said, "We shall sleep the night at an inn in Le Touquet. One bedchamber, one bed. No bolster. You have until tonight to change your mind."

"I won't change my mind," she said softly.

He fetched her horse and boosted her up into the saddle. He frowned, his hand on her booted ankle. "Where did you get that horse?"

"I asked the ship's captain to help me find one. You were right; he was very helpful. I was able to get the money back for my ticket, too. Do you want your purse back? I spent some of your money on this riding habit, but I got it at a pawnbrokers, so it was very cheap. It's very good quality and will wear well."

He gave her a frustrated look and stomped off to his own horse. Damn, damn, damn!

Faith watched her husband's tall figure stride away. The taste of him was still in her mouth. It had been a very . . . intimate kiss. She licked her lips, and a ripple of sensation washed through her as she tasted him again.

His words came back to her: *"You have until tonight to change your mind."* She watched him swing lithely onto his horse, and something inside her seemed to settle into place. She wouldn't change her mind. She was determined to go forward, not back.

Tonight she would become Mrs. Blacklock in the flesh.

Chapter Eight

∞

License my roaving hands, and let them go,
Behind, before, above, between, below.
JOHN DONNE

THE NIGHT HAD COME, AND IN THE SMALL INN CHAMBER FAITH awaited her husband. She wore the nightgown that Marthe had given her after her wedding. Made of creamy lawn, it was so fine as to be almost transparent. The bodice was made of beautiful handmade lace and cut low across her breasts.

"My *maman* made it," the old woman had said. She'd added, "It has only been worn once, you understand." Faith knew at once what she meant. Marthe had worn this on her own wedding night. It was a special nightgown; one made for love, not sleeping.

Faith had bathed, soaking her stiff limbs in hot water in a large tin bath in the bedchamber. She'd been taught to ride as a girl and, since it was the only area of their education Grandpapa hadn't ignored, Faith was a competent rider. But she didn't adore riding the way her twin sister did, nor did Faith ride daily. She was very out of practice, and her day in the saddle was making itself felt.

A candle flickered on the nightstand. Where was he?

She'd come upstairs nearly an hour before and was on tenterhooks, waiting.

He'd said little at dinner. His face was pale and austere, and for the most part his jaw remained clenched. He'd hardly touched his dinner. He'd barely responded to her attempts at conversation. He paid her little attention—he paid little attention to anyone, in fact.

Faith couldn't read his mood at all. She wasn't sure if what she observed was tamped-down anger or some dark preoccupation with something else. A nervous tic flickered in the jawline beneath his left ear. His grim, remote expression did nothing to calm her nerves.

His knock, when it finally came, made her jump in fright. He entered quietly and sat down heavily on a hard wooden chair. "Will you help me get my boots off?" His voice was quiet.

She hurried to help, kneeling in front of him and dragging his boots off one by one, his stockings, too. She glanced shyly up at him, wondering if he liked what he saw in the beautiful nightgown. She was shocked at his expression. Instead of the intense, heated gaze she'd expected, his eyes looked dull and glassy. His face was pallid, and the skin around his eyes looked dark, as if it were bruised.

She laid a hand on his knee. "Are you not well?"

He started to shake his head, then stopped, as if the movement hurt him. A rueful expression flickered briefly across his face, and he said in a careful voice, as if each word hurt, "Sorry . . . wedding night postponed. Again. Got . . . another blasted headache."

"What can I do? Will I see if the landlord's wife has any laudanum or—?"

"No!" He winced as if the sharply spoken command had pained him. He managed to grate out, "No laudanum . . . Filthy stuff. No, this . . . gone by morning . . . usually."

He struggled out of his coat. Faith hurried to help. He let her remove his waistcoat, neckcloth and shirt, but when she reached to unbutton his breeches, his hand stopped her. "I will do . . . well enough from here. Get into bed . . . Your feet . . . chilled."

He was worrying about her feet? They were chilled, but as if that mattered, Faith thought. He looked shocking. Willow bark tea, she thought suddenly. Her little sister, Grace, used to get severe headaches when she was young, and Cook used to make willow bark tea for her. It always seemed to help.

She pulled on a dress over her nightgown and hurried to the door in bare feet. In a moment she was knocking on the door of the room Stevens and Mac were sharing. Stevens answered.

"Mr. Blacklock has another headache. Will you see, please, if the landlady has any willow bark to make a tea? I'm sure it will help."

"But, miss—"

"Please, Stevens, now! Make a pot and bring it up to my—our chamber." She hurried back to her room.

Nicholas Blacklock had climbed into bed and dragged some bedclothes over him. He was in an undershirt and drawers. His eyes were closed, but she did not think he was asleep. His forehead was deeply furrowed, his mouth grim and tight. White lines of pain grooved his skin from nose to mouth and between his brows. His breathing was labored. The tic in his clenched jaw jumped harder than ever. She straightened the bedclothes around him and smoothed his pillow and his tumbled, dark hair.

The moment Stevens arrived with the willow bark tea, she took it from him with whispered thanks. She let it draw and poured it into a spouted invalid cup, sending a silent thanks to whoever had thought of it.

She lifted his head and slipped the spout between his lips. He made as if to resist. "It is just tea, willow bark tea. It will help," she said softly. "Please." she said again when he still resisted, and after a moment his mouth relaxed, and she was able to pour some of the bitter liquid into him. He swallowed and shuddered at the vile taste of it, but she made him drink a good quantity.

She placed the cup on the bedside table and climbed into bed beside him. Her movement jolted him, and he groaned.

"Sorry." She smoothed his brow. His eyes opened, and in the light of the candle she saw in them pain, stubborn endurance, and a stark loneliness that called to her.

Faith acted purely on instinct. She opened her arms to him. "Nicholas." She drew him toward her. He resisted at first, then with a deep sigh, he locked his arms tight around her and buried his face between her breasts. He held her so tightly that she thought for a moment she wouldn't be able to breathe. But she could. Just.

He gave another deep sigh, and she felt him get heavier, as if he was finding some ease.

Faith looked down at the dark head cradled between her breasts, and she felt somehow tearful, she did not know why. He held on to her body like a man drowning. His body was rigid with pain.

Faith smoothed her fingers over his neck, his arms, and his sleek, dark hair with a featherlight touch. She could feel every breath enter and leave him. His breath warmed her skin, and her skin absorbed it. She stroked him and held him and breathed in the scent of him and knew that this was why she'd been guided to the man in the sand hills that terrible night.

Slowly, slowly she felt the rigidity seep from him. His convulsive grip of her eased, and his breathing slowed until it became even and regular, and he passed from pain into sleep.

She pulled the covers more securely around them both. This was not what she'd expected to happen in this bed. It was less. And it was more. She held the big, supine body to her and, with a prayer of thanks, drifted into sleep.

Faith woke slowly to a delectable sense of . . . pleasure. She was having the most wonderful dream. She kept her eyes closed, clinging to the sensations of the dream, prolonging the delightful sensation of being . . . loved. Needed.

Big, warm hands smoothed, kneaded, caressed her skin. She felt desired in a way she'd never before felt. Warm, sleepy, smiling, she stretched and moved sensually, squirming pleasurably in the grip of the marvelous dream. Her skin felt alive as his hands moved, sending delicious shivers through her body, shivers that had nothing to do with the cold and everything to do with . . . desire.

His mouth came down over hers, softly, tenderly, possessively, nipping gently at her lips.

"Open up, Mrs. Blacklock," he murmured huskily.

Her eyes flew open. It wasn't a dream; it was Nicholas Blacklock. Nicholas Blacklock recovered apparently from his headache, recovered enough to push her nightgown right up to her waist. Even as she realized it, he tugged it even higher.

She opened her mouth to ask him how his headache was and what he thought he was doing—and found her mouth filled with the taste of Nicholas Blacklock. He tasted dark and male and wildly exciting. His tongue tasted her, learned her, possessed her, and she learned him in response.

Her hands found the hard, rough planes of his jaw, and she smoothed her palms along his jawline, reveling in the friction of his unshaven skin outside and the smooth insistent warmth of his tongue inside.

Hands slipped up her thighs and caressed her hips,

and she moved restlessly, her legs trembling. He was naked, she realized dazedly. When had he removed his clothes? She hadn't felt him move all night.

A large, warm hand dipped into the low neckline of her nightie and cupped one breast, and she felt her flesh move silkily against the rougher skin of his hand. Her breasts seemed to swell under the caress, and when she felt warm breath through the lace against her skin, she clenched her eyes shut and felt her body arch with pleasure. Her fingers slid into his hair, his cool, thick hair, and clutched it, holding him to her but not as she had the night before.

"You smell so good," he murmured against her flesh. "Like roses . . . and new-baked bread . . . and the sea." The deep sound of his voice seemed to rumble through her bones. He feathered moist, warm kisses over her skin, and she trembled in helpless, blissful response.

Their bed was a rose-walled arbor, golden glints of sunshine breaking through the slits between the dark red bed-curtains. Her bones were melting. She was drowning in pleasure. Ripples of delight lapped the deepest recesses of her body, like waves foaming up the sand, finding every secret hollow and filling it.

He lifted the nightgown right up, tugged it over her head, and tossed it aside. Hot gray eyes devoured her, but before she had time to feel self-conscious, he was kissing her again, his tongue tangling with hers while his hands created exquisite friction against the tender skin of her breasts.

"Like silk," he murmured. "My silken-skinned girl."

He kissed her in a slow pathway along her jaw, down her neck, caressing the hollow of her throat, and she melted and tensed, melted and tensed. His tongue teased her nipple in lazy, leisured circles around and around until she was dizzy with wanting. And when she was poised on the brink of who knew what, his hot mouth closed over her breast, and she arched and shuddered uncontrollably, helpless in the grip of a force she had never experienced. He sucked hard, and she almost came off the bed as hot spears of ecstasy drove though her body and into a realm where she'd never been before.

When the shreds of Faith's awareness finally began to gather again, she found she was already climbing that dizzy spiral once more: she couldn't think, only feel. Her hands gripped his shoulders, and she leaned forward and tasted his hot, damp skin, glorying in the spicy masculine taste of him and the leashed power of the smooth, muscled body under her palms.

A large, calloused hand smoothed down over her belly, sliding between her legs, caressing, smoothing, teasing . . . Her legs fell apart, trembling with need. He growled, a low, masculine sound of satisfaction, and his mouth followed his hands, tasting the soft, smooth skin of her belly while his fingers explored her. She was as tense as a bowstring, vibrating with need, when she dimly heard him murmur, "And you taste even better than you smell." She bucked beneath his mouth, once, twice, three times, and with a groan of masculine satisfaction he lifted himself over her and entered her in one smooth, powerful motion. Arched beneath him, Faith hovered on the brink and then he began to move and she felt . . . she felt . . .

Far in the distance she thought she heard a faint, high scream as she plunged into glorious oblivion . . .

When Faith awoke the second time, she was alone in the bed. The sun no longer shone through the cracks between the bed-curtains, and Nicholas Blacklock, from the sounds of things, was getting dressed.

She found her nightgown and put it on again, feeling shy to be naked in front of him, despite the recent events. She parted the curtains and peeked out.

"Good morning."

He jumped and whirled guiltily. He scrutinized her face intently, his face serious. "Good morning," he said in a gruff voice. "Are . . . are you all right?"

She swung her feet over the bed, stood up, and began to stretch. "Ow!" she exclaimed.

"What's the matter? Are you hurt?"

She shook her head. "No, it's just . . . ooh!" She tried to stretch again and winced at the stiffness in her back and legs. "Yesterday's unprecedented exercise. It's . . . oohh." She stretched again, her face screwed against the protesting muscles.

He blanched and looked even guiltier. Faith caught the look and said, "Oh don't worry, it's not serious. It's just a few muscles protesting. I am rather out of practice, you know."

"Out of practice?" His eyebrows snapped together, and he scowled.

"Yes, but it will get better. The more I do it, the better it will be." She gave him a rueful look. "You did warn me, after all, that I would have to endure all sorts of discomfort and hardship."

His scowl grew blacker and more grim. "Yes, I did. And so let this be a lesson to you, madam!" He sounded offended. "If you wish to return to England now, I will send Stevens to escort you."

"Oh I have no intention of leaving. I am sure I will learn to adjust. It is just a matter of practice, I know."

He snorted. "I suppose that blasted Bulgarian had more finesse!" he snarled.

She stared at him in amazement. "What on earth do you—" And then she saw what he had been thinking. And started to giggle.

He glared at her. "What is so blasted funny, madam?"

When Faith could speak, she said between giggles, "I don't know what *you* were referring to." *Oh, what a fib!*

She had to stifle another giggle at the thought. "But *I* was talking about riding. My muscles are stiff from spending all day on the back of a horse, not from, um . . . you know." She giggled again, then gave him a warmly intimate smile. "That part of the journey has been very nice so far."

He stared at her, and a dark red color crept up his throat and face. He cleared his throat noisily and looked around for his jacket as if in a hurry. "I will see you downstairs at breakfast, madam," he said in a gruff voice. He turned to leave, but she flew across the room barefoot and stopped him.

"Wait!"

"What is it?"

"My morning duty. As a wife. Remember, you explained it to me the other day," she murmured and, winding her arms around his neck, she stood on tiptoes and kissed him.

He stood, stiff, passive at first, as if indifferent. Faith opened her mouth and shyly ran her tongue over his, greedy to taste him, needing to return a little of the pleasure he had given her earlier. His jaw was rough-bristled, and she caressed it with her palms, enjoying the friction. He stood like a hard mountain, resisting her, and she closed her eyes and simply kissed him. She kissed him with all the burgeoning feelings that were growing inside her, as if a new person was emerging, a bold, sensual Faith who wanted to reach out to him and let them be new together.

But he stood there, unmoving, letting her kiss him, refusing to respond. She was just about to give up when with a low moan he pulled her closer and deepened the kiss, and the heated, spice-dark sensation of Nicholas shivered through her, swamping her very bones with helpless love for him.

Her knees sagged, and he wrapped his arm around her,

hard, lifting her higher, so that their mouths could merge more fully. She slid her fingers into his soft, thick hair, damp from where he'd splashed cold water on his face, clutching it in her fists as she lost herself in him.

When the kiss finished, she slowly released her grip on him and let herself slide back down his body. They stood a few inches apart, chests heaving, staring at each other. His pupils were huge and dark.

"Good morning, Mr. Blacklock," she said softly, willing her jelly legs not to buckle.

He mumbled something under his breath and left the room. She heard him stomping down the stairs in his boots and smiled. It was a beginning, a glorious beginning.

"Stevens, did you know many soldiers' wives in the army?" Faith asked. They were traveling side by side on a narrow road around the coast. Nicholas had galloped ahead, and Faith took the opportunity to drop back and chat with Stevens. He was a very easy man to talk to. Unlike her husband.

"Yes, miss. Plenty. Some wives and some . . . common-law wives."

"Common-law wives?" She didn't know the term.

"Yes, miss. Not legal marriages, as such. Soldiers being rather short-lived as a rule, some of the women simply moved on to the next man when their own was killed."

Faith was shocked. "Just like that?"

"Yep, just like that." He nodded, then seeing her dismay, explained, "I know it sounds a bit callous, but you have to understand, miss, in wartime it's different. Men and women, well, they seek comfort quick-like, and there ain't no time for long mourning periods. The survivors have to move on, make what they can out of life. A woman needs a man to protect her, and men, well, they need women, too. A good wife—common-law or legal—can make a real difference to a soldier's life."

"In what way?" Faith urged her horse closer to hear his response. This was why she'd raised the subject in the first place, though he'd given her something else to think of as well.

"Well, some women have the knack of making a home anywhere. A hot meal waiting, a warm bed—even on the ground—a few small, precious comforts, soft words in the night. You don't know what a difference that can make to a man, 'specially one who might die tomorrow."

"I see." And she did. If Nicholas had been a soldier so long, it might explain why he was so unwilling to think about the future, to make a commitment to her, even though she wasn't a common-law wife. It would be quite disconcerting to think that if you were killed, your wife of today would calmly move on to your best friend tomorrow. She could see how that would make a man reluctant to speak of love.

Comfort, now, that was another matter. She thought of what they'd shared in the morning and smiled. Comfort was hardly the word. Bliss was more like it. Nicholas Blacklock might not want his wife's love, but he did not seem averse to a little shared marital bliss.

Stevens, oblivious of her straying thoughts, continued, "There was one woman now—Polly MicMac, we called her—I heard she went through a half-dozen husbands one year. Some o' the men reckoned she was bad luck, but there were never any shortage of suitors when Polly's latest man died. A grand girl, Polly; bonny and generous-natured and never a complaint out of her, no matter how hard things got. And cook—always seemed to find a hare for the pot or a brace of pigeons. Brewed up something hot and tasty every night." Stevens shook his head reminiscently. "Even when the army was starving, Polly managed something." After a while he added, "I never did find out what happened to Polly. Lost touch when the capt'n was injured at Toulouse."

"He was injured? What happened?"

"Oh, no need to look so worried, miss. That wasn't the first time. Capt'n Nick, he's been shot many a time and lived to tell the tale. He's been blown up, and I don't know how many bits of shrapnel got pulled out of him after Waterloo—and still the ladies come a'fluttering around him." He patted his own cheek ruefully. "Me, I get hit just the once, and look what a mess it made of me."

"Nonsense!" Faith clutched his arm and said warmly, "No lady worth her salt would care a jot for that. Character and kindness is what real women look for in a man, and those, Stevens, you have in abundance."

He grinned at her. "Why, thank you, miss."

Faith grinned back. Stevens had given her a lot to think about. Nicholas had lived the life Stevens had described since he was sixteen. No wonder he had such peculiar ideas of marriage. And attachment.

Faith had until Bilbao to show him differently.

They had been riding for a good part of the day, stopping for short rests and varying the pace of the horses so they would not tire too much. Most of the time they had been within sight of the sea, a sight Faith never tired of, but since they'd passed through the ancient medieval town of Saint-Valery-sur-Somme, they'd cut inland. Faith was thrilled to have visited the last place William the Conquerer had stayed in before going off to conquer England. She would have to remember to tell her sisters in her next letter.

She'd written several letters home by now, to each of her sisters and to Aunt Gussie and Great Uncle Oswald. In the first letters she'd simply assured them she was safe and well and married to a man named Nicholas Blacklock. She hadn't gone into much detail about the disaster with Felix—only to Hope. Twins hid nothing from each other.

She'd written a couple of letters since, describing their journey and telling her family they were heading for Bilbao, in Spain. She didn't want them to worry.

They were crossing an area of neglected-looking meadowland scattered lightly with clumps of beech and birch and an occasional clump of brambles. There were some berries, Faith saw, but they were small and green and not yet ripe. She was determined to become a good soldier's wife, and not only because that was what Nicholas wanted in a wife.

In that miserable period after leaving Felix, she'd been at her lowest, and the days spent trudging along dusty roads had given her plenty of time for reflection about her life. The realization that she'd been looked after most of her life—that she'd left it to others—hadn't been a comfortable one.

She never wanted to feel so alone again, but nor did she ever want to feel as though she was dependent on others. From what she had gathered, soldiers' wives were strong and independent women, partners with their husbands, rather than dependents. That's what Faith wanted to be, a partner with Nicholas. A partner for life.

It was late afternoon. The horses were ambling along in single file when Faith noticed it: a large hare sniffing and nibbling at a clump of sweetgrass. Now was her chance.

She carefully pulled out her pistol, cocked it, and shot. The hare fell over, and for a moment she felt hugely triumphant. Then, to her horror, it got up. Slowly and agonizingly it scrabbled its way lopsidedly into a small clump of brambles. Faith felt sick. Its shoulder was shattered and bleeding profusely. She'd missed! And worse, she'd injured the poor thing. It must be in agony.

"What the devil do you think you're doing?" Nicholas came up behind her. His voice was sharp, cold. Angry.

She pointed. "I—I shot at a hare, only . . . only—"

"Only it's not a clean kill! You missed, madam!" His voice was accusing.

"I know," she wailed. She felt bad enough without him snapping at her as if she'd deliberately missed.

The others had gathered around. Mac had dismounted and was on all fours, peering in under the brambles. Beowulf pushed in with him, sniffing eagerly.

"I'll see to it," Mac growled. "You get on. Dusk isna too far off, and ye'll need to get to town. I'll catch up wi' ye."

"Right," Nicholas said, tight-lipped. "Come on," he snapped at Faith. He wheeled his horse around and trotted off.

Feeling guilty and upset, Faith followed.

He ignored her for several minutes, then he reined in his horse and waited for her to come level with him. As she did, he unleashed a tirade on her.

"What the devil were you thinking of to pull such a stupid, irresponsible stunt? I bought you that pistol for self-defense, not for shooting hares!" His face was tight with anger, his eyes chips of stone. He spoke so coldly it was like knives slicing into her. "Nobody asked you to come along on this journey, madam, and if you're bored already, it's your own fault! If you think you're going to ride along whiling away the tedium by taking potshots at the local wildlife, you can think again. I won't tolerate it, do you hear me! I shall have Stevens escort you back to Saint-Valery, and you can catch a boat to England! I loathe and detest the attitude that wild creatures are there for our sport!"

"It wasn't for sport, it was for *dinner*!" she burst out,

dashing away the tears that were rolling down her cheeks. "And I wasn't bored. I have been enjoying every single minute of this trip. I . . . I just saw the hare and I . . . th-thought I could help fill the pot. For dinner."

"In God's name why?"

Faith scrubbed at her eyes and tried to explain. "I thought . . . I wanted to be like . . . I mean, you were happy enough for me to catch a fish. And you ate it!" She pulled out a handkerchief, mopped her eyes, then blew into it, hard.

He watched her in silence, and when he spoke again it was in a much more normal tone. "I have no objection to fishing. Nor to hunting animals for food. It is ripping them apart for the sake of mindless entertainment which I abhor."

Her eyes flooded again at his words. "I didn't mean for the poor hare to be r-r-ripped a-apart. I've never k-killed any animal before in my life. I thought it would be d-dead before it knew. But it m-moved at the last m-minute and I m-missed," she finished on a wail of distress.

She took out her handkerchief and looked at it doubtfully. He sighed, reached into his pocket, and handed her a clean handkerchief, which she took gratefully.

When she was more composed he said, "But why on earth would you suddenly take it upon yourself to hunt for our dinner? I am sufficiently in funds to command whatever we may need."

"I was t-trying to be like P-Polly MicMac."

"Polly MicMac? *Polly MicMac?*" He started at her in incredulity. "Why on earth would you want to model yourself on a thieving light-skirt like Polly MicMac?"

"Thieving?"

He made an impatient gesture. "The biggest light-finger I ever met. Ask the farmers and villagers she passed. Never a farm was passed without Polly MicMac 'finding' a cockerel or some apples or a stray piglet. Could glean a feast from the desert, that wretched woman. And besides, that was in wartime!"

Faith suddenly saw a different side to Polly MicMac's activities. She supposed officers and men would be inclined to see things from a different point of view. And especially if the men concerned were getting the benefit of the lady's larcenous activities.

"And how the devil did you hear about Polly MicMac in the first place—?" He broke off with an exclamation. "Stevens, of course! Bloody hell! I might have known. Romancing on about his days in the army. He always did have a *tendre* for that woman, but she was—" He suddenly realized where his speech was heading and broke off.

He regarded her from under black brows. "Well, from now on, madam, you are forbidden to shoot at any more hapless creatures. For heaven's sake—you don't even know who owns the land that wretched hare was grazing on. You do realize that if we were in England you could be arrested for poaching!"

"P-poaching?" Faith faltered. She hadn't thought of that.

"People get transported to New South Wales all the time for taking hares that didn't belong to them. Lord knows what they do to poachers in France."

Faith bit her lip. "I didn't think."

"No, you didn't! So let us have no more shooting. Keep that gun where it belongs. It's for frightening off footpads and brigands, not for killing dinner."

He urged his horse to a faster pace and moved ahead.

Faith felt small, stupid, and cruel.

"Don't fret, miss." Stevens came up behind her. "You just happened to hit one of Mr. Nick's sore points. It's just, he's been powerful fond of wild creatures ever since he was a little 'un and used to go off into the woods all day with my Algy."

"But he's right. I didn't think. And I feel just terrible about the poor hare. I didn't even think. I assumed it would be over in a moment—quick and painless, like it was with the fish when you stabbed it." She shuddered, feeling queasy.

"Never you mind, miss. You didn't mean to make a mess of it, I know. Mr. Nick knows you meant well."

"No he doesn't," she said miserably.

"Ah, don't you take it to heart, miss. He knows it was a mistake. He'll come around, just you see."

"I just wish . . ." She bit her lip.

"There now, miss. It'll blow over. Mr. Nick will calm down, you'll see, and Mac will find that hare and put it out of its misery quick enough."

"I suppose Mac thinks it's a sin to waste the meat." Even as she said it, she felt petty.

"No, you're wrong about that," Stevens said with gentle reproof. "Mac is there because he can't bear to let any living creature suffer. He'll find it and dispatch it quick and clean this time. A legacy from the war."

Faith felt even worse about her mean-spirited remark when he said that. "What do you mean, a legacy from the war?"

"Mac saw a great many men die in slow agony. We all did, but it seemed to hit Mac worse than most. Some men took days to die, some weeks or more. There was nothing anyone could do to help them. Mac hated it. He made all of us promise that if he was ever in that situation, one of us would shoot him, make it quick, and he promised to do the same for us."

"How dreadful."

Stevens shook his head. "No. You don't know what it's like, miss. Better to die quick and in dignity. I'd take a clean quick bullet from Mac any day over a slow death. That hare is lucky."

Faith bit her lip.

Mac rejoined the party a short time later. His hands were scratched, and from his saddle dangled a limp and bloody rag of fur. Faith shuddered when she saw it. She felt like a brute.

"I'm sorry you had to do that, Mr. McTavish," she said. "I'm sorry the poor hare suffered so."

"Aye, well next time ye go to kill a creature, make sure ye do it quick and clean."

Faith swallowed. "I will. Though I don't think I'll kill so much as a spider, ever again," she muttered ruefully.

He eyed her from under his bushy brows and said in a gruff voice, "Ach, dinna take on, lass. If a fox had caught this hare, it probably would have suffered just as much. Life isna kind to creatures for the most part, and death is no kinder."

It was undoubtedly the nicest thing Mac had ever said to her, and the fact that he'd meant to comfort Faith only made her feel guiltier and more wretched than ever. He rode ahead, and the bloodstained, dead hare bounced floppily against his horse's flank. Faith felt every bounce.

That night, as they were getting ready for bed, Faith told Nicholas how awful she felt about the hare. She hadn't liked to bring it up when they'd been dining below with the others.

He looked at her in surprise. "But that happened hours ago. Have you been brooding about it all this time?"

She frowned at his tone. "Of course."

He shrugged out of his jacket. "Live in the moment, madam—remember? You made a small mistake, it wasn't serious, so move on from it. However ill-informed your action was, you meant well. The consequences, apart from the unfortunate ones for the hare, were immaterial; there was no serious delay, you learned an important lesson, and Beowulf enjoyed the fresh meat." He sat down to pull off his boots.

Faith was inclined to feel a bit indignant at his casual dismissal of her feelings, but he began to unbutton his breeches, and she turned away hastily. She was not yet so comfortable with him that she could watch him disrobe with equanimity.

She unbuttoned her dress and slipped out of her petticoat and chemise and into her nightgown with as much modesty as she could manage. She knew it was foolish, as he had already seen all of her there was to see, but she was new to this marriage and still felt a little shy and self-conscious at moments such as these.

She slipped under the bedclothes and waited for him to join her. She felt the give of the mattress as he joined her in bed, but instead of sliding in with her, he ripped the bedclothes back, exposing her completely. Her mouth went dry, and she swallowed, half nervously, half in anticipation.

"Turn over. On your stomach," he ordered.

She turned over. She tried not to jump when he took the hem of her nightgown and pushed it up as far as it would go.

"Lift up," he instructed, and she lifted her stomach as best she could, while he pushed the nightgown right up past her waist.

She waited, feeling very exposed, wondering what her bottom and the back of her legs looked like. For a long time he did nothing, but she heard small odd sounds and a sort of sticky noise, like bare feet on a sticky floor—only he wasn't on the floor.

She swallowed. Was this what she had released with that wanton kiss this morning? Or was it to be some sort of punishment for the hare? He'd said it was in the past, but people said all sorts of things they didn't mean.

He moved closer. She braced herself. She could feel the warmth of his body close to her chilled, exposed skin.

Then something cold and slimy touched her thigh, and she gasped in horror and tried to push away from it.

"Don't move. It's a bit cold, I know, but it'll soon warm up." He started rubbing her thigh in small, circular movements.

She groaned. Her muscles were still stiff and sore from the unaccustomed amount of riding she'd done in the last few days.

"That's it, relax," he said. His hands stroked her thighs with long, firm movements. She felt her aching muscles protest.

"Ouch! I'm a bit sore there," she told him.

"I know. That's why I'm rubbing this salve into you. It'll make you feel better."

Faith doubted it. The pungent smell tickled her nostrils. Camphor and mint, cloves and something else. He'd used it on her ankle once, to good effect, but that was out of doors. In this small room . . . She wrinkled her nose. She wasn't too fond of the smell of camphor. This was the life of a soldier's wife, she reminded herself. She gritted her teeth, pushed her nose into the pillow, and set herself to endure it.

He put cold salve onto her other thigh and started to massage it in, squeezing and pulling and rubbing. It hurt at first, but wherever his hands moved, her skin tingled and heated. Eventually the movement and the heat seemed to penetrate into her body, and her aching muscles began to loosen and relax.

Soon Faith found herself stretching and squirming pleasurably under his hands. "Oh, this is so good," she gasped.

He grunted. His hands never stopped.

After a while he said, "Lift up, I'll do your back now."

With difficulty she lifted her midriff, and he pulled the nightgown right off her. A glop of salve hit her square between the shoulder blades, and she gasped and waited for his big warm hands to start their magic again. He smoothed it over her skin gently, then rubbed and stretched and stroked for what seemed like hours. His long, strong fingers seeming to seek out every knot and work at it to dissolve it.

"Oh, Nicholas, this is heavenly," she purred, stretching sensuously into his movements.

Again, all he did was grunt in response.

By the time he'd finished, Faith was a boneless mass of pleasure. "Sit up," he said, and when she did, he dropped his shirt over her.

"Your shirt?"

"It'll be easier to wash the salve out of that than the flimsy thing you were wearing."

"Oh." She snuggled into his shirt. It felt lovely, wearing his clothes. He pulled the bedclothes up around them and lay down beside her.

"Don't you want me to massage some salve into you?" she asked. "You must be a bit stiff, too."

There was a short silence.

"No, thank you."

"Aren't you even a bit stiff?"

There was another short silence.

"No," he grated. "Good night, Mrs. Blacklock."

She felt a small trickle of disappointment that they were not going to make love again tonight. Though probably he found her dreadfully unattractive, reeking of camphor as she did.

She leaned over and gave him a quick kiss. "Good night, Mr. Blacklock. Thank you for the massage. It was truly wonderful." She snuggled down in the bed, feeling warm and relaxed and well cared for. And as she snuggled, her hand brushed something, and she froze.

A little smile fought to escape her. He obviously didn't object to the smell of camphor in the least. "Mr. Blacklock."

"Hmm?

"You didn't tell me the truth, Mr. Blacklock."

"Go to sleep; you're worn out."

"But you are stiff, and I think you do need a massage. Or something." Her hand encircled the stiffness she had encountered.

He groaned. "Are you sure you're not too tired?"

"Oh no, I feel just wonderful," she said and squeezed.

They left the inn in midmorning.

"We will not leave so late again, madam. It is imperative that we travel as far as possible each day," Nick informed his wife in a brusque voice.

"Yes, certainly. Perhaps you could wake me earlier tomorrow morning." She gave him a mischievous smile, and he looked away, knowing full well whose fault it had been that she'd needed to sleep late. Again.

He had been watching her for any signs she might be getting overly attached, but apart from a tendency to share her smiles with the world, she seemed quite normal.

"Your hat is on crooked," he said, needing something to say. She adjusted her hat to better shade her face and gave him a look of bright query. He nodded. It was bad enough she was on this rough trip without having her delicate skin scorched to pieces. The weather had turned warm, almost hot.

By early afternoon it was even hotter, and Faith's face was glowing with heat or exertion, Nick wasn't sure which. Catching a glimpse of sea in the distance, he announced they would rest at the beach for a little while. Mac and Stevens gave him odd looks, but he ignored them.

The beach was sandy and deserted. They found some shade and ate bread with sausage and cheese, and crisp local apples to follow. On a blanket in the shade, Faith lay back and closed her eyes. She was asleep in moments, he thought guiltily. He'd worn her out. She slept, the sun beat down, the sea sparkled a brilliant blue.

Nick eyed it longingly. They would have to turn inland for a while soon. It might be his last chance. He stood abruptly.

"I'm going for a swim."

Mac and Beowulf joined him. Stevens shrugged. "I'll stay here with the mistress. I might even have a snooze, myself."

Faith woke to the sound of snoring and seagulls. She sat up, hot, sleepy, and disoriented. Stevens lay on another blanket a few feet away, sound asleep with his mouth open.

She stood and stretched. Her muscles had loosened a little with the riding, but she'd slept in an awkward position. Where was Nicholas? She looked around and saw Beowulf standing at the very edge of the waves, looking intently out to sea. Two heads bobbed in the waves. They were swimming. So much for traveling as far as possible each day.

Faith watched them enviously. She would have loved to swim, but she didn't know how. It was such a hot day, and the water looked so cool and fresh and inviting. She'd paddled her bare feet in it earlier, and it was bliss. The thought of putting her whole body in the coolness was heavenly.

In her mind, she heard her twin's voice saying, just as if Hope were right here, "Turn down no opportunity for joy, however small."

Just yesterday she'd agreed to live for the moment. And this was the moment. Without further thought Faith snatched up her blanket and ran down the beach a little. She glanced back at the sleeping Stevens. He was sound asleep and barely visible. There was not another soul around, so she unbuttoned the jacket of her habit. She removed the skirt, folded it, and placed it beside the boots and stockings she'd removed when they first arrived at the beach. She kept unbuttoning things until she stood on the beach wearing nothing but her chemise and pantaloons. Feeling a bit exposed, she shook out the blanket, wrapped it around her, and walked down to the water's edge.

Beowulf gave her a sideways glance and growled but otherwise ignored her. He was only interested in his master.

Faith dropped the blanket and, feeling immensely daring, waded in up to her knees, gasping as each small wave splashed her hot skin. The water was freezing at first, but very invigorating. She waded deeper, her excitement growing, until she stood almost waist deep. She did not dare go deeper; she was frightened of being swept off her feet. The waves were small but quite strong. She jumped and splashed and patted the cold salt water on her hot face and arms. It was heavenly. She would have loved to immerse herself completely, but she was too nervous.

She looked out to sea at her husband, his sleek, dark head bobbing in the waves. His back was turned; he hadn't noticed her yet. She wondered if he'd agree to teach her to swim.

"Have ye no modesty, woman?"

A large, wet, irritable Scotsman was standing chest deep in the sea to her left. She hadn't noticed him coming to shore.

A tangled mass of seaweed floated in the clear water near her feet. Faith wasn't fond of seaweed. Creatures lurked in seaweed. She carefully stepped around it.

"Well?" Mac demanded.

"Well, what?"

"Will ye no remove yer person?"

She frowned. "Why should I?"

"Fer the sake o' yer modesty!" Mac said, bristling

with indignation. "It should be obvious, even tae the likes o' you!"

"I am perfectly modest," she retorted, crossing her arms across her breasts defensively. After all, she might be in her underwear, but her chemise and pantaloons covered her decently, whereas he was no doubt naked, as he'd been that first day.

"Not if ye can face a nekkid man wi'oot a blush, ye're not! Now, move, woman!"

"I will not! I have a perfect right to cool myself just as you have!"

"Mebbe, but I wish to get oot!"

She shrugged. "I'm not stopping you!"

"Ye are! Did ye no' hear me? I'm nekkid, ye shameless creature!"

"I am not a shameless creature, and I utterly refuse to move. Go ahead, leave the water, I am not stopping you. See?" She turned away from him. "I won't look!"

He snorted. "I wouldna trust ye no' tae peek."

"I gave you my word." Faith was furious. Not least because the other day she had peeked. But not at him. And she hadn't given her word then.

He snorted again. "Aye, the word o' a hussy!"

She turned, enraged. "I am not a hussy! And if you ever call me one again, I—I will—I will—oooh!" She could think of no fate terrible enough. Without a thought, she bent and scooped up the floating mass of seaweed and hurled it at him with all her might. It landed directly on him.

He staggered back in the water, clutching the mass of dripping seaweed to his chest. It may have contained creatures, but Mac was made of sterner stuff.

"Ye'll no' budge then?"

"No!"

He glared at her. "No shame at all," he declared and

stalked out of the water clutching the seaweed strategically against him to preserve his own modesty, if not hers.

"It's full of crabs!" Faith called after him.

He recoiled and flung the seaweed from him. Faith instantly turned her back. She was not a hussy! As if she would want to stare at a big, nekkid, hairy Scotsman! A naked Greek god, now . . . As she peered out to sea, looking for her husband, his dark, wet head bobbed up beside her, like a seal in the water.

"That, Mrs. Blacklock, was very naughty of you."

She said defensively, "Well, he was very rude."

"Yes, but also very embarrassed to be caught naked by a woman. I expect you've given him food for thought. Tell me, were there really crabs in that seaweed?" He was amused, she saw with relief. His eyes were dancing with laughter.

"I don't know. I hope so. I hope they were big and angry, and I hope they bit him. Hard and in a sensitive spot!"

He laughed out loud then. Faith beamed, her temper forgotten in the joy of hearing him laugh, and without hesitation he reached out and pulled her under.

She surfaced, spluttering and splashing, and eyed him with outrage. "You beast! Whatever did you do that for? I could have drowned!"

He laughed in what Faith thought was a very callous manner and pointed out, "You're standing on the sea floor and you're only up to your waist."

Having no words to retort in a fitting manner, she splashed him. He splashed her back, and the fight was on. Water flew in all directions, until they were both panting and dripping and laughing. It was wonderful fun, but eventually Nicholas stopped it by diving under the waves and swimming out of Faith's reach.

She watched him with a mixture of frustration and wistfulness. "Not fair," she said when he surfaced a few yards away. "You know I can't swim."

For answer, Nicholas dived back under the waves and disappeared. He was gone for a long time, and just as Faith was getting anxious, a dark shadow arrowed toward her under the water. She shrieked with fright, even as she realized who it was. He gripped her around the thighs and lifted her high out of the water.

"Do you want to learn? I could teach you if you like."

She clutched his shoulders, but said eagerly, all thought of water fights forgotten, "Would you?"

"Of course," he said and let her slide back down the length of his body, into the sea. Friction, hot and cool. "Now, the first thing you need to learn is how to float."

Disappointed, she wrinkled her nose. "Just float?"

"Floating is both harder than you think and easier. It's important. For a start, you need to know that you can float, and that therefore you can swim. Also, if ever you get tired in the water, you can always float." He scooped one arm around her waist. "I'll keep my hand here, in the small of your back. Just lean back and put the back of your head in the water and let your feet float up to the surface."

She leaned back against his hand, but her feet refused to rise.

He slid his other hand under her hips. "Don't worry, I'll support you; you won't go under."

She squeezed her eyes tight closed and pushed backward. It was scary, but after one or two false starts, she managed not to struggle when, murmuring encouragement, he gently but surely tipped her backward and pressed her hips upward. She was as stiff as a board, certain that at any moment, she'd go under.

"Head back, that's right, now breathe . . ." He waited. "It's all right to breathe . . . In fact, you *need* to breathe." He waited a little longer, and then said in his officer voice, "Faith, breathe."

She opened her eyes, took a huge gulp of air, and went under. She came up spluttering. "You said I wouldn't—"

And stopped. He was laughing. She thumped him on the arm. "How dare you half drown me and then laugh about it!"

Still laughing, he said, "That was quite good. You were floating almost by yourself, you know, only you need to learn the art of floating *and* breathing."

Ignoring his teasing, she tried again, insisting he keep his hand under her back, just in case. She put her head back in the water, feeling the cool water lapping around her ears, and pushed her feet up.

"Now breathe," he said. "It helps keep you buoyant."

Faith floated and breathed, big, deep breaths. It was amazing. She felt weightless, but his big hand was still supporting her. Breathing did aid buoyancy. Faith breathed even deeper.

He groaned. "God give me strength."

Her eyes flew open. "Am I too heavy for you?" Her feet thrashed around, and she immediately sank.

He hauled her to her feet. "Of course not. In water you weigh nothing at all."

"Then why did you ask God for strength?"

"Not physical strength, moral." With a rueful expression, he glanced at her body. "I'm sure you thought you were well covered when you began, but now that you're wet all over . . ." His mouth quirked at her puzzled expression. "I don't suppose you know the effect of water on white cotton underwear."

She followed his gaze and gasped. The effect of water on white cotton was to make it almost totally transparent, and she looked as near to naked as made no difference. She clapped her hands over her breasts and crouched down in the water.

He smiled then. "I have seen you before, you know."

She didn't know where to look. She felt her face heating. "Y-yes, maybe, but not outside in the open air. Oh heavens! Mr. McTavish!" she turned, horrified. "He would have seen—"

Nicholas shook his head. "No, he wouldn't have seen anything except your underwear. Your bottom half was under the water, and your top half didn't get wet until you bent to pick up that bunch of seaweed." He grinned. "I seem to remember that he was somewhat occupied after that."

Faith thought it over, then relaxed. "Yes, and I turned my back to prove I wasn't a peeking hussy."

"A *what*?" His brows snapped together.

"He said I was a shameless hussy who likes to look at naked men. And it's not true, not really. I only like to look at—" She broke off, flustered. What would he think if she discovered she had, in fact, shamelessly ogled a naked man?

"What do you only like to look at?" he prompted.

She didn't answer. She was sure her face was on fire. She longed to sink into the cool, salty water and just hide there, only his hands were still holding her upper arms.

"Faith?"

He obviously wasn't going to give up. "Greek statues," she said in a small voice.

There was a short silence. "Greek statues?"

"Yes," she said airily. "Haven't you seen Lord Elgin's marbles? They are most cleverly wrought."

"No, I haven't." He frowned again. "So, Mac called you a shameless hussy?"

"Yes. I suppose it was a bit hussyish of me to be in my underclothes. But at least *I* was covered," she said quickly, glad of the change of subject. "He's very *bear-ish*, isn't he?"

He gave her a doubtful look.

She explained. "Grumpy and mean-spirited and expecting the worst from me all the time. Why does he dislike me so? I've never done anything to him."

He shook his head. "It's not you. He's had very bad luck with women in the past. He expects the worst from all women." His brow darkened. "But I'll not have him upsetting you or speaking disrespectfully to you. I shall deal with—"

"No!" She laid a hand on his chest. "I will deal with Mr. McTavish myself. Since he expects the worst from women, I won't disappoint him," she declared. "I don't care if he is your friend, Nicholas. I will not put up with his—his bearishness anymore. I am fed up with men being rude to me!"

He gave her a thoughtful look. "Very well. I'll leave it in your hands . . . for the moment. Now, shall we return to the beach?"

Her face fell. "What about my swimming lesson?"

Nick stifled a groan. A man shouldn't have to deal with a rosy, near-naked water nymph and not be able to do anything about it. Especially now he knew the texture of her skin, the shape of her body under his hands, the taste of her breasts . . .

He should never have consummated the marriage.

"Just one little lesson? Please?"

He took a deep breath. He could do this. Ever since he'd first pulled Mac and Beowulf out of that river, he'd instructed any number of young officers and men in swimming techniques. Soldiers needed to cross rivers without drowning. And wounded men healed quicker after bathing in the sea. Teaching Faith was no different, he told himself. She had the requisite number of arms and legs. She could be taught to use them in the same way. It was just a matter of discipline.

He said curtly, "Very well, let me see you float."

Obediently she lay back in the water against his hand, and with grim concentration thrust her hips, her belly, and her breasts up. Nick clenched his jaw.

She bobbed, rosy and wet, the translucent shrouding

of her wet underclothes only adding to her allure, like a treasure wrapped in tissue, half-revealed and enticing.

"Breathe," he ordered and tried to remember to breathe himself.

She breathed, and her breasts rose and fell, her nipples hard like little berries. Water pooled and lapped in the vee of her thighs, swirling the dark gold curls beneath the folds of her drawers.

Desire rocked him. Clamping down on it hard, Nick removed his hand from the small of her back. She floated. He moved away from her. She continued to float.

"How long do you think it will take before I can do this by myself?" she asked.

From several yards away, he said, "Open your eyes, Faith."

Slowly she did, and saw she was floating. She managed another minute, saying, "I can do it. I can float!" She stood and splashed over to him. "I can float, Nicholas!"

He tried not to laugh at her excitement. There was a hard knot in his chest. She was so damn beautiful. So full of the joy of life. It was almost painful to watch her.

It was fitting punishment, he told himself sternly. He should never have offered to teach her to swim.

"Now, show me how to swim," she commanded.

He really ought to call it quits now. Go in, get dressed, and get back on his journey. Time was passing. He glanced at the shore. There was no sign of his men. Possibly they were seeing to the horses, he told himself. Allowing Nick privacy to frolic with his wife.

"Very well. It is much the same process, only on your front, not your back. I place my hand on your stomach, like so, and you . . . Yes, that's right. Now, have you ever watched a frog swimming?"

Frowning in concentration she followed his every instruction.

His hand cupped her belly, supporting her while she "swam" in circles around him, moving her arms and legs like a frog's. From time to time she would accidentally gulp in a mouthful of seawater and choke and sputter, or he would take his hand away, and she would sink. But always she bobbed back up, laughing and undaunted, water streaming from her lithe young body.

Nick wasn't sure if he was in purgatory or heaven. All he knew was that teaching soldiers to swim had never been like this.

"Now try it by yourself," he snapped.

Her face fell a moment, then it cleared. She glanced at the sun. "Oh, yes, sorry. I am delaying everyone, aren't I? Right, one more try, and then I promise you I will go in."

Her face a study in grim concentration, she launched herself into the water and swam clumsily and doggedly toward him. The closer she got, the more he moved away until, when she had swum nearly ten yards by herself, he stopped and let her swim up to him.

"I did it!" She panted as she found her feet. "I can swim, Nicholas! I can float and I can swim! Oh thank you, thank you!" and without warning, she surged up out of the water, flung her arms around his neck, and kissed him. She planted kisses on the corner of his mouth, on his chin, on his cheek, exuberantly and without finesse; she simply rained kisses all over his face.

Chapter Nine

∞

*To see a world in a grain of sand, and heaven in
a wild flower, hold infinity in the palm of your hand,
and eternity in an hour.*

WILLIAM BLAKE

THERE WAS ONLY SO MUCH TEMPTATION A MAN COULD STAND,
Nick decided. He wrapped his arms tight around her and
took firm possession of her mouth.

Her lips were salty and cool, but they parted under
his, and inside she tasted hot and tangy sweet. The contrast was intoxicating, and Nick could not get enough of
her. She was soft, her skin cool and petal-smooth, and
she kissed him back with shy eagerness. Her arms
twined around his neck, and she returned each kiss with
a heartfelt response that rocked him to his soul.

Her hard-berry nipples pressed against his naked
chest, and he caressed her with his hands first and then
his mouth, tasting salt through the fabric, and woman
underneath. She arched against him, her hands clutching and caressing his shoulders, his jaw, locking in his
hair, kissing every piece of his skin she could reach.

"Wrap your legs around my middle."

Her eyes widened, but she obediently lifted herself
against him and wrapped him in her thighs. Warm and soft.

"It's easy to move around in the water, isn't it?" she said between kisses. "I'm so light. Do you think fish feel like this?"

"I don't know," he murmured. "I've never tried kissing a fish. I prefer you. Fish are cold and clammy. You're warm and soft and lovely."

She gave a soft laugh, and he kissed her long and deep, glorying in her female vitality.

He reached for the ties on her drawers, praying she hadn't knotted them. They were tied in a small, neat bow. Women were amazing creatures. He tugged at one end, and the bow fell away. He loosened the drawstring at her waist and slipped his hands between the drawers and her flesh. Her warm, wet, silken flesh.

She shivered in his arms, and he felt it clear to the bone. He caressed her gently, and she shuddered again. He couldn't wait. He pushed the drawers down over her bottom, caressing the smooth curves.

"Move your legs."

"I think they've dissolved." But she unlocked her legs, and he stripped off her drawers. He drew her legs back around him and, finding her entrance warm and waiting, he surged into her.

She clutched him tight to her, making small moans as she took him deeper and deeper. His eyes closed, Nick gave himself over to the urgent demands of his body and the urges of the woman twined around him. Her movements became more frantic and demanding, and he gave her what she wanted, what he needed, until she arched and shuddered in climax, taking Nick with her.

It was some time before he came to an awareness of what he had done. He was half standing, half floating in the water, Faith curled against him, her legs locked around his waist, her arms around his neck, and her face pressed against his jaw. She was limp and panting. He felt simultaneously exhausted and full of life.

But oh, Lord, he'd just made love to his wife *in the sea*! In full sight of anyone passing.

He looked over her shoulder at the beach. There was still no sign of Mac or Stevens—or anyone else. Thank God.

"We should go in now," he said quietly in her ear.

She stirred. "Yes. I'm a little bit cold."

Faith still in his arms, Nick started to wade toward shore.

"Stop!" she said, pushing at him. "What do you think you are doing?"

He gave her a blank stare. "Going in. You said you were cold."

"Yes, but I'm not going in like this!"

"Like what?"

"Without my drawers! You took them off me. Where are they?" She looked at him as if somehow she expected him to have a pocket into which he'd tucked her drawers.

Nick shrugged. "I don't know. Somewhere out there." He gestured toward the sea.

"Well, I'm not going in, in front of your men with—with my bottom all bare."

"You won't. The men have gone off somewhere."

"They might come back."

"Well—I'll get a blanket so they won't see."

"You'll have to do that anyway. The effect of water on white cotton, remember?"

"Well then?" Nick was baffled. She'd be covered by a blanket anyway, so what possible difference would it make? But logic didn't seem to apply, or if it did, it was some female logic, because she would not budge.

"Blanket or not, I am not going out onto an open beach without my drawers, Nicholas! I won't give that McTavish any further excuse for rudeness. And, do you think I'll be riding a horse with no underwear?" She made a scornful female noise. "You lost my drawers; you find them!"

He gave her a harassed look, but she wriggled out of his arms and said with determination, "They won't have gone far, the tide is not yet turning, and the sea is very calm."

Shaking his head, he waded back to where they had been before and cast around, looking for her drawers. It was impossible. He dived and dived, feeling crosser and crosser. It was his fault for letting her seduce him. He should have had more discipline. It was her fault for being so damn prissy about going to shore without her drawers. After his tenth fruitless dive, he glanced back at her.

She stood in the water, her arms folded, watching him anxiously. She looked chilled but determined. He should just pick her up and cart her to shore and forget about the damned drawers. One more dive, he decided, and if that proved unproductive, he would give up and fetch the blanket and damn well drag her out of the water, bare bum or not.

He dived and, just as he was about to surface, caught a glimpse of something pale wafting in the deep. He dived again and with a growl of triumph retrieved the wretched things.

"Here." He handed her the soggy bundle.

"Oh, I knew you would find them. Thank you, Nicholas!" She beamed at him as if he'd performed some sort of heroic deed, and he felt some of his irritation dissolve. He watched as she tried to put them back on. The fabric clung, and she could not seem to get even one leg into them. There was a great deal of splashing around and muttered feminine cursing. Nick stood it as long as he could.

"Here, let me help." He took the drawers from her hand. "Now, you float, and while you're doing that, I'll get these things back on you."

She floated, her golden hair swirling around her

head, rosy-tipped breasts bobbing in their translucent covering, and her lower half as naked and beautiful as God made it. Nick set his jaw and forced himself to shroud God's handiwork in one of the most pointless garments ever invented.

She struggled to her feet. "Thank you," she said softly and gave him a smile that dazzled him. "It was very good of you to do that for me. I know you probably think it was foolish—"

"Not at all," Nick lied. His throat was thick with desire. For two pins he'd have had those drawers off her again and be buried deep within her. She seemed to sense it. She gazed at him, and it was as if he was drowning in her eyes, bluer than the ocean and just as wide and deep.

"I had a lovely time just now," she said almost shyly. Her face glowed. "In fact, it's been one of the loveliest days in . . . forever."

He nodded, unable to think of a thing to say. He'd never experienced anything like it.

They stood in the warm water, waist deep, neither one of them apparently able to move. She looked glorious, golden and so damned beautiful he could hardly believe she was real. But she was, real and wholly female, soft, rosy curves wrapped in damp, white tissue. His wife.

Her eyes moved over his body in fascination. "Amazing," she murmured. She was staring at a certain part of his anatomy. He supposed she wasn't used to male nakedness. Despite her previous experience, in some ways she was an innocent.

He gave her an indulgent smile. "What is amazing?"

"It floats."

Nick looked down at himself and indeed, it did float. He stepped hastily out of the water. He needed to fetch a blanket.

• • •

"You're humming."

Faith jumped. For the last few miles she'd been miles away, Nick could tell from the dreamy look on her face. All unconscious, she'd been humming a pretty little tune to the rhythm of her horse's hooves as they ambled along.

"I'm sorry," she gasped, turning a guilty countenance toward him. "I didn't mean to, I promise. It won't hap—I won't do it again."

He frowned. Her anxious expression disturbed him. "I didn't say I minded. I didn't recognize the tune."

If anything, her look of guilt deepened. She mumbled so that he had to lean over to catch what she was saying. "I made it up."

"It's a very pretty tune. Do you make up tunes often?"

She gave him a wary look. "Why do you ask?"

He shrugged carelessly. "No particular reason. I just wondered." Her behavior baffled him. She acted as if he'd caught her in the middle of robbing a church or an old lady instead of commenting on a tune she'd hummed.

An elusive memory teased him. When Stevens had given her that cheap little flute for her wedding present, she'd received it as if it were the most precious thing in the world. What had she said? Something about having a flute when she was young and her grandfather had smashed it. That was it. Her grandfather had forbidden her to play music.

And from the look on her face when he'd startled her out of her reverie, the bastard had backed up his edict with more than just words. She'd flinched automatically, as if half expecting a blow. Fury flared within him. For anyone to dislike music was beyond him, but to hit a sweet young girl, especially one in whom music bubbled as naturally as water bubbled out of a spring . . .

"You said once that your grandfather smashed your flute. Was it deliberate?"

Her eyes darkened. "Yes. It was a terrible day."

"I can imagine. It must have been upsetting," he said carefully.

She hesitated, then darted him a glance that was half-ashamed. "It was worse than that. My twin, Hope, was beaten, and it was my fault."

"Tell me about it."

"I had been playing my flute—Grandpapa had forbidden music and didn't even know I owned it. He saw me from an upper window and saw where I had hidden it. He came looking for me and instead he found Hope. Unfortunately she had taken off her rope, and so he didn't realize which twin she was—"

"What do you mean, she had taken off her rope?"

"Hope is left-handed. Grandpapa tied her hand behind her all the time so she could not use it, but Hope was more defiant than I. She sometimes got one of the servants to cut the ropes off."

She said it in such a matter-of-fact way, he was appalled. "Good God! He sounds like a complete brute!"

"Yes, he was a terrible man. Anyway, he grabbed Hope and accused her—thinking she was me. And he found the flute and smashed it and then he beat Hope." She bit her lip, remembering. "I didn't even know until afterward."

Nick urged his horse beside her, reached out, and caught her hand in his. "Poor little girls. Poor little twin. She did it deliberately, didn't she? To protect you."

Faith nodded. Her voice was husky as she said, "She always tried to protect me from him. She is very brave, my twin sister."

"Very brave, and very special, just like you." And he lifted her left wrist and kissed the inside of it tenderly. She looked at him, and her eyes were bright with unshed tears.

He tried to think of a way to ease her tension, to comfort her. She'd said she didn't want to dwell in the past, and he could well understand why.

"That is the past, though. We live in the present, now, remember?" he said softly. "Wasn't Hope the same sister who taught you to embrace the joy in the present?"

She nodded dumbly.

"I make up tunes, too," he said diffidently.

"You?" She blinked, startled at his admission. "Of course! I'd forgotten for a moment you played the guitar. So much has happened—and you haven't touched your guitar for ages."

He shrugged. "There hasn't been much time for playing music." He glanced at her. "But now's as good a time as any. Stevens, pass my guitar, please."

From the packhorse, Stevens pulled out the guitar. Nick knotted his reins so they rested on his horse's withers, took the guitar, and began to tune it. His horse walked on without so much as a flick of an ear, testament to the fact that this was no unusual occurrence. Nick started to play, a Spanish tune, and as he played he watched her relax and gradually give herself over to the music.

"It's lovely," she exclaimed.

"Play your flute, miss," called Stevens, and she glanced at Nick.

"The more the merrier," he said.

Needing no further encouragement, Faith pulled out her flute and joined in, hesitantly at first. The tune he'd been playing was unfamiliar to her, but she soon picked it up and began a bright counterpoint to the slow, rather sad song. Slowly both the tempo and the mood of the song picked up.

"Ah, that's grand, miss," said Stevens when they finished. "Now how about something me and Mac can sing to."

Faith glanced at the dour Scotsman in surprise.

"Oh, he can sing if he's a mind to," said Stevens, understanding. "He can play as well—if you can call it music, that is. There's a set of bagpipes in here." He jerked a thumb at the bundles on the packhorse and winked at Faith as he spoke.

"Ach, it's music a'right, ye ignorant wee Sassenach, but it's only fer important occasions. Bagpipes are no' for time-wasting frivolity."

Faith wondered what sort of important occasion he'd brought his bagpipes for. Perhaps he planned to pipe a lament for fallen comrades when they visited those battlefields. Where was it that Algy had died?

Just then Nicholas began an army marching song and instantly Stevens joined in a cracked, lusty voice, and after a moment, Faith chimed in with her flute. From time to time she even caught a deep rumble that could have been Mac, but she wasn't sure. They continued on for some time until the horses were sufficiently spelled and it was time to put the instruments away and pick up the pace again.

She was still feeling moved, not just by the pleasure of the music, but by Nicholas's response to her story of the smashed flute. He'd understood instinctively that Hope had taken her punishment, and he knew how the guilt of that flayed Faith. No one outside her family had so easily understood or accepted the twinly bond she and Hope shared.

"Over there is Dieppe." Nicholas's voice broke into Faith's thoughts. She was happy, she thought. Really happy. A simple sort of happiness that she'd thought she'd never feel again. She was agreeably tired and her skin tingled—no doubt she'd caught a little too much sun—her complexion was probably ruined forever, but she didn't care. It could also be the salt dried on her skin that made it tingle. Whatever the case, she didn't care. She was happy.

She looked at the town in the distance but could see no particular reason why he'd pointed it out. They'd passed by several small villages and towns. Dieppe looked larger, and she could see turrets. "You mean I should look at the castle? It is a castle, isn't it? Do you know much about it?"

"No. And I didn't mean the castle. Dieppe is a port."

She waited for him to continue, but he said no more. "Is it?" she said encouragingly. "Is it a large port?"

He gave her an impatient look. "Its size is immaterial, madam. It is a port."

Faith sighed. So they were back to *madam* again, were they? She'd hoped they progressed beyond that, particularly after the night they'd spent together and then her lovely swimming lesson and those glorious moments in the sea together afterward. And then the final joy of playing her flute, making music with friends. She refused to let him ruin her happy mood with his officer voice and his *madams*!

"Yes, I understand it is a port. You made that quite clear."

He gave a satisfied nod, as if that cleared everything up. Faith was more at sea than ever. "Umm, why would I be interested in a port?"

He said, a little impatiently, as if she was being obtuse, "Boats sail from Dieppe to England quite often. It is a longer trip than from Calais or Boulogne, but—"

"I have no wish to sail to England." Now she knew what he was getting at, and she would have none of it. She would not be dumped on a boat and sent back!

He gave her an intense look. "It would be better for you if you did."

"I disagree," she declared loftily. "I am having a perfectly lovely time. I am not holding you up—" She broke off, recalling their idyll in the sea. But that delay was as much his fault as hers. Almost. "Well, only a little," she amended. How he could think of sending her packing after the happy day they had had!

That was it, she thought, suddenly arrested. It was as if he did not trust anything that made him happy. Anything that made him feel. Or was it her feelings he did not trust? Whatever it was, she would not be dispatched like an inconvenient parcel!

"That is the point."

She said incredulously, "You would force me onto a boat because of a delay at the beach while you—we—"

He cut her off hastily. "No, of course not because of that." He frowned. "Or at least, not in the way you think." He urged his horse closer to hers and said in a low voice, "I have been observing you for the last few hours."

She arched an eyebrow. "And?"

"You, madam, have had a—a—*look* on your face!" he accused her.

"A look? Dear me. What sort of look, pray?"

He rolled his eyes, apparently frustrated by her lack of understanding. He leaned across and growled, "A *dreamy* look, madam!"

"Dreamy? How shocking," she said placidly. "It has always been a besetting fault of mine. Never mind, I'll try to concentrate better in future."

He made a growling sound under his breath. "Madam, it is partly my fault, I know. I should never have, er, done what we did in the water—"

She deliberately misunderstood him. "I shall never regret learning to float and swim."

"You know what I mean. What we did *afterward*!"

"Oh, that."

"Yes that." He sounded nettled. "And ever since, you have been looking dreamy."

She shrugged.

"And you have been *humming*!"

"You said you didn't mind the humming," she flashed. "You said it sounded pretty!"

He rolled his eyes again. "It's not the humming I mind—it's what's behind it."

She frowned. "What do you think is behind it?"

He looked uncomfortable, then he said deliberately, as if uttering an unpalatable truth, "I think you may be spinning castles in the air, madam. Against which I particularly warned you."

So she was right; her feelings did unnerve him. Faith squinted at the castle on the horizon and said, "Heavens, is that what it is? It looks quite solid to me. Fancy it being an illusion. What causes it, do you know?"

"I am not talking about the castle at Dieppe," he snapped. "I am talking about your becoming *attached*! Thinking thoughts about the future! Planning things, when I have warned you repeatedly that there is no future for the two of us!"

Faith gave him a long look. "You're quite wrong, you know," she said after a moment. "The only thing I'm attached to at the moment is my lovely new flute." She waggled the flute, which was on a string around her neck. "And if you want to know what I was dreaming about, it was the idea of a hot bath. I wasn't planning anything apart from that."

He looked even more displeased at that, so she gave him a bright smile and further reassurance. "Attached? To *you*? How silly. You specifically ordered me not to get attached, didn't you?

"I did."

"And I said I agreed to your terms, didn't I?"

He nodded. "You did."

"Well then. That's all right then, isn't it? We don't need to go to Dieppe after all—that is unless you would like to look over the castle?" She peered at him inquisitively. "Do you?"

"No, I don't want to look at the blasted castle, madam!"

"Neither do I," she agreed, resisting the temptation to remind him she could spin her own castles, ones that floated, what's more.

"Then take a last look at the sea. We'll be turning inland for a while now, and when we reach the coast again it won't be the English Channel you'll see, but the Bay of Biscay."

"The Bay of Biscay—isn't that famous for its blood-thirsty pirates?"

"Not anymore," he said dampeningly. "They were all eradicated. Besides which, we won't be sailing across the bay; we shall be riding around it."

A thought occurred to her. "If there are no pirates any longer, and since you are in such a hurry to get there, why didn't you just sail direct to Portugal from England? Why waste so much time going to Calais and then riding all the way down?"

There was a muffled choking sound from Stevens, but when she looked at him to see what the matter was, he was staring ahead with his face completely wiped clean of all expression. She glanced at Mac, and he, too, looked completely wooden faced. It was an improvement on his usual scowl.

"The horses," Nicholas said after a moment. "The horses don't like sailing."

"Yes, miss," Stevens agreed loudly. "It was coz of the horses. Nothing to do with people at all. Nobody here would turn green when he so much as stepped on a boat, no indeed. It were entirely fer the benefit o' the horses."

She glanced at Nicholas's face, which was rather redder than it had been a moment earlier, and bit her lip.

"It is true I am not the best of sailors," he said with stiff dignity. "But the horses don't like sailing either."

"Good then, that's settled. None of us wants to get onto a boat!" She urged her horse into a trot and joined the others. She tried to keep the smile on her face, because after all, she'd won this little skirmish, hadn't she?

The trouble was she didn't feel victorious. The thought troubled her that if she had admitted that she was "getting attached," he would have put her on the first boat leaving Dieppe.

They'd shared such a joyous afternoon, with swimming and sunshine and laughter—and then they'd shared music. Faith couldn't have imagined a more heavenly day. And suddenly he was ready to turn her off and send her back to England. She couldn't understand it.

Why was he so determined not to let her love him? What was he afraid of? Didn't he want to be loved? Faith couldn't understand it. She'd yearned for love all her life.

Why would anybody fear love? She glanced across at her hard-faced husband and wondered.

He found them a bed to sleep in the next night, too, above a village tavern. A small room under the eaves, it had a crooked roof and a floor that sloped to one corner, but it was clean, and the bedding smelled fresh.

So much for sleeping rough on the cold, hard ground, Faith thought to herself with a smile. Beneath his tough talk of her needing to endure the privations of a soldier's existence, her husband was very protective of her comfort. Though . . . her smile widened . . . his motive might not be solely her comfort.

All her initial reservations about sleeping with a man she barely knew had flown out the window after that first night. When he came to bed, Nicholas Blacklock left the steely eyed officer behind him and became a smoky-eyed lover who made love to her with a concentration and intensity that melted her very bones.

Faith and her twin sister had been called beauties by the London ton. And though she enjoyed the parties and the balls and the admiration of elegantly dressed men and women, it had touched her far less than the way Nicholas looked at her the instant before he touched his mouth to her skin. At that moment she *felt* beautiful in a way she never had before.

Faith had never seen herself as a beauty. Any girl who had grown up with Grandpapa knew that physical beauty was a two-edged sword and vanity a sin that courted a thrashing. There were no looking glasses at Dereham Court, and no visitors to admire. There were only sisters.

In any case, when Faith looked in the mirror, it was like looking at her twin's face. To outsiders, she and Hope might look pretty and glamorous and confident, but they both knew that deep inside, they felt none of these things.

But when Nicholas Blacklock looked at her with that dark, smoky gaze, she felt a deep feminine unfurling in some core of her that had never been touched before, a sense that he was not just seeing one of the Merridew Diamonds—not that he knew of that silly title—but that he was seeing Faith, a Faith she hardly knew existed.

When he took her in his arms and loved her, she didn't feel like the girl who had spent half her life frightened of her grandfather's rages, nor like the foolish dreamer who had fallen for a shallow impostor and made a mess of her life. She didn't feel like the girl who now distracted him from his journey and argued with him. When he planted a line of warm, drugging kisses from the shell of her ear along each curve and hollow of her body to the inside arch of her feet and back, as if he were trying to absorb and learn her essence, she felt more than special, more than beautiful. Her body and heart overflowed with love, and she wondered if he could feel it spilling over him, too, if that was what he was absorbing.

And floating on air in the aftermath, she felt . . . almost . . . loved.

But he never said the words.

And in the morning, it was as if he denied the truth of the actions of the night. For it was always the same.

"Do not get attached, madam."

"Do not spin dreams out of moonbeams, madam."

"There is no future for us, madam."

"Tell me about your Algy, Stevens. What was he like?" They were riding down a track that threaded narrowly through a maze of green and gold patchwork fields. Harvest time was over for some crops, and the ground was newly ploughed and dark. The fresh-turned earth smelled glorious.

"Algy?" He gave her a surprised look, then smiled reminiscently. "He was a good son—not a good boy, mind—chock-full o' mischief, he was! Him and Master Nick, both. Inseparable they was—not that the master was too happy about that."

"No?"

"No. Sir Henry didn't like his son hobnobbing with the son of a groom. Oh, it was all right when they was little lads, but later on, when there should have been a gulf between them . . ."

"A gulf?" Faith prompted.

"Master Nick, he was sent off to school when he was seven, and if his older brother—young Henry, named after his pa—was any guide to go on, Master Nick should have come home changed. But he didn't. Came home from school looking neat as a pin, like a stiff little gentleman, but he'd head straight down to the stables, and the two boys would be off to the woods like a shot." He chuckled. "And come back hours later looking like a pair of gypsies."

"What did they do in the woods?"

"Everything. Played at Robin Hood and Guy of Warwick and Richard Coeur de Lion and such games when they was little, but as they got older, it was the wild things that drew them—well, it was Master Nick mostly, but my Algy liked them, too. Those two—they knew that land better than the gamekeepers—where the peregrines nested, where the badgers slept, where the vixen hid her cubs . . ." He grimaced. "That was the beginning o' the trouble. Old Sir Henry—as I said, he was mad on foxhunting."

Faith nodded. "My grandfather was a great one for the chase, too. It was a great disappointment to him that none of us were boys."

"Old Sir Henry—he was down on Nick for lots of things. The music, for one."

"He forbade music? My grandfather did that, too."

Stevens gave her a sardonic look. "Not forbade it as such. Just didn't want no son of his playing it. Music was women's business, he said. And books. A great one for stories was young Master Nick, but his pa reckoned it weren't manly for a boy to like music and books. And oh, Master Nick, he did love his stories. He used to read 'em to Algy and me—well, that's where they got their games about Richard Lionheart and such from."

Faith smiled. She could just imagine Nick as a young boy, acting out tales of derring-do in the forest with his friends.

"In Sir Henry's eyes, the boy's sole saving grace was that Nick was horse mad from the time he could walk—him and Algy, both—and Sir Henry expected Nick to be like himself and his brother; mad for the hunt."

Stevens shook his head. "Hunted just once, when he was a little lad. I'll never forget it, his little face smeared with the fox's blood, his father so proud and Nick sick to his little stomach and white with fury. After that, he refused to join in the hunt, no matter how much Sir Henry roared and beat him and punished him.

"Didn't go down well with his pa, I can tell you. Hunting-mad, old Sir Henry was, even though it killed him in the end. Broke his back on a hunt, he did. Came off at a hedge." Stevens grimaced. "A bad end he came to, as well—confined to a bed and wasted slowly away."

"That's terrible. How old was Nicholas when that happened?"

"Oh, he was well off at the war by then. But it was interfering with a hunt that got him sent into the army in the first place. The hunt was after a vixen he and Algy knew had cubs, and so they ruined the trail with rotten fish and suchlike, got the hounds all confused. When his pa found out, he was like to kill the boy." He gave a snort of disapproval. "Gave him the beating of his life and sent him off to the army to make a man of him. They were sixteen, the boys."

"He—they must have found it difficult in the army, then."

There was a short silence. "Aye, they did—Nick more than Algy. Some aspects of soldiering he took to, but the killing . . . A good fighter is Capt'n Nick—none better, but Algy reckoned it was like something took him over. They say he has berserker blood in him, a cold fighting rage. But when it's over . . . ah, then Master Nick hates himself."

He glanced at Faith. "Been a lot of death in Mr. Nick's life. Pretty much all his mates in the army got killed at some battle or other. And then there was his pa, dying the way he did. And his brother."

"His brother?"

"Died of a septic cut just before his pa broke his back. I have to say, it nearly killed Lady Blacklock— that's Mr. Nick's ma—what with seeing young Mr. Henry, the heir go, then having her husband die slow and painful-like—took him months to die, it did—and with Capt'n Nick away with the army, risking his life daily. Poor lady. It turned her hair white, it did, the worry of it all."

Poor, poor woman. What a dreadful burden to bear, thought Faith. "I suppose Nicholas went home to help his mother."

Stevens's old battered face crinkled into an enigmatic expression. "No."

Faith was shocked. It didn't seem like the Nicholas she knew, not to help, and she said so.

"Ah, but they never told him, miss. His pa forbade any mention of it to Mr. Nick. Not of his own broken back, nor of young Mr. Henry's death."

"But that—that's terrible. To shut him out like that . . . when he was so needed . . ."

Stevens nodded. "Fair ate at him, it did, after he found out. Went home after they'd died, o' course, though it was all too late. Too late even for the funerals. He was like a lost soul, then. Blaming himself for what was no fault of his. It didn't help that my Algy had been killed by then. Mr. Nick blames himself for that. Feels as if he should never have let Algy follow him into the army." Stevens snorted. "As if anyone coulda kept my boy from doing what he wanted, but Mr. Nick, he takes things like that hard. Thinks it's his job to look after everyone."

Faith nodded, her eyes prickling with tears. He did look after people, her Nicholas.

"That's why I joined up and went soldiering after my Algy died. Someone had to keep Mr. Nick from brooding." His face crinkled in a crooked smile as he added, "I think you've taken that duty over now, miss. And may I say, you're doing a better job than I ever did. He's a lot happier when he's with you than I've seen him in a long time."

Faith pondered his words. Coming from a man who'd known Nicholas all his life, she had to accept that he knew what he was talking about, and the thought that he was happier since he'd married her was one she would love to accept.

But it didn't seem to her that Nicholas *was* particularly happy. He had his moments, but for the most part, Faith sensed a darkness, a deep sadness in him that she hadn't been able to touch. Now she knew a little about where that darkness came from. What a terrible, terrible story. She understood more of why he was so wary of attachment. Loving people was wonderful, but it could also be painful—more than painful if you lost them. And Nicholas had lost so many people . . .

"Do you really think he is happy, Stevens?" She looked at him searchingly as she asked it, and after a moment, he looked away.

"Happier, miss. A lot happier. We can't always have perfection."

Chapter Ten

∞

There is no such thing as pure pleasure;
some anxiety always goes with it.
OVID

NICHOLAS HAD BEEN SILENT AND GRIM FOR SOME TIME NOW. His face was set, and he was frowning as he rode. He was either cross or deep in some unwelcome memory, Faith thought, but then she noticed the tic in his jaw.

"Are you getting one of your headaches?" she asked him softly.

He jumped, as if he had been miles away. "What makes you think that?"

She eyed the tic in his jaw. "Oh, no special reason, just a feeling . . . and you do look a little pale." *And getting paler by the minute.*

He shook his head and rode on. Faith said nothing but observed him narrowly. He was in pain, she was sure, the stubborn man, and when finally he started to squint, as if his eyesight was affected, and sway ever so slightly in the saddle, she said, "You should lie down. I will get Mr. McTavish to ride ahead and find us an inn."

"Nonsense!" He grimaced. "I'll just have a quick nap under those trees up ahead. I shall be right in a few hours."

Faith frowned. "I'm sure the bright sun makes it worse. My sister always found sleeping in a darkened room was beneficial."

"It won't make any difference to me."

"You can't know until you try it," she said firmly. "Your headaches seem very severe and painful, but at least they pass relatively quickly. Poor little Grace would sometimes be ill for several days."

"Mine will be over soon."

"All the more reason to find a place where you can sleep. Mr. McTavish?" She rode ahead and quickly informed McTavish of the problem. "See that farmhouse?" She pointed. "Ride ahead and see if they can accommodate us. We will pay. I am not sure how long it will be before Nicholas's headache passes. They seem to be lasting longer."

McTavish opened his mouth—to argue, Faith was sure, so she snapped, "Go at once and do not argue! I have no time for your nonsense. Nicholas is ill!"

He gave her a look from under his brows. "Aye, I ken that well, lass."

"Well then, hurry!" she ordered, and he rode off toward the farmhouse.

It only took ten minutes for Faith, Nicholas, and Stevens to follow him to the small, neat farmhouse, but by the time they got there, Nicholas's face was ashen gray. He held himself on his horse by willpower alone, Faith was sure.

McTavish and a burly Frenchman stood in the yard arguing. A plump woman in an apron watched, an anxious expression on her face.

"He'll no' let us in the house," Mac declared as he came to help Nicholas dismount. "But he says we can use the barn fer a price."

"In the barn?" Faith exclaimed. "But Nicholas needs dark and quiet." She hurried over to the man and woman and introduced herself. She explained the problem and asked for their help, ending with an offer to pay.

The man began to shake his head, and in desperation Faith turned to the woman. She took her hand and pleaded in her best French, "Oh, please, madame, my husband is in a great deal of pain. If we could just put him in a bed, in a dark room . . . I'm sure it would help him. We will make no trouble, I promise—"

The woman looked across at Nicholas and said uncertainly, "He looks sick. I want no trouble."

She meant she would not deal with disease or drunkenness or vomit, Faith realized. "Oh no, madame, no mess, it is just his head, a migraine, *un mal de tête très grave*—he just needs to sleep in a dark, quiet room. And perhaps a pot of willow bark tea—I have some willow b—"

The woman cut her off. "I understand *la migraine*."

"Well then . . ." Faith wrung her hands uncertainly.

The woman's face softened. "You are very young, *p'tite*. How long have you been married?"

Faith stared at her. Of what possible relevance was that? But she responded, "Two weeks, madame. We were married two weeks ago."

The woman gave a decisive nod and said something rapid and incomprehensible to her husband. She nodded. "Your man can sleep upstairs. Tell your friends they can help him up—anyone can see he cannot manage the stairs like that—but first, off with their boots. No man tramps mud into my kitchen!"

"Oh *merci*, madame. Thank you so very much!"

"Not *madame, s'il vous plait*; call me Clothilde, *p'tite*."

The house was immaculate, scrubbed and shining, and the men made no demur about removing their boots. Ignoring his protests that he could manage by himself, Madame and Faith helped Nicholas upstairs to a small, simple bedchamber with the bed set into an alcove in the wall. Clothilde drew back the deep, soft quilt and helped Faith strip Nicholas of his breeches and coat. By this time he was in so much pain he could hardly see. He said not a word; all his reserves went into coping with his pain without it showing. He looked severe and distant, and he shut her out completely.

With obvious reluctance, he swallowed some willow bark tea and lay back, his eyes closed, unmoving. Faith sat on the edge of the bed, watching him anxiously. She reached out and stroked his tumbled hair back from his forehead. His skin was tight, his brow furrowed with pain.

She didn't want to leave him to suffer alone. She smoothed his forehead with featherlight touches. She fancied the tight muscles relaxed minutely, but she could not be sure. She wondered whether stroking his head might add to the pain. She took his hand in hers, but it was clenched with pain into a hard fist, so she held that instead and stroked the inside of his wrist.

Such a big, strong hand. Protective and powerful, clenched so tight and hard against his current weakness. He so obviously hated to be vulnerable, hated these headaches. They were the only chink in his armor.

She sat there, cradling his fist against her breast, willing his pain away, watching his face, his dear face. White lines of pain bracketed his mouth. His eyes were closed and shuttered. Shuttered against the pain. Shuttered against Faith.

She ached for him to love her.

When she was a young girl dreaming of love, it had seemed so simple. She was wrong.

She'd been dazzled by Felix, but she saw now that she hadn't loved him. She looked at Nicholas, at his tanned, narrow face grooved with pain and hard experience, his beautiful mouth tight with pain, and she ached with love for him.

Love he didn't want.

Why didn't he want her love?

He wanted her body, and that was wonderful, but it was as if a starving child had been given a taste of a feast and was then shut outside to watch through the window. Because for Faith, desire was just a part of the love she felt for him.

Was she desirable but not lovable? She was flawed—she knew that—Grandpapa had told her, told all of them, over and over that they were ugly inside, that they were flawed, misbegotten creatures.

Faith shivered. The old man's hatred could reach out to touch her, even here, even now. She wished her sisters were here; they could banish Grandpapa's poison. It only struck when she was at her lowest.

So why was she so low now? It didn't make sense, she told herself in a silent, bracing voice. Her skin still tingled with salt from her afternoon swim. She'd swum in the sea. She'd even made love in the sea and felt closer to Nicholas than ever. It had been glorious, utterly glorious.

A perfect afternoon, and if she felt a little low, well, that was understandable, with Nicholas in so much pain and she unable to relieve him of it. She would not give in to Grandpapa's poison. She should not wish for the moon when what she had was perfectly satisfying . . .

Only . . . She looked at his strong, sleeping face. She yearned so much for him to love her, it was like a physical pain.

Behind her, Clothilde murmured, "He will sleep now."

Faith carefully replaced his fist, smoothed his brow one last time, and stood up.

"You love him very much, your man, don't you, *p'tite?*"

"Oh, yes." She did. She loved Nicholas Blacklock. Very much. And at that soft admission of her love to the first living soul she'd confided in, she felt her face crumple. The tears she'd been holding off spilled down her cheeks.

Clothilde bustled forward and took her in a comforting embrace. "There, there, *p'tite*. There is no need to cry about it. Oh, but I was the same after my marriage, all tears one moment and laughter the next."

The tears continued to flow, and as she ushered Faith out the door and shut it behind them, Clothilde asked, "You are not crying about *la migraine*, are you? It is something more serious, his illness, no?"

Faith shook her head and mopped her eyes with a handkerchief. "No. I'm sorry, madame. I don't know what came over me. No, it's just a migraine. My little sister used to get them, too, though not as often as Nicholas does. She grew out of it . . . or it might have been caused by living with Grandpapa. We aren't sure. They stopped after our oldest sister Prudence was married." And Grace no longer feared being taken back to Grandpapa's . . .

She frowned as a thought came to her. If excessive worry had caused Grace's headaches . . .

"You have many sisters?"

"There are five of us."

Clothilde threw up her hands in horror. "No boys?"

"None. But I am a twin," she offered wryly. It was always the same. People seemed to think it remiss to have so many girls in a family and no boys, as if it were something people chose.

"A twin?" Clothilde was interested. "My daughter has twin girls."

"Really? How old are they?"

"Just six months old. Beautiful they are, but oh, what a handful!"

"I would love to see them," exclaimed Faith. "My sister and I are what they call mirror twins; I am right-handed, she is left-handed; I have a mole here, and she has it in the exact same place on the opposite side. And we share everything. It is wonderful to be a twin."

Clothilde beamed at her, her ruddy face lighting with pleasure. "Maybe you will see my granddaughters, then. Now, I must get on, *p'tite*. Work on a farm never stops."

After she'd left, Faith wondered about Nicholas. Could his headaches be caused by anxiety and fear, also, as Grace's were? And if so, what was he worried about?

This *thing*, whatever it was, that he had to do or face after Bilbao. She couldn't imagine what it was. The war was long over, and Napoleon was incarcerated on Saint Helena. In any case, she couldn't really believe he'd fret over some military mission. He didn't seem afraid of anything or anyone.

But there were times when something seemed to weigh dreadfully on his mind.

What was so important about this trip into Spain and Portugal? Mac seemed to know all about it, but she was the last person he would confide in. Perhaps Stevens . . .

But when she stepped outside, Stevens was nowhere to be seen. There was only Mr. McTavish standing on his own, staring out over the rolling hills of farmland. That reminded Faith. She marched up to him.

"Mr. McTavish, I have a bone to pick with you." She was utterly determined to have it out with the contentious Scot once and for all.

McTavish turned slowly. "Oh ye have, have ye?" His bushy red brows were raised in a sardonic manner, his attitude intimidating.

Faith stiffened her spine. "Why are you so hostile toward me?

He gave a snort. "Ye dinna ken what hostile is."

"I do, too. I was reared in an atmosphere of hostility, and it was completely horrid. So I take leave to inform you, Mr. McTavish, I will not have any more of it. Do you hear me?"

"Ye'll not have any more of it, eh?"

Faith refused to be intimidated. "No. Which brings us to that bone: you will explain to me, if you please, what injury I have done you, so that I may apologize and we can be done with this unpleasantness."

Her question took him so much by surprise his red brows almost disappeared into his hair. "What injury ye've done me?"

"Yes. Obviously I have done something—wittingly or unwittingly—to earn your enmity. The others seem to believe it is not me, that you are motivated to be horrid to me because of some Spanish girl who treated you abominably, but I believe that's nonsense. A man such as yourself could not possibly be so petty and mean spirited. Nor so completely unjust. The Scots are known for their passion for justice, are they not?"

He was too dumbfounded to respond, so Faith swept on. "So it must be something I did when first we met. So, what was it?"

His brow knotted. He looked at her, perplexed.

"Do not be shy, Mr. McTavish. Anyone who lived with my grandfather is accustomed to being called the most vile epithets. You need not hesitate to spare my feelings."

He glowered at her.

Faith gave him a smile. "I can see you are bent on being gentlemanly, but truly, I wish to know." She peered at him hopefully a moment, then continued, well satisfied with her tactics. "I have been giving that incident at the beach some thought. About my being a hussy—"

"No! No, I didna—"

She ignored the strangled outburst. "I did not, at that point, understand. I assumed that since you were stark naked in public that you had no sense of modesty, and when you called *me* a hussy—well, I lost my temper, which I am very sorry for. But my husband has assured me that you are in fact terribly shy and modest—"

McTavish dashed sweat from his brow and muttered something Scottish and inaudible.

Faith suddenly realized he was a lot younger than she'd assumed. "I failed to take into account your very delicate sensibilities, which were shocked—quite understandably—at seeing a lady in her underwear. All I could think of was that I was so hot, and the water was cool. I realize now I must have ridden roughshod over your delicate sensibilities—"

"Och, will ye stop going on aboot ma delicate sensibilities—"

"And I apologize for offending your modesty. And for the crabs." She held out her hand to him.

He made a strangled noise in his throat, but after a moment's hesitation, he took her hand in a big paw and shook it.

Faith continued in a bright tone, "Now, you have been hostile toward me since the beginning, and whilst I can appreciate your protectiveness toward the best interests of my husband, you must surely see by now that I mean him no harm. On the contrary, my sole desire is to make him happy."

"Aye." He didn't sound as if he meant to agree.

She frowned. "And what is wrong with that, pray? It seems to me as though Nicholas has had a very hard life, one without a great deal of happiness in it. He deserves better."

"Mebbe, but that's no' the point."

"Not the point? The whole purpose of life is to be

happy and to bring happiness to others. That is what love is all abou—"

"Love?" He stared at her.

"Love? Did I say love? I'm sure I didn't. I said . . . er, er, life—yes, that's it. That's what life is all about."

"Ye said love."

"I deny it. I did not mean for any such word to slip out. And if you so much as—as hint to Mr. Blacklock that I said so, I will—I will strangle you, McTavish! Understand?" She poked him in the chest with her finger to emphasize her words. "I do not—most emphatically not—love Nicholas Blacklock, and I am not attached to him in the least! Is that clear?"

He gave her an enigmatic look. "Aye, it's clear." His expression was not very convincing.

"You will not say a word?"

His response was a Scottish look and a heavy silence. "McTavish?"

"Verra well. I'll no' tell the cap'n ye love him."

"Good."

He shook his head gloomily. "Ye're stirring up muddy waters, woman."

Faith wrinkled her brow. "In what way?"

But he just shook his head and refused to explain.

"If I am hurting him in any way, I wish to know it."

He gave a lugubrious sigh, then said, "I fear ye're making things a great deal harder for him, lass."

"What do you mean? You mean harder for him to do this job, whatever it is?"

"Aye."

"But I haven't held your journey up—well, not by much. And I do my share, don't I? And I don't complain."

"Aye, ye're no' a bad traveling companion."

The grudging praise lifted her spirits a little. "Then how am I making his life harder?"

"He's no' on a pleasure trip, lass. When he gets to the end, he's got to do something, face things; things that wouldna be easy for any man. You'll not be making it easy for him to do what he has to do."

His tone worried her. "What does he have to do?"

McTavish just shook his head and clammed up. She wouldn't get any secrets out of him.

"Very well. I understand that you cannot confide in me, but will you at least advise me how I can make it easier for him to do what he must?"

He gave her a long, grim look. "Leave now."

"That is not an option," she said firmly. "As it is, I only have a short time with him until Bilbao, and I will not give that up."

He shrugged.

It must be very terrible, whatever it was that Nicholas had to do; she could tell by the look on McTavish's face. "That is what weighs on his mind so heavily at times, isn't it?" she asked quietly. "The thing that makes him quiet and withdrawn." The only thing that seemed to draw him out of that mood was music. And sometimes, Faith. Sometimes, she was sure, she did help.

"Aye."

"Is it so terrible to contemplate?"

"Aye."

"But there must be something I can do to help."

"There isna."

Faith bit her lip. It wasn't in her nature to give up. "McTavish, you see this period until we get to Bilbao as a waiting period, something to be got through until the real work starts, is that not so?"

"The real work?"

"This job. Whatever it is you and Nicholas have come to do."

"Aye. Everything else is but a prelude."

"Yes, but don't you see, for me the prelude is everything. It is my chance to create something."

His eyes dropped to her stomach. "A babe?"

She shook her head. "No, though if one came it would be . . . most welcome." She sighed, "But it is Nicholas I'm talking about. I've promised him that when we reach Bilbao—and if he asks me to—I will leave him and return to England, and I will." She gave him a look. "I don't break my promises. But I'm thinking about after that, when he's done whatever it is he has to do. If I can build something between us now, something good and strong and enduring, then whatever Bilbao brings—for I know from everyone's refusal to speak of it that it must be something terrible—we will be able to go on afterward. Before Bilbao, we only have a short time, but after Bilbao . . . well, we will have the rest of our lives."

There was a long silence. "Till death do ye part?"

She nodded, relieved that he finally understood the depth of her commitment to Nicholas. "Yes."

He shrugged and said heavily. "So be it."

"You will help me?"

"If ye want to build something with Cap'n Nick afore Bilbao, then go ahead. I'll no' stand in yer way."

"And afterward, will you help me, too?"

He pursed his lips, then shook his head. "No, lass. After Bilbao, you're on your own."

Faith nodded, undaunted. "Just Nicholas and me, then."

She sighed. One never could talk properly with men—she needed her sisters. She needed her twin. She went back to Nicholas's bedside and got out her writing materials. She would unburden herself to Hope. Her twin would understand.

Mac found Stevens in the stables. "'Tis a bad business, Stevens. That wee lassie truly loves him, ye ken."

"I know."

"It will destroy her when she finds out."

"As she must, soon," Stevens said in a somber voice. "We were warned this would happen."

"Should we not prepare her?"

Stevens shook his head. "That's for Mr. Nick, and you know he doesn't want to upset her any more than he has to. Why upset her to no purpose? Give her till Bilbao."

"Aye, I suppose."

Nick awoke disoriented. He parted the curtains of the alcove and looked out. Nothing looked familiar. The room was tiny and very simply furnished. He tested the door, and it opened. He was not locked in then. That was a relief.

He padded to the window and looked out over neat patchwork fields. A farm. He was on a farm somewhere in France. He had no memory of this place, no memory of coming here. From the look of the sun, it was sometime in the late afternoon; the shadows were long and the light mellow. His head was still throbbing with a residual ache; he knew what had caused the problem. But where was he, and how had he arrived there? And how long had he been asleep? Or had he blacked out again?

It was worrying. His headaches had produced small gaps in his memory before, but this was the worst yet.

He found a ewer filled with clean water and a large basin. He splashed his face in the water and dried it on a clean rag folded next to it. His head felt marginally clearer, though he still had no recollection of coming here. His boots lay on the floor, and his jacket and breeches hung from pegs on the back of the door. He dressed and went downstairs in search of answers.

His nose caught the scent of meat stew, and he followed it to a large, open kitchen.

Faith sat in a chair beside the fire, a golden-haired baby in her arms. She was singing softly to the babe, a song he didn't recognize, and rocking gently back and forth.

Nick stopped dead, thunderstruck. His sense of disorientation increased. The scene made no sense to him. Faith looked serene and happy and too damn beautiful to be real. But she was real. She was his wife. Only . . . where had the baby come from?

She looked up and smiled at him. As always, when their eyes met, he felt a thud in the region of his chest.

"Oh Nicholas, how is your head? You slept for a very long time."

"Tolerable, madam, thank you," he said brusquely. She knew he didn't like to talk about it. He stared at the baby. "Er?"

Faith jiggled it in her arms. "Isn't she lovely?"

"Very nice," he said cautiously, racking his brains. "Er, where are Stevens and Mac?"

"I'm not sure; outside, perhaps." She didn't even look at him, just smiled at the baby and resumed her song.

Nick beat a hasty retreat.

Outside, things slowly came back to him. He remembered the journey he was on, he even vaguely recalled the layout of the farm buildings. But there was no sign of either Stevens or Mac. He returned to the kitchen and stopped dead.

There were two babies now, two golden-haired babies, one in each of Faith's arms. She looked blissful.

He must have made some strangled sound, for she looked up. "Come and see, Nicholas," she said softly. "Hope and I must have looked like this when we were babies."

Feeling as if he'd stepped into some bizarre dream, Nick moved closer and peered at the babies. Yes. There were definitely two of them. Identical. Both golden-haired and blue-eyed, like his wife. He swallowed.

"I've never seen any other twins before," she told him. "Apart from my sister and me, that is. Hope and I have such a strong bond." She gave the babies a soft look. "I wonder if these little ones are the same. Oh, I wish Hope could see them, too."

Nick made a noncommittal sound.

"The one with her face buried in my neck is Clothilde, named after our Clothilde, of course, and the one blowing you bubbles is Marianne, after her other grandmother."

Our Clothilde? As far as Nick could remember, he'd never owned a Clothilde. Nor was his mother called Marianne. She was Matilda Jane Augusta Blacklock, née Alcott. Thank God he remembered that, at least.

"It was nice of Clothilde to get her daughter to bring the twins over for me to see them, wasn't it?"

Relief trickled through him. "I've never seen them before, have I?"

She gave him a puzzled look. "How would you? They arrived when you were asleep."

"Yes, that's right," he said, satisfied. One of the babies waved a chubby fist and, without thought, Nick reached out a hand to it. The child latched onto his finger with a determined grip and gave him such a look of triumph that he laughed aloud. "Strong little thing, isn't she?"

Faith laughed. "Yes, and determined. I've never had much to do with babies before. It's amazing how much personality they have, even at this age. I can see that Marianne—she's the one who has your finger—is going to be the adventurous one, and Clothilde will be the shy one."

He said curiously, "Is there always an adventurous one and a shy one?"

Faith shook her head. "I'm not really sure about always. But with Hope and me, there was, certainly."

"So Hope is the shy one."

She gave him a surprised look. "No, Hope is the brave one."

He raised his brows and said, "She must be a force to be reckoned with, then."

"No, not if you mean she's bold and pushy. She's not," She came to her twin's defense hotly. "She's lovely. She's brave and clever, and—" She blinked rapidly, and he realized her eyes had filled with tears.

Her hands were full of babies, so Nick pulled out his handkerchief and dried her cheeks for her.

When she could speak, she said, "I'm sorry. I didn't mean to turn into a watering pot. It's just that having these little ones here has made me think of Hope and how much I miss her. She's very special, my twin sister. All my life she has tried to protect me."

"In that case she must be a wonderful girl," he said softly. "Nearly as wonderful as her sister."

She gave him a misty smile and busied herself with the babies. After a minute she said, "Why would you think I was the adventurous one?"

She was so in earnest, so genuinely puzzled that he could not help but smile. "I have no idea. It must have something to do with you living in sand hills and learning to fish and swim and riding after us and preferring to travel long hours on horseback and sleep on the cold, hard ground in a foreign country than to dwell in comfort in England."

She considered his words, then dismissed them with a shake of her head. "Most of that I had no choice about. And the swimming and fishing and traveling have been fun—as long as someone else kills and cleans the fish. And as for sleeping on the hard ground, we haven't slept out of doors since that first night. You are too chivalrous to allow it."

Chivalrous? He felt his face warming and moved away so she wouldn't notice. There was one reason and one reason only why she hadn't slept a single night on the ground, and it had nothing to do with chivalry. It was so he could make love to her every night. And again in the morning. To his chagrin, he couldn't seem to get enough of her.

He cleared his throat. "I'll see if Stevens and Mac have returned."

He stepped outside, grateful for the silence in which to think. The gaps in his memory were disturbing. Thank God he'd recalled in time.

But it meant he couldn't trust his memory.

He'd probably dreamed that he'd heard his wife say she loved him. He didn't want anyone to love him. The thought was unbearable. He had enough of a burden to bear.

Was dreaming she loved him a form of madness? he wondered.

One of the horses had lost a shoe, and Stevens had taken it into the nearby village to have a new shoe fitted by the local blacksmith, so they ended up staying the night in the farmhouse. Mac and Stevens bedded down in the barn, while Faith and Nick used the room he'd slept in earlier.

"Aren't these sheets nice?" Faith said as she climbed into bed.

Nick looked at them. They looked like ordinary sheets to him, and he said so.

"Yes, but they've been soaped and scrubbed and dried in the sun; you can smell it." She sniffed. "Heavenly! In England, sheets often have to be dried in the kitchen or in front of the fire. And some have a faint damp smell. They don't get the sun baked into them like this. I'm sure it helps you to sleep better."

"I'll take your word for it." He slipped between the sheets and automatically reached for her. She turned to him with a soft blush and a welcoming smile, and that thud in his chest happened again. There was something about the way she looked at him . . . almost tenderly.

It gave Nick pause. They were only a week or so away from Bilbao. He frowned. It would have been better for her if they'd slept in the barn. Or if he'd slept in the barn, leaving her with her precious sun-dried sheets.

"You're not getting attached, are you?"

For a moment she said nothing, just gave him a searching look. "No, I'm not getting attached." She said it quietly, calmly, but something in her voice disturbed him.

"Are you sure?"

"I'm sure." And she sounded sure, this time. It should have reassured him. It didn't.

"Good."

Her face was fresh-washed and glowing in the candlelight. She was wearing that nightgown again, the one that the old woman had given her with lace in all the right places. She smelled faintly of roses, and how she managed that—smelling so sweet and fresh no matter where they were—he didn't know or care. All Nick knew was that he wanted her, wanted to take that nightgown off her and explore the woman underneath, to feel her warm silkiness wrapped around him and taste her sweetness and her warmth. He wanted to bury himself in her, not thinking about Bilbao and what it would bring, not thinking about anything except Faith and the glorious oblivion of making love with her.

He shoved the doubts and uncertainties from his mind and moved closer to her and then suddenly the image of her in the kitchen came to him. Of Faith with a babe, two babes, in her arms.

He hesitated. "What if you fall pregnant?"

She blinked. "I would be delighted. I would love to have a baby. But I'm not thinking about that!"

He was a bit surprised by her unconcerned tone. "Not thinking about it? Not at all?"

"No, of course not." She gave him a smile. "Why would I?"

There was no "of course" about it as far as Nick was concerned. And as for why, well, he would have thought that would be obvious.

She explained. "We're living in the moment, remember? Not making any plans or considering the future in any way. Wasn't that what you wanted?" Her wide-eyed query made him uncomfortable.

Yes, it was what he wanted, but it disturbed him to think she was taking him so very literally. She needed to be prepared for if . . . or when . . .

Oh God, he ought to be more responsible. He'd meant simply to help her: to marry her, restore her good name, and send her on her way. Instead she'd become embroiled in his problems. Oh, he could argue that she'd done that herself by disobeying his orders, but it was his responsibility. If he hadn't been so weak, so unable in the face of that sweet smile to drive her off with harsh words . . .

He couldn't help himself. He'd been so strong up to now, but this girl . . . she undermined his every resolution. A small taste of heaven before . . .

She raised herself, leaning on one elbow, and looked at him. "I thought now was what you wanted, Nicholas." She hadn't done up most of the tiny buttons on the nightgown. One pearly shoulder slipped from the neckline, satiny smooth in the candlelight. The open neck of her nightgown dipped temptingly into shadow, and Nick's eyes followed.

"Oh God yes, now is all I want," he muttered and, drawing her to him, he began to explore the shadowed mysteries, feathering kisses onto her silken skin in a trail of exploration.

He woke before her in the morning and found himself watching her sleep. So beautiful, her hair in tumbled clusters of gold, her long lashes caressing her cheeks. Asleep, she looked so young, such an innocent, it was hard to believe she was the same person who welcomed his lovemaking with such natural sensuality and joy.

He'd never experienced anything like it. She made him feel powerful, ten feet tall, and yet at the same time humble . . . and needy.

Yes, needy. He wanted her again. It was unforgivable of him to keep her like this. He prayed she meant it when she said she was not the least attached.

Nick slipped out of bed and began to dress.

A sleepy voice greeted him. "Good morning, Nicholas." She stretched and held her arms out to him in an expectant gesture. He bent and kissed her quickly. He was a damned fool ever to have invented that "morning duty" notion. It was one she took very seriously. But it played merry hell with a man's resolution.

She lay back on the pillow and watched him as he continued dressing. Then she asked, quite as if they were continuing the conversation of the night before, "Why are you so worried that I will get attached to you? I mean, we are married, after all."

"Women get attached."

She gave him a quizzing look.

"You are a woman," he pointed out.

"Yes. Yes I am," she agreed in a thoughtful tone. "So, don't men get attached, then?"

He started to shake his head, but some shred of fundamental honesty asserted itself, and he found himself saying, "Some men do." He retrieved his position quickly. "But not soldiers."

"Not soldiers. I see."

"Yes, and I will warn you again that there is no possibility of me getting attached to you. Despite our marriage and despite any, er, *proximity*." He was not yet up to admitting he'd rutted on her like a stoat at every opportunity, so he gestured vaguely to the rumpled bedclothes and her naked shoulder rising from them.

"Because you are a soldier."

"Correct, madam." It was the only reason he could think of. And there were elements of truth in it.

"I see," she said again. She seemed to think it over a few moments, then she said, "I still don't quite understand why it would be a problem if *I* got attached. I mean I'm not, of course. No, not at all. Not the least little bit, in fact," she assured him with a bright smile. "I'm just interested in the *theory* of attachment."

Her assurances should have relieved him. For some reason, they didn't.

"You see, all of this is new to me." She shrugged, and the bedclothes slipped a little lower. "As you pointed out, I am a woman and not a soldier, so . . ."

As she was all but naked, and his body was thick with desire, he was of no mind to contradict her.

"So there is a possibility—a very slender one, mind—that I might get attached. Would that be so very bad?"

"Yes," he said firmly. "Very bad indeed. It would distract me from my purpose, and I would have to send you back to England early."

She lay back against the pillows. "Well then, what a good thing that I'm not attached, because I'm enjoying this journey very much and have no wish to distract you from your purpose." She stretched again sleepily, and the bedclothes pooled around her waist. Venus, rising from the bedclothes.

Nick groaned and had a quick tussle with his conscience. It lost. He put down the coat he'd just picked up and began to unbutton his shirt buttons.

Delay was not the same as distraction, he told himself. And besides, it was just a few more days to Bilbao. He would do what he must do then. Besides, she had said she wanted a child. He could at least try to give her that.

Chapter Eleven

*Seldom, very seldom, does complete truth belong to any
human disclosure; seldom can it happen that something is not
a little disguised, or a little mistaken.*
JANE AUSTEN

DARKNESS WAS FALLING. A CLUSTER OF BUILDINGS WAS JUST
visible in the distance. A village. Faith hoped they
would stay the night there. They'd ridden longer and
farther today than any other day since their journey had
begun.

Nicholas was trying to make up for the time he'd
lost, Faith surmised. Not that he discussed such things
as headaches. He'd almost bitten her head off earlier
when she'd asked him if perhaps they might be made
worse by anxiety.

"That topic is dreary, madam," he'd snapped. "I do
not wish to hear you ever again refer to . . . to my temporary indisposition. I find the whole matter a bore."

And that was that.

Faith's back was aching, and she felt unutterably
weary. She felt herself sagging in the saddle and jerked
herself upright again. She was determined to prove to
him that she had what it took to be a soldier's wife. She
would endure any hardship and discomfort if it meant

she could sleep in his arms every night. And wake to find him watching her with tender possessiveness—even if he did hastily disguise it.

This life might not be a life of ease and comfort, but she had never been happier. He could talk all he wanted about being attached or not attached, but Faith felt loved. More, she felt cherished. Even his attempts to prevent her from "getting attached" were based, she believed, on some strange kind of protectiveness, though protection from what, she had no idea. He might try to disguise it as soldierly indifference, but it wasn't indifference Faith felt when he took her to heaven each night.

If he called that building castles in the air, then she wasn't going to waste time arguing. Happiness was happiness. She'd known all her life that happiness was temporary; she would wallow in it while she could.

As they turned the corner into the village, they became aware of a commotion farther up. There were flaming torches and the sounds of yelling. A woman was screaming.

They halted. "We should give it a miss, Cap'n," said Mac. "It doesna do to interfere in local matters."

As he spoke, there was a shrill feminine scream of pain.

"Nicholas?" Faith was horrified at the suggestion they should leave. "I was once in trouble like that."

"I know." Nicholas nodded. He gripped her hand in reassurance. "We'll see to it. You stay here," he ordered Faith. He, Mac, and Stevens galloped forward, then pulled their horses to a sudden stop.

"Women!" Mac said in surprise.

A crowd of women were gathered in the village square, screaming and hurling abuse at someone or something in the center. A few men stood around the edge of the crowd, but it seemed to be a largely female riot.

"'Tis a lass they've got there," Mac said. He watched for a second, then said uneasily, "They look angry enough to kill her, Cap'n."

The three men looked at each other.

Faith watched anxiously, telling herself they were used to this sort of thing, being soldiers. As the crowd shifted, she caught glimpses of the girl in the center of the throng. She was young, dark-haired, and stood alone against all the rest. They were hitting and kicking her, grabbing at hunks of her hair and screaming abuse at the top of their lungs. It was horrible.

Faith didn't know why these women were punishing this young girl; she didn't care. In any situation where a raging crowd was ranged against one person, she would side with the underdog.

Save her, Faith willed Nicholas silently. *Save her!* She waited for him to wade in and rescue her.

He and Stevens had dismounted and were trying to talk to the women, to find out what was going on, to calm things.

As she watched, a woman leaped at Nicholas and swung a punch. She missed. But it started something. Some of the women turned on the two strangers. Nicholas fended them off without too much trouble, holding them at arm's length, ducking blows and kicks, but from the looks of things, Stevens didn't escape unscathed. But neither of them struck back, she saw, torn between pride and frustration.

Mac, the inveterate woman hater, seemed not to notice. He sat on his horse, staring at the girl in the middle, a black frown on his face, his big fists bunching and flexing.

The girl was fighting back like a young Amazon, scratching and kicking like a wildcat. But she was no match for a dozen or so grown women. Faith watched with growing anxiety.

"Come on, Nicholas!" she yelled. They might be hampered by their reluctance to lay violent hands on women, but Faith had no such inhibitions.

Drawing her pistol, she rode forward. "Stop this at once," she screamed at the top of her lungs, but there was so much noise, no one could hear. So she fired over the top of their heads. There was a sudden silence, and everyone turned to face her. She quailed before the hostility on their faces.

"Grab her, Mac," yelled Nicholas. "Get her out of here."

He meant grab Faith, but Mac misunderstood. Roaring like an enraged beast, he forced his horse forward into the crowd. Women scattered before him, and he bent, snatched up the beleaguered girl, tossed her across his saddle, and rode out of the village before anyone quite realized what happened.

Stevens mounted his own horse and returned the way he came, to collect the packhorse.

"Now, let's get out of here!" Somehow Nick was back on his horse and at Faith's side. "This way." He pointed. "Now go!" He slapped her horse, and Faith found herself galloping out of the village and then veering in a wide circle across the fields.

"Where are we—"

"Just follow me!" he growled.

"But—"

"Shut up and ride!"

By that time she'd caught a glimpse of his face. She'd never seen him so furious. She shut up and rode.

They galloped in silence, riding as if the Devil himself were after them. But in fact nobody was in pursuit. The speed and fury of the pace he'd set was a direct reflection of his mood. The horses' hooves echoed in the night, thudding over the ground, eating up the miles.

As the first rush of excitement drained away, dread slowly pooled in the pit of Faith's stomach. She'd seen his cold anger; that was something to be feared. Now rage simmered under his skin, and it was far from cold.

As a child, she'd learned to hide from Grandpapa's rage by hiding in the cupboard under the stairs. Now she was out in the open, riding *ventre à terre* into the dark unknown. She was alone with him, and there was no place to hide.

Eventually, the tired horses could keep up the speed no more. They came to a small clearing, wooded on one side and with a stream running through it, and he turned off the road. He flung himself off his horse, and set it free, still saddled, with a slap on its flank. He took Faith's reins from her, dragged her from the saddle, and set her horse free, too. Both animals headed directly for the stream. Faith would have liked a drink, too, but she had no time for anything except to brace herself as a furious tirade erupted from him.

"What the *devil* possessed you to ride into that pack of harpies, when I *specifically* ordered you to stay put?" He gripped her upper arms fiercely. "Don't you know that *anything* could have happened? Those women were in a mood to *kill*!" He shook her for emphasis.

"I know. I wanted to save that girl," she managed in a shaky voice.

"You little fool! What the devil do you think Mac and Stevens and I were going to do?" He glared at her. "We are soldiers! We know what to do!"

She braced herself and retorted, "You weren't doing much that I could see."

"You shouldn't have even been there to see!" he roared.

A small thrill ran through her as he roared. She blinked at him. His face was dark with rage, and he looked as fearsome a man as any she had seen. Yet—the thought dropped into her mind like a huge stone into a pool—she wasn't terrified.

He'd been nearly this angry about the hare. And he hadn't touched her.

The knowledge trickled through her numb body like slow bubbles of champagne. She wasn't afraid. She was arguing with him. He was in a red-hot fury and roaring at her like a bull, and she was shaking, but not with fear. It was reaction, the shaking. And so, perhaps, was his rage.

She said, "Yes, but I was there. And I could see that your chivalry was hampering you in dealing with those women."

"Chivalry!" He rolled his eyes fiercely. "Will you stop ascribing chivalry to my every action. I am not a chivalrous person!"

She shrugged, suddenly feeling exhilarated. "I acted as I thought best."

"You didn't think *at all*! Nobody there was thinking! Those women were a mob! There is *no reasoning* with people in that state."

"I know. That's why I used my gun." She smiled at him. She wasn't afraid of him. She wasn't afraid.

He stared at her, as if unable to believe she could smile at him while he was roaring at her. Faith could hardly believe it herself.

"I was *mad* to have given you the blasted gun. You only have *one shot*, don't you know that? After you'd fired, anything could have happened, and you couldn't have defended yourself!" He shook her again. "When people act in a crowd like that, it's a *pack* mentality, d'you hear me? A pack mentality. Like wild dogs! They could have turned on you and *torn you apart*!" He stared at her wildly and repeated, *"They could have torn you apart!"*

And then he groaned and wrapped his arms hard around her. "Oh, God, don't you ever, *ever* frighten me like that again." And he held her so tightly she could barely breathe. She could feel his blood pounding through his body, his muscles straining to hold her to him. His breaths came in great gasps. She leaned into him, breathing in his warmth, his strength, his scent.

After a few moments it was not enough simply to be held—heaven as that was—and she struggled to free her arms so she could hug him back in the same way.

And then his mouth was on hers, and he was devouring her: embracing her, running his hands, his mouth over her body, part caress, part reassurance that she was in one piece.

Faith had never felt so treasured, so valued, so cherished in her life. And oh, how she loved him.

"I not go with you. I kill you first, cochon! Monstre!" The furious female voice pierced their consciousness.

Mac rode into the clearing with the rescued young woman clamped tight under one arm. She didn't behave like any grateful damsel in distress, however; she was fighting and hurling abuse in a mixture of broken English, French, and Spanish. "I *not* go with you. I *hate* you. I *kill* you! Let me *go!*"

"Get it through your thick wee skull, woman, that I rescued ye. I'm not going to hurt ye, ye silly wench!" As she thumped him again, he added, as if to himself, "I have to have rocks in ma head . . ."

She tried to rake his face with her talons. They tangled in his beard, and Mac laughed. His laughter spurred her to further fury.

"Let me goooo!" the girl screamed in rage.

"Fine then." Mac opened his arm, and the girl

dropped to the ground. She didn't land sprawling in the dirt, as Faith was sure she would have done, but landed on all fours, like a cat. She straightened with a lithe movement, shook herself like an animal, and smoothed her ragged clothes, glaring at Mac through the dark tangles of her hair and muttering under her breath.

She glanced at Faith and Nicholas, and at Stevens as he rode into the clearing with the packhorse. She tossed her head back and regarded them defiantly, bare legs braced and hands on hips.

She was a flamboyant-looking girl. Her long, gathered skirt left her ankles and part of her calves quite exposed, and her feet were bare, except for a decorative silver chain around one ankle. She was good-looking in a wild, gypsy manner, with liquid dark eyes, currently flashing with rage and defiance, and a thick mane of curly black hair. She was small and slender but voluptuously built, with generous curves above and below the tightly cinched waist. Her blouse had been ripped at the neck more than once and roughly mended.

Mac dismounted and said something they did not catch. She whirled and said something in Spanish—something abusive by the sound of it. Mac responded in the same language.

She recoiled. "How you know my language, English?"

Mac started unbuckling saddle straps. "I'm no' English. My name is McTavish. I was in Spain for some years, with the army, and picked up some of the lingo."

"I *hate* soldiers!" She tossed her hair at him in a clear challenge.

Mac shrugged and lifted the saddle off his horse.

"I hate the English, too!"

He shrugged again. "I'm no' English."

She watched in frustration. "I know about soldiers. If you try to touch me, I kill you!"

Mac made no sign he had heard. He set about methodically rubbing down his horse. The girl stepped forward and poked him, hard, in the back. "You hear me, English? If you touch me, I kill you!"

Mac turned. "For the last time, I'm no' English, ye daft wee besom!"

She frowned, and then glanced down at her front. "What mean wee—is small, yes?"

"Yes."

"But my besom not small!" Mac didn't reply, so she turned to the rest of the group, who were watching the exchange in fascination. She plucked at the low-cut blouse and said in an offended tone, "My besom not small, no?"

Faith was about to explain that besom was a word for witch, but Nick stopped her with a gesture and shook his head. He was trying not to laugh. "No, your besom not small."

She nodded in satisfaction, turned back to Mac, and punched him on the arm. "You think my besom small, yes?" she said belligerently. "Then why you look so much—eh?"

Mac's face was red. "Bite your tongue, girl! Shame on you to speak of bosoms to the cap'n like that!"

The girl bridled indignantly. "Shame on me? Who speak of my besoms in first place? Who say are too small? Is shame on you, you hairy great Englishman, for looking at them in first place! And for insult them. I am Estrellita, and I no accept insult from any man, English or not! I know English from war, and I no—"

"*I. Am. Not. An. Englishman!*" Mac roared.

Beside Faith, Nicholas choked. Stevens mopped eyes that were streaming and watched the girl in fascination.

Estrellita gave Mac a scornful look. "Well, what are you then? You not Spanish or Portuguese, of course, and not French, not with that great red bush on your face. Frenchmen stinking pigs like all soldier, but they have elegant."

"I am a Scot, woman!"

She frowned, puzzled. "Scot? What is Scot?" Then her face cleared, "Ah, I know, the ones who wear dress, no?" She gave him a dubious look. "You wear dress?"

"Not a dress, the kilt!"

She cocked her head, like a curious sparrow. "What is kilt?"

Mac groped for words. "It's a tartan, er, traditional pattern, and it's draped around a man. Fastened around the waist and sometimes wi' the plaid coming up here. And it finishes here." He gestured with his hands.

She pulled a face and shrugged, "Is dress. You wear dress but show hairy knees."

"How do you know my knees are hairy?"

She gave him a slow look, silently pointing out that if the visible parts of him were this hairy, his knees would be, too. "So, you wear dress, but not shave off that thing." She waved a disdainful hand in the direction of his beard. "Is very strange."

Goaded, Mac growled, "I don't wear the kilt anymore."

She pouted. "Is pity. I think maybe you look pretty in dress, Tavish. Now . . ." She glanced at Stevens and Nicholas, who were still struggling with mirth. She regarded Nick a moment with an odd look on her face, as if a thought had occurred to her, then she turned to Faith. "I am Estrellita. You shoot gun for me back there in village, yes? For this I thank you. The women of my family, we pay debt."

Faith hurried forward and put an arm around her. "Oh, I am so glad you have not lost your spirit," she said. "What a horrid thing to have happened to you. Those women looked terrible. My name is Faith—that is, I am Mrs. Blacklock, but you may call me Faith, as I'm sure we shall be friends."

Friends? Nick blinked as he wiped the laughter from his eyes. He knew his wife was friendly to a fault, but to offer her friendship to an unknown, grubby, gypsy-looking girl, one who'd been attacked by a wild mob of women who he presumed were otherwise normally respectable, was taking rashness a little far. He cleared his throat.

The girl threw a suspicious glance at him over her shoulder.

Faith continued, oblivious, "The tall man clearing his throat is my husband, and that is Stevens over there with the handkerchief, and of course you have met Mr. McTavish. And we will look after you. You are safe now, and nobody shall hurt you. My husband is a wonderfully gallant man and so is Stevens and"—she faltered, then said with a challenging glare at Mac—"and Mr. McTavish will protect you, too. As he already has."

The girl sniffed and sent a darkling glance at Mac.

Faith, apparently blind to any undercurrents, was focused wholly on the girl's needs. "I'll see to those scratches at once. Stevens, have you any of that salve left? And some brandy to settle our nerves. It's wonderfully fortifying after a bad fright," she confided to the girl. "And how soon can we get hot water? This young lady needs to wash, and we could all use a nice hot drink. Nicholas, is there a fire lit?"

He responded to her question with a sardonic look. She knew very well there was no fire. She'd been in his arms the entire time. He wished she was, still.

"Well, go on then!" She flapped her hands at him in a shooing motion. "We need hot water at once!" She turned back to the girl while Nick went off to build a fire. He wondered whether he'd be expected to produce a bath as well. The girl certainly needed it.

• • •

"So," Nick addressed the gypsy girl as the fire burned low after dinner. "Why did those women attack you?"

Estrellita stiffened as she was confronted with the question she'd expected from the beginning. Faith had refused to allow anyone to question the girl until all her hurts were tended to and she was washed, and they were all fed. But now she was clean, well-fed, and though she'd refused to borrow Faith's pink dress, saying it was too new and nice, she'd conceded her clothes needed washing and had consented to wear one of Mac's shirts, which hung down well past her knees, and his jacket over the top. She was sitting huddled into the jacket now.

She was not the sort of female who would ever look entirely respectable, especially not in those garments.

Faith had ordered the men out of sight while she tended the girl, but Nick had watched from a distance. He didn't trust his wife alone with the sort of girl who'd stir up an entire village full of women. But as far as he could tell from his vantage point, she'd been quiet and docile, and she and his wife seemed to get on well.

But now, as he asked her why she'd been attacked, she stiffened, and all signs of docility vanished.

She gave a defiant, unconvincing shrug. "How should I know? You were there, too!"

Mac leaned forward. "Dinna speak to the cap'n like that. Now, answer, girl. We'll no' hurt ye, but ye must have done something to get that mob o' women all riled up like that."

Faith was surprised by Mac's tone of voice. He'd all but snapped Faith's head off when she'd arrived in camp, and yet with this girl, he was almost . . . gentle. She was about to comment, but Nick, who was sitting with his arm around her, squeezed her and shook his head in a silent message.

Estrellita bridled at Mac's tone, tossed her mane of

black curls back over her shoulder, and snarled, "What I do? I bewitch their men, poison their water, curdle their milk—and the milk of their cows—turn their wine to vinegar and cure—interfere with their babies, that is all!"

Mac raised an eyebrow and said in a mild tone, "Is that all? Ye didna put the evil eye on their unborn as well, did ye?"

She glared at him. "No, but I'll put the evil eye on you, you big red bear!"

To everyone's amazement, a fleeting grin appeared on Mac's face. "So, what was the matter wi' the bairns—the ones ye cured?"

She frowned, puzzled and suspicious. "Bairns?"

"Wee ones. Weanlings. Babes."

She shrugged. "A fever."

"And what did you do?"

She said savagely, "I fed them with live toads and then I roasted them and ate them and after that I danced naked with the Devil. What do you think I did?"

Apparently unperturbed by her outburst, he said, "So you brought down the fever. What with?"

"Catnip, hyssop, and thyme, with a little licorice root," she muttered sulkily.

He nodded. "Verra good. So, why were the women angry?"

Her dark eyes flashed with anger. "Because I bewitched their men, of course, and lay naked with them in the village square."

Mac frowned thoughtfully. "So the problem started with the men." He eyed her speculatively. "What did they want you to do?"

She glared at him in silent fury.

Mac said calmly, "You're a bonny-looking lass, but while they might desire you, they'd no' be asking it of you in front of their women. So, did they take you somewhere?"

She said sulkily, "To the inn. I thought they were going to pay me for curing their babies, but they wanted—they wanted—" She spat belligerently into the fire. "They wanted me to do what I do for no man!"

"And the women found out."

She shrugged.

"And they blamed you, didn't they?" said Faith. "The same thing happened to me!"

The girl started at Faith in amazement. "You?"

Faith nodded vehemently. She leaned forward and patted Estrellita's hand. "Oh yes, if you're friendless and alone and . . . and pretty, men will want . . . things of you . . . but for some terrible reason, everyone blames the woman. It is so unfair."

The girl glanced at her, looked down, and nodded. "*Sí,* señora, they always blame the woman." Nick caught a sheen of tears in her eyes that surprised him. Perhaps she was not as tough as he'd thought. And, now he came to think of it, she was not as old as he'd thought she was before she'd washed.

"How old are you?" he asked.

She narrowed her eyes suspiciously, but could see no hidden threat in the question. "Nineteen summers."

Faith beamed. "I am nineteen, too!"

"And where are you from?" Nick continued.

"Why do you want to know?" she demanded.

"No particular reason."

"What my husband means is that we are traveling south—to Bilbao in fact," Faith interjected. "And if your home is anywhere in that direction, we could escort you. It is not safe for a woman to travel alone."

Nick looked at her in mild exasperation. That was not what he'd planned to offer at all. For a start, this girl was a gypsy, and if he knew anything about gypsies, it was that they stole.

Estrellita looked from Faith to Nick to Mac and then back to Nick. "As it happen," she said slowly, looking at Nick as if her words should challenge him, "My great-grandmother is just beyond Bilbao, and I am traveling to meet her."

Nick raised his brows. Something in the way she said it niggled him. As if there was some kind of silent challenge going on. He decided she wasn't telling the truth. "Indeed? Where exactly does she live?"

"I not tell you! I never tell you!" Her eyes dared him to push it any further.

Nick tried to keep his tone even. "I have no interest in where your blasted granny lives."

"Why are you visiting her?" Faith interjected.

"She very old. I been away for few months, but now she send for me to come home. And now I see him," she gestured at Nick with a jut of her jaw, "I know why she need me to come."

Nick ignored her incivility. She was a fractious female. He would have liked to ask how this supposed summons had arrived. He'd bet his last penny the girl could neither read nor write. But gypsies had their ways, he knew.

He glanced at Mac, who had hardly taken his eyes off the girl, and made his decision. Mac would undoubtedly watch her like a hawk, and if she tried to steal anything, he'd pounce. Other than that chip on her shoulder, she seemed harmless. And there was no denying her interactions with Mac were very entertaining. Besides, Faith was already fond of the girl, gypsy or not, thief or not. He didn't have much choice.

"Can you ride?"

She snorted as if the answer was too obvious to give. Gypsies were famous for their horse skills.

"Stevens, would you mind if Estrellita rode—"

"I no ride with him. I ride with him." She stabbed a finger in Mac's direction.

"That's for me tae decide."

"There is the packhorse, Capt'n," began Stevens.

"No packhorse. I ride with him!" She flung a challenging look at Mac as she said it.

Nick was inclined to agree. It didn't make sense to let her have the packhorse, with the possibility she'd ride off with all their things. And she clearly needed a strong hand.

"Mac?"

Mac gave the girl a long look. "Aye, orright, but I have no doubt she'll drive me mad."

Instead of showing gratitude, the girl narrowed her eyes, as if her suspicions were confirmed.

"Lovely!" exclaimed Faith, apparently oblivious of the silent interplay. "Now, I don't know about anyone else, but what I would love, Nicholas, is for you to play your guitar. Would you, please?"

He was not proof against the appeal in her eyes as she asked, so he fetched his guitar and played quietly for perhaps half an hour. He played mostly Spanish music that he'd learned while a soldier, the flamenco style that had so appealed to him in those days, and several times he noticed the gypsy girl's head come up as he started a new song. He thought of asking her if she knew them, but the instant she noticed him looking at her, she hunched her shoulders and looked pointedly away. A petulant piece indeed.

But then he noticed his wife's sleepy eyes, and he finished his song and put the instrument away.

"Time for bed," he announced and held his hand out to Faith. She put her hand in his, and he drew her to her feet and led her to where their bedding had been spread out.

As on the first night Faith had joined them, they slept on the ground around the fire, the men taking it in turns to keep watch. Mac drew first watch. He glanced across at the gypsy girl, hovering uncertainly.

He took his blankets over to her and thrust them gruffly at her.

She turned on him like a cornered vixen. "What you want? Because I tell you now I not fack with you! You try, and I kill you!"

Mac darted a glance at where Faith and Nick were and said in a low, angry voice, "Shut your trap, girl, I never bloody well asked you, and in any case, we don't use that word here!"

"What word. Fack? You do, too. English soldiers use word all the time, want all girls do it with them—and French soldiers, too, but I not do it with them. I not fack for no man!"

He clamped a hand over her mouth. "Hush up, I said! We don't use that word, and if you keep saying it, I'll throttle ye!"

He held her till she gave a sulky nod, then released her. "What word I can use then? What word Scotsmen use?"

"You don't need a word for it!"

She made a scornful sound. "I need when every man I meet want me to f—" She made a loud blowing noise instead.

A hunted expression on his face, Mac thought for a moment. "Um . . . diddling. We say diddling."

She considered it for a moment, then shrugged. "Well, I not diddle with you, English, so do not be thinking I will!"

"Will ye get it through your skull I am no' English! My name is McTavish, woman."

"How do you do, Tavish. I am Estrellita. And I diddle with no man. Understand that, and we can be friends!"

"God save me!"

"I hope he does," she said politely. "Now why you try to drag me away if you not try to diddle me?"

Mac gave a long-suffering groan and said, "I brought you blankets! The night is mild, but it will be cold on the earth."

She sniffed. "Do you think I not know what is like to sleep on the ground? I no some delicate flower!"

"No, I ken well ye're a bloody wee thorn thicket!"

Faith was watching the exchange tensely, ready, Nick thought, to jump up and defend the gypsy girl from Mac's apparent hostility.

"Don't worry," Nick whispered in her ear. "She will be all right. She has the look of a girl well used to battle."

"Yes," Faith whispered back. "But it is very hard when one has to battle alone."

McTavish towered over the girl, looking like a great, angry bear. "Now, I dinna care whether you've slept up a tree or down a pixie hole, tonight ye're going to use these blankets!"

"They are your blankets," she retorted.

"Aye, ye stubborn wench, but I'm on watch! I'll not be needing blankets! Besides, I have ma greatcoat! Now get into them. If I find ye're not using them when I come off watch, ye'll not relish the consequences! I'll no' be trying tae diddle ye, but I'll no' promise not to spank ye!"

With that threat, he tossed the blankets to Estrellita and stomped off to a place where he could see the camp and also up the road.

Estrellita watched him go. She stirred the blankets with a disdainful toe, glanced again at the large man standing like a rock at the edge of the camp, and tossed

her hair back defiantly. With reluctance in every movement, she picked up the blankets and shook them out
fastidiously. She folded one and left it in a neat pile
where Mac would be sure to see it, then wrapped the
other one around her and curled up on the ground. Beowulf padded across the clearing and stood staring at
her.

Faith wondered if she should warn the girl that the
hideous hairy beast hated women, but even as she
opened her mouth to speak, the girl grabbed a handful
of the dog's fur and pulled the huge beast down next to
her. Faith gasped, but the dog just heaved a great sigh
and closed its eyes. Amazing!

Faith relaxed after Mac stomped away. She watched
Estrellita settle down for the night and whispered to
Nick, "It's a shame those two dislike each other so
much. It's going to make the journey rather awkward
for us all."

Nick wrapped an arm around her and drew her toward the bed he'd prepared. "On the contrary, my innocent, it's going to make the remainder of the journey
extremely entertaining."

She gave him a puzzled look but did not pursue the
question. He'd made up one sleeping space for both of
them. She raised an eyebrow, just to tease, but he pok-
ered up and explained in his officer's voice, "As Mac
said, it might be fine and mild now, but it will get cold
later on. It is only sensible to sleep together. For
warmth."

"Yes, of course, for warmth," Faith agreed, a small
bubble of happiness rising inside her. It was not simply
desire he felt for her. There was no question of marital
congress here, but he still wanted to sleep with her and
hold her through the night.

She sat down on the blankets to remove her boots
and outer clothes, and Nicholas sat down beside her to

do likewise. He had just pulled off his boots when she turned to him and kissed him impulsively. "Thank you for the music tonight. It was just what I needed after the ugliness in that village. It made everything beautiful again."

He cupped her chin and turned her face gently to the moonlight. "I'm glad." He lifted a corner of the blanket. "Now, slide in. You look exhausted, Mrs. Blacklock."

She slipped into the cocoon of blankets he'd made, and he followed. Their bodies curved together so naturally Faith felt a small jolt of pure contentment. This was the way she wanted to sleep for the rest of her life; well—not on the ground—but curved together like two halves of a whole, with Nicholas Blacklock wrapped around her.

Realizing the direction of her thoughts, she resolutely pushed them out of her mind. Worrying couldn't help the future; it only poisoned the present. She had promised to live in the moment, and she would.

Right now she lay beneath a velvet dark sky scattered with a million bright stars, with a warm fire crackling gently nearby. And best of all, she had the warmth and strength of her husband's arms around her. Why worry about nights of the future when she could enjoy what she had now?

She heaved a big sigh.

"What is it?" he asked.

"Oh, nothing. Just that I must thank you for this . . . this . . ."

Oh God, here it comes, Nick thought. The declaration.

"This whole notion of living in the moment, looking neither forward nor back," she said. "You cannot imagine what a difference it has made to me."

Nick felt his tension subside. With relief, he decided. "What sort of a difference?" he asked cautiously.

"Look at those stars. Have you ever seen so many stars, and sparkling so bright. A night so velvet and peaceful? Just to be here, safe and warm and well-fed—it's enough for the moment, isn't it? Enough for a moment of perfect happiness." She sighed again. "In fact, a whole string of perfectly happy moments."

Nick didn't reply; he couldn't. There was a lump in his throat. She never failed to surprise him, this wife of his. Not many gently bred young ladies would slide happily into a makeshift bed on the hard ground, let alone with a smile of pure delight. And then lie on the cold, lumpy ground and rapturize about how perfect it was.

She went on, "I used to worry so much, before you." She half turned her head and nuzzled his bristly jaw with unconscious sensuality. "Before you taught me about living in the moment, I mean. I used to brood about the past and plan exhaustively for the future. I used to dwell in that imaginary future." She paused for a moment, thinking. "That was why I fell so easily for Felix, I think . . ."

He waited. He wanted to know what appeal the bastard had. For a moment it seemed as though she wouldn't continue, so he squeezed her gently and said, "Go on."

"My twin and I dreamed of our future husbands and future lives, and they were filled with music and laughter and sunshine and love and happiness—all the things we'd never had as children."

She grimaced. "You have no idea how I yearned for that future. It was the summit of all my dreams, to find a love like Mama and Papa had, like my sisters Prudence and Charity have. Even my twin, Hope, found love with such an unexpected man . . . I've never seen her so happy." She was silent a moment. Nick thought there were probably tears in her eyes.

Nick didn't know much about dreams these days. He

knew how easily dreams could be crushed. He wished things could be different for her, but he had a terrible conviction that his interference was only going to make it worse for her in the end. He should have sent her back to England at the start. His arms tightened around her. He would send her back, only not just yet.

He'd thought he could face this trip alone. He was used to being alone, managing alone . . . but now . . . since Faith came into his life . . . He buried his face in her hair.

"And when Felix came along, he was the most brilliant musician I'd ever heard, and so very handsome and, well, I never really looked past that. I simply imagined him into the role. I didn't know the difference between reality and dreams."

She leaned back against him and sighed again. "And now I know. This is reality . . ."

Nick felt bleak. He wished he could give her that life—what had she said?—filled with music and laughter and sunshine and love and happiness. But it was not possible. Not for them. She had no part in what lay ahead for him, and Nick vowed to keep it that way.

"And reality is studded with small, perfect moments, if you let yourself see them." She turned in his arms and gazed into his eyes. "It's a priceless gift you've given me, Nicholas Blacklock, and I thank you from the bottom of my heart. Thanks to you, I know that whatever the future brings, my life need never be as cheerless and unhappy again."

Nick couldn't speak. Nor could he bear to meet the tender honesty of her gaze. He pulled her against him and kissed her, seeking oblivion from the turmoil her words had caused in him.

Nick woke at sunrise to find the gypsy girl standing over him, hands on hips.

"It is you!" she accused him in a belligerent voice.

Nick sat up. "Well, who else would it be?" he said irritably.

"You are The One!"

"What one?" He scratched his head. The woman made no sense. He wished she would go away. Beside him, Faith was stirring, sleepy and beautiful.

"The one who come to take the life of The Old One."

"What old one?"

"The Old One—my great-grandmother."

Nick stared at her. "You think I've come to kill your great-grandmother? What a load of rubbish!"

"It is true. I know it here!" And she thumped a fist between her breasts, over her heart.

Nick snapped, "Look, you foolish chit, I've never harmed a woman in my life, and if you think I'm going to start now—and on an old lady—well, all I can say is, you've got rats in your attic!"

"Rats in . . . ?" Puzzled, she turned to Mac for enlightenment. He tapped his temple, and she turned back furiously to Nick. "I not crazy. You are The One. I think it last night when I see your eyes cold and gray as stone, but last night I dream all again, just as it was foretold."

"Foretold by whom?"

"By The Old One. 'Three foreigners will come; the first, his blood in the earth at my feet, the second a man of fire, blood of my blood, and the third with eyes of ice, whose blood will take my life,' she say." She glanced significantly at Stevens, at Mac, and at Nick. Three foreigners, and one, a man of fire. She nodded at Mac's red hair and beard.

"What nonsense!" Nick declared. "Prophesies before breakfast! Enough to give anyone indigestion. Look, you foolish girl, I'm not going to hurt your old granny, and you can see for yourself Mac is not made of fire—

though I admit, with that red beard of his, he could be confused with a burning bush!"

Estrellita said in a low, throbbing voice, "I warn you now, *Capitaine*, I not let you kill The Old One."

Nick rolled his eyes. "Take her away, Mac, before I lose my temper."

Mac took Estrellita by the arm and marched her away, still muttering and casting malevolent glances toward Nick.

Nick lay back and groaned. Just the traveling companion they needed, a demented gypsy girl. As if he didn't have complications enough on this trip.

He glanced at his sleepy complication, planted a light kiss on her nape, and rolled out of bed. He gathered a few things and headed for the stream. A swim was what he needed to shake the irritability out of his system.

Chapter Twelve

∽

But at my back I always hear
Time's winged chariot hurrying near.
ANDREW MARVELL

THE COFFEE WAS BREWING BY THE TIME NICHOLAS RETURNED from the stream. Seeing him return, barefoot and only half-dressed, Faith regretted not following him to the stream. He wore just his breeches and shirt, which was still unbuttoned, and both clung to every muscle, as if he'd pulled them on over a damp body. His hair was wet, and his chin was scraped clean of whiskers. She had a vision of him standing naked in the stream, shaving. Her own personal Greek god.

She hurried to greet him, her "wifely duty" to perform.

"Good morning, Mr. Blacklock." She rose on tiptoe, put her arms around his neck, and kissed his firm lips. He wrapped his one free arm around her waist and kissed her back. His skin was cold from the stream, and he smelled of soap and Nicholas.

"Good morning, Mrs. Blacklock, I hope you slept well on the ground last night."

She gave him a sunny smile. "I always sleep well

with your arms around me, even on the ground." And it was true, Faith thought with wonder, and not just about the ground. She hadn't had a nightmare or a bad dream of any sort since her marriage to Nicholas. "Marriage to you agrees with me, Mr. Blacklock."

His smile faded, and he released her abruptly. "Have you broken your fast?" he asked curtly.

"Not yet. I was waiting for you."

"I'm not hungry. Make haste. I'd rather we got on the road as soon as possible." He strode off, leaving Faith staring after him, dismayed and wondering what she'd said.

And then she noticed it. A trail of blood where he had walked. Nicholas was bleeding.

"Nicholas, wait!" She ran after him. "Did you cut yourself? Where does it hurt?"

He stared at her as if she was talking nonsense. "What are you talking about?"

"You're bleeding." She pointed to the blood on the ground and crouched down in front of him. "I think you've cut your foot." She examined his feet as she spoke, and sure enough, one of them was cut and bleeding.

"It's nothing," he said. "I can't even feel it." He made to keep walking, but she held on to him.

"You're not moving, Nicholas, so don't argue with me! Now sit down and let me look at it. At the very least, let me clean all this dirt off it so I may see how badly—or not—it is cut."

She made him sit down and called to Stevens to bring some hot water and a cloth. Stevens came, and Estrellita followed, watching curiously from a short distance.

When she had washed the dirt from his foot, she saw it was quite a deep cut. It was bleeding profusely. "You must have cut it on a sharp rock or some broken glass. How could you not have noticed?"

He shrugged indifferently. "I suppose the cold water numbed my foot. Clap a bandage on it, and let's get on."

Stevens bent over Faith's shoulder and peered at it. "I think it mebbe ought to be stitched, Capt'n. It's pretty deep."

Nicholas shrugged again. "Then do it. I don't want to sit around here all day."

"I'll fetch the necessaries." Stevens stomped off to get them.

Faith felt a bit ill at the idea of stitching up her husband's flesh. To cover it, she said, "You're being very brave about it. I'm sure I would be crying at such a deep cut."

He shook his head, but there was a pucker between his brows. Obviously it hurt him more than he was letting on.

Stevens returned with the needle and thread, the pot of salve, and a bottle of brandy. He handed it to Nicholas, who waved it away impatiently.

"No, I don't need it."

Stevens frowned but said nothing. He nudged Faith aside. "I'll do this, miss."

Faith nerved herself to say it. "I—I thought perhaps I ought to do it. It's one of the duties of a soldier's wife, isn't it?" To her chagrin, her voice trembled a little.

Stevens gave her a shrewd look, but all he said was, "Be quicker and less painful for the capt'n if I do it, miss. You watch and see how it's done, and then next time he needs sewing up, you'll know what to do."

"Very well." Relieved, Faith moved aside and braced herself to watch.

Stevens splashed the cut with brandy. Nicholas didn't even flinch. His frown, however, grew. Stevens glanced at him and frowned also. He opened his mouth to ask a question, but— "Get on with it," Nicholas growled.

Stevens got on with it.

He was obviously used to this task; his hands moved quickly and deftly as he sewed and knotted, sewed and knotted. Faith felt ill each time the needle pierced Nicholas's skin. By the third stitch, she felt clammy and faint.

Nicholas noticed. He took her hands in his and said in a low, almost savage voice, "Don't watch if it makes you ill. I'm really quite all right. Go and have your breakfast, Faith. That's an order."

But Faith shook her head. She was determined to stick it out. If he could endure it, she could watch. She was determined to prove to him that she could fit in to his rough-and-ready life.

He wanted to wrap her in cotton wool and send her back to lonely comfort in England. She had to make him see that she relished this life with him, even the hard parts. Despite the discomforts, she had been happier on this journey with Nicholas than in any other time of her life, and she was not going to jeopardize her future with him by getting missish and fainting at the sight of a needle entering flesh!

She clutched his hands, battling waves of nausea, and watched as Stevens's needle pierced the ugly gash in her husband's skin. She tried not to wince as he tugged the thread tight, pulling the two pieces of flesh together to make a neat seam. Every now and then he dashed some more brandy on it, to wash away any blood and, he said, to keep the wound clean.

All through the procedure, Nicholas neither flinched nor made a sound. Soldiers were different, she thought. It had to be hurting him terribly, but he sat there in silence, apparently unmoved, apart from a black frown.

His hands held hers as if she were the one who needed comfort, his thumbs stroking her. He watched her; she could feel the touch of his gaze like a warm ca-

ress, willing her to look at him, not his wound. But
Faith would not be distracted. She would not lift her
gaze from the stitching taking place. She was determined to show him she could manage whatever this trip
threw at her. She was totally resolute: she would travel
on with him after Bilbao, facing whatever he had to
face, side by side.

His big thumbs rubbed back and forth across her
skin, soothing, rhythmic, and immensely comforting.

"Miss, do you know what plantain looks like?"

Faith blinked in surprise at Stevens's question.
Botany seemed rather irrelevant at the moment. "It's a
weed, isn't it?"

"Yes, but a very useful one. Would you recognize it
if you saw it?"

Faith frowned, trying to remember. "I don't know all
that much about herbs, only the ones Cook used to use
when we were sick. Is plantain the one with purplish
green flowers, not particularly pretty?"

"That's right, miss. Low growing with broad green
leaves. In the army we used to call it soldiers' herb, and
if you could find some, it would do Capt'n Nick's cut a
power of good. A real healer it is."

"Is it? Then I could go and look for some immediately. I'm sure there will be some growing around
nearby. It grows nearly everywhere, doesn't it?" Faith
looked at Nicholas. "Will you be all right by yourself if
I go and look for this herb?"

"Yes," he said gravely.

She dropped his hands and scrambled to her feet, al-
beit a little shakily. She felt better having something ac-
tive to do.

"I help you find it," Estrellita said from behind her.
Faith jumped. She had forgotten the gypsy girl.

"You want plant for stop blood, yes?" Estrellita confirmed with Stevens.

"That's right. You fetch us some, and we'll use it to help the capt'n here."

Estrellita snorted. "I not do it for him, I go with her so she not lose her way."

Nicholas watched the two young women hurry off toward the woods. They were a strange pair; the gypsy girl despised and mistrusted him but seemed to have adopted Faith.

"Hope you don't mind, Capt'n, but I thought it best to get Miss Faith out of the way. Turning green she was."

"I know."

"Determined to see you through it, she was."

"I know."

"She's a good 'un, Mr. Nick. A real good 'un."

"I know."

Stevens frowned and seemed about to say something more, then changed his mind. He bent over the cut foot again. "That gypsy girl will keep an eye on her, make sure she don't get lost in the forest. No flies on that one. Interesting how Mac treats her, don't you think?"

"Interesting how she treats Mac, too," Nick responded.

Stevens worked in silence for a few minutes. Then he carefully tugged the final stitch tight and knotted it. "Is it my imagination, or can you not really feel what I'm doing to you?"

Nick gave him a level glance. "It's not your imagination."

Stevens grunted and cut the thread with his knife. "Not good, that."

"Depends on how you look at it. Some would say it's a blessing," Nick said wryly.

Stevens grunted, unimpressed, and began to bandage the foot. Nick didn't want to think about it.

• • •

They had not gone far when Estrellita caught Faith's arm in both hands and forced her to stop. "I not come to help you find the soldiers' herb," she said in a low, intense voice.

Faith's curiosity was roused. "Then why did you come?"

Estrellita glanced around her in a furtive manner. "I come to beg for The Old One's life."

"What? You mean your great-grandmother? But none of us would dream of harming her, Estrellita. Why ever would you think so?"

The girl obviously didn't believe her. "Your husband—I watch you with him. He listen to you. He care for what you think." She clutched Faith's arm tighter. "Please, lady, tell him not to hurt her. Tell him not to come near her."

Faith found the girl's anxiety distressing. She, better than anyone, knew how protective Nicholas was toward women. She took Estrellita's hands in hers, squeezing them comfortingly. "Nicholas will not hurt her, I promise you. He might look fierce—and he can be—but with women, he is the gentlest creature. I should know."

The girl shook her head. "No! You his wife. He not hurt you because he love you. But The Old One he not know, not love. But you, lady, he will listen to. So tell him not hurt her."

"No, it's not simply because I am his wife. He rescued me—just as he rescued you—when I was a complete stranger to him, an unknown girl running from terrible men."

But Estrellita wasn't convinced. "You beautiful. Of course he help you. The Old One, she old and wrinkled and no man call her beautiful—but every mark and wrinkle on her face beautiful to me." Her eyes filled with tears. "She is last of my family. All dead now, except her and me."

"Looks would make no difference to Nicholas. When he saved me, it was dark, and he couldn't even see my face, but that's not important. If Nicholas was the sort of man who could hurt an old woman, why was he unable to hurt any of those women who were attacking you in that village? He wanted to rescue you, but even though those women were hitting and scratching him, he didn't hurt any of them, just fended them off and lifted them aside. Does that sound like a man who would hurt any old lady, let alone your great-grandmother?"

Estrellita's eyes clouded briefly with doubt, but after a moment she shook her head and said in a flat voice, "In my dream I see it. The Old One on the ground, her breast covered in blood. And your husband, too, with blood on his hands. What else can it mean? My dreams, they do not lie." She added in a tragic voice, "The Old One and I, we are last of our line. If she die, I am all alone in the world."

Faith bit her lip. In the face of Estrellita's doomed certainty, it was not possible to say that sometimes dreams were just dreams. The girl would not believe her. Besides, Faith was a believer in the power of dreams. But dreams had let her down before, whereas she would stake her very life on Nicholas's essential goodness.

She put her arms around the girl and gave her a hug. "Estrellita, I assure you, my husband will not hurt your great-grandmother. He is not that sort of man."

Estrellita shrugged fatalistically. "He will kill her; I know it."

"No, he will not," Faith said firmly. "I promise you."

"We will camp the night here," Nick announced as they reached a forest clearing in the foothills of the mountains.

Faith slumped in the saddle. It was disappointment as much as tiredness. Ever since Estrellita had joined them, they had camped out of doors. Faith was not sure whether it was because Nicholas didn't think any inn or lodging house would accept the gypsy girl or whether he simply preferred it. The weather had been fine, and Faith had to agree she found it pleasant under the stars. It was amazing how one's body adapted to sleeping on the ground. It felt like no hardship at all, these days.

But she was worried his decision to camp was caused by a desire to keep her at a distance. When they camped, she and Nicholas did not have marital congress.

Nicholas reached up to help her out of the saddle. "Not too long now," he said gruffly. "I realize this journey must seem endless."

Endless? She wanted it to be endless. She wanted to be with him forever.

"My guess is we'll reach Bilbao in another three days."

"Three days!" Faith gasped. It could not be so soon. She glanced at the unyielding profile of the man beside her. She just knew he was going to make her leave once they got to Bilbao.

She had just three days in which to make him love her!

She avoided his hands and tightened the reins, causing her horse to take a few steps backward. "I don't want to camp here," she declared. "I'm tired, and my back is aching. I want a hot bath, and I want to sleep in a proper bed." She avoided his eyes in case he divined her scheme.

He scowled. "I told you to expect hardships, madam."

"You did, sir," she retorted. "And I've endured them so far without a murmur. But now I want a bath and a bed." She gave him a friendly smile. "You can stay here and camp. I still have the money you gave me in Calais. I'm sure it will be enough to pay for a bedchamber and a hot bath at the next town." And before he could respond, she wheeled her horse around and cantered down the road.

He followed a few moments later, thundering after her, as she knew he would. She refused to slow her pace, and he was forced to canter along beside her while he shouted, "What the devil do you think you're doing, madam?"

She called back cheerily, "Finding myself a bedchamber and bath, sir. Didn't you hear me?" It was a shame her horse was tired. She would have loved to have raced him, but even at a canter, the poor horse wouldn't be able to keep up the pace for long.

"You married a soldier, madam, and as my wife—"

"But you're not a soldier anymore, surely? The war is long over—isn't it?" She gave him a challenging look. If he wanted her to treat him as a soldier, let him explain his mission in Spain and Portugal.

"I told you at the very beginning—"

"And I listened." It felt gloriously freeing to be riding along like this in the twilight, tossing arguments back in her husband's face. "I think I have done quite well. I have learned to fish and—" She broke off, flushing, remembering her disastrous attempt at hunting, then hurried on, "And although Stevens has done most of the cooking, I have helped."

His mouth quirked. "Yes. I remember some charred and blackened chunks you claimed were toast."

"That was entirely your fault," she retorted airily. Recalling that he didn't know she'd been watching him naked at the time, she continued before he could demand an explanation, "And I have learned to wash in streams and set up a camp and sleep on the ground and

I have tended wounds—or at least learned how they are tended—"

"But—"

"And now, having been a good soldier's wife, I want a hot bath and a bed. It's not too much to ask, is it?"

He hesitated, then said, "No, it's not." And he gave her a smoky, dark look, which sent a small bubble of hope rising inside her.

The bathtub was made of enameled copper and was heavy enough to require two men to carry it up the stairs and set it in front of the fire. Buckets of steaming hot water followed, carried in by several maidservants and men. Faith stopped one of the girls as they were leaving and asked her to bring up a cup of white vinegar. Nick could not imagine why.

The maidservant brought the cup of vinegar just as the last girl set her bucket down beside the bath, for rinsing purposes, Nick assumed, and then the two girls carefully set up a folding screen around the bath.

And then suddenly their small bedchamber was empty. There was just Nicholas and his wife. He lounged on the bed, bootless and in his shirtsleeves, watching her careful preparations for the bath, enjoying the feminine ritual of it; the combing out of the hair, the careful unwrapping of the sliver of rose-scented soap, which was all that remained from her wedding gift from Marthe. Nick made a mental note to buy her some more. The scent of roses was now inextricably linked in his mind with Faith, her skin, her hair, the warm, sensuous feel of her in his arms.

He felt privileged to be part of this, even as an on-looker. He'd had lovers before, though not many; he was too fastidious to dally with camp followers, and he was reluctant to make promises he knew he could not keep. So for the most part he'd enjoyed temporary, lighthearted liaisons of the sort common to soldiers the world over, mostly with older, experienced women who wanted nothing more from him than his body and protection. Ladies they were, for the most part, widowed or with long-absent husbands, wanting Nick in their bed—discreetly—but not in their life. When the army moved on, they'd parted with few regrets.

Never had he experienced this, this daily . . . intimacy. The intimacy of knowing every garment she owned, the feeling of her small, soft body curled against him every night, of holding her through the night without making love, oblivious of the hard, uneven ground, drinking in the scent and feel of her and the small sounds she made in her sleep. Of days and nights filled with kisses both light and passionate, of small gestures of affection: a touch, a look, an unspoken shared reaction to small events, conveyed by a look or a smile.

Intimacy. It terrified him. And yet he could not resist its pull.

She removed her shoes, stockings, and outer garments, then stepped behind the screen for the final disrobing. Nick grinned. Such a modest little creature she was. He'd explored every inch of her body in bed, and she'd explored his, shyly at first, then with growing confidence. In bed she'd learned to shed her modesty and made love with an enthusiasm and passion that stole his breath away.

He found it endearing that now, after a few nights of not making love, she'd grown shy with him again. He loved the contradiction of her: this wife who'd made love to him naked in the sea and then sent him to fetch her drawers, this wife who'd slept naked with him night after night and now stepped behind a screen to bathe.

What if they'd never met? What if she'd run the other way that night, when she'd fled? He shuddered to think what would have happened. What if she'd stayed on that ship he'd put her on, and gone to England as he'd told her to?

He'd never have learned what intimacy could be.

He wondered whether the lesson would be worth the pain. Whether she would think so. He pushed the thought aside. He had this moment, now, and by God, he would live it to the fullest.

Her silhouette was outlined by the glowing fire. He watched as she unbuttoned the bodice of her chemise, then lifted it over her head. His mouth dried as she bent and pushed down the legs of her drawers, lifting out first one leg, then the other. She stretched, arching her back, and he almost moaned aloud at the enticing sight she made.

He heard the splash as she cautiously put one toe in the water and swished it around. He watched as she stepped in and slowly, by agonizing inches, lowered herself into the bath. She settled back with a sigh of satisfaction, and that was enough for Nick.

He stepped behind the screen and placed his hands on her shoulders. She jumped and instinctively covered her breasts. "N-Nicholas, what are you doing?"

"Bathing you. It's a husband's privilege." His voice sounded hoarse. She was all pink and peach and warm, wet curves, and his body craved to pull her from the water, throw her on the bed, and take her at once, without finesse, without preliminaries. But he knew the power of delay and anticipation. And the divine pleasure of seduction.

He took the soap and lathered it between his fingers, then slowly rubbed it over her skin, her fine white skin, starting with her shoulders. She was tense. He kneaded her shoulders and felt her muscles gradually relax and loosen under his ministrations.

"Ohh, that's better," she said. "I'm a bit stiff."

"Me, too," he said with irony. He was hard as a rock.

She didn't notice. "We rode a long way today, didn't we?"

"Mmm. Lean forward, and I'll do your back." He didn't just soap her back, he rubbed it hard, massaging it with his fingers. She moaned with pleasure as his hands slipped down along her spine, kneading and soaping.

Without warning he slipped his hands around her ribs and cupped her breasts, warm and silky, bobbing in the water. She arched against him as he brushed his fingers over her nipples. They hardened at once. He stroked and caressed her breasts, arousing, teasing, soothing. She gasped and made little movements in the water, sending the water splashing at the edges. He took the washcloth and gently abraded the distended nipples, and she moaned and pressed her head back against his shoulder, and he felt one of the pins holding up her hair.

He pulled it out and took out the remainder, letting her hair tumble down around her nape. It was not long, but it was silken and curly, and he loved the texture of it in his fingers. He lathered her hair with the soap, and she smiled. "This is bliss. I think I will always require your attendance at my baths, Nicholas."

He said nothing; there was nothing to say. They had now.

He massaged her scalp, and she rubbed against his hands sensuously, her eyes squeezed shut against the soapsuds, and he could not help himself; he slid his hands down her front, over her breasts, and between her legs, soaping the golden curls there, delicately at first and then with greater urgency. She gasped and writhed and clutched him, leaning forward and planting small, clumsy kisses on any part of him she could reach. The water slopped over the side.

"Now, Nicholas, now," she begged, but Nick knew the value of delay.

"I'll just rinse your hair," he said, and she opened her eyes and looked at him almost indignantly, as if she could not believe he could think of such a thing at such a time. But he was hard as a rock, and his whole body ached with need, and it was himself he was torturing, not just her. He focused on the task at hand, concentrating on each step, the tension and anticipation building in his body, knowing that soon, as soon as she was ready . . . The pleasure-pain of delayed gratification.

Carefully he rinsed the soapy bubbles off her body. "Bend your head, and I'll rinse your hair," he said.

"Use the jug on the table and add that cup of vinegar."

"Why?"

"It clears off the soapy scum and makes my hair shinier."

"But then you'll smell of vinegar, not roses."

"No, I won't, or at least not for long. I always do this, and you've never yet complained I smell of vinegar."

Doubtfully, Nick poured the vinegar into the warm water in the jug. "Close your eyes," he said and carefully rinsed her hair.

"Now stand up, and I'll rinse the rest of you."

She tried to stand, but her knees buckled, and she made a grab at him that soaked them both and the floor a good deal more. And if he thought he was torturing his body before, it was nothing to having to hold a wet, naked, giggling, amorous wife upright while he rinsed soap bubbles off her. It was, in fact, not humanly possible.

"Oh, to hell with rinsing you! That soap is good enough to eat, anyway!" And he lifted her from the bath and carried her to the bed. She was ripping at his shirt, pulling it off him and covering his chest with kisses and nips. She found his nipple and fastened onto it with her mouth, teasing it softly with her tongue. Then she bit it, lightly, experimentally, and Nick almost came off the

floor as exquisite sensation burned through him. She
kept nibbling on him, even as her hands were busying
themselves with the buttons of his breeches.

"Aha!" she declared triumphantly as her hands found
their object, closed around it, and squeezed.

Nick heard himself groan.

So much for his modest, shy little wife. And thank
God for contradictions.

Faith woke to an odd feeling. Something was wrong.
Her husband's warm bulk lay beside her, and she nudged
him, saying, "Nicholas, are you awake?"

He didn't move. Not surprising, since they'd made
love half the night. She could not shake the uneasy feeling, so she turned and shook him, "Nicholas, I don't
know what it is, but . . ." Her voice trailed off. He
hadn't responded. He lay in the bed, unmoving, breathing evenly but almost imperceptibly.

"Nicholas!" She shook him again, harder. He didn't
move.

This was no normal sleep.

She flew out of bed and grabbed the jug of water that
stood on a table. She scooped a handful of cold water
from it and splashed his face. He didn't stir. She threw
another and another and shook him hard, but he lay
there passively, unknowing, uncaring.

He wasn't asleep; he was unconscious.

She ran out onto the landing and called for help. The
landlady produced smelling salts, and when that produced no effect, burned feathers under his nose. All to
no avail.

In the middle of the chaos, Stevens, Mac, and Estrellita arrived. Faith quickly explained the problem, and
they all crowded into the small bedchamber and stood
around the bed.

"Do you know what it is?" she asked Stevens.

"Not exactly." Stevens sounded evasive. "I think we should leave him be."

"What, just leave him and do nothing? I can't do that! He's sick, can't you see? I must help him." Faith was beside herself. She needed to do something—anything. She dipped a cloth in the water, wrung it out, and went to smooth it over his face.

Mac stopped her by the simple expedient of catching her wrist. "He looks wet enough already, lass."

Faith flushed. "I tried to wake him with cold water."

"Aye, I can see that." Mac bent over Nicholas and examined him carefully. "Stevens is right. We'll let him sleep it off."

"He's not drunk! And he's not asleep!" Faith almost yelled. "He's insensible! He needs a doctor. One of you must fetch one immediately."

Mac and Stevens exchanged glances. Mac answered for both of them. "Nay. The cap'n gave orders we were never to do that."

"But how could he know—"

Stevens patted her shoulder in a fatherly manner, "Now, now, it's just another one of his headaches; no need to fret and carry on."

She flung off his hand in frantic irritation. Stupid men, acting as if she was making a fuss over nothing while Nicholas lay there insensible and unmoving! "But he didn't have a headache last night; he was perfectly well. You must fetch a doctor! If you won't go, I will!"

The landlord poked his head into the conversation and said sorrowfully. "There is no doctor here, señora. The closest is Bilbao, and he is not so good." He made a quaffing gesture with his hand to signify the doctor in Bilbao was a drunkard. He glanced at the still man on the bed. "I could fetch the priest, perhaps."

"No!" all three of them said at once.

Faith wrapped her arms around herself and stared in

helpless frustration at each of the men in the room. She was frightened. She had no idea what to do.

Mac, who had been in quiet conversation with the landlord, raised his voice. "Breakfast will be served in twenty minutes downstairs, lass. Ye can do no good sittin' here and fashin' over the cap'n. Have a wash, get dressed, and come downstairs. Estrellita here will help you." He gave the girl, who had been hovering near the doorway, a little push.

"You expect me to eat breakfast?" Faith began incredulously.

"Aye. The cap'n will wake when he's ready, and in the meantime, starvin' never did nobody any good. Now do as I say and don't argue."

He spoke quite softly, but Faith blinked. McTavish had been Nicholas's sergeant in the war, she remembered. It seemed even sergeants had habits of command. And though her mind screamed that she ought to be doing something, she couldn't think what. It made sense to dress and break her fast; she didn't know what else to do.

"I don't want Nicholas to be alone."

"I'll stay," Stevens offered. "Mr. Nick would never forgive me if you let yourself starve a'cause of him, miss."

"Very well," she said unhappily. "But I'm coming back up here straight afterward, mind."

Nicholas lay insensible for the rest of the day. In the afternoon, Mac forced Faith to go out for a walk with Estrellita. When Faith was inclined to argue, he just pushed her out the door, saying in a low rumble in her ear, "Estrellita isna used to being cooped up indoors. You'd be doin' the lass a favor as well as yoursel' and Stevens and I will stay wi' the cap'n. Take the dog, and nobody will bother you."

Put like that, Faith reluctantly agreed, though she

was by no means sure about taking his big, ugly, un-
friendly hound.

Estrellita jumped at the chance and linked arms with
Faith happily. The moment they were outside, she gave
a shrill whistle, and the dog bounded out from nowhere.
To Faith's horror, Estrellita produced a thin length of
twine and pulled the dog closer to tie the twine around
its neck.

"Be careful, he'll bite you!"

Estrellita laughed. "This one? Never!" She rumpled
the dog's fur in a rough caress, speaking to it in her own
language. To Faith's amazement the beast not only endured it but leaned its big, rough head against the girl's
legs as if enjoying such treatment.

"That's amazing."

Estrellita gave her a surprised look. "What?"

"I thought he hated women. He's always growled at
me."

The girl grabbed the huge dog and shook him play-
fully by the scruff of the neck. "You been growling at
Faith here? You stop that, Wulfie—you hear me? She
good lady!" The dog's tail waved gently, and its big,
pink tongue lolled in a horrible grin.

Faith couldn't help but laugh. "Come on, we'd better
get moving if we're to have any sort of a walk. Those
clouds look like rain to me."

Their walk was cut short. Heavy, leaden clouds
rolled in and, as the sky darkened, they turned back,
reaching the inn just as the rain began to pelt down.

Faith was about to hurry back upstairs to Nicholas,
when Estrellita detained her by a tentative hand on the
arm. "You and me friends, yes?" She looked embarrassed.

"Yes, of course." Faith wondered what would make
the normally bold and self-confident girl look so diffi-
dent.

"I want ask you something? So nobody can hear us talk. Is all right?"

"Yes, certainly." Faith couldn't imagine what she wanted to talk about. She glanced around to see where they could be private. "There is a balcony upstairs overlooking the sea. I'm sure we can talk there and still be sheltered from the rain. Is that private enough?"

"*Sí.*" They went upstairs and found the balcony. It was a little cold and damp, but not enough to be uncomfortable. They found a narrow bench and sat down, side by side.

"Now, what did you want to ask me about?" Faith said.

"About diddling. You like it or not?"

Faith wrinkled her brow. "Diddling? I'm not sure I know what you mean."

"What you do with Capitaine Nick." Estrellita made a crude gesture with fingers and thumb.

It took Faith a moment to realize what she was doing, and when she did, her face flamed. "Estrellita!" She stared at the girl, half-shocked, half-amused, but she quickly realized her reaction had upset the girl.

She did her best to swallow her embarrassment and hastened to reassure her. "I'm sorry, you surprised me, that's all. I've never seen . . . or heard anyone refer to it quite like that. In fact, I've never really heard anyone refer to it at all—except for my oldest married sister, once and very briefly."

Years ago she and Hope had hounded Charity to tell them about it, after Charity was married. But they'd just said "it," and Charity had blushed bright red and said nothing much, only that the husband would explain, and that it was nothing to worry about. When they continued to pelt her with questions, she'd blushed even redder and added in a whisper that it was very agreeable.

"I have no sister to ask," Estrellita said baldly.

Faith swallowed, knowing she must also be bright red. She wondered how much detail the girl wanted to go into. A girl who could make such graphic movements with her fingers needed no explanation, surely. "Wh—what do you want to know?"

"When you do it with Capitaine Nick, you like it or not?"

"I like it."

Estrellita pursed her full lips, dissatisfied with her brief answer. "Like it much or is bearable?"

"I like it very much." She took Estrellita's hand. "It's wonderful, Estrellita. The best feeling in the whole world."

"Better than a full belly?"

Faith blinked. Estrellita was only too familiar with hunger, she realized. "Yes. Sometimes I feel like I've been hungry all my life, and now, with him, I will never feel hunger again."

The gypsy girl nodded thoughtfully. "Better than kissing?"

"Yes, better than kissing. In fact, you kiss at the same time."

The girl's eyes opened wide in surprise at that. She rose and paced a few steps back and forth along the narrow balcony, deep in thought. Then she turned. "I only do it once, and it terrible."

"The first time can be a little uncomfort—"

The girl stared out to sea, her body stiff, and said without looking at Faith, "A soldier, he rape me."

Faith jumped up and put her arms around the girl's hunched shoulders. "Oh, Estrellita, I'm so sorry."

"After the battle at V—" Estrellita cut herself off suddenly. "After big battle," she amended. "He alone—I think he coward, maybe, run and hide from battle. I, too, hide. All girls in Spain know what soldier do if find girl alone." She shrugged. "But I young and stupid. Not hide well enough. Not know how bad it be." She fell silent, brooding over the unchangeable past. And then she shuddered with remembered horror.

Faith held her tighter, taking in the implications. The fighting in Spain had been over for years. Estrellita was the same age as she was. With trepidation she asked, "How old were you?"

"Fourteen."

"Oh, dear God."

After a while Estrellita gave a loud sniff and said in a matter-of-fact tone, "I kill him after, when he sleep. I slit his throat."

Faith, horrified, stroked the tangled curls and said fiercely, "I'm glad you did, Estrellita. So glad you did! It was the right thing to do."

The girl nodded. "I lose my honor, but I get my revenge."

"I lost my honor, too," Faith said softly. The girl's head came up in surprise, and Faith explained. "It was before I met Nicholas. I ran off with another man and though I thought we were married, he had tricked me. It wasn't rape, but I still lost my honor. I thought no decent man would marry me." She felt her eyes prickle with tears. "But Nicholas did. He hardly knew me, he knew what I'd done, and still he married me. That's why I say you don't have to worry about him and your Old One."

They sat for a long time, staring out to sea, thinking their separate thoughts. Then Estrellita asked, "This other man—the one who trick you—you like diddling with him?"

Faith considered it. Oddly, since that first night with Nicholas, she hadn't really considered the matter. "It was all right," she said. "Quite pleasant. But I often felt lonely afterward. With Nicholas, it's different. I feel so much . . . more. And afterward he holds me, and I feel so happy that sometimes I wonder that my heart hasn't burst." Her eyes blurred with tears again, and she wiped them away. "I'm sorry, it's just—"

Estrellita laid a grubby brown paw on Faith's hand. "You love him much and so you worry much. But he not die, Faith—not here, not now." She spoke with solemn certainty.

Faith looked into the girl's deep brown eyes, trying desperately to make herself believe her words were true. But she didn't believe anyone could know the future. "I'm sorry, Estrellita, I hope you don't mind if we finish now. I really have to go to my husband."

She gave a sad smile. "I not mind. You help me, Faith. Thank you. I owe you much."

Faith stepped inside and turned to tell Estrellita that friends didn't have debts, but the words that came out were different. "Estrellita, I have four sisters who I miss very much. I cannot imagine what it would be like to have no sisters at all. And right now, I need a sister with me, and I think you do, too. If you like, you and I could become sisters, sisters of the road."

The gypsy girl stared as if unable to believe her ears. Finally she whispered. "You mean this, Faith—true?"

Faith nodded, feeling too emotional to speak.

Estrellita's eyes flooded with tears, and she leapt forward and hugged Faith hard around the neck. Then she drew back and with grave dignity kissed Faith on each cheek. Their tears mingled as she repeated the words like a vow, "Sisters of the road."

Nicholas remained insensible for a day and a night. Faith was beside herself. She paced up and down. She forced Stevens to fetch the doctor, but took one look at his red face and drunkenly swaying form and sent him away.

Not even the sight of Estrellita braiding red ribbons

into Beowulf's woolly coat comforted her. Nor the roar of fury Mac gave when he saw his dog turned into what he called "a bloody sissy!" Even the spirited argument that resulted failed to distract her. The only thought in her mind was of Nicholas.

He woke around eight the next day. He was a little disoriented at first, but after he'd eaten, and drunk a few coffees, he seemed quite as usual. But Faith was still anxious. It was simply not normal to sleep so long, especially the kind of sleep from which he could not be woken, and she said so. "I want you to consult the next sober doctor we find, Nicholas."

"Absolutely not! I've had enough of quacks prodding and poking at me."

"But—"

"No!" The word was explosive, and she flinched. Her reaction made him notice how worried she was. He sat her down on the bed and took her hand in his. "I'm sorry to snap. When these headaches first started, I consulted a doctor—in fact in the end I saw several, some of the finest doctors in England. I know what the problem is, and it's nothing you need worry about. It is a minor inconvenience, that's all."

"But—"

"We've lost a little time, that is all. If I can cope with it, I'm sure you can, too."

Faith had no choice but to accept his word for it. He was not going to change, she could see that. But she'd caught the implication; he'd consulted doctors—in the plural—which meant it was serious. Not just migraines, something like epilepsy, perhaps? A minor inconvenience, he'd called it.

What would a soldier call a minor inconvenience?

Chapter Thirteen

∞

Gather ye rosebuds while ye may, old Time is still a-flying. And
this same flower that smiles today, tomorrow will be dying.
ROBERT HERRICK

ACCORDING TO NICHOLAS'S CALCULATIONS THEY WOULD REACH
Bilbao in one more day. After some discussion, he and
Faith decided to spend the last night camping on the
beach near the small fishing village of Biarritz.

It was a warm, balmy night. Stevens had bought
some fish from the local fishermen, and Faith had
helped him cook up a magnificent dinner, which they
ate around the campfire.

After dinner, by request, Nicholas pulled out his guitar
and played. He played a number of familiar airs, a couple
of Faith's favorites, at least one for Stevens, and the "Mingulay Boat Song" for Mac. Faith knew the words and sang
along, her voice cracking with emotion as she always did
when she got to the women's part of the song:

> We are waiting by the harbor,
> We've been waiting since break of day-o,
> We are waiting by the harbor
> As the sun sets on Mingulay.

Waiting for the men who didn't come home. Women's part in life was one of such helplessness, with no option but to wait for their men to come home, praying for their safety, not knowing how they fared. Why did men never take their women with them? It would be so much kinder than leaving them behind, waiting and wondering.

And then as Faith blew her nose and tried to recover her composure, Nicholas switched to a flamboyant Spanish song, and after a few bars, Estrellita rose to her feet with a swish of skirts and began to dance.

Faith had never seen anything like it. She knew instinctively that this was true gypsy dancing and nothing like the silly imitation Felix used in his performances. How long ago it seemed. Felix had had no idea. Of anything, she thought, and dismissed him forever from her mind.

Estrellita danced barefoot in the sand, her small brown feet stamping and twirling, her toes delicately pointing up one minute, stamping her heels the next. It was passion and discipline, ancient tradition and the fire of the moment, all wrapped together. Her body moved in lithe coils, twirling, bending, swaying. Each part of her was magic, the movements of her hands, sometimes clapping, sometimes making a rhythmic clicking noise.

The song ended, and before anyone could clap, "Another," she demanded like a small queen. Nicholas obliged, his fingers almost invisible as he plucked fiery music from the strings of the guitar. It was magic.

Estrellita danced to song after song: fast ones which were a mad frenzy of gypsy spirit, slow ones which were so sensuous Faith felt as if she might be witnessing something private.

"You are good, *Capitaine*," she said after three songs. "But do you know this one?" And she said a name that Faith didn't catch.

Nicholas thought for a moment. "Is this it?" He strummed a few chords.

"Ah *sí, Capitaine*, it is that one. So play!" she demanded with an imperious gesture. She stalked to the middle of the clearing and waited, her head cast down, her body poised, as if she were on the stage in some great capital.

Nicholas played, and her head snapped up, and she began to dance. The song started slowly. Estrellita's movements were mesmerizing, slow at first, then faster.

It was a story she was telling, Faith thought, of innocence and betrayal, of pride, and of hopeless yearning. Her movements plucked the heartstrings, each gesture laden with emotion. Faith did not fully understand it, but she had tears in her eyes by the time Estrellita sank to the dust, exhausted, as Nicholas played the dying chords of the song.

There was a long silence afterward, and then Estrellita rose in one lithe and fluid movement, flung a gauntlet of a glance at McTavish, and stalked from the camp.

After a moment, Mac got up and followed her.

"You've stolen every word from my mind, lass. You're magnificent." Mac reached to take Estrellita in his arms.

She slapped him and shoved him away. "No, don't touch me! I can't! I won't." Her chest was still heaving from the dancing, and she looked sweaty, dusty, and disheveled. Mac had never seen anyone more beautiful in his life.

"I haven't even tried." Mac was confused. She had seduced him with that dance, deliberately and explicitly, and now she wouldn't even kiss him?

She retreated back into the shadows. "I will have respect, Tavish!" Her voice rang out in the darkness. "And I choose! Me! Not the man! Estrellita!"

Mac heaved a sigh. Seduction? He'd imagined the

whole thing, pathetic desperado that he was. He said heavily, "Aye, I know, lass, and I'll no' press ye. Why would ye want such as me, anyway? You're so graceful and beautiful, and I'm just a big, ugly lummox, and clumsy to boot."

She ventured a little closer, where he could see her face again, and said in a softer voice, "You not ugly, Tavish. You very manly looking man. Only that beard make you ugly."

He stroked the offending article. "But it's a grand beard. It took me years to grow."

She rolled her eyes. "You man, Tavish. Of course man like beard, I am woman. We different. And you not clumsy. I watch you with knife. You have big hands, but you clever with them." Her eyes ran over him. "And you big, but . . . big in man is good, sometimes." Her eyes showed deep though wary feminine approval of what she saw, and Mac's hopes rose again.

He reached for her, and this time she allowed herself to be drawn against his body, stiff, like a little piece of wood. He kissed her gently and she sighed and seemed to relax, so he kissed her again, deeper. She opened her mouth under his, untutored but naturally sensual, and he reached for her breast, and in a flash he had a vixen in his arms, biting, scratching, and clawing to be free.

He released her, and she stared at him, poised to flee, breasts heaving, eyes wide with fear and passion mixed.

"Gently, lass, gently," he murmured, holding his hands up pacifically. "I'll no' hurt you, I'll never hurt you, no matter what you do to me." He reached for her again, gently, saying, "Now, let us try that again. Dinna fash yerself, lass, I'll no do anything ye dinna want, just try—"

She stepped back and glared at him suspiciously. "Why you talk to me like this?"

"Like what?"

"Like wild animal. You think I need be tamed?" She narrowed her eyes at him. "You talk to Faith about me, maybe?"

"No, I've never discussed you with anyone."

"Liar!" She punched him on the arm. "You know, don't you?"

"Know what?" He said evasively, rubbing his arm. "You pack quite a punch there, lass."

"Know what happened to me after that battle."

"Aye," he admitted after a moment. "I overheard you telling the cap'n's lady about it on the balcony, and I want to say—"

"So you know I am not virgin!"

"Aye, but that's no' a problem. I'm no' a virgin eith—"

Her hand flashed out and slapped him. "Do not be making fun of me, Tavish, or I will slit your throat the way I slit his—the English pig who rape me!"

"Lass, I'd never make fun of such a wicked thing done to you, especially when ye were little more than a bairn. The man deserved killing, and worse."

She stared at him, and he saw her throat move as she swallowed convulsively.

"You're a brave and bonny lass, Estrellita, and as beautiful as moonlight on the mist. And whether you can ever bring yourself to suffer my hands on you or not, I want you to know I will protect you with my life, for as long as you need me."

He heard a sniffle. "You speak beautiful, but I am sorry, Tavish. I cannot, not now."

"It's marriage I want from you, lass," Mac said softly. "I'm not interested in a quick tumble. I am young and strong, and I work hard. I have some money saved. I will take good care of you."

There was a long silence, and Mac thought he heard another sniffle. "I consider you, Tavish, that is all. I . . .

consider." There was a pause, and she added, "But I promise nothing!"

"Did you hear that?" Faith stiffened. "Someone slapped someone."

Nicholas said quietly, "Unless I miss my guess, that was Miss Estrellita slapping Mac, not the other way around. Don't worry, Mac won't hurt her."

"Are you sure?"

"I'm sure." Nick chuckled. "Haven't you noticed that our misogynistic Scotsman has become deeply enamored of our little gypsy? And she knows it, too. He's putty in her hands."

"He cares for her? And she for him? Truly?"

"Truly. They haven't been able to take their eyes off each other since they met. All that scratching and snarling is just part of the courtship game."

They heard a deep Scottish rumble and and answering female murmurs, but no words were audible. Nick rose and held out his hand to Faith. "But though I hope it works out for them, I don't feel comfortable eavesdropping like this. Would you care for a moonlight swimming lesson, Mrs. Blacklock?"

She jumped up eagerly. "I'd love one, Mr. Blacklock."

Nick picked up a blanket, shook it out, and draped it over his arm.

"What do you want that for? It's not at all cold."

He winked but did not explain.

They walked down to the water's edge. The sand was clean and white, the water gleamed like a still, dark mirror edged with faint frills of lacy foam, which caught in the moonlight. The moon was a slender crescent, low in the sky. They were a mile or so from the sleepy fishing village of Biarritz, and everything was still except for the lazy ebb and slap of tiny wavelets against the shore.

Nick spread the blanket and stripped off his clothes. Faith stripped to chemise and drawers.

Nick grinned. "Now, Mrs. Blacklock, you know what's going to happen to that chemise and those drawers, and I take leave to inform you now, if they float away, I am not fetching them."

She glanced around her warily.

"There is nobody for miles," he assured her. "Take them off."

She slowly unbuttoned her chemise, then, glancing around her several more times, she pulled it off, dropped her drawers, and ran down to the water.

The sight of her naked in the soft moonlight had a predictable effect on Nick, and he followed more slowly. She stood in the shallows, turning as he joined her.

"Oh," she said, glancing down at the evidence of his desire. She smiled a small, feminine smile.

"Yes, oh," he said. "And what are you going to do about that, Mrs. Blacklock?"

She regarded him thoughtfully. He stood knee-deep in the water, naked and waiting, as rampant as a bull, thick with desire. She bent and examined him intently. His breath stopped in his throat. She reached out and with one fingernail gently stroked him from the underside to the tip. A shudder racked him.

The feminine smile grew, and she murmured, "My, my, if we're going to have a swimming lesson, we really ought to do something about that first, shouldn't we?"

"Yes, we should," he managed to croak.

"Very well, I will." She bent down even closer, and her rosy, damp lips pursed, then parted just inches away. Nicholas could almost feel her breath, warm and sweet, on his exquisitely sensitive skin. He might never be able to breathe again.

And then she splashed him.

It took Nick a moment to recover, and when he did, he roared, "You little witch!" and plunged after her in pursuit.

Shrieking with laughter, she splashed her way deeper into the water, fleeing his masculine wrath as best she could, but he dived under the water and pulled her down.

She surfaced, spluttering and laughing.

"For that piece of impertinence, witch, I am going to have to punish you!" he growled and planted a hard, deep kiss on her mouth. She twined her arms and legs around him and kissed him back, saying when they broke for breath, "I am your penitent servant, sir."

He looked at her dancing eyes and snorted. "Liar, there's not a shred of penitence in you."

She giggled and tried to look apologetic, but it was such a hopeless failure that he was forced to kiss her again. And again.

They floated in the glassy, dark sea, kissing and caressing, when suddenly Faith became aware of an unearthly glow around them.

"Look, Nicholas! What is that in the water?" Hundreds of tiny lights, green and gold and turquoise, floated in the sea around them, like stars fallen into the water. She looked up to see if they were a reflection, but the night was dark; the shred of moon had vanished, and only a few stars were visible.

But all around them there floated a hundred tiny lights.

She dipped a hand out to try to touch whatever it was, and wherever her hand trailed, the glowing lights formed a gleaming, magical trail. She wiggled her legs and left streams of fire behind her.

"I've heard of this," said Nicholas beside her, "but never before seen it myself. The sailors call it 'fire in the water,' and they don't like it, because it clings to the nets and warns the fish away."

"It's beautiful," she said, dipping her fingers in and swishing them around her in a circle, leaving trails of glittery sea fire behind her. "I feel like a magician or a sorceress."

"You are a sorceress," he murmured, but low, so she didn't hear him.

"Look, I can write my name in the water," she said, doing it. She wrote her name, she wrote his name, and then she wrote in the black, black water, "Faith loves Nicholas."

And Nick felt a hard knot in his chest and said not a word and made no sign that he had seen. And after a minute the words faded.

"I wonder if it will cling to my hair," she said in such a determinedly cheerful voice, he knew his silence had wounded her.

But it would be worse to respond, he knew. Worse to get her hopes up. Better to say nothing. Pretend he didn't see.

She held her nose and bobbed under the water, and when she came up her hair was full of glittering sea fire and she looked beautiful and magical and more than ever of a world he knew he could never share with her.

They made love on the blanket on the beach in silence, joined, yet separate, like lovers communing across a chasm. There was a frantic edge to their lovemaking that made it the most intense and powerful Nick had ever experienced, but once it was over he was flooded with melancholy, as if it were their last time, which he knew it wasn't. Not yet.

They returned to camp in silence, hand in hand, and went to bed for the first time since their marriage, without a good night kiss. They held each other tightly in the darkness, and it was a long time before either one of them slept.

It was raining when they arrived in Bilbao, a soft, relentless drizzle that hid the mountains behind the town in a shifting veil of gray. They sought out the town's only inn, intending to dry out as soon as they could, but as they walked in the door, a voice rang out.

"Miss Faith!"

Faith turned, surprised to hear her name called out in such a place and blinked as a small, neat man walked toward her with an uneven gait. It was Morton Black, her brother-in-law Sebastian's agent. What on earth was he doing in Spain? "M-Mr. Black? Can it really be you?"

Morton Black took her hands in his and, beaming, bowed low. "It is indeed, Miss Faith, and I'm delighted to see you, just delighted. And looking so well— blooming you are, positively blooming."

"I'm very pleased to see you, too, Mr. Black, but why—how—? Nothing has happened to Hope, has it?"

"No, miss, blooming like yourself, she was, when last I saw her."

"And the others, Prudence and Gideon? Are they well?"

"In fine fettle."

"And Charity and Edward—nothing has happened to the baby, has it? Little Aurora?"

"No, miss, they are all perfectly well, as is young Grace and the two little girls and everyone in your family, Sir Oswald and Lady Augusta included, though strictly speaking, Lady Augusta isn't famil—"

"Then why are you here? Is it some business of Sebastian's?"

He gave her a troubled look. "No, miss, it's you I've come to find. It's your sister—she was that worried about you that Mr. Reyne sent me to search for you."

"Would you introduce us, please, my dear?" Nicholas, who had listened to the entire exchange, slid a possessive hand around her waist.

"Oh, yes, of course, sorry. Nicholas, this is Mr. Morton Black, my brother-in-law's agent; Mr. Black, my husband, Mr. Nicholas Blacklock. The most incredible thing, Nicholas, Sebastian—that's Hope's husband—sent Mr. Black to find me—and he did!"

The two men shook hands and eyed each other cautiously.

Faith returned to the question most puzzling her. "But I don't understand. Why was Hope so worried about me?" She turned to Nicholas and explained, "My twin and I have a special bond and can feel when each other is upset or hurt, so she must have known how happy I was." Blushing faintly, she turned back to Mr. Black. "And besides, I'd written to her. Didn't she get my letters?"

"Yes, miss—and by the way, I have a fat packet of letters for you upstairs, from all your sisters. But that's how I knew to come to Bilbao. You mentioned you were coming here. She was still anxious, though." His glance flickered toward Nicholas and back, and Faith realized that despite all her letters of reassurance, her family didn't believe her that Nicholas was a good man. She wasn't surprised. His rescuing her had been almost too good to be true.

"Will you stop calling her miss—she's a married woman!" said Nicholas irritably. "She's my wife!"

Faith gave him a surprised look. Stevens called her missie all the time, and Nicholas hadn't once objected.

Morton Black narrowed his eyes at Nicholas. "Excuse me, sir, but would you be the Blacklock who was a junior officer under Lieutenant-General Cotton at Talavera?"

"I was, and still wet behind the ears. I gather you were at Talavera."

"Indeed I was, sir, with the Sixtieth Foot. Copped this at Waterloo, and I reckon you was there, too." He rapped his wooden leg loudly. "I hadn't made the connection until I heard you snap just then. A lot younger you was back then—and I'm not just talking years, sir. Well, well, small world, isn't it, sir?"

Nicholas gave him a cool look. "Spit it out. What are you after?"

But that wasn't Morton Black's way. "Couldn't get work to save my life after the war—not until Mr. Reyne offered me a job. Do anything for Mr. Reyne I would, sir." He looked Nicholas straight in the eye and said, "And Mr. Reyne would do anything for his wife, sir, and what his wife wants is her twin sister home, safe and sound."

Nick gave him a long, assessing look, then came to a decision. "Good," he said briskly. "In that case you can escort her home, with my blessing."

Faith gasped. "What?"

He ignored her. "I was wondering how to achieve that. I would have sent Stevens with her, only he wants to visit his son's grave at Vittoria. And I wouldn't trust my wife's safety to just anyone. But I know you. You lost that leg rescuing one of your fellows, didn't you?"

"Yes, sir, I did. Not that it did him much good, poor fellow. He died anyway, and I was left, a peg leg."

"You look fit enough to me. Your arrival is extremely timely, Black."

"Excuse me, but I think I have some say in this, and I'm not going anywhere! I'm staying with you!" declared Faith.

As if she hadn't said anything at all, Morton Black said, "There's a boat leaving tomorrow, sir. It's a small cargo ship, transporting wine to England, but there are two small passenger cabins. We could obtain passage on it, I'm sure."

Faith was furious. She pushed in between the two

men who were disposing of her like a package and said, "Obtain as many passages as you like, Mr. Black, but I'm not going!"

Nicholas took her arm. "We will discuss this in private, madam."

"Don't madam me, Nicholas! We will not discuss it at all. I am not leaving, and that's that!"

His lips compressed firmly, and he marched her in silence up to the bedchamber they'd been allotted.

"Now, madam, you knew this was coming, sooner or later. I would be grateful if you didn't make a fuss about what you know is an inevitable parting and left with the quiet dignity I know you can assume."

"Why is it inevitable?"

He made an awkward, impatient gesture. "You know I have a . . . a task before me."

"Yes, you told me, and I've prepared myself for it."

His brows snapped together. "What do you mean, I told you? I did not tell you anything!"

"No, I know it is some sort of deadly secret," Faith assured him, "and I know that whatever it is will be terribly difficult for you. But I have learned so much in these past weeks, Nicholas. Surely you can see that I will be able to manage now."

He stared at her, clearly at a loss.

She explained, ticking off each point on her fingers as she spoke, "I can now cook over a campfire—not well, but adequately; I have learned to catch fish and scale and gut them; Estrellita has taught me how to forage for wild greens and herbs; and whilst I was not able to stitch that cut in your foot, I am sure I could stitch a wound if I had to; and I can shoot." She took his hands in hers. "Oh, Nicholas, I know when you married me I was a useless, helpless creature, but now I can truly be a good soldier's wife. I won't hold you up or demand your attention. I know this task you have to do is very difficult and of life-and-death importance, but I promise you, I won't get in the way. Only please, Nicholas, do not send me away."

Her words devastated Nick. She'd said much the same to him before, about all the things she'd learned, but he hadn't taken it in. He hadn't realized she was learning them for him, all those skills; training herself to be a good soldier's wife. He turned away, rubbing a hand over his eyes, hardly able to stand the pain the knowledge caused him. To be a good soldier's wife. What an irony.

"Do you have a headache?" she asked quickly.

He took her hand and kissed it. "No. Not this time." Though it wouldn't be long before it came again, and Nick had no idea of the state in which he would wake. The doctors had been unanimous—the periods of unconsciousness would increase, as would the disorientation and the loss of sensation in different parts of his body. He might even go insane—though they were not unanimous about that. What they all agreed on was that something was wrong in his head—something growing, perhaps—and that he would die slowly and in great pain.

And he was not going to put Faith through that.

He groped to think of a way he could save her dignity and get her away from him and safely back in England with her loving family.

"I'm sorry, my dear, but you have to leave. You cannot be with me when I do what I have come here to do."

She opened her mouth to argue. He drew her toward him and said gently, "You have become a magnificent soldier's wife. A man couldn't ask for a better wife—soldier or not. You are not the problem here; I am. If you are with me, I will be distracted." He gave her a wry look. "You distract me even when you try not to.

The thing is, my love, you have become the most important person in the world to me."

Her eyes filled with tears. "I'm sorry. I tried so hard n-not to get a-at-ttached." Her voice wobbled on the last word. "But I couldn't help it."

He sighed and smoothed a golden curl back from her brow. "I know. I tried, too, but it was an impossible task, wasn't it?"

"You? You got attached, too?" Her voice was a mixture of incredulity and hopefulness.

"I did, but I should not have let myself. I tried to hide it from you, tried to stop you from telling me how you felt . . . I thought if we didn't say the words it would somehow keep it in bounds, manageable." He gave her a rueful look, "But the words are only part of it, aren't they? They are important, but actions convey truth as well. So whether we speak of love or not, the feelings are there. And that is the problem."

"How can love be a problem?" she whispered.

"A soldier must devote his full attention to the task. Your presence would complicate things enormously."

She asked in a voice that trembled, "You mean if I stayed, it would be more difficult for you to do your duty."

"Much more difficult."

A tear rolled down her cheek. "And there is nothing I can learn or do that will make it easier for you to do what you must do?"

He gathered the tear on the tip of his finger. "It is not a matter of skills; it is a matter of who you are. You are Faith, for whom I would do anything. Faith, who I love with all my heart and soul and body."

"Nicholas!" The tears poured from her eyes, and she clung to him for a long time, unable to speak. Eventually she recovered her composure enough to respond. "I love you so much, too, my darling. And I do not think I can bear to part from you."

He kissed her gently, with a restraint that told her as much as any words that he was already pulling back from her. "You can. And you must."

She knew what he was saying. He loved her. So much that he feared he would neglect his duty for her. For Nicholas, who took his honor and duty very seriously, that would be a terrible thing.

She had to leave. Whatever this mission he had been sent on, it must be very important. He had been a soldier since he was sixteen, putting honor and duty to his country before all else. It would destroy him, destroy them both, if she stayed and prevented him from doing his duty.

Nicholas loved her. Was there ever such a bittersweet declaration?

Morton Black obtained the passages and returned with the information that the boat would leave soon after dawn, weather permitting. They had one last night together, and though they didn't discuss it, Faith and Nicholas were agreed: their last precious moments would not be wasted in sleep.

She greeted him in bed wearing the nightgown Marthe had given her, the fine lawn with exquisite handmade lace, creamy with age and stitched with love.

Nicholas caressed her through it, the old lace abrading her skin deliciously. With shaking hands, as if it were their first time, he undid each tiny mother-of-pearl button, one by one by one, carefully and deliberately slow, until it was open to the waist. He kissed her breasts though the fabric, once, twice, then suckled her through the lace. Then he peeled the nightgown from her and made love to her with a concentration that threatened to shatter her heart, caressing her all over, as if he was learning her, learning each curve and hollow, laving each patch of skin, tasting her, storing up memories, saving her.

He tasted every part of her from her fingertips to her toes, and then he worked his way back up the inside of her thighs and tasted her there, where the damp vee of golden curls clustered, and she gasped and clutched his hair as sensation shivered through to her very bones. His tongue explored her delicately at first, then deeper and more demanding. And he suckled her there, where she had not known it possible, and before she knew it she was shattering in fierce, helpless ecstasy. And as she began to shatter, he surged up and in one movement, buried himself in her and took them both to paradise.

They lay in each other's arms, stroking languidly, murmuring of this and that, small, inconsequential things.

And later Faith took her turn to make love to him, sitting astride him, tasting him as she'd never tasted him before, suckling him where she had not thought to do so before. And she was filled with deep female pride and love as she watched him buck and writhe in helpless pleasure beneath her, until he flipped them over and buried himself in her again, and she felt the hot spurt of his seed inside her.

"We might have a baby, Nicholas. Would you like that?"

"I would, my love. I've given Morton Black instructions to take to my solicitor. You and any babe will be well taken care of."

"You don't need to worry about me. I am an heiress."

"How nice for you," he murmured, uninterested. "If there is a babe, would you take it to show my mother? She would love to see it."

"Of course I will, we will both go—we will all go when you return," she amended. "And we'll stay with her often. And she can stay with us."

He kissed her again with such tenderness that Faith wanted to weep. But she was determined not to. She was going to make this night a happy one if it killed her. If Nicholas was going off to risk his life on some important mission, she would make sure he had only happy memories to take with him, not memories of a blotchy-faced wife with red eyes.

"Tell me about your mother," she asked. "Will I like her?" She was more worried that Nicholas's mother would not like her. What mother would welcome a chance-met, strange, convenient bride?

"My mother is a wonderful woman," he began, and Faith's heart sank. "She adored my father, even though he was a bully and seemed to show her no affection." He thought for a moment and looked at her with sudden awareness. "Though perhaps in the bedchamber it was different. I had not realized—until you—the depth of intimacy . . . and love . . . possible."

Faith smiled tremulously and rubbed her cheek against the hair on his chest. She had dreamed of it, had been promised it by her mother. Mama's dying promise to all her daughters: sunshine and laughter and love and happiness. Nicholas had given her all that and more.

"They seemed happy enough, and she openly adored him. But then, a few years ago, my father had an accident. He loved to hunt, and he came off at a fence one day when his horse balked at the last minute. He broke his back."

"I'm sorry," she breathed.

He glanced at her. "I—he and I were never on good terms," he admitted, "but his accident nearly killed my mother."

"In what way? Did she fall, too?"

He caressed her back absently. "No, she didn't ride. My father took more than six months to die. He died slowly and in great pain. Watching him suffer and die like that nearly killed my mother. She nursed him to the very end."

Faith hugged him silently.

"She was a dark-haired beauty when Father fell. She was a white-haired old woman when he finally had the grace to die." He was silent for a moment, then shuddered. "He should never have put her through that, never!"

"He could not help it," she offered tentatively.

"He could. He could have taken something to end it quickly, spared her the sight of his suffering when she was helpless to alleviate it, except with laudanum. But he wouldn't even take that. He was determined to draw out the whole filthy process as long as he could, damn him!" There was anguish as well as rage in his voice, and she knew it was not as simple as he was making out, that he had been deeply torn by his father's decision.

"You had to watch him die, too," she suggested.

"No, I didn't! He loaded it all onto Mama's frail shoulders. I didn't even know he'd been hurt until I received the letter saying he was dead. It reached me a month to the day after he'd been buried. I wasn't even there to help her with the funeral!"

She hugged him silently, knowing the hurt of being shut out from the family at such a time would have made the grief bite all the deeper, fester longer. "But your mother is well now?"

He sighed. "Yes, she is well."

"I will visit her as soon as I get to England. She may not like me, but I want to tell her how much I love her son and how you are. She will want to know you are well."

He looked at her with anguished eyes. "Yes, she will want to know I am well. And she will love you, Faith, have no doubts. She won't be able to help herself."

And then he made love to her again, silently and with a desperate edge, as if he was seeking oblivion in her, seeking forgetfulness. And Faith sought oblivion, too.

Live in the moment, forget about the past, don't worry about the future. The moment was all that counted, this moment, here in this bed in the inn in Bilbao with Nicholas, her husband, her miracle, the love of her life.

The door of Mac's bedchamber creaked open. He feigned sleep, but his fingers stealthily secured the knife that was never far from reach.

"Tavish, you awake?"

He put the knife away and sat up. "Aye, lass. What do you want?"

Her face was wet with tears. "I have bad dreams again, Tavish. Can I stay here with you?"

He pulled back the covers. "Aye, lass."

She faltered and stared. "You have no clothes, Tavish. I not come here to diddle with you."

He sighed. "Just get into bed, will you, lass? I give you my word I'll do nothing you don't want."

She narrowed her eyes at him. "You think I stupid gypsy girl who just believe what man say? When man is naked in bed? If you try force me, Tavish, I fight you. And then I will have to kill you—even if it break my heart."

"I think you're a foolish gypsy girl who is standing there freezing us both for no reason. I gave ye my word, Estrellita, and I'll no' break it." He looked at her scantily clad body and sighed theatrically, "Even if it kills me."

Cautiously she padded across the room and climbed into bed beside him. "I mean it, Tavish!"

"Just lie down and shut up, will ye?" He reached out and pulled her against him. She was stiff and awkward, like a wild animal that had been trapped, but gradually he felt her body relax.

"You nice and warm, Tavish."

"Aye, I am," he agreed glumly.

She snuggled down, wriggling against him until he groaned and clamped an arm over her. "Be still, will ye, little witch. A man can stand only so much."

In answer she turned in the circle of his arms and faced him. "I think you good man, Tavish," she said softly. She stroked his chest, pushing her fingers experimentally through the fur on his chest. "You like big warm bear, Tavish." She darted him a look and explored further. "I like bears."

"And I like little gypsy cats." He groaned. "Estrellita, lass, you're killing me."

She snatched her hand away. "You no like?"

"I like, too much."

She stared at him thoughtfully. "You want diddle with me much, I think, Tavish."

"Aye, I want ye much, Estrellita."

She swallowed, and her eyes slowly filled with tears. "Sorry, Tavish, I cannot. I only came because of terrible dreams." She started to get out of bed, but he caught her and pulled her back.

"Hush now, lass, ye needn't leave. We'll stop all this . . . fondling for now, and sleep. That's what ye came here for, sleep and comfort, no' a big, hairy, lustful Scot." He pulled her down beside him and tucked her into the curve of his body, pulling the bedclothes around them. "Now sleep, my little cat," he said. "Nothing shall harm ye."

She curled up against him and slept; just closed her eyes and slept. Women were amazing, he thought, his body aching and unfulfilled. She was amazing. She didn't trust him enough to lie with him as a woman, but she could sleep in his arms as trustful as a kitten.

She stirred and rubbed her lush little bum against him. It was going to be a long, sleepless, uncomfortable night, Mac thought. But he wouldn't trade it for the world.

Chapter Fourteen

∞

The greatest happiness is to transform one's feelings into action.
MADAME DE STAËL

THEY WALKED DOWN TO THE DOCKS, HAND IN HAND, IN THE faint gray light that precedes dawn. Stevens followed, carrying Faith's meager baggage and chatting quietly to Morton Black. Mac and Estrellita trailed behind, walking close together but not quite touching. Even the dog, Beowulf, had come to see Faith off. Probably to make sure she was gone, Faith thought dismally.

A gentle breeze blew, and the morning sky looked clear and calm. A perfect day for sailing.

Faith desperately didn't want to go. She was ragged with the effort of not weeping. "Why can't I stay in Bilbao? You can go and do whatever it is you have to do, and—"

Nick cupped her face between his palms and said gently, "Hush, my love. We've been through this a dozen times. It's just not possible. Your presence here would be just as distracting for me. You must go to England, to your family. You will be happy to see them, won't you? You said you missed your sisters—"

"Yes, of course, but that's not the point. I could wait for you, and we could go home togeth—"

Abruptly Nicholas released her and walked the last few paces to the dock alone. He stood, his back to her, staring out to sea. The breeze was picking up, and canvas and rope flapped and slapped impatiently as sailors shouted and went about their business. They were the only passengers, and the captain had been waiting for them to arrive. He was impatient to leave.

Morton Black took their bags and walked up the gangplank.

Stevens came forward and touched her on the arm. "Don't make it harder for him, missie. The more you ask to stay, the more it tears him apart."

Her face crumpled, and she fought back the tears. "I know. I'm sorry. It's just . . . I cannot bear to leave him, after . . . just . . . now that we know how much we love each other. He loves me, Stevens. He said so."

The wise, battered face crinkled. "I know, my dear. I've known for a long time. But you cannot stay. If you love him, you'll do what's best for him and leave."

Faith wiped the tears from her eyes. "I suppose this is truly what being a soldier's wife is about."

Mac spoke at her shoulder. "Aye, lass, it is. Now, make him proud o' ye. Go, and bid him farewell with a brave and bonny smile and a sweet kiss."

They were right, Faith knew. Nicholas had his duty to perform, and her duty was to smile as she saw him off and then wait for him to come home to her, as the women of Mingulay waited. Only she was the one going to sea . . .

She scrubbed at her face with the handkerchief to remove every trace of tears and took several deep breaths to calm herself. "Do I look all right?" she asked Nicholas's friends.

"That's my brave girl," Stevens told her.

"Aye, lass, you look bonny."

Her face crumpled briefly as she looked at them, these two men, who such a short time ago had been strangers to her. Stevens had taught her so much, he was a bit like the father she'd missed so much, growing up. And Mac, who had started out so horrid—astounding to think how fond of him she now was. She hugged them both and kissed them on the cheeks, then embraced Estrellita.

"Good-bye, my sister of the road," the gypsy girl whispered in her ear. "I never forget you, Faith."

Faith nodded and hugged her again. She couldn't speak.

Bracing herself, mustering all the control she could, she closed the gap between herself and the tall, dark man standing still and alone on the wharf.

She touched his arm, and he stiffened and turned to her. He wore his officer's face; still, remote, controlled. But he was breathing hard as if he'd been running, and she felt the intensity radiating from him.

Her beloved man.

This was just as hard on him as it was on her, she realized suddenly, and the knowledge fortified her resolution as no amount of argument could.

"Farewell, my dearest love. I will wait for you." Tears blurred her vision again, but it didn't matter because he was holding her in his arms, so tightly she couldn't breathe, but it didn't matter. He kissed her deeply, once, twice, and then released her, stared down at her with a still face and ravaged eyes, then grabbed her again for one last anguished kiss.

"You have been the best thing in my life," he said in a voice that cracked. "I will love you till I die—and beyond. Remember that always."

She nodded dumbly. "Keep safe, my love, keep safe. I will see you in England."

He gave her one last, devouring kiss, then turned and strode away.

"Come along, my dear." Morton Black was at her elbow. Faith allowed him to steer her up the gangplank and onto the boat; she was blind with tears.

She stood at the rail, dimly aware of the bustle of sailors scurrying around hoisting sails and heaving on ropes as the boat cast off.

She gripped the rail with white-knuckled hands as the narrow silver band of water widened. Slowly the boat swung around, and she walked around the edge of it like a sleepwalker, never taking her eyes off the still figure watching on the shore.

And then the sun spilled over the mountains and blinded her, and Nicholas was lost in a golden haze. She tried shading her hands and squinting, but try as she might, she could no longer see him, only the burning rays of the rising sun.

The tears came in earnest then, and she slumped down on the deck, weeping.

"I'll go doon an' fetch him then," Mac told Stevens after a while. They'd packed up, ready to leave on the last stage of their journey, leaving Nick in privacy as he watched his wife sail away. The boat was a tiny shape in the distance, the size of a child's toy.

"He'll no mind a wee detour to Estrellita's gran, will he, d'ye think?"

Stevens shrugged. "Depends where that is. The girl's been mighty close-mouthed about where that is, exactly."

Mac shook his head. "Aye, she still has it in her stubborn wee noggin that the cap'n means her gran ill. But I'll talk sense into her." A bit self-consciously he added, "She and I have a better understanding of each other now."

Stevens raised his brows. "I should hope so, after she spent the night in your room!"

Mac flushed. "It isna what ye think. And anyway, I aim to marry the wench, so dinna be thinkin' disrespectful thoughts of her!"

Stevens grinned. "Congratulations. She'll make you a good little wife, I think."

Mac looked glum. "As to that, she hasna said yes, yet. As I said, she's a stubborn piece."

Stevens nodded. "Off you go, then and fetch the capt'n. We should get on the road straightaway—it's no good to let him brood."

When the two returned, Nick mounted his horse in silence. He looked as weary and defeated as ever Stevens had seen him.

"Cap'n, you'll no mind a short detour to Estrellita's great-granny, will ye?"

Nick shrugged indifferently. "Of course not. Where is it?"

"I'll ask her. She'll have to tell us now. Estrellita?" Mac called, looking for the girl. "Where is the wench?" He walked back into the inn but could find no sign of her.

"Stevens, have ye seen Estrellita?'

"Not since she said good-bye to—" He glanced at Nick. "Since she was down at the wharf. She slipped back here then, before the boat left. I figured she had something to do."

They looked everywhere, but it soon became clear; sometime in the last forty minutes, the gypsy girl had slipped away.

"Where the devil has she got to?" Mac growled. He was refusing to admit she'd gone, was certain she'd just popped out for a moment, the way women did, and would be back.

"What's that around Beowulf's neck?" Stevens asked.

Mac whistled, and the dog came shambling up. He

still wore the red ribbons that Estrellita had plaited into his fur, but around his neck was something blue and frilly. Mac felt suddenly hollow inside.

He pulled it off the dog and said dully, "It's a garter—blue satin ribbons and lace." He stared at the scrap of bright fabric. "It's Estrellita's. She canna write, but this—" He crushed it in his hand with a fierce, angry gesture. "This is her farewell note." He stuffed the garter in his pocket and strode toward his horse. "No point waiting. And no need for any detour—we might as well get straight on to Vittoria, then see where your Algy is buried."

"I'm sorry, Mac," Stevens murmured.

Mac shrugged. "Women! I should ha' known better. They never take to me."

"Estrellita was different."

Mac was silent a long time. Then he said softly, "Aye, that she was." And he pulled the garter from his pocket, stroked it with a big thumb, and tucked it into the bosom of his shirt.

After a time he added, "She was too full of life to be goin' on a journey such as this, anyway, goin' from bat-tlefield to battlefield, visiting the dead—and waiting for him to"—he nodded toward the silent figure of Nick, riding up ahead—"you know."

"He's a fine man, Lady Blacklock," Morton Black said once Faith's tears had dried. He handed her a flask. "Drink this; you'll feel better."

Faith took a sip. Sherry. It didn't burn the way that first sip of Nicholas's brandy had that first night. It seemed like a lifetime ago he'd given her his flask and told her to drink to settle her nerves. She handed back the flask and thanked Morton Black. Then it registered, what he'd called her. "Lady Blacklock? Isn't that Nicholas's mother?"

"Yes, and you, too. Your husband is Sir Nicholas Blacklock, didn't you know?"

She shook her head. "No, he never mentioned it. Are you sure?"

"Ah, well maybe he preferred not to draw attention to himself while traveling, but there's no doubt about it. The Blacklocks are an old, established family."

Faith thought about the story Nicholas had told her during the night. He was still very angry with his father . . . Might that be why he'd rejected the title?

They stared back at the land, and though the sun was no longer dazzling her, Bilbao was now just a huddle of buildings, and she could see no tall, dark figure standing on the wharf. She felt empty inside. It was foolish, she told herself firmly; she was only experiencing what every soldier's wife experienced, and though she didn't know what Nicholas's mission was, she ought to have more faith in him. He'd been a soldier since he was sixteen; he had to be good at it to have survived as many battles as he had.

"You'll marry again, I suppose."

Faith looked at him in surprise. "Marry again? Why? Do we need to? I thought a marriage in France would be legal in England. And we were married in a church, as well as at the town hall—though it was a Catholic church. I don't suppose Great Uncle Oswald would be too pleased about that."

"No, no, you misunderstood me. This marriage is legal, all right." He patted her on the arm, awkwardly. "I don't suppose you want to think about such things yet, anyway. But in case you're wondering, he'll leave you well provided for. His cousin will inherit the title, of course, unless you are, er—" He touched his stomach lightly and arched his brows in a delicate inquiry.

She gave him a blank stare as she considered the matter. It had been some time since she'd had her monthly courses. On the other hand, she was often irregular . . . "I have no idea." She thrust the thought aside and focused on the present. The tone of his conversation niggled at her belatedly. Something wasn't right. "Why are you talking about who will inherit the title? You just said it was Nicholas's. It's a little early, surely, to be speaking of who will be stepping into his shoes."

Morton Black coughed and looked away. "I mean after . . . of course. I apologize, it was indelicate of me to be presuming before—er, anything had happened."

Faith frowned. "Please don't speak in such negative terms. I won't have it! You cannot know how dangerous this mission he's on is. He has emerged from a number of dreadful battles with only superficial wounds, and I, for one, am certain he will manage to survive thi—" She broke off. "What is it? Why are you looking at me like that?"

Morton Black's jaw had dropped open with surprise. "You don't—!" He broke off and swore under his breath. When he looked at her again, his face was deeply troubled. "I was certain from the way you was crying fit to break your heart just now that you must've known."

"Known what?"

He shifted his feet uncomfortably and looked away.

"Known what?" she repeated more anxiously. She clutched his arm and said, "Mr. Black, if it is something about my husband, you must tell me!"

Morton Black's face puckered with concern. He hesitated, cleared his throat, and said, "There's no easy way to say this, Miss Faith, so I'll just spit it out. He's dying."

"Dying?" she whispered, unable to take it in. "How can he be—?" She thought about the long period a few days back when he hadn't woken. But he was just insensible, and he'd recovered perfectly. "No! He can't be dying!"

Morton Black patted her shoulder awkwardly and said in a sorrowful voice, "It's true, I'm afraid. Some disease of the brain—the doctors don't know what has caused it."

Faith stared at him, profoundly shaken. "But, they're just migraines."

He shook his head somberly. "No. I'm sorry, my dear, but there's no hope."

"How do you know? There's always hope."

He said nothing.

"How did you discover this?"

"Mr. Reyne and your sister had me investigate Mr. Blacklock on your behalf. Mrs. Reyne was worried; she wanted to find out what sort of man you'd married. So I did."

"And what did you find out?"

Morton Black glanced around. The port of Bilbao was just a speck in the distance, the breeze was freshening, and their boat was bobbing up and down. He took Faith by the arm, "Come on, miss, let us go below, where we can talk in comfort."

She shook off his hand impatiently. "No, tell me here, tell me now!"

"Very well, Lady Blacklo—"

"Don't call me that! He never called me that. He always called me—calls me Mrs. Blacklock." Her voice broke. "Tell me what you found out."

"You say he gets headaches. Have the headaches been getting worse? More frequent?"

She nodded dumbly.

"I spoke to his mother and to his doctor. His doctor said it was only a matter of time, that the headaches would get more frequent and more severe, and that eventually he would most likely descend into—" He broke off suddenly and cleared his throat. "That eventually he would die, Miss Faith."

"That isn't what you were going to say, is it?"

He cleared his throat again and looked impenetrable.

" 'Eventually he would most likely descend into' . . . What is it that people descend into?" she pondered. "Descend into . . . madness?"

Some flicker of emotion passed across his face, and she took a swift intake of breath. "Madness!"

"From the pain, I gather. But it's not certain."

She gripped the rail with white-knuckled hands and stared unseeing at the distant shore. "So . . . there's no military mission?"

"Not that I'm aware of. That Stevens chap, we had a bit of a yarn last night, and he said they were revisiting the various battlegrounds where Mr. Blacklock fought. A lot of his friends died and are buried in various parts of Spain and Portugal—Stevens's own son was one of them. It's a kind of pilgrimage, I gather."

She gripped the rail harder and nodded her head slowly. "So, there's no military mission, and my husband is dying of a nasty and painful unknown disease, which in the end might drive him mad with pain."

Morton Black blinked at her blunt summation. "Yes, that's what his doctor said. He had several others confirm the opinion—though they are not unanimous on the question of the ma . . ." He tailed off, awkwardly.

"And Nicholas has taken himself away from his home and his country and everyone who loves him so that he can die alone in an obscure foreign village somewhere." She felt sobs thicken in her chest and forced them back down. Now was not the time to give in to emotion. She had to think.

"Apparently he prefers it like that. Not wanting a fuss, I expect."

Faith understood now why Nicholas had told her

about his father last night, why he'd told her how his mother had been forced to suffer along with her husband. He knew she'd find out eventually. He meant her to understand why he'd done it this way.

But if his mother really had loved her husband, she'd have wanted to be there. Even if she'd had the option, wild horses probably wouldn't have dragged her away from her husband's side in his hour—or weeks or months—of need. Not if his mother had felt about her husband the way Faith felt about Nicholas.

She said in a distant voice, needing to get it all clear in her mind, "And he has sent me off in complete ignorance of it, so that I will not have to be subjected to any unpleasantness."

"Yes, I must say it is very considerate and gentlemanly of—"

"Considerate? Gentlemanly?" She turned, and her eyes were wet with tears and blazing with fury. "How dare he?"

He took a step backward. "I beg your pardon?"

She dashed the tears from her cheeks. "How dare Nicholas decide what I can or cannot bear! How dare he conspire to keep me in ignorance, while he goes off to suffer and die alone!"

"It's a very noble act, Miss Faith."

"Pshaw!" She snapped her fingers. "I don't give a fig for nobility. If my husband is going to suffer and die, he will not damn well do it alone!" Her face crumpled. "He will have every comfort I can possibly give him!"

"My dear, I know it is hard, but you must face—!"

She cut him off. "Turn the boat around! I'm going back!"

"Now, Miss Faith, you know you can't do that—"

"Why not? We're the only passengers, and we're only a few miles offshore. Please inform the captain that I wish to return to Bilbao immediately."

"But—"

"I am not leaving my husband to face the unimaginable alone."

"He has his men—"

"But I love him, Mr. Black, really love him!" Her voice cracked with emotion. "If Nicholas has to face the worst, then I will face it with him. And I will do my utmost to make every single day he has left of his life as full and joyful as I can possibly make it." Now, finally, she understood why Nicholas only wanted to live in the moment, why he refused to think about the future. Because he had no future. Every moment counted. The thought stiffened her resolve.

"And that is why you must tell the captain to turn the boat around."

"But—"

She could see he was going to try to reason with her. "At once, if you please. Mr. Black!" Not for nothing had she watched Nicholas give orders.

Morton Black opened his mouth to argue, then apparently thinking better of it, trudged up to where the captain stood at the helm. Faith watched as he spoke to the captain. The man looked at Faith, then shook his head. Morton Black said something more. The captain shook his head more vigorously and waved his hands as he gave some explanation.

Black returned. "He said he cannot, that he is making good time and wishes not to be any further delayed."

"Offer him money," Faith said bluntly. "I am going back!"

Morton Black blinked. "You've changed, Miss Faith."

"Yes, I have, more than you know. And from now on, please call me Mrs. Blacklock, not Miss Faith. As my husband pointed out to you yesterday, we are married"—she gave him a determined look—"until death us do part. Only death will part me from my husband, not muttonheaded, well-meaning, misguided Englishmen or Scotsmen or stubborn Spanish sea captains! Now offer him money and get this boat turned around."

Black returned and attempted to bribe the captain, but returned unsuccessful. Faith swallowed. "I shall speak to him." She could see only two courses of action open to her. She hoped the captain would succumb to the first.

She picked her way delicately between the ropes to where the captain stood at the helm. She introduced herself and found her hand being kissed by a dark-haired piratical fellow with a gleaming gold tooth and an earring in one ear. He looked exactly as she imagined a Bay of Biscay pirate would look, except he wore no eye patch. He was Basque, but also spoke Spanish, Portuguese, and some English.

"Captain, I believe Mr. Black has informed you of my urgent need to return to Bilbao," she said in a voice that attempted to be crisp and decisive.

The man shook his head with sorrow that was patently insincere. "Not possible, beautiful lady. The wind, she is fresh, and the sailing good. Is bad luck to put back to port."

"What if I offer to pay you?" She named a sum that was large enough to have Morton Black hissing between his teeth at the unwisdom of letting such a man know how much money she had, but Faith didn't care.

It was a large enough sum to give the captain pause, but he shook his head and repeated the nonsense about bad luck. He was just being stubborn, Faith decided, unwilling to bow to the wishes of an Englishman or a woman.

"Then perhaps I can help you change your mind."

The captain turned a smile full of raffish charm on

Faith, "Ah, perhaps, beautiful lady. What did you have in mind?"

"This," said Faith, and pulled out her pistol and pointed it at him. Behind her she heard a strangled moan from Morton Black.

The captain's smile froze.

"Now, turn the boat around, please," she ordered in a voice that shook. She had never before pointed a gun at a man.

The captain noticed her shaking voice. He eyed the pistol shrewdly. "Is not loaded, I think."

"It is loaded, I promise you."

"But your hand is shaking too much to be of danger to me or any of my men."

She steadied the gun by holding it with both hands.

He smiled, though his eyes were sharp and hard. "Beautiful lady, you are too gentle and lovely a creature to shoot a poor man—"

"I will shoot any man who stands between me and my husband, and right now, you are in my way, Captain. Now, are you going to turn this boat around, or—" She cocked the pistol.

He met her gaze squarely. "I do not think you have it in you to shoot anyone."

Faith swallowed. "I have killed before," she said, and thinking of the hare, she shuddered uncontrollably. "It was—" She shuddered again and licked dry lips. "It was dreadful, and I had nightmares about it for weeks. But—" She looked him full in the face so he could see just how determined she was. "I must return to Bilbao and find my husband. It is the most important thing in the world to me, and if I have to shoot you to achieve it, I will." It was a desperate bluff.

He looked at her for an endless moment, eyed her shaking hands, her trembling lips, and her determined eyes. He pushed the cap back on his head and scratched his thick curls meditatively. Then he gave a shrug, "Very well, señora, I turn the ship."

Faith's knees sagged with relief. She fought not to let it show. She said as coolly as she could manage, "Thank you, Captain. I knew you would see reason." From the corner of her eye she saw Morton Black pull out a large handkerchief and mop his face with it.

In a short time they were back in Bilbao. As the sailors dropped the gangplank and hurried to fetch her belongings, the captain held out his hand to help her to shore. "You not shoot me, I think."

She bit her lip. "I don't know," she admitted. "Probably not."

"Before, when you kill—who you kill?"

Faith stepped down onto the wharf before she answered. "It was a hare," she confessed.

His jaw dropped. "But you go all pale and shaky when you tell me!" He threw back his head and laughed. "The face of an angel, the heart of a lion, the cunning of a fox! You are crazy, beautiful lady."

"No." Faith tucked the gun back in her reticule. "Just desperate."

"Your husband, he lucky man, I think."

Faith bit her lip and shook her head. "I wish that was true."

"Is true! God go with you, beautiful lady."

The road to Vittoria was just a narrow track that zigzagged up into the mountains. The air was cool and moist, and the track was slippery with mud, making progress slow, but none of them minded. There was no hurry.

The higher they climbed, the lower Nicholas felt. It was the right thing to do, but oh, God, if only he'd realized how she'd interpreted his words, all that time ago. In retrospect he could see her learning all the skills she thought a soldier's wife needed: food preparation, taking care of her own horse, setting up a camp—the shooting of that damned hare! She'd even forced herself to stay with him while Stevens stitched the cut in his foot. She'd stubbornly seen it through, her face pale green and clammy, her stomach queasy.

He hadn't understood it at the time, but now he saw; she was earning her right to stay, a right that didn't exist; he'd always intended to send her home. It was just a matter of when.

He'd been, he saw now, inadvertently cruel. His evasiveness in explaining exactly what he'd come to Spain to do had rebounded to hurt the person he'd most intended to protect.

His horse plodded on, skirting terrifying drops. Nicholas barely noticed.

God, he would miss her. But it was better this way. She would force herself to cope with his illness the way his mother had forced herself. The idea of his golden, joyful, sensual Faith fading into a pale, sad wraith of a woman, worn out by witnessing his suffering, was a prospect Nicholas could not, would not bear. Better by far that she think him on a mission and be taken by surprise by news of his death . . . Eventually she would learn the truth, but she would remember him telling her about his mother, and she would understand why.

Ahead of him rode Mac, hunched over his horse in deep Scottish gloom. Maybe they should have tried harder to trace the gypsy girl. Mac would never go after her; he had no belief in his power to keep a woman. He was fatalistic about the loss. But the girl had been so careful to keep her great-grandmother's dwelling place a secret from them all. God knows why she thought he'd want to hurt the old woman.

Anyway, this part of the trip was for Stevens. And for Nick. He'd built a cairn of stones over Algy's grave. He was sure he could find it again. It was on the heights overlooking the battlefield. He'd carried Algy's body up there, not wanting him to be buried in the mass graves that were being dug. Not for Algy, his lifelong friend.

The mist swirled up ahead, thickening, enclosing them in a moist chill. "Capt'n, if this gets much worse, we won't be able to see. I think we'd better look for lodgings in the next village," Stevens called from behind.

Nick shrugged indifferently.

"Are you sure that this is where they're going?" Faith asked for the third time, urging her horse around the sharp bend. She averted her eyes from the chasm on her right.

"I don't know for sure," Morton Black responded with weary patience, "but that fellow Stevens did say they'd be going to Vittoria eventually. His son is buried there."

"Yes, he is. But they might have gone to take Estrellita to her great-grandmother."

"They might. Wherever that is. We don't know anything for sure, Mrs. Blacklock. But I am good at finding people, and I say we go to Vittoria and wait."

"Yes, yes, I suppose so." Having left the boat in such a dramatic fashion, Faith had imagined she'd be able to gallop up to Nicholas as she did that other time, surprising him on the way after an hour or so. But another day had passed, and she was feeling tired and dispirited. It was taking an eternity to get through these mountains, and she was wet and cold and very much afraid that they had taken the wrong route and that she'd lost Nicholas forever.

The mist thickened and grew heavier, and as the afternoon wore on, it settled into a steady, streaming downpour. Faith pulled her hat lower on her forehead and plodded on, blindly trusting in her horse to find the path.

After some time Morton Black came level with her. She looked up, surprised. The narrow track had opened up into a sort of natural terrace overlooking a wide valley. Faith's spirits rose marginally; in the valley would be a village or town, and shelter.

Morton Black leaned across and said in her ear. "Hush, I heard a voice up ahead."

Faith could not see or hear anything. "Nicholas!" she exclaimed, but before she could urge her horse forward, Black grabbed her reins and led both horses off the track, behind some bushes.

"Don't be foolish! These mountains are full of bandits. I will investigate. Wait here, off the track, behind these bushes. Get your pistol ready, but keep it under cover so it does not get wet. And keep your powder dry, too." He did not wait for her to answer but climbed stiffly off his horse—he'd done amazingly well for a man with a wooden leg—handed her the reins, and disappeared into the night.

Faith waited. And waited. She fingered the pistol nervously. This time she might actually have to use it on a man.

After what seemed like an endless time she heard a shout. She clutched the pistol tighter and braced herself.

Then it came again, and this time she heard the words. "Faith? Faith? Where are you?" It was Nicholas, her Nicholas.

Joyfully she urged her horse forward, and in seconds she'd been plucked off it and was in her husband's arms being soundly kissed. "I'm furious with you," he growled and kissed her again. "Look at you—you're soaked to the skin! And freezing, dammit!" He unbuttoned his greatcoat and drew her under it against his big, warm body. "I probably ought to beat you for disobedience,

Mrs. Blacklock," he growled, kissing her again, hard. "But first I'll get you to some sort of shelter."

Faith didn't answer. She was laughing and wiping tears or rain from her eyes and kissing him back. There would be a reckoning on both sides, but not just yet.

He rode on with Faith on the saddle in front of him, wrapped in his greatcoat, clasped against his heart. Morton Black followed, leading Faith's horse. They found the others and were swiftly on their way, a bedraggled group of travelers. Even Beowulf looked cold and wet and miserable, the once jaunty red ribbons limp, muddy, and bedraggled.

They traveled in single file for nearly an hour more, Beowulf leading the way, and then suddenly the dog snuffed the ground, then started barking.

"Hush up, Wulf! We're nearly there. Get on, ye stupid beast," Mac shouted, but the dog kept barking, his tail wagging furiously. Ignoring his master's shouts, he ran a short way along a narrow, almost invisible trail up to the right, then came back, barking and leaping with excitement.

"Come, Wulf!" Mac urged his horse along the road.

But the dog stood in front of his horse and growled and barked. Not surprisingly, the horse wouldn't proceed.

"What's wrong with that blasted dog?" Nicholas swore. "Get him out of the way, Mac! I want to get my wife to shelter!"

Mac shook his head, mystified. "I've never seen him act like this, Cap'n." He glanced at the direction the dog was making short runs toward. "He doesna want us to go on the road. He wants us to go up this wee track." He gave Nicholas a doubtful look. "Mebbe the main road is dangerous—a rockfall or something. Maybe the beast can tell, wi' his animal instincts."

Nick swore again. "Very well, let's try the track if

that's what you want, but I'm warning you, Mac—if it leads nowhere, I'll throttle the blasted dog myself!" He tightened his hold on Faith, and she felt warmed by his concern. She knew he'd never hurt the dog. It was all bluster, worry for her comfort.

They followed Beowulf for another ten minutes or so until the track petered out at a ramshackle stone cottage, built into what seemed to be a natural hollow or cave in the hillside. A chink of light showed through wooden shutters.

Nicholas was none too happy. He cut Mac's apologies short, snapping, "Well, get down man, and see if they'll let us shelter here the night, or at least until this wretched rain ceases. It's damn near sleet! There's room enough in that cave, for the animals and us as well, at a pinch!"

Mac dismounted and rapped on the cottage door.

One of the shutters opened, and a small, piquant face peered suspiciously out. Suspicion turned to shock, then joy, then back to suspicion.

"Wulfie? Tavish?" It was Estrellita, her face far from welcoming. "Stop that noise at once, Wulfie!" The dog immediately stopped and wagged his tail ingratiatingly.

She looked around suspiciously. "Where is Cap'n Nick?"

"I'm here," Nick said. "Let us in, Estrellita. My wife is wet to the skin and frozen."

Estrellita shook her head. "Why you follow me? Go away, Cap'n Nick. You not hurt The Old One!"

"We didna follow you; the dog brought us here," Mac growled. "I've better things to do than follow runaways!"

Nick added, "And I'm damn well not going to hurt your great-grandmother, you stupid girl! How many times do I have to tell you? Now let us in. Faith is soaked to the skin!"

"Don't you shout at me!" Estrellita shouted back. "Faith, she can stay, but the rest of you, go away!"

The scene looked set to degenerate into a farce, with Estrellita shouting from the window and Mac and Nicholas shouting back, and the dog, who'd started barking again, but in the middle of it all, the door opened and a tiny, ancient woman dressed in dusty black shuffled out.

There was a sudden, shocked silence. Even the dog stopped barking.

She was small and frail, her face a mass of wrinkles. "Welcome to my house," she said in careful Spanish. "You are expected." She stood back, clearly inviting them in.

They dismounted. Stevens took the reins of all the horses, and he and Morton Black led the horses into the cave shelter, saying they'd see to the horses while the others sorted out what was what.

Estrellita hurried to the door and stood arguing with the old lady in some incomprehensible language. She saw Faith and said hastily, "Sorry, but I not want your husband here. Come in. Faith—you all wet! You can come, but no mans!"

The old lady snapped something, and waved her aside. Estrellita looked mutinous but obeyed.

The old woman looked at Faith. "You are wet, child. Come. Is warm and dry here." She held out her hand, and Faith took it. She felt a tingle and, startled, glanced at the old lady's face. Her dark eyes seemed to glow with warmth and kindness as she looked at Faith.

She looked at the waiting men and said, "You welcome also. Hush, Estrellita!" She turned back. "My house is your house. Come!"

Mac entered first. She tipped her head back and looked shrewdly up at him. She held out her hand to

him, unsmiling. "You I have heard of." It did not sound
like a compliment.

Mac took the wizened little claw in his big paw and
shook it gingerly, as if fearful it would break. She held
on to his hand a long moment, then nodded as if satisfied. Mac bent his head and entered the small cottage,
rubbing his hand with a thoughtful expression.

Nick, following Mac, offered his hand, but the old
woman pulled back, refusing to touch him. Remembering Estrellita's absurd fears, Nick decided not to take
offense. He simply nodded as he stepped inside.

The cottage consisted of one room and smelled deliciously of herbs and soup and warmth. There was a bed
in one corner, a table in the middle, and a bench and
shelves along several sides. Brightly colored handmade
rugs were scattered thickly on the floor. They would be
necessary, Faith thought, as the floor was the stone of
the cave and would be very cold.

It was an oddly shaped dwelling, nothing like anything Faith had ever seen before. The walls were
crooked and curved, and the whole structure had been
built to fit the shape of the cave. Only the wall with the
door and the shuttered window was straight, and they
looked out across the valley into the sky.

Her little sister, Grace, would love this, she thought
suddenly. It was exactly the sort of cottage a pixie or an
elf would live in.

A fire was burning, and there was a large pot of soup
hanging over it. The smell was delicious. The old
woman ordered a blanket hung up and behind it, Faith
was stripped of her clothing, rubbed dry, and under the
old woman's supervision clad in clothing brought out of
a chest. Clearly it was meant for ceremonial occasions,
for it was stiff and heavy with embroidery. Faith was reluctant to wear it, but the old lady insisted. She had an
imperious air.

On the other side of the blanket the men stripped and wrapped themselves in blankets. Mac draped his blanket around his body like a Scottish plaid, fastening it around the middle with his leather belt, and the others copied. Soon the small room was steaming with the scent of wet wool—and wet dog, for Estrellita had insisted Wulfie be brought inside—not so much because she wanted him close, but because she feared for her great-grandmother's chickens outside.

Once the dividing curtain between the men and women had been removed, however, the room grew silent and tense.

Nicholas looked Faith over in her gorgeously colored peasant dress, but said only, "Would you care to step outside, madam? I think we have things to discuss."

She met his look with a defiantly lifted chin. "By all means, sir. We do indeed have things to discuss."

It was still pouring, but the cottage door opened into the shelter of the big, shallow cave, so they didn't get wet. They were forced to talk in the cave, however, with several goats, their horses, and a dozen chickens watching. Nick strode into the center of the space. His lower limbs were bare, and he wore a blue and white striped blanket wrapped around his middle, then up his back, coming over his shoulder and tucked into a belt at his waist. He looked like a cross between a Scottish Highlander and a Roman senator.

"Why the devil did you follow me, madam?"

"Don't madam me, Nicholas. You lied to me!"

"Nonsen—"

"You did. You let me believe you were on a military mission!"

He looked uncomfortable. "I said no such thing. You put that interpretation on my words—"

"As you meant me to."

He looked away awkwardly. "I meant it for the best."

All Faith's hurt and anger drained away at the anguish in his eyes. "I know," she said softly. "But it doesn't work like that. I want to be with you, Nicholas."

"No! You cannot know what—"

"I know. Morton Black told me. He spoke to your doctor."

Nicholas swore softly. "He had no business to blab!"

"I am your wife. I have the right to know."

"You don't need to be with—"

Again she cut him off. "You worry that I will suffer like your mother—and yes, I probably will. But I will suffer more if you send me away, unwanted."

"Not unwanted," he croaked.

"Unwanted. That's how I felt before, when you sent me away."

He shook his head, but she continued, determined to make him understand. "And how do you think I would have felt later, knowing you'd—you'd died alone, without me? I married you for better or worse, Nicholas my darling, and, and—" She bit her lip, unable to say the words. "And no one, not even you, can make me break that promise. It is my right, Nicholas."

And still he said nothing, so she said quietly, "If I were the one who was dying, would you abandon me to my fate?"

His head came up at that. No, he would not, she saw, and left him to digest the realization in silence. Eventually he said, "I warn you, it will not be pretty!"

She stared at him in disbelief. "Pretty?" she whispered. "Pretty? You stupid, bloody man. As if I care about that. I would face anything, endure anything for you. I would die for you if I could. I love you. I don't care about anything else." Her face crumpled, and she ran at him and thumped him on the arm, "And if you must die, you stupid bloody stubborn man, you'll damn well die in my arms, where you belong!"

Chapter Fifteen

∞

If our two loves be one, or thou and I
Love so alike that none do slacken, none can die.
JOHN DONNE

"THE OLD ONE, SHE WILL TALK TO STEVENS FIRST, THEN Faith." Estrellita hovered at the edge of the entrance. The rain had stopped, and watery sunshine lit the valley below. "You—" she jerked her chin at Nick, "You stay out here."

"I've told you," Nick began, exasperated. "I'm not going to lay a finger on—"

"Everybody must be out here. She want talk to Stevens, then Faith alone."

"Me?" Stevens looked surprised. "What would she want with me?" He opened the cottage door and went inside.

The old lady was sitting on a bench near the fire. She beckoned him closer. When he stood in front of her, she lifted her hand and laid it gently on his chest, then seemed to listen.

After an interminable silence, she nodded and said slowly, "You find what you search for on hill below cottage. You not see it from here. Go on foot. Take your friends. Send the English girl to me." Mystified, Stevens left.

He sent Faith in, then told the others what she'd said to him. They looked down into the valley. Below them, a river snaked in a silvery line. Nick stiffened. "I think that might be the Zadorra River. Estrellita?"

She nodded sulkily. *"Sí, Río Zadorra."*

"Then over there is Vittoria, and below us, in that valley down there is where we fought Boney's brother and the French." He looked back and forth, taking his bearings. "If we go down to the river, to that hairpin bend there, I'm sure I can find my way back to Algy's cairn." He looked at Stevens. "Shall we go and see?"

Stevens swallowed and nodded. The three men and dog set out. "I come with you," Estrellita announced. "You maybe get lost. And also . . ." Her eyes wandered to Mac. "I think maybe I need protect you."

Mac frowned. "You? Protect us?" His voice was scornful.

"Sí," Estrellita said. She cocked her head to one side and examined Mac thoughtfully. "See, I say before you look pretty in dress, Tavish, and you do," she said. "Verrry pretty. Basque girls like pretty man too much, but don't worry, I protect you." And she skipped off, full of cheek. With a mock growl, Mac followed her, a swirl of hairy legs and blue blanket. The bleak look in his eyes had completely disappeared.

Faith entered the cottage cautiously. The old woman beckoned her over with a gentle smile. She pointed to a stool and indicated that Faith was to bring it close and sit down in front of her.

"You are the one who call my little star your sister of the road, no?"

"Yes." Faith nodded.

She gazed into Faith's eyes for a long time and then nodded. "It is good. You may call me Abuela."

It meant grandmother. "Thank you," Faith whispered.

The old woman hesitated, then said, "The big red bear man—he is good to my little star? Not hurt her?"

"My husband says Mac loves your Estrellita, if that is what you mean. He has known him for years. He says Mac would never hurt any woman."

The old woman pursed her lips and considered her words. "And your man, he is good man?"

Faith nodded emphatically. "Oh yes, Abuela. A wonderful man." She felt her eyes fill with tears and blinked them away. The old woman watched, unembarrassed, her wise old eyes, deep in their wrinkled pouches, noticing everything.

"It is good. You great lady, I think. I have short time now to live. Will you be sister of the road to my little star when I am gone?"

"Yes, of course I will."

"Will you take her from this place? After I am gone it will have only bad memories for her."

Faith glanced around, thinking that this was Estrellita's home. The old woman seemed to read her thoughts. "She is last of our line; we have no family left. Estrellita like to call herself gypsy, but in truth in our blood we have Basque, we have Moorish blood, we have Spanish, we have French and Portuguese. This place was my home, and it was good, mostly, but an evil thing happened to my little star in the valley below when she was young girl. It better for her to make home in some new place."

Faith said, "I understand, and I promise you, I will take care of her. Estrellita can come with me back to England, after . . . after . . ." She blinked again, rapidly. They would need each other, she and Estrellita, having lost the two people they most loved in the world.

"Give me your hands, child." She held out her hands, and Faith put hers into them. Again she felt that tingling sensation. The old woman closed her eyes and seemed to listen.

She opened her eyes, and the old brown eyes seemed to glow. "There will be a child." She glanced at Faith's stomach. "Remember that. Do not fear for what must come now. The coming of your husband to this place was foretold. Three foreigners will come; the first, his blood in the earth at my feet, the second a man of fire, blood of my blood, and the third with eyes of ice, whose blood will take my life.

Faith held her breath. The old woman patted her hands.

"This was said at my birth, more than ninety years ago. Remember that, help my little star to remember it, and know that I am content. Now, I must sleep. He have take long time to arrive, your man with eyes of ice." She thought for a moment and smiled. "I think maybe you melt that ice, Faith. Only the color is same, now."

"Here it is, the cairn. See?" They climbed up to the pile of stones, about three feet high. Nick had spent the last hour reliving the battle of Vittoria for Stevens's benefit. He'd pointed out where they'd camped the night before, where Anson's Brigade, of which the Sixteenth was a part, had been deployed.

He'd shown him the place where Algy died; said it was quick and clean. He would die before he admitted anything else to Algy's father. Stevens probably knew, anyway. He'd been at Waterloo. Few deaths were quick and clean.

And now they'd found the cairn under which Algy's body lay, Nick had carried the body up there himself and fetched every stone with his own hands, protecting the shallow grave from predators, animal and human.

He straightened the stick, which had fallen crooked in the pile of stones. On it was scratched these words: "Algernon Stevens, Sixteenth Light Dragoons, 1792–1813. A true friend." Around the cairn grew one or two weeds and thick clumps of wildflowers.

Stevens knelt down and wordlessly started to tidy around the cairn. Nick put a hand on his shoulder and then knelt beside him and started weeding, too.

When they'd finished, Stevens sat back on his heels. He looked at the horizon and frowned. He stood, looked down at the river and up to the top of the hills. "The old lady was right. You can't see the cottage from here. But it's directly above us, hidden by that ledge there."

He looked down at the small pile of weeds and up at where the cottage lurked, invisibly. "Someone's kept Algy's grave tidy all these years."

Nick frowned. It was true. There were a lot fewer weeds around Algy's cairn than around any of the normal rocky outcrops scattered across the mountainside.

"And those flowers didn't grow there by accident." Stevens called to Estrellita, who was in quiet conversation with Mac. She turned, looking unhappy.

"Estrellita, do you know who planted these flowers here?" Stevens asked.

She shrugged. "Me."

"Why?"

"The Old One, she tell me I must keep this place nice."

"But why?"

Again she shrugged. "It is something to do with the prophesy. She know you will come, Stevens."

"But how? And how could she possibly know it was my son under those stones? She told me, right up there, not an hour ago—she said, 'You will find what you search for on the hill below the cottage.'" He stared at Nick, mystified, and then at Algy's grave. "But how could she know? How in the world could she know?"

The wind whistled up the valley. Nobody had an answer.

From his pocket, Stevens took a small gold chain with a cross on it. "It was Algy's mother's," he explained, though no one had asked.

He looped it over the stick with Algy's name on it and tucked it out of sight, under a rock, then bent his head and said a silent prayer for his son. The men snatched off their caps and bent their heads, too.

The wind soughed through the mountains.

"Your man in pain. Bring him to me." The old woman addressed Faith. Faith jumped. How could she tell? Faith had only just noticed that faint, telltale tic jumping in Nicholas's jaw.

Estrellita, coming in from collecting eggs for breakfast, heard her and dropped to her knees, breaking several of the eggs held in her skirt. "No, no, Abuela. No! You must not!"

The old woman cupped her cheek tenderly. "Tend to your eggs, child."

Estrellita sobbed, "But you know how it will end."

The old woman kissed her tear-soaked face and repeated gently but firmly, "Bring him to me." Estrellita started wailing, and she said, almost sharply, "Hush, little star. Be brave. You know it was foretold long before you were born. He is my destiny, and I am ready."

Sobbing, Estrellita stumbled to the table and started to clean up the mess of eggs. "She want the Capitaine, now," she mumbled to Faith as she passed.

Faith, puzzled and a little apprehensive, reached for Nicholas's hand. "Come on, she wants to see you. I think she thinks she can help your headache."

He snatched his hand away. "I don't have a headache."

"You know that's not true," Faith said quietly. "Come."

But Nick refused to move. "There's nothing she can do. I don't believe in superstitious mumbo jumbo!"

"That does not matter!" Faith exploded. "Please, Nicholas, do it—if not for yourself, then for me and for the old lady." She held his hands tightly and tried to explain her feelings to him. "Before, when she held my hands in hers, I felt the oddest tingle. And it was as if . . . I don't know . . . something flowed from her to me, something good. I don't know if she can help you, but you said yourself the finest doctors in England could do nothing for you, so why not let Abuela try?"

"Abuela?"

"She told me to call her that. It means grandmother."

"I know what it means," he said impatiently. "You seem to be mighty chummy all of a sudden with this old witch."

She gave him a reproachful look. "Nicholas, that's not worthy of you." She squeezed his fingers. "I don't know why, but I believe in this old woman. And she believes she has been waiting all her life for this moment."

He snorted. "You want to believe."

"Don't you? Don't you want to have faith?"

"I have Faith." He put his arms around her. "And you are all I need."

Her eyes filled with tears. "Not for much longer if your doctors are to be believed. Please, Nicholas, let her try."

Mac stepped forward. "Cap'n, if she tries and fails, what have you lost?"

"Mac? Don't tell me you believe in this nonsense, too!"

The big man shrugged. "I don't speak of it much—most folk think it superstitious nonsense—but my mam has The Sight. She sees things sometimes, in dreams, that come true. So I say try, Cap'n. I dinna ken what the old woman has planned for ye, but if it doesna work, what have you lost? And if it kills you the quicker . . ." He shrugged again. "No loss there either."

Faith was horrified at his words. No loss, indeed! But before she could spring to his defense, Nick stopped her. "He means a quick death would be a merciful one. What the doctors told me would happen was—"

"I know. Morton Black spoke to them, and he told me."

"Did he tell you one doctor recommended having me tied to a bed in a madhouse?"

"I would never let anyone do that to you," she said fiercely. "Never! No matter what!"

There was a long pause.

Stevens added his mite. "That old lady knows things. Like why I was here and exactly where Algy's grave was. And I felt that tingle, too, when she pressed her hand to my chest."

"She's never so much as touched me, so I wouldn't know," Nick said.

"There might be a good reason for that," said Mac somberly.

Nick looked at each of them in turn, the people he trusted most in the world, then threw up his hands in defeat. "Oh, very well, if it will make you happy, I'll let the old woman have her way with me."

The old woman held out her hand to Nick.

"Nooooo!" Estrellita screamed and flung herself in between them.

The old woman turned to her, took her face in her hands, and spoke in a language no one else could understand. Gradually Estrellita calmed, though tears still poured down her cheeks. The old woman blessed her, making the sign of the cross on her forehead. She pulled a cross on a silver chain from around her neck, placed it around Estrellita's throat, then kissed her three times. Her hands caressed Estrellita's face, smoothing tears away.

It was obviously a farewell.

The old woman looked up and gestured to Mac to come to her. She said something to him the others didn't catch and placed Estrellita's hand in Mac's. Mac said something in a low voice; it sounded like a promise. Estrellita glanced at Mac, shook her head vehemently, and snatched her hand away. She kissed her great-grandmother again, three times, then stepped aside with ragged dignity, tears still streaming from her eyes. The old woman gave an approving nod.

The people watching exchanged uneasy glances. "Is this going to be dangerous?" Faith asked. "I thought you were just going to try to heal him."

The old woman turned and said gently, "All healing dangerous, with result uncertain. We are in God's hands."

It was not a reassuring answer.

Nick stared into the old woman's eyes and shivered with prescience. He turned and kissed Faith hard and possessively. "Never forget that I love you." Then he stepped forward and knelt at the old lady's feet.

The old woman glanced around the cottage one last time, then took a deep breath and reached out her hands to Nick. Estrellita's gasp was audible; she pressed her knuckles to her mouth and watched with agonized eyes. The old woman placed her gnarled old hands carefully on either side of Nick's head, the long fingers cupping the back, her thumbs pressing just behind his ears.

She closed her eyes and for a long time didn't move at all, then she started to move her hands slowly around and across his head, as if feeling for something. It went on for long enough for Faith to start to wonder if it was all an act; then suddenly the tiny body arched back and gave a huge, terrifying shudder, as if an invisible bolt of lightning had passed through her.

She arched again and again, her frail old body seemingly racked with pain. Then Nick began to shudder in the same way, as if waves of pain rocked through the old woman into him. His hands came up and tried to pry her fingers away from his head, but he didn't seem to have the strength.

Faith stepped forward, sure this could not be right, but Mac stopped her. "Once it's started, ye canna stop it or they will both surely die." With a whimper of fear and distress, Faith buried her face in his coat sleeve, but then Nicholas groaned, and she pulled away. It was unbearable to watch but worse not to watch.

The old woman started shuddering uncontrollably, bucking and writhing, and Nick did the same. Suddenly he gave one last, terrifying arch, then slumped at the old woman's feet, apparently insensible.

Or dead.

His collapse pulled the old woman off her chair, but she never let go. They lay together curled on the floor, Nicholas unmoving, the old lady quivering and shuddering around him. Her fingers clung to him like talons, and suddenly Faith saw . . .

"Blood!"

She wanted to run to him, pry him loose, but again Mac barred her. "It's too late to have second thoughts. Ye must see it through to the end, lass, good or bad."

Eventually, with an unearthly shriek, the old woman pulled back from Nick and dropped her hands. Faith stared at the bloody talons, sick to the heart at what she'd talked him into enduring. A trickle of blood ran down the side of Nicholas's face.

Faith flew to him. He didn't move, didn't even seem to breathe. His head and hands were covered with blood.

Mac bent over him. "Dammit, old woman, I think ye've killed him." The old woman didn't move. Her hands and breast were red and sticky with blood.

Stevens laid his head on Nicholas's chest. "No, he's

alive! He's still breathing. Here, Mac, help me lift him onto the bed."

They lifted him gently onto the bed.

"The Old One, too," instructed Estrellita, so Mac lifted the tiny, shrunken body and placed it next to Nick in the bed.

Faith saw with enormous relief that Nick was still breathing, though very shallowly. But blood flowed copiously from his head.

"Head wounds always bleed a lot," Mac told her in a matter-of-fact tone that made Faith want to scream. How could Nick get a head wound from an old lady's fingers?

Stevens took a cloth, splashed it with brandy, and pressed it to the wound on Nick's head. "I've seen worse in the field, missie," he said, meaning to be of comfort. "In fact, Capt'n Nick has survived worse head wounds than this."

Faith shoved her fist against her teeth. All this calm matter-of-factness was driving her to hysteria. Her husband hadn't come from a battle; he'd been wounded by an old witch! And she—Faith—had convinced him to do it. And there was nothing—nothing!—she could do to help!

"She nearly killed him!" Faith said.

"No. She kill herself for him." Estrellita bent over her grandmother and cleaned the wrinkled old face and hands lovingly. "Look!" she exclaimed.

The old woman's palm fell open. There was something in it, covered in blood. Something sharp and metallic.

Mac took it from her and wiped it clean. "By God, it looks like—"

"A piece of shrapnel," Stevens finished for him. "Well I'll be damned!"

"Did that come out of Mr. Blacklock's head, then?" Morton Black asked.

"*Sí,*" Estrellita said shortly. She was bent over the old woman, who now resembled a frail bundle of rags. She instructed Faith in a preoccupied voice, "When bleeding stops you must put that stuff in pot on his wound and wrap his head with clean linen. And keep him warm. You, Tavish, build up fire and move bed close to the window. The Old One will die with the fire behind her, but she must look out to the stars and moon."

Faith blinked at the girl's calmness. She stared dumbly at the jagged sliver of metal lying on the table.

"How could that possibly have come from Nicholas's head?"

Stevens explained, "Shrapnel's like that, missie. They pick out what they can, and the rest either stays there or works its way out. This bit must have escaped the surgeons when Capt'n Nick was wounded at Waterloo." He shook his head with wonder. "Though how the old lady knew about it, let alone got it out, beats me."

Stevens and Faith cleaned Nick's head wound. With a dubious expression, Stevens picked up the pot the girl had indicated. He opened it and sniffed cautiously. His brow cleared. "Smells right," he murmured and smeared the strong-smelling salve over the ragged wound. He covered it with a pad and then wound a bandage of clean linen around Nick's head, as instructed.

Mac, having set up the frail old lady as Estrellita ordered, returned and helped Stevens make pallets of hay for them all to sleep inside. The cottage was tiny, and they would all be cramped, but there was no way any of them wanted to remain far from the two who slept.

Faith slept on the floor beside Nicholas, reaching up to hold his hand through the night. On the other side of the bed Estrellita did the same with her great-grandmother.

•   •   •

For two days and two nights Nick and the old lady lay still and comatose. They were long days and very long nights. Nobody slept well.

On the second day, Stevens and Mac went hunting. Food for the pot, they claimed, but in truth they were quietly going mad, living in such cramped quarters, listening to nothing but the almost inaudible breathing of the two on the bed.

On the evening of the second day, Morton Black reminded Faith he had brought letters for her from her family, and she took them gratefully. She read and reread them, smiled a little, wept a lot, and read bits of the letters to the others.

In some ways the letters were comforting, but in others they made her feel so distant. Their concerns were from another world. Faith's world lay in a bed, silent and unmoving.

Then at dawn on the third day, Nick woke for a few moments. He muttered something, and Faith flew to his side.

"Nicholas, can you hear me?"

His eyes fluttered open again, and he stared at her as if trying to think. Then, "Good morning, Mrs. Blacklock," he muttered and, closing his eyes, he fell into a natural sleep.

"Good morning, Mr. Blacklock, oh, a very good morning to you, my darling Mr. Blacklock," Faith sobbed, kissing his face and his hands and his face again. She stayed with him the rest of the day, watching him sleep. Finally, exhausted, she fell asleep, her hand curled under the covers with her sleeping husband's hand in hers.

At dusk on the same day, the old lady died.

The first anyone realized it was when Estrellita gave a low moan and started to rub her face with ash from the fire.

Faith hurried over to her. "Oh, Estrellita," she began.

Estrellita looked up, her face wild and pagan-looking in the firelight. "You promise me he would not kill her, but he did. He did!"

Faith did not immediately make the connection.

"In my dream I see them, blood on her breast, blood on his hands, you remember, Faith?"

Her words hit Faith like a blow. She had promised her that Nicholas wouldn't kill the old lady, but there was no denying, Nicholas was alive and getting stronger by the minute, and the old woman was dead. The gypsy girl's dream had been right after all.

And the worst of it all was Faith could not regret it.

"I'm sorry," she whispered. "I didn't know how it would be."

"Nay, lass," Mac interrupted. "Look at your great-granny's face, Estrellita. Tell me what do you see."

They all looked. The old woman's face looked smoother, as if the cares and vicissitudes of her ninety years had been wiped away. On it was an expression of great peace and happiness, as if at the moment of death she'd been exalted.

"Ye said when ye first saw the cap'n that his arrival had been foretold. Your granny said it had been predicted at her birth. She knew what was to come, and she wanted it to happen."

Estrellita made a vehement gesture of denial. "How can you say that? Who want to die? Not you! Not me! Not nobody!"

Mac smiled wryly. "Aye, but we are young, my bonny. We have our lives ahead of us. But if ye were old, and had only a short time left to live, how would ye prefer to go? Slowly, your powers fading, eaten away by pain and illness until you are helpless and dependent . . ." He paused to let his words sink in. "Or quickly and magnificently, in a blaze of eternal glory such as we saw here three nights ago?"

Estrellita looked up, her expression arrested.

"She died like a warrior queen, lass," he said softly. "She chose her death, and ye must honor her choice, and her."

Tears poured silently down Estrellita's face, making tracks in the gray ash smeared on her skin. She whispered, "*Sí*, she die like warrior queen."

Estrellita sent everyone away while she washed and dressed her beloved great-grandmother in her finest clothes.

Nick was still unsteady on his feet, so they made a bed of straw for him in the shelter of the cave, and he lay there, sleeping on and off, Faith never far from his side.

Mac paced helplessly outside the cottage, respecting Estrellita's wish for privacy, wanting to offer support and comfort and love, but the girl held herself aloof from him, from everyone, her face drawn, her eyes swollen and red from weeping.

She spoke to him only once, and then it was indirectly. "Faith, please tell Tavish and Stevens to dig grave for Abuela. There." She pointed down the hill. "Next to Steven's Algy."

Stevens looked up, startled. "Next to Algy?"

Estrellita said to Faith, "*Sí*, she tell me this long time ago. And four days ago she tell me again. So dig."

Estrellita sat watch over her grandmother for three days and nights. On the morning of the next day she emerged from the cottage dressed in a brilliant red outfit, its cheerful effect ruined by the ash smeared over her face and hands and hair. "Is time to lay The Old One to rest."

It was a very small funeral; only Estrellita, Faith, and the four men. Mac was disturbed by this realization of how isolated they were. "Do ye not want a priest, Estrellita love?" Mac asked. "I'll go down to Vittoria an fetch one if ye wish."

She addressed Faith. "No priest. Abuela and I, we are— were part of the village, but not belong in same way as others. The priest, he will come after, and bless grave. And village women will come after and pray for her." She scrubbed at her swollen eyelids with her fists. "Is why Abuela say to put her in ground next to Algy. Village women much respect Abuela. She help with babies, sickness, everything. Women will come every week, keep grave clean, bring flowers, leave food, say prayers, talk to Abuela. Stevens's Algy and my Abuela, they never be lonely now."

Stevens pulled a handkerchief from his pocket and blew into it loudly. "Thank you, my dear," he said.

The old lady's funeral was quiet and very poignant. They carried Abuela down the hillside, wrapped in a rug and carried on a wooden pallet by the men of the party. Nick had almost fully recovered by then and wanted to do his part, to pay his respects to the old lady who died to give him life.

They laid her carefully in the deep hole beside Algy's cairn. Around her Estrellita placed a pair of fine leather boots, an embroidered shawl, a skirt, a black cooking pot, a copper kettle, a bowl, spoon, and cup, a string of jet beads, and a fistful of coins. Then she covered them all with a white woven cloth.

Estrellita made a long speech in the language she and Abuela shared, then bent and threw a handful of dirt into the grave. Soundlessly, racked with grief, she gestured for the others to do the same. They came forward one by one, each person saying something, a prayer and something personal. Each of them threw a handful of dirt in.

Mac went first and disappeared soon afterward. Nick was the last to stand beside the grave. He stared down into the hole at the small figure wrapped in the rug. This could have been his grave, here, on this stony, foreign hillside, along with Algy, his lifelong friend. What did one say to a woman who'd given her life to heal him? He could think of no words sufficient to thank her. He simply recited the twenty-third psalm.

"The Lord is my shepherd, I shall not want, he maketh me to lie down in green pastures . . ."

As he spoke, the English members of the funeral party joined in, reciting the beautiful prayer.

"Yea, though I walk through the valley of the shadow of death . . ."

Estrellita started sobbing, and Faith's arms went around her, as Faith recited the prayer and gazed sightlessly out over this valley of death below. This was for Abuela, and for Algy, and for all of the young soldiers who'd died here, far from home and their loved ones.

And as the last words of the prayer were blown away on the wind sweeping up the valley, a low moan came, followed by the sound of an unearthly tune.

Estrellita looked up, shocked, wondering. "What—?"

Nick explained. "It's Mac, he's playing the bagpipes for your gran. It's a Scottish tradition." He listened. "The song he's playing, it's called 'The Flowers of the Forest.' It is a traditional lament—that means song for the dead." He softly spoke one of the lines in time to the music, *"The flowers of the forest are all withered away."*

"Is beautiful," Estrellita sobbed. "I not expect this. Abuela, she would love this. My people also play these pipes."

They listened. The music was poignant and hauntingly beautiful. The strains of it echoed down the valley and faded away into the mountains.

"He brought the pipes thinking it would be Capt'n Nick's funeral he would be playing at," Stevens said softly in Faith's ear, and the information made her hug Estrellita all the tighter.

Chapter Sixteen

◈

O, thou art fairer than the evening air
Clad in the beauty of a thousand stars.
CHRISTOPHER MARLOWE

NINE FULL DAYS OF MOURNING WERE REQUIRED. AFTER THE
death. It was the tradition of her family, Estrellita explained to Faith. "And I must do it properly, to show respect. I am the last woman of my family." She added,
"With us the bloodline is traced through the woman."

She spoke only to Faith during that time, though Mac
several times attempted to speak with her. She would
not communicate with him in any way; she refused even
to look at him. She looked appalling. She did not wash,
her face and hands were covered in ash and soot, and
her hair was tangled and filthy. Her bright red funeral
clothes were soon torn, ragged, and covered in soot and
ash.

She went about the business of clearing the cottage of
everything that had belonged to her great-grandmother. She
smashed what she could and burned the rest: clothing,
linen, pots, and pans. She did not cook, she refused to eat
what Faith and Stevens cooked for her. She did not mind
them cooking, she told Faith—they were not bound by her

traditions—but she would do nothing that might show disrespect.

Mac's frustration built until at last, on the sixth day, he found her alone, burning more of her great-grandmother's things.

"What are your plans, Estrellita, lass? Cap'n Nick and the others plan to leave in five days. The cap'n's lady says you will be mournin' for nine days, so that'll be finished by then. So I need to know, lass. Do I stay or do I go?"

She ignored him, acted as if he wasn't even there.

He grabbed her arm and swung her around to face him.

"I'm asking ye again, Estrellita. Will ye wed me?"

She averted her face and said nothing.

"Ye have nothing to stay for—and by the looks of what ye're burning, ye'll have nothing left anyway. So come home wi' me, lass, and we'll be wed." He drew her close to him, and uncaring of the ash-smeared state of her, bent to kiss her.

She fended him off with a flurry of kicks and punches. In deep fury she hissed, "You! Do not speak to me! You are being disrespectful! And anyway, I am the one who choose. I, Estrellita! Not the man!"

Mac clenched his fists. His face ached from where she'd lashed out at him. "Disrespectful, ye say?" He snorted. "For a man to ask a grubby little witch to wed him? There's plenty who wouldna bother wi' such niceties, ye ken!"

For answer she tossed her hair in sublime indifference and marched off.

He stared after her, swore and kicked a rock over the edge, listening with a sour expression as it bounced down the hillside. When he had his temper under control, he rejoined the others.

"She'll no say what she's doing. I dinna ken if she'll stay or come wi' us."

Nick gave him a sympathetic glance. "Well, it must

be up to you. You are free to choose now." He put his arm around Faith. "It's been six days since I've had a headache. It's early days, of course—"

"I believe it," Faith interjected. "She really did cure you. The doctors didn't know there was a piece of shrapnel pressing on your brain, but now it's out—"

"And how the hell she did it is more than I can fathom," said Stevens.

"Does it matter?" Faith asked. "All I care about is that Nicholas is well and that we can have—" Her face crumpled, but she mastered herself and continued, "Nicholas and I can have a life together. A future." Her eyes flooded, and she buried her face in her husband's chest and hugged him. She had been so emotional lately. Given the circumstances, it was not surprising, but really, why was she such a watering pot now, when her husband was cured and the future looked so rosy?

She touched her stomach and wondered. Was the old woman right about that, too?

"How are you going, Capt'n?" Stevens asked.

Nicholas smoothed Faith's hair. "We'll sail from Bilbao."

"By boat?" Stevens and Mac exclaimed in unison. "You?"

Nicholas pulled a face. "I can endure it, and I'd like to get back as quickly as possible." He shook his head ruefully. "Black says my mother knew of my illness. She will be expecting any day to hear of my death. Damned blabbermouth doctor!"

There was a short silence, then Mac said, "So ye'll not be needing me after all?"

Nick shook his head. "I never thought I'd be so glad to sack a man."

"Aye, Cap'n, and I never thought I'd be so glad to be out o' a job!" He gave Nick a clout on the back that nearly sent Nick and Faith flying.

"Of course," Nick said, "If you do decide to come back to England, there will always be a job waiting. You know that, I hope."

Faith had been trying to follow the conversation. "What do you mean, you've sacked Mac? What job?"

There was an awkward silence. Mac said hastily, "Oh, just the arranging of the journey, you know—that sort of thing, missus."

"Then why wouldn't you be needed for the return journey? I would imagine you'd be especially necessary if Nicholas is to be incapacitated by seasickness."

"Ah, yes . . . but Stevens can see to that," Nicholas said.

"Stevens has been here all along," Faith pointed out.

There was another silence.

"It can't hurt to tell her now, Capt'n," Stevens said. "Now that it's not going to happen."

Faith looked from one grave face to the other and said slowly, "You mean now that Nicholas isn't going to die."

Mac looked uncomfortable and suddenly decided Abuela's bonfire needed stirring. Nicholas said in a bracing voice, "Stevens, you have plenty to do, I think, if we're to leave in a few days. Mac, whatever you choose is acceptable to me." He released Faith and walked into the cave to see to the horses' tack.

Faith detained Stevens as he went to pass her. "Tell me, Stevens."

Stevens hesitated, then said slowly, "Remember that hare, missie? And what Mac did? Can't stand to see a living creature suffer, Mac." He gave her a significant look and then went past her.

Faith felt her stomach clench as the unspoken meaning of his words penetrated. Nicholas had come to Spain to die, and it was Mac's job to see that he didn't suffer.

Oh, God! What an appalling thing those three men had been facing. One to die, one to kill, and the other to watch it happen. Thank God for Estrellita's Abuela. Thank God they'd met Estrellita in the first place. Thank God the piratical ship's captain had believed she might shoot. There were so many things to be grateful for. She sent up several quick prayers of thankfulness. And then made up her mind not to dwell on the narrow escapes they'd had. She had the present to dwell in, and the future with Nicholas to look forward to.

"I don't want you to stay behind alone, lass. Come wi' me. Ye dinna have to marry me, and I'll no touch ye if ye want it that way."

Estrellita glared at him and walked past without a word.

He followed her. "I'll no' press ye, lass, but 'twill drive me mad to think of you alone, wi' no family and no man to protect ye."

Estrellita addressed the air. "Why would I want come with a mutton-head, hairy great bush who not even know what mean respect!"

Mac flung up his hands in frustration and rage. "Well, if that's the way you see it!" he yelled after her and stormed off.

When the others sat down for dinner that night, Estrellita's gaze revealed she had noticed his absence, and the number of times it wandered to the door told Faith she was worried, but the girl said nothing. Nor did she eat anything except green leaves and drink water and coffee.

Mac was gone for the next two days, and each day she looked more and more worried. But each time Faith tried to talk to her, she just shrugged and pretended indifference.

"But why won't you even talk to him?" Faith pleaded on Mac's behalf.

Estrellita regarded her with amazement. "For respect, of course. Woman and mens must not talk together until nine days after." She spoke as if it would be obvious to any but a simpleton.

"Of course," Faith said gently. "We do not have this custom, Estrellita. Mac thinks you are angry with him, that you don't like him."

The girl shrugged, as if indifferent. "I am angry. He show no respect. He must wait nine days." She hunched her shoulder. "If he no can wait nine little days, he no good for me."

Faith decided to find Mac and tell him. She did not think she could sort out the differences between two such prickly people, but she thought it might help if Mac knew Estrellita's silence toward him was part of her mourning ritual.

But Mac was nowhere to be found.

On the morning of the tenth day Estrellita emerged from the cottage looking like a new woman. She had bathed from head to toe and looked fresh and young and sweet-smelling. Her hair, newly washed and combed, clustered in glossy elflocks around her head and flowed down her back. She was dressed in a new red and black flounced skirt and a fresh white embroidered blouse.

"Estrellita, how pretty you look!" Faith exclaimed.

The girl preened, stroking the new clothes and said, almost shyly, "Everything from the skin out, must be new." Her eyes wandered around the area, as if searching for someone.

"He's not back yet," Faith told her. "But I'm sure he will come back. He wouldn't leave without saying good-bye."

Estrellita looked doubtful. He had not been seen since their last quarrel. He hadn't even returned at night.

"We are leaving tomorrow," Faith told her. "You must decide if you want to come with us or not. I would very much like you to come, my sister of the road." She gave her a quick hug. "But it must be your decision. You will have money, to do whatever you want with. You are free to choose."

The girl scowled and stepped back. "I no want your money!"

Faith touched her on the arm. "Hush. I promised your abuela I would take care of you. I cannot force you to come to a foreign land, Estrellita, though I hope you will. But I will insist you have enough money so you shall not want for the necessities in life. A woman alone must be prudent—I know—and there is nothing worse than being alone and having no money."

"There is worse," said Estrellita soberly.

"Well, yes, but you know what I mean. You will take this money, Estrellita."

The girl looked mutinous, but Faith suddenly had an idea. "It is your dowry. A gift from me on behalf of your grandmother for saving my husband's life." That was a different matter, she saw at once. This was something Estrellita could accept without loss of pride. "So we are agreed?"

Estrellita gave a gruff agreement, but she was pleased, Faith saw.

But there was still no sign of Mac, and as the day wore on, Estrellita looked more and more anxious.

The sun had dropped behind the mountains, and the stars were beginning to peep from the dark velvet night. They had eaten a good meal, and for once, Estrellita ate everything, but with little relish for a girl who'd fasted for nine days. Her mouth drooped with sorrow, and her eyes were dark with a different kind of woe. Mac had not returned.

No one had raised the topic, but all were beginning to worry. They were to leave first thing the next morning.

But as the moon showed her pale face above the mountain peaks, an unearthly sound pierced the soft night air. It was the sound of bagpipes.

Estrellita sat up, her face suddenly glowing as if a fire had been kindled inside her.

"What this song?" she asked. "Is beautiful."

"It's the 'Eriskay Love Song,'" said Faith softly. She sang:

> *Bheir me o, horo van o*
> *Bheir me o, horo van ee*
> *Bheir me o, o horo ho*
> *Sad am I, without thee.*

"'Sad am I, without thee.' Oh, is pretty." Estrellita wiped her eyes. "What mean '*Bheir me o, horo van o*'?"

"I don't know. It's Gaelic—the Scottish language. You'll have to ask Mac," said Faith and kept singing.

Estrellita sniffed and got to her feet. "Is muchly beautiful song. Stupid man! If he so sad without me, why he hide?" She stalked off into the darkness.

Faith sighed rapturously. "Oh, I hope it works out, Nicholas."

"So do I, my love. But it strikes me that it's a beautiful night, and we can sit here speculating fruitlessly, or we can go outside and . . . enjoy the moonlight." He kissed her deeply.

Faith's heart swelled with joy. She knew what he meant. "Oh yes, my love, let us go out and enjoy the moonlight." And they strolled, entwined, into the moonlight, only stopping to snatch up a blanket.

Estrellita climbed the hill, following the sound of the bagpipes. In an open circle, surrounded by scrubby trees, she saw the lone piper, standing tall and strong among the shadows. She suddenly felt strangely shy and lurked in the darkness, waiting, until he'd finished the beautiful song. Then she took a few steps into the circle, so the moonlight shone full on her.

He saw her and put down the pipes; they squawked dolefully as the air sagged from them. Then he straightened and folded his arms.

He would not come to her, she realized. This time it was she who must go to him. She took a deep breath and padded toward him. She got close enough to see his face and stopped dead.

It was a stranger.

"Who you?" she demanded. "What you do with my Tavish?"

"It's me, ye daft little witch."

She peered suspiciously at him through the dim light. "You not look like my Tavish."

The stranger rubbed his chin self-consciously. "Aye, well, since ye seem to despise it so much, I shaved my beard off. I wouldna do that for any other woman, Estrellita, lass."

"You take beard off—for me?" Her eyes ran over him, assessing the new look, and she gave a small, satisfied nod. "Is pretty, Tavish." Then her face clouded. "Faith tell me you not understand why I no talk to you before."

"Aye. I was only tryin' to help ye." He was hurt; she could hear it in his voice.

She nodded. "Tavish, with my people, after close relative die, woman must not talk with man, not for nine days. Is for show respect for dead one."

His breath came out audibly. "So that was it."

"Aye," she said seriously. "So is all right now, Tavish?"

"Aye, is all right."

"Good. Now can talk. Can do . . . anything."

"Is that so? Then come here to me, lass, and we'll see what 'anything' might be."

She closed the gap between them with a joyful bounce, reached up, and rubbed the clean-shaven jawline. "Mmm, nice. You have good chin, Tavish. Strong. Look and feel good."

He reached for her, and she skittered back teasingly. She gave him a smile filled with shy female promise. "I shave my beard off for you, too, Tavish."

Her beard? For a moment Mac thought she'd got the word wrong, or that she didn't understand what she'd said, but then he saw she was lifting her skirt, slowly, enticingly, and all coherent thought flew from his head. His throat thickened as the crimson skirt with the black lace edging rose higher and higher, exposing the prettiest legs he'd ever seen.

"Oh lord, lassie, you're killin' me."

The black lace crept higher and higher. Mac was locked on it, unable to tear his glance away. She stopped just short of showing her privates. He held his breath, hoping for more. And then she smiled and lifted the skirt all the way.

And his jaw dropped. He stared, unable for a moment to comprehend. And then he saw. She had indeed shaved off her "beard." He nearly choked.

"In my family, this how bride come to her husband." She said it almost as a question.

Mac couldn't move, couldn't speak. He was filled with lust, love, gratitude, and elation.

Estrellita explained, a little impatiently, "I choose you, Tavish. But I not virgin. You still want marry me?" Her voice was thready with anxiety.

"Och, aye, lassie, I want marry you. God, how I want!"

She still hesitated, wanting him to be sure. "The women in my family, once we choose, we choose until death. We take no other man."

"That's grand," said Mac with enormous satisfaction, "I wouldna have it any other way. I'm a one-woman man meself. Now come here, my bonny bride, and kiss me."

She gave a triumphant shriek and, bunching her skirts above her waist, she ran to him and leapt into his arms, locking her legs around his waist. She kissed him fiercely, planting rapid kisses all over his clean-shaven face. And Mac knew he would never grow a beard again.

Faith and Nick lay on the cool earth, gazing up at the myriad twinkling stars. They'd made love and now lay wrapped in a blanket, enjoying the tranquil beauty of the night.

Nicholas's arms tightened around her. "Do you know what I'm thinking about?"

"What?"

"I'm thinking about the future. Making plans!" He kissed her. "I've never done it before—I've never had a future to plan for. You don't when you're a soldier—it's tempting fate. And since I stopped being a soldier . . . well, I never had a future then, either." He pulled her close. "It's all thanks to you, my dearest love. You gave me a future. You *are* my future."

"Oh, Nicholas. And you did the same for me."

After a time he asked, "And what are you thinking about?"

"Darkness," Faith answered with a happy sigh.

"Are the moon and stars too bright for you?"

She laughed. "Of course not. No, I was just remembering my dream—you know, the special one I told you about—the one that made me think Felix was my destiny. I had forgotten about the darkness. In my dream, the music came out of darkness, played by a man in darkness."

"Oh?"

She sat up on her elbow and looked at him. "Don't you see? Felix was *never* in darkness. He was always on a brightly lit stage. *You* were the man in darkness."

"I certainly was. And you brought the light to me."

She kissed him. "No, what I meant was—"

"What *I* meant was, you're very beautiful bathed in starlight and moonbeams, my love, and if you think I'm planning to lie here and discuss old dreams when we can make new ones, you're very much mistaken." And he rolled over, bringing her with him, and began to make love to her with tender deliberation.

"I thought you'd ordered me not to spin castles in the air," she murmured.

"Yes, but that was before I realized we had a future and would need somewhere to live," he murmured. "I love you, Mrs. Blacklock. Now, do you want to talk or make love?"

She locked her arms around his neck and pulled his head down to hers. "Guess."

Epilogue

∞

Love is love's reward.

JOHN DRYDEN

CARRADICE ABBEY. NOVEMBER 1818

"AND AS WE SAILED AWAY ON THE EVENING TIDE, PORPOISES followed the boat, leaping and diving in the most playful way and leaving trails of magical gold and green glowing fire behind them, like comets in the water. It was a truly marvelous sight to behold," Faith finished telling her sisters.

She sat curled on a sofa with her twin, Hope. Prudence and Charity sat in squashy, comfortable chairs on either side of the fire, baby Aurora gurgling on a rug on the floor, her toes being tickled by her youthful aunts, Grace and Cassie. The last of the small aunts, Dorie, was showing baby Alexander to the dowager Lady Blacklock.

Faith watched them poring over the babies and smiled to herself. She squeezed her twin's hand and whispered, "I'm not completely sure yet, but I hope to be making that lady a grandmother sometime next summer."

Hope looked at her in surprise. "Me, too," she whispered, and they hugged each other, laughing and wiping away the odd tear.

"It's a secret," Faith said, when the others wanted to know. "Twin stuff." She wanted to tell Nicholas first, and she wanted to be sure when she told him. But her twin was different. They'd done everything together all their lives.

"Oh it's so good to be home," she exclaimed, hugging Hope for the hundredth time.

All the Merridew girls had come together again at Carradice Abbey, not to greet Faith—for her homecoming was a huge surprise all around—but to welcome to the family its newest little member, Alexander Gideon Oswald Carradice, nearly three weeks old. The christening was set for the following week.

Faith and Nicholas had arrived in London to find nobody home at Great Uncle Oswald's. His butler had informed them that everyone was gone to Carradice Abbey for the new baby.

They'd gone next to see Nicholas's mother, who broke down in tears when she beheld the son she thought never to see again, alive and well and with a beautiful, warmhearted wife. They'd brought her with them to Carradice Abbey to meet the rest of the family.

"I remember the fire in the water in Italy, too," said Prudence suddenly. "You know, I'd forgotten all about it until you described it just now. It truly does look magical."

"Prudence says you can swim, Faith," added Charity.

"Oh yes, it's the most wonderful feeling." She glanced at the younger members of the family and added with a discreet twinkle, "But it must be a husband who teaches you." She winked. Her sisters blushed and smiled secret smiles.

"I shall insist on it," murmured Prudence.

"I wish you had brought Estrellita with you," Grace said, oblivious of adult concerns. "I'm longing to meet her. She sounds fun!"

"She is, and you will meet her eventually, but Estrellita and her husband are in Scotland now. She's meeting the rest of the McTavish clan. But Mac is coming to work at Blacklock, so you will meet Estrellita soon enough." Faith added, "And if Stevens succeeds in his mission, you might even get to meet the lady who called me '*la petite tigresse.*'"

"The French cook lady you wrote to us about?" Charity asked.

"Yes. Stevens said he was inspired by all the romance in the air. He was off to propose to her. He thought she might agree to cook at Blacklock, but Nicholas remembered that the landlord of Blacklock Inn was looking for a buyer, so he bought it. A much better solution, I think, as I suspect that lady would not take at all well to being a servant."

"Speaking of inns," Aunt Gussie interjected majestically, "I've just recalled some news that would interest you, Faith. It seems that a certain Count Felix Vladimir Rimavska was set upon in Paris by a group of ruffians who bundled him in a sack and ran off with him. Yes, shocking, I know!" She glanced around at her avid audience. "The count seems to have vanished from the face of the earth. Isn't that extraordinary? It happened around the same time as Sebastian and Oswald made that visit to Paris, but alas, men never pick up gossip."

Ignoring the immediate outbreak of questions, she selected a sweetmeat from a silver dish and inspected it closely. "Oh, and the other news—much happier—is that a Bulgarian lady called Mrs. Yuri Popov had her missing husband—he'd been missing for years—restored to her. And just as happily, she came into a small fortune." She bit into the sweetmeat. "Being a woman of enterprise, she purchased a pig farm. Now dear Yuri Popov is up to his knees in pig swill by day, and by night he performs in the inn owned by Mrs. Popov's

four brothers. Four, large, very protective brothers."
She gave Faith a bright smile, "I do so enjoy happy end-
ings, don't you?"

"Pig swill?" Faith giggled. "Do you know, I haven't
given that man a thought for ages. Nicholas has quite
ousted him from my mind."

Aunt Gussie patted her knee. "Good girl."

Just then the gentlemen came into the room; Great
Uncle Oswald first, followed by Gideon, Edward, Sebastian, and Nicholas, all talking and laughing as if
they'd known each other for years.

"Brr, it's gettin' demmed chilly." Great Uncle Oswald declared as he made straight for the fire. "Well,
young Faith, you've ended up with a fine husband, even
if he did beat me at billiards! I must say, I thought you'd
jumped from the fryin' pan into the fire when you wrote
to tell me you'd married a feller you just met—and in
France of all peculiar places! D'ye know what sort of
crazy risk you took, girlie, marryin' a perfect stranger?"

Faith slipped off the sofa and hurried to slip an arm
around Nicholas. "No risk at all, Great Uncle Oswald.
You said it yourself."

Great Uncle Oswald looked up. "Eh? What's that?
What did I say? Gussie, what was it I said?"

"Lord knows, Oswald. But he does have lovely big
hands, I noticed." Aunt Gussie winked at Faith, who
blushed, recalling Aunt Gussie's scandalous theories
about the size of men's hands.

Faith leaned against her husband, marveling yet
again that she'd been so lucky. "You just said he was a
perfect stranger, Great Uncle Oswald, and he is. The absolutely perfect stranger for me." She looked at her sisters and added in an increasingly watery voice, "And
he's given me laughter and love and sunshine and happiness, just as Mama promised."

Nicholas gazed down at the woman who'd given him

so much. "Whatever I may have given you," he said quietly, "You have given me much, much more." And in front of her entire family he gathered her to him and kissed her hard and long.

"That's all very well," said Aunt Gussie testily when the cheering and clapping had died down, "but if you had a grain of sense, young man, you'd have kept her *out* of the sun! Sun is ruinous for a young gel's complexion, utterly ruinous!" She looked at Faith and shook her head. "You're brown, my girl—brown as a berry! It's face packs for you, my gel, face packs of lemon and crushed strawberries for the next few weeks—if not months—though where on earth we'll find strawberries at this uncivilized time of year—and in the country!— I have no idea!"

Award-winning author **Anne Gracie** spent her childhood and youth on the move. The gypsy life taught her that humor and love are universal languages and that favorite books can take you home, wherever you are. In addition to writing, Anne teaches adult literacy, flings balls for her dog, enjoys her tangled garden, and keeps bees.

Visit her website at www.annegracie.com.